CITIES OF SALT

Abdelrahman Munif was born in Jordan in 1933 into a trading family of Saudi Arabian origin. He was stripped of his Saudi Arabian citizenship for political reasons. He earned a licence in law from Baghdad and Cairo universities, and his Ph.D. in oil economics from the University of Belgrade. During his career in the field of oil, he served as director of crude oil marketing. In Baghdad he was editor-in-chief of *Al–Naft wa; Tanmiya (Oil and Development)*, a monthly periodical. He now devotes his time to the writing of novels.

THE TRANSLATOR

Peter Theroux was born in Boston in 1956 and educated at Harvard and the American University of Cairo. He has lived and travelled in Iraq, Syria and Saudi Arabia, and is the author of *The Strange Disappearance of Imam Moussa Sadr*. He lives in Long Beach, California.

Abdelrahman Munif

CITIES OF SALT

TRANSLATED FROM THE ARABIC BY
Peter Theroux

VINTAGE

Published by Vintage 1994

2 4 6 8 10 9 7 5 3 1

English translation copyright © 1987
by Cape Cod Scriveners Company
Originally pubished in Arabic under the title
Mudun al-milh by The Arab Institute for Research
and Publishing, Beirut, Lebanon, in 1984

The right of Abdelrahman Munif to be identified as the author of this
work has been asserted by him in accordance with the Copyright,
Designs and Patents Act, 1988

First published in Great Britain
by Jonathan Cape Ltd, 1988

Vintage
Random House, 20 Vauxhall Bridge Road, London SW1V 2SA

Random House Australia (Pty) Limited
20 Alfred Street, Milsons Point, Sydney,
New South Wales 2061, Australia

Random House New Zealand Limited
18 Poland Road, Glenfield
Auckland 10, New Zealand

Random House South Africa (Pty) Limited
PO Box 337, Bergvlei, South Africa

Random House UK Limited Reg. No. 954009

A CIP catalogue for this book
is available from the British Library

ISBN 0 09 938811 1

Printed and bound in Great Britain by
Cox & Wyman Ltd, Reading, Berkshire

To Ali Munif . . .
who departed too soon

Translator's Acknowledgments

I am deeply indebted to two people for their help: to my brother Paul for his invaluable support and encouragement, and to Nayef Al-Rodhan, M.D., whose patient advice regarding Arabian dialects was crucial to the accuracy of this translation. Heartfelt thanks.

P.C.T.

1

WADI AL-UYOUN: AN OUTPOURING OF GREEN
amid the harsh, obdurate desert, as if it had
burst from within the earth or fallen from
the sky. It was nothing like its surroundings, or rather had no
connection with them, dazzling you with curiosity and wonder:
how had water and greenery burst out in a place like this?
But the wonder vanished gradually, giving way to a mysterious
respect and contemplation. It was one of those rare cases of nature
expressing its genius and willfulness, in defiance of any explanation.

Wadi al-Uyoun was an ordinary place to its inhabitants, and
excited no strong emotions, for they were used to seeing the
palm trees filling the wadi and the gushing brooks surging forth
in the winter and early spring, and felt protected by some blessed
power that made their lives easy. When caravans came, envel-

oped in clouds of dust and weakened by hunger and thirst, yet redoubling their efforts, in the last stage of the journey, to reach Wadi al-Uyoun as quickly as possible, they were overtaken by an almost frivolous enthusiasm. They controlled their exuberance and headed straight for the water, feeling sure that He who had created the world and humankind had created, at the same time, Wadi al-Uyoun in this very spot as a salvation from death in the treacherous, accursed desert. When the caravan lingered, unloaded its cargoes and watered its men and beasts, a kind of narcotic restfulness set in, a powerful contentment induced by the climate or the sweet water, or perhaps by a sense of danger passed. This affected not only men but camels, who were distinctly less willing to bear their heavy packs and resume the journey afterward.

For caravans, Wadi al-Uyoun was a phenomenon, something of a miracle, unbelievable to those who saw it for the first time and unforgettable forever after. The wadi's name was repeated at all stages of a journey, in setting out and returning: "How much longer to Wadi al-Uyoun?" "If we make it to Wadi al-Uyoun, we'll rest up for a few days before going on," and "Where are you, Wadi al-Uyoun, earthly paradise?"

This urgency in invoking the wadi's name was genuine, for in addition to it being a salvation for caravans and travelers, its peculiar location enabled the caravan traders to learn a great deal: when other caravans had passed through and where they were headed, what they were carrying and in what quantities, what prices were and who was selling, and other information. Thus the men of a caravan would decide whether to sell here or elsewhere, to speed up the journey or slow the pace for a few days, and what to take on in the way of men and supplies.

Left to himself to talk about Wadi al-Uyoun, Miteb al-Hathal would go on in a way no one could believe, for he could not confine himself to the good air and the sweetness of the water available every day of the year, or to the magnificent nights; he would tell stories which in some cases dated back to the days of Noah, or so said the old men. There was a special relationship, a rare passion between Miteb al-Hathal and Wadi al-Uyoun. Those who had lived there in both periods—the one when Wadi al-Uyoun was as Miteb knew it, and the following period— would speak about it differently. They would say that this wadi, with its palm trees and plentiful water, which soothed and sup- plied travelers on their way to better places, was indispensable; without it there would have been no life or movement, no road; no tribes would have come; there would never have been Miteb al-Hathal and his tribe, the Atoum.

The wadi stretched for about three miles or perhaps a little more. This broad expanse tapered until it became at the end a narrow ribbon with a few scattered palms, which survived on what water there was, and what was left behind by the few men and animals that strayed there. The end of the wadi was no- ticeably scragglier, and anyone who stood by the last tree could tell that the salty, sandy earth began there. This particular patch of land linked the wadi and the desert, for it rose bit by bit until it became one with the desert. When the wind blew, sand drifted on this land since the fine-branched tamarisk, wormwood and lotus trees, thickly planted at the end of the wadi, prevented the sand from mounting, preserving the blackness and solidity of the soil and keeping the encroaching sands at a distance.

Hills surrounded the glen, shifting sand hills, but the direction of the winds and the nature of the soil made them immovable, presiding over the wide stretches of surrounding territory. These made good landmarks and had names: Zahra rose from the east, Watfah and Umm al-Athal on the northern side. The hills bor- dering the wadi on the west and south meant little to travelers or even to the wadi but were named anyway since names were so important in the desert. They were named not through desire or caprice but by nature itself, which had determined the importance, features and location of each hill.

People who traveled and were familiar with the area knew that the sea was not far from Wadi al-Uyoun—perhaps seven or eight days away—but the caravan road passed nowhere near it, following, as it did, the trail of freshwater wells and oases. As to the desert, on the other side, no one could guess where it ended. It might have ended far away or not so far after all, but everyone regarded this as an unknowable secret.

Omens of a good year to come always appeared first in Wadi al-Uyoun, for in addition to the abundant water that filled the three reservoirs and encircling streams the good years brought the waters which flowed down to where water was never expected to reach. In these years vegetables were planted and green plants appeared with the early rains, making the people of Wadi al-Uyoun behave in a way that astonished travelers used to passing through dozens of similar places. The people would overdo their insistence that all travelers stay there longer, take little for what they gave out and dream up occasions to postpone the traveling plans of their visitors. Their generosity would reach the point of extravagance, leading some travelers to consider them silly and rash people who never thought about tomorrow or remembered the hard times they had known in years past.

But during the years of drought—which is what most years were—the people of Wadi al-Uyoun behaved differently, were sadder and more introverted, leaving the travelers to act as they pleased, without interfering. If they were offered goods in exchange for dates, water or any services rendered they accepted them thankfully, and if they asked anything from a caravan it was only to seek places for new passengers who had prepared and waited a long time to travel. After they had all left, the wadi felt relief and hope, for it was rid of burdens and yet could look forward to the good things to come from the day they returned, for all travelers came back sooner or later. Between the relief and the hope, with the steady supply of water and caravans, Wadi al-Uyoun continued to be strong, never fearing or wavering, for it always found a way to confront and overcome its misfortunes.

Wadi al-Uyoun's people, like its waters, flooded out in times of overabundance: emigration had been a necessity for a long time. One day they would feel that there were too many of them for the wadi to support, and the young men able to travel would get ready to head out to new places to live and work. This impulse seemed strange and mysterious, for it was not always related to the rains or the seasons as was the case elsewhere. For regardless of a given year's rainfall, in spite of the grazing lands that surrounded the wadi, in spite of record floods, a crazed notion grew up slowly and secretly in men's hearts. This notion, which grown men felt but repressed and rejected, slept and started in the hearts of women and youths, but the desire to discover the world, the dream of wealth, the nameless longing nagged young men to the point where they lost patience with their elders' advice and made these hard decisions by themselves.

There was not a single man in the wadi who had not at some time been seduced by the urge to travel, and it was a rare old man who had not traveled to some distant place or other. To be sure, their dreams and journeys had widely different time spans and outcomes, since some trips lasted for years or a lifetime and others for just a few months, after which they would return triumphant or disappointed but in either case full of nostalgia, encumbered by ideas, memories and the dream of another journey. The experiences of Wadi al-Uyoun's travelers could not be summed up in a few words, for every traveler had expectations and fancies different from everyone else's. Everyone had his own idea of success and failure, of rich and poor. Often the travelers who returned with innumerable new ideas and tales, and long

nights of dreams remained poor, but they could not desist from
telling dozens of stories about their adventures, the money they
had come into and how they had spent it, and how short life
was.

The repetition of these and other stories in Wadi al-Uyoun
aroused irresistible dreams in young men who swore that they
would not travel for long, that they would be back come spring
or fall. They knew that their elders did not believe them, but
that despair and resignation would force them to go along. If
death were mentioned and a mother's tear fell, or a father said
anything, the sons felt the haunting nearness of departure together with a diabolical urge to be cruel and scornful, but at the
last minute they relaxed and changed their minds.

Wadi al-Uyoun's talk of travel was a beginning for any person,
but it had no end. Young and old alike knew it; they were so
used to it that leaving no longer created insupportable sorrow.
Even the mothers who wanted their children to stay in the wadi,
to live and die there, out of their fear of other places and conviction that no place better existed, had to give in sooner or
later, but theirs was an impotent and despairing resignation, and
it always mingled with the hope that the children would come
back, having had their fill of travel.

The wadi's people were known for their strange mixture of
gentleness and obsession. Peaceable and happy, they were always
quick to help out and expected little in return, but they were at
times prone to laziness and daydreaming. Even bedouin who
stayed in Wadi al-Uyoun only for short periods knew them to
be this way and so tolerated behavior that they would never
have accepted elsewhere. "The people here are just big children,"
they would say. "A single word overjoys or kills them. You

have to know just how to speak to them and how to deal with them." They did need special treatment even beyond how you spoke to them, for they watched strangers' gestures and mannerisms closely, and once they formed an opinion or conviction they stuck by it, never changing their minds. If they differed among themselves about any person or thing, one would say, "Don't be too quick—we've seen thousands of people come through here and life has taught us much. Just wait." Such a statement would end many a discussion, for after the implied challenge only time would show who was right and who was wrong.

Travelers often reminded each other that the people of the wadi had to be dealt with carefully, for even a simple mistake would stigmatize the whole caravan and sour relations for a long time. Traders who were careful to sleep beside their goods and merchandise, never leaving them for a moment or trusting anyone else to guard them, felt a unique confidence when they arrived in the wadi, for they valued the people's trustworthiness. People of the wadi preferred quick buying and selling free of haggling and coercion, practices they regarded as suspicious and unfriendly, especially when two caravans met and tough, long-winded bargaining ensued, marked by pretensions of unwillingness to buy and the buyers' professed disgust at the goods they were offered. Even when the bargaining suddenly ended, with the prices and conditions set out by the buyers and endorsed by the sellers, there were shows of surprise and sometimes shouts of anger and denunciation. The eventual laughter of both sides, indicating satisfaction, moved the wadi's men to observe, "These traders are devils in men's clothing—they haven't the slightest idea of right and wrong."

If it were pointed out to them that commerce depended on haggling and bargaining and satisfaction in the end, and that there was nothing sinful in making money, they would respond with a mixture of pity and mockery, saying either aloud or to themselves, "How can you compare someone who works all year for his wage with another who makes more profit in a single moment?"

The people of Wadi al-Uyoun were thus distinct from the Atoum, who lived in their chosen habitat on Mount Zahra and had close ties with their great tribe in all regions of the desert. The Atoum had a special view of life—they were not obliged to welcome caravans the second they arrived, for they presided at the highest reaches of Zahra, looking down on the caravans hurrying toward the water and the nearby caravansary, and they would descend with some deliberation long after the caravan's arrival. Being part of a great tribal confederation gave them self-confidence, so they viewed money and possessions with haughtiness and sometimes outright scorn; no matter how life dealt with them it could never crush them, and these feelings sometimes made them rough and boorish. Nonetheless if they trusted or loved anyone they would give him all they had, expecting nothing in return and with no bitterness.

The Atoum were the poorest people in Wadi al-Uyoun, and the proudest. Perhaps it was the very poverty that gave rise to the arrogance, because any one of the Atoum, who could never become rich even if he wanted to, could suddenly squander everything he possessed without any trace of sorrow or regret and begin saving anew, wearily and patiently. As soon as he had anything extra the game began again.

In the wadi itself, people were poor, but they were happy with the life they lived and praised it extravagantly. At times they would complain about the constant diet of dry dates, milk and stale bread and the intestinal pains they got, the dryness of their faces and limbs and weakness that affected some men so badly that they'd stand up only to get dizzy and fall down again. So many children were skinny and sallow, and were afflicted with vomiting and diarrhea in the summer. The persistence of the symptoms frightened them and made them think that they needed more meat to strengthen their bodies; they would anxiously await the next caravan, whose arrival would change the atmosphere; and perhaps the travelers would slaughter a few head of sheep in return for what they got from the wadi. If no caravan came, some excuse would have to be found for slaughtering a camel so that everyone might eat.

When things got better, the people acted differently, talking more and spending long nights socializing. On summer nights it was not enough to sit around the coffeepots telling stories; they wanted to sing and sometimes dance, to unleash endless ideas, sorrows and memories. Some men would be overcome by sleep and others by an urge to fight, all for unknown reasons or even no reason at all. If their guts were still tormented by hunger and the vessels of sour milk were no longer making the rounds, someone would shout to the rest, "Grilled meat! Yes, that's just what we're going to eat tonight!"

And in fact some nights they would decide to slaughter a camel at dawn. Skill, dexterity and boundless cooperation came into play as one group gathered firewood, another prepared the pots or made new bread and volunteers carried out the actual killing and butchery work. Before long the whole wadi was a hive of a special kind of activity, showing the will to stay and fight and creating the will to resist poverty and hardship.

This kind of life endowed the people of the wadi with distinctive physical features: good height, strong backs, symmetrical frames and straight, slender limbs, hips and shoulders. To see them you might think of them as horses run and trained to the point of overleanness, but still strong, sturdy and beautiful.

Their faces were longish and symmetrical, with thin lips and smooth cheeks set high but not prominent. They were not nearly as prone to facial or bodily defects as people in other areas.

Because everyone in Wadi al-Uyoun was so similar, in both physical appearance and general attitudes, it was possible to distinguish one from the other only by age or personality, or by the exact kinship to the ancestor al-Aoun, who was considered the wadi's chief in spite of the fact that he had died long years ago. Stories of his courage and generosity were still told, and the selflessness that marked all his deeds revered, so that he was still seen as their genius and guardian.

If Ibrahim al-Aoun and his tribe, the Atoum, had come in from the far-off desert to settle in Wadi al-Uyoun, then nature and places also had their unknowable laws.

The al-Aoun clan, to which Jazi al-Hathal and his father Miteb before him had belonged, had been sown in this place like the palm trees. They were torn between a longing to go back whence they had come and a longing to move on to new places, but they were held in place by some mysterious force. People still remembered Jazi al-Hathal and what he had done to the Turks forty or fifty years before, making their occupation of Wadi al-Uyoun an unbearable hell. He would lie low for so long that he was thought to have died or been killed, and was almost forgotten by everyone, including the Turks themselves. Then he'd burst onto the scene, killing, burning and destroying, only to escape back into the desert with what he had seized, staying there long enough to be forgotten again; then he'd be back, making the wadi a veritable hell.

Jazi did that many times, even before the people had begun to think of the Turks as enemies, and he kept it up until the forces withdrew. The Turkish command's attempts to pursue and arrest him ended in the deaths of the leaders of the two campaigns against him and the defection of soldiers who joined

Jazi's raids and helped to cut roads. It was said that they stayed with him until the end.

This cause, which took over and obsessed the al-Hathal clan, manifested itself to them in many forms; perhaps it was the reason they chose this central place, a way station for travelers, so that they too could be witnesses to an era of life and history that would come once and never recur, so that they could tell others of the wonders and prodigies they had seen.

2

O N THAT DAY SO LONG AGO, LIKE SO MANY THOU-
sands before it, the last of Miteb al-Hathal's
sons was born. It was in late spring, in the
afternoon. The heat had been merciless for days, with the fruit
of the date palms budding and plumping out. Miteb was just
unyoking Umm Khashab from the plow and tying her up firmly
so he could go to his house on Zahra and check on his wife and
prepare the coffee early when he saw his son Fawaz racing toward
him, his face radiating joy. Then he knew that his wife had given
birth, that a new son had come. He stayed leaning against the
palm trunk, waiting for Fawaz to arrive with the good news,
and as he waited he looked around several times. At that moment
the wadi seemed to him greener than ever. "We got good rains
this year," he said to himself.

"Father—father! Good news!" cried Fawaz while he was still far off.

"If it's come, it's come," said Miteb to himself.

Just as in the past, he did not hesitate in giving the boy a name, as if he had been ready for a long time. Scarcely had the lad's feet touched the ground, his face covered with dust, sweat and joy, when Miteb looked him in the eye and calmly asked, "Tell me, boy, has Mugbel come?"

The lad looked at his father in confusion, thinking his father did not understand what he had told him. After catching his breath he said, "We have a new brother."

"You say Mugbel has come, hah?" asked Miteb, putting his large hand on the small boy's head. He laughed loudly. "God bless you, boy."

He took off his belt and loosened his robe, and after he dusted off his hands, the two walked quietly back to the house on Zahra. They walked in silence, but an inner glow more like a tumult filled Miteb al-Hathal. Zahra seemed unbearably far, and he thought of speeding up or running, but changed his mind, saying to himself, "If the boy were my first, or I not so old!" He looked at Fawaz several times and then said laughingly, "We'll marry him off to little Shaqra Mubarak!"

Miteb gave a huge banquet that evening, killing a sheep and inviting everyone. Late that night, after the men had all left, he sat alone in the moonlight. His whole life passed in front of his eyes like a long ribbon. He saw his days and nights. He remembered his boyhood and his first journeys. He smiled when he remembered Wadha and the first son she gave him. She had been afraid, and late at night she'd wept and looked at him. Tonight when he looked at her she was tired and neither laughed nor wept. Miteb al-Hathal did not understand why he wanted to claw the hard earth under the carpet with his fingernails, as if putting a mark on it, wanting to leave some indelible trace. He went into the house late that night to get out his old rifle and shoot off a few rounds. The idea came to him suddenly, like a flash of lightning. He did it every time a boy was born; the first time had been with Thweiny, his first son, who had died long ago. That night he had taken out the rifle before all the men and shot off a whole clip, and all his friends who had pistols had joined in. He remembered that Ibn Mubarak al-Huweizi and Fahd had shot off bullets unceasingly, and that al-Huweizi had used up all the bullets he had the day Shaalan was born, and that al-Qahtani had tried too but his pistol had failed after firing the first bullet. The men were happy and excited; they feasted, laughed and fired their rifles for hours. This time was not like it was before. That time the joy had been overpowering, though Thweiny had died young. Tonight they ate, drank and were merry; al-Qahtani said that Mugbel was a sign of good times ahead, but they did not get out their guns. Miteb did not even think of it, and now he told himself somewhat sadly, "The old days were good—better than these days."

He wanted to make some noise, in order not to create any fear or surprise, as he was fetching the rifle. He stood by Wadha's bed as his sister Sarah sat rocking the baby. It seemed she had just finished feeding him some honey.

The two women looked at him. Wadha was exhausted, half asleep, and when she saw the gun she jumped slightly as if suddenly penetrated by fear or joy. She watched Miteb closely and rose up on her elbow a little. Feeling proud, he struck the rifle butt on the ground as if giving an order of some kind. Sarah was speaking to the crying child: "You'll grow big, little boy, you'll grow strong, and tomorrow you'll be a man. Men have to be men." When she heard the thump of the rifle on the ground she turned and looked at Miteb questioningly, then glanced at Wadha.

"Listen," said Miteb. He spoke slowly as if beginning a long speech. When he saw the two women looking at him, looking curiously at the gun, he went on exultingly. "He was telling the truth, whoever said, 'Whoever has children never dies.' "

He paused a moment, smiled and nodded his head, and went on sadly. "God rest our parents and their parents."

Very calmly, he took up the rifle, shot the bolt and put a shell in the magazine, then turned and went out.

There was silence, and a moon. Miteb al-Hathal was in the great desert alone. He contemplated the sky and stars and breathed deeply. He felt like doing something extraordinary.

"Midnight! Take this!"

He raised the rifle to the sky, to the moon, and fired. The shot ripped the night and echoed, and its fragrance filled his lungs. He drew the bolt and dropped the empty shell, and the smell of the gunpowder filled his nostrils. He remembered past days and told himself, "God, give us good days. Make us stronger and more patient!" When he inserted the second shell into the magazine he heard movement inside the house, and guessed that it was not the sound of Wadha or Sarah; one of the children had been woken by the sound of the gunshot. He turned slightly and saw no one at first, fell to the carpet, and after a moment Shaalan came out looking curious and a little afraid.

"Hah, my boy, were you frightened?" asked Miteb, laying the rifle on the ground.

Shaalan smiled and looked at his father questioningly, and seeing him calm shook his head no.

"When you came into the world we lit it up with gunpowder until morning," said Miteb, his face joyful in the moonlight.

The boy nodded, filled with pride.

"Today, my boy, you have a brother."

Shaalan laughed in acknowledgment and agreement, and Miteb added, "Your brother has to smell gunpowder, so it won't scare him when he's bigger."

"Make more coffee, Abu Thweiny," called Sarah from inside the house, where she had been listening to Miteb. "You'll have another batch of men coming from Wadi al-Uyoun."

"The coffee's all ready, Sarah. They are most welcome."

"If they come you'll be shooting until morning!"

"Daddy, give me the gun," said Shaalan excitedly.

Miteb al-Hathal proudly handed his son the rifle. He wanted someone to share this mysterious, invigorating game with him. He was flooded with strong, fleeting feelings, with a lightness more like exultation. Shaalan raised the rifle and fired, and the whole wadi resounded with the shot. To Miteb the shot sounded louder and more resonant than the first, and the scent of gunpowder filled the air with an eerie sweetness. When silence returned, he heard Sarah's voice again. "The best is yet to come, and we'll have more than odors, Abu Thweiny!"

"Trust in God, Sarah. Time is long!"

When the third shot rang out, Miteb told his son, "That's enough, my boy." He paused a moment and then laughed, adding in a loud voice, "We know our own people. Day or night, one more shot and they'll all be here in Zahra!"

He laughed again. Miteb was talking to himself, talking to the others; he felt that everything around him was moving forcibly. Even the moon and stars seemed to him different than in the many days past. He felt that the icy cold gripping the air at that moment infused him with strength and confidence; he wanted his body to swell out to hold the erupting joy that filled his soul, to say something that would not only stick in the memory but reside in the heart. He gazed at the moon and Shaalan's face, at the open door where Sarah stood, and said: "If your boy grows up, give him a brother."

"With luck, Abu Thweiny, a hen can lay eggs on a tent peg!" said Sarah, won over by the air of joy and excitement.

Miteb guffawed and replied, "If I manage it, Sarah, donkeys can piss on lions!"

"Trust in God!" shouted Wadha from inside the house.

3

M UGBEL BIN MITEB AL-HATHAL WAS BORN IN
Wadi al-Uyoun, that much was for sure; what
was not for sure was the year of his birth.
What caused the dispute was confusion over similar events.
His aunt Wasma said he was born the year of the locusts. That
was a bad, black year, yet when he was born Miteb al-Hathal
had said, "The bad days are over; the good times are coming."
It was to emphasize that conviction that he had named him
Mugbel. Wasma added that her brother Saad had come that year
after a long absence; all the sugar, flour and cloth he'd brought
with him had made the family decide to stay in Wadi al-Uyoun
instead of leaving the way so many others had done. She was
sure because she had been wearing a new dress Saad had brought
her when she put Mugbel on her shoulder and he pissed on it.

Even then she was happy and said that their hard times would soon be over.

Sarah—Umm Thunayan—said Mugbel was born the year the brooks flooded; the year of the locusts Wasma was talking about had been three years before that. The bedouin had come to Wadi al-Uyoun later than usual that year, she said, because it had been a good year in the desert and the wells had been full of water. She was positive, because the truffles and mallow and other herbs were everywhere; she had never seen anything like it. As to Mugbel's name, that had been her idea; she had suggested the name and insisted on it, "because Miteb wanted to name him Thweiny or Ziyab, Thweiny for the baby that passed away and Ziyab after that sheep incident in the wadi."

Sarah and Wasma's dispute over the year of Mugbel's birth was never settled, because neither would give in and the witnesses each woman cited refused to change their stories no matter how much the other pressed them to; they could not betray their memories that much.

If births in Wadi al-Uyoun did not stand out or cause arguments, what really did complicate things that season was the government's three-man commission sent to record the names of all the males and new births. The commission had passed through many different parts of the desert, carrying their papers and heavy ledgers, but no one knew why they had come or the real reasons behind the census. This fear led the people of Wadi al-Uyoun to deal warily with the commission: they concealed much information, said nothing about traveling family members, and did not so much as mention their daughters. Some of the males were registered and some not, and as an added precaution all boys from eight to fourteen years old were told to go away and play in the gardens all day long. Fathers pretended to remember only the vaguest details about the years their sons were born.

That was what almost everyone in Wadi al-Uyoun did, because weeks before the arrival of the commission there was a rumor that the military was going to take the young men. It did not, however, keep three or four families in Wadi al-Uyoun from doing just the opposite, registering all their sons and traveling relatives and even some of the recently deceased. They did that because one of the men on the commission told them in the strictest confidence, on condition they tell no one else, that quantities of sugar, flour and cloth would be distributed in the wadi and elsewhere according to the number of family members. Most people scoffed at that story, saying it was just a trap, because the government had never done that before, even in years when people were dying of thirst.

Later, when Suleiman al-Hadib was told the year of Mugbel's birth, he hesitated before agreeing or disagreeing, and when he was told that government records didn't lie, he smiled scornfully, and said, shaking his head, "If they go by their book, then they are wrong most of the time."

He remembered how the townsfolk of al-Hadra had dealt with the commission that year.

Aunt Wadia, the wadi's matriarch, had a completely different theory regarding the year of Mugbel's birth. She said he was eight or nine years older than Anoud. She remembered that because Mugbel was the same age as Halima, who had died at one year old, and she had had two children between Halima and Anoud, meaning that Mugbel would have been born the year of the world war, because her husband Hazaa' had been imprisoned in Egypt during the war for refusing to sell his sheep. He had smuggled them, or tried to smuggle them, but he'd been arrested and thrown in prison. Hazaa' said, and Aunt Wadia agreed, that the world war between the Germans, the Italians, the English, the Indians and the Senegalese would have driven him to Tripoli in Libya had it not been for God's grace. They said that the war had lasted for years and years, and that Halima had been born five months after her father left.

Aunt Wadia would often strenuously defend her version of events, because Mugbel was one of the strongest contenders for Anoud's hand. After a long wait, however, with Mugbel still hesitant and unable to give his final word, one of Hazaa's clan came along, got Anoud's father's permission to marry her and did so. Then Aunt Wadia stood by her story less vehemently, saying she did not exactly remember. But she went along with her sister Wasma, saying that Sarah's information was all wrong, nothing but fabrications to help one of her relatives make a match with Mugbel.

So there was really no need for anyone to plumb his memory trying to remember Mugbel's birth year; it was such a complicated question, with nothing to gain from settling it. He might have been born in the year of the locusts or the year of the floods, or before or after, but he was certainly born before that frightful year of the storm, because then the wadi, the caravan road and the people had all been reduced to a state of utter poverty and devastation. Echoes of the outside world reached the wadi intermittently by way of caravans or relatives absent for long years, some of them forced to return out of fear of being drawn into the war; and because they had lost their livelihoods.

News of the world reached them garbled and confused. Fawaz was then a boy nearing young manhood, for he had begun to sit in the men's encampment, Sarah recalled, and one night, as the men told stories and recited odes, and the wolves howled afar off, she first heard that Fawaz wanted to travel.

If the arrival of a caravan meant much to both old and young, sending them all scurrying off in some direction, it did not interrupt the peace and equilibrium of the men, who took their time getting to the brook and the caravansary. They knew a lot about the caravan even before it got there, thanks to the children who ran around like cats bearing the news of how many men and camels were in the caravan, what it carried, where it came from and where it was going. The children's immoderate curiosity made them want to know everything and confirm it themselves, and they would instantly tell the adults what they had seen. It happened with every caravan. The adults listened with an attentiveness they did not show, for they had already heard something from other caravans, from a passing messenger a few days before, or from counting the time between journeys and places. When the adults finally went to the brook or the caravansary, they took notice of everything, even the beasts' droppings, and drew their own conclusions.

About this time Fawaz stopped racing along with the other children. He joined the men of the Atoum in delaying their arrival at the brook, but he was annoyed by his father's still later arrival. When the caravans began to prepare for resuming their journey after a break of two or three days, he would be there to assist the travelers, at the same time trying to convince his father to let him go. With every bundle handed up and tied to a camel, with every rope wound around to secure the luggage he showed skill and strength, and he never stopped trying to persuade his father.

When the hour of departure finally came, with the sweaty brown hands offered in firm but gentle farewell, Fawaz would be filled with vexation and bitterness at not being included in the caravan. Soon he would join another caravan, he told himself.

"In two or three years, when you're bigger, you can travel, my boy," Miteb al-Hathal would say when a new caravan had left.

When Fawaz pestered him and took a stubborn stand, trying to act like a grown man when a caravan took its leave, Miteb al-Hathal would say, "My boy, this place is better than others."

After a thoughtful silence he would add, "What has travel to offer besides weariness?"

Sometimes Fawaz would tell his father that he had seen two boys of his own age or even younger in the caravan that had left that day, or in the one that had passed through two weeks before.

"Wadha," Miteb would say to his wife, "Shaalan still hasn't come back from his travels and Fawaz wants to set off. Get his things ready to go, and trust in God."

At this point Miteb would step aside to let his wife play her part, for if he were ready to discuss the matter and give in, at least outwardly, to please his son, Wadha's refusal to consider the idea brooked no argument: her nature, and what she possessed of hidden strength and sometimes a sad or dejected look usually defeated Fawaz and made him put the idea aside for a while. She would assure him that in a few years' time he would be stronger and better capable of handling the trials of a journey that might last ten years; in the meantime (for he had not even begun to grow a beard yet) the thought of travel would have to remain a hope. She talked about his father and his relatives who had traveled, how long they were absent and how much trouble and pain they endured, and she kept at him until he was convinced or pretended to be convinced.

"If you're a big strong man now, then go and water the animals and come back safely," Miteb would tell him when watering time came.

He meant that a boy of Fawaz's age could herd some of the animals by himself, if he were strong and knew what he was doing, for sundown in the wadi, when the animals went to drink, was one of the hardest and most dangerous times. In addition to making it to the brook at the right time, controlling the beasts, not mixing them up and all that was entailed in the way of discussions and sometimes arguments could only be handled by men or the strongest youths. It often took two men to water the animals quickly and without incident.

So when Miteb al-Hathal asked his son to go on his own, Fawaz felt pride and daring; when his mother motioned to his younger brother Ibrahim to accompany him, Fawaz refused firmly and told her somewhat challengingly, "By myself! I don't want anyone and I'll be the first one back."

Fawaz went off by himself but did not make it back early as he had promised. He returned very late indeed!

When he reminisced later about the first day he went to water the animals by himself and returned so late, he recalled that his delay was due not to any difficulty in getting the job done, but to another, more important reason, the same reason that would subsequently prevent him from traveling.

After the sun sank from sight and the light shadow covered everything, when the camels and sheep stirred and bleated in the compass of the dappled, fast-retreating light, the air was filled with the beasts' heavy movements and friction and their scattered lowing. Fawaz felt alarmed and confident at the same time, and confined as well, and in spite of the blind sounds he drove before him, as he urged the cattle to move faster their pace remained plodding and even slow. He realized too late that he had succumbed to this hidden inducement and stayed an hour or more roaming between the animals and the small circle of men near Ibn Rashed's encampment. When he got back to Zahra he found the old lady sitting in the foremost place, as if by sitting there, close to the earth, she was trying to penetrate the shadow and the distance as men did in daytime when they stood erect or sat on a hill with hands over their eyes so as better to scrutinize the distance and detect shadows and movements. Thus the old lady sat in the near-darkness, overtaken by unease and fear. Ibrahim was pacing around mockingly, not saying a word, trying to show how serious and useful he could have been had he gone along with Fawaz.

Fawaz went on his way without stopping to explain his lateness, but some nervous instinct took over his movements and made him shout at the sheep to hurry into the corral, and at the camels to kneel so he could hobble them. He shouted at Ibrahim, who was still wandering around, to finish the rest of the chores.

He could not make excuses just then; he wanted to tell his father about what he had seen and heard. No sooner had he looked at his father's face, however, in the faint light of the last snapping embers, than Miteb's eyes had shone with a sarcastic but somewhat pitying smile, as if he wanted to say once again, "That's enough stubbornness—you're still too young to travel. You have to wait!" He lowered his eyes and continued to stoke the small fire, and Fawaz felt that his father wanted no explanation or excuse for his tardiness. He placidly kept stirring up the live coals with light expert movements preparatory to making coffee.

Fawaz felt frustrated and threw himself down to lie propped on his elbow. His mother's squatting away from the house, Ibrahim's flippant provocation, his father's quick glance, heavy with rebuke and disappointment, and their complete silence, all of it filled him with frustration and a sense of grave injustice. He imagined that the hour he had spent moving between Ibn Rashed's encampment, the animals and the faces of those mysterious foreign guests, and his sprint back to see that the camels and sheep were unharmed and had drunk, had made him wonder if he should return quickly or stay behind to look at what he was seeing for the first time.

"Ibn Rashed has foreign guests," he told his father, who was still busy with the fire.

His voice fell among the coals and the clinking coffeepots as his father kept at his task, as if he had not heard or did not want to hear excuses for the delay. Fawaz spoke again, more loudly and with something of a challenge in his voice. "They're Franks, and they speak Arabic."

His father raised questioning eyes at these words and waited to hear more. They sat across from each other with the fire and coffeepots between them.

"Three foreigners with two marsh Arabs, and they speak Arabic." He raised his voice for effect. "They speak differently than we do—it's comical. But you can understand what they say."

He saw a sudden change in his father, whose concentration now gleamed in his eyes as he looked at Fawaz sternly, as if he wanted to read in his face and eyes what he had seen and what impressions had been left, in order to know what kind of men these had been. Miteb spoke slowly. "Did you find out where they came from and what they want?"

"The people at the encampment said they were Christians."

"What do they want?"

"I heard Ibn Rashed tell one of them, 'Say "There is no god but God and Muhammad is His prophet" ' and the man said after him, 'There is no god but God and Muhammad is His prophet.' "

"What are they after?"

"People say they came to look for water."

"You—what did you hear them say?"

"There were too many people around them—I only heard a word here and there."

With the same vigor that had shown in his eyes when Fawaz said they were foreigners, that had drawn him out of his original disappointment and censure, Miteb pulled himself together and got up.

"I have to see for myself," he said.

He and Fawaz quickly saddled the two horses. Mugbel tried

to cling to him to go along, but Miteb snapped at his wife: "Take the child—get him away from us."

"God knows how late we'll be. We might sleep at Ibn Rashed's," Miteb called when he had mounted his horse and they were ready to gallop off.

They were off, both silent. There was no sound but hoofbeats. When they reached Ibn Rashed's, Miteb al-Hathal sat near the guests and Fawaz sat with boys his own age near the entrance to the encampment.

4

MITEB AL-HATHAL QUICKLY AGREED TO SPEND the night at Ibn Rashed's and stayed there until sundown the next day, always watching the three foreigners closely, speaking to them, asking himself and others what had brought these men here. This and the slow, sad ride home, with its stops and discussions, the way his son talked and acted—all this made Fawaz al-Hathal a man before his time and left an indelible memory in his heart.

Miteb chose a long road for the ride back to Zahra, one he almost never used, and when he got back he was a changed man to all those who saw him and knew him. He was confused and depressed. He spoke in a way he never had before; his tone of voice, the kind of things he said and the many questions he asked his son—which in fact he was really asking himself and others—

were all different. To Fawaz, who was careful to remain silent during the whole trip back, his father's words were strange in an unforgettable way.

"They certainly didn't come for water—they want something else. But what could they possibly want? What is there in this dry desert besides dust, sand and starvation? They say they'll be here a long time? How will they live? They look like chickens when they eat. And the questions they asked were damned crafty. Saying they weren't like the ones who came before. 'Have any foreigners besides us come?' 'Have you heard about any foreigners, English or French coming here?' 'Did they stay long? Did they do anything?' They're afraid—they've done something. You know very well that whoever does anything wicked is afraid of others. If they were honest people who came to look for water, why everybody knows where the water is. They don't want to stay here—they want to travel around, to go and then come back, and others will come after them. That's what they said. They said, 'Wait, just be patient, and all of you will be rich!' But what do they want from us, and what does it concern them if we get rich or stay just as we are? Watch their eyes, watch what they do and say. They're devils, no one can trust them. They're more accursed than the Jews. And the bastards memorized the Koran. Strange."

When he paused and asked his son for his opinion, Fawaz did not say a word, for he did not understand what was happening. True, he had heard the young men say bad things about the strangers, and point at them and laugh. He had seen them eat and talk, but he did not know what was happening around him; even when they got back to Zahra and Miteb told the other men some of what he had seen and heard, his father had looked at him, wanting him to corroborate in some way what he was saying. All his life his father had taught him to be silent when adults were talking and remain standing when they had guests, to move and act politely. This time Miteb al-Hathal acted differently.

"My friends, you wouldn't believe it. One of them, God knows, their sheikh, knows Arabic, but he doesn't want to speak it. I am positive. I noticed him. He was like a hawk, watching everything and trying to hear. I asked him if he spoke Arabic or not and he said, 'A little, a little.' The son of a bitch knows it better than all of them, but he's crafty. When he wants something he talks in his own language and has the others ask. Water? Wadi al-Uyoun has water enough—we don't want any more than that. If they want water, if they want people to help them, let them go somewhere else."

In the days that followed, Miteb al-Hathal took care to water all the animals by himself, and to test his suspicions he had all the men go and see the foreigners for themselves. He had Fawaz take the animals so that he could go to Ibn Rashed's. Each time Miteb returned with new ideas, which all confirmed his first suspicions and convinced him more firmly that "those devils are incapable of any good."

They were busy all day long. They went places no one dreamed of going. They collected unthinkable things. They had a piece of iron—no one knew what it was or what they did with it— and when they returned in the evening they brought with them bags of sand and pieces of rock. Once they brought tamarisk and wormwood branches, and bunches of clover. They broke the branches in a strange way and attached pieces of paper on which they had written obscure things. That was not all: they placed wooden markers and iron poles everywhere they went, and wrote on them, and wrote things no one understood on the sheets of paper they carried with them everywhere. The markers were hidden or moved around whenever they went away—the boys of the wadi moved and gathered up some of the markers, and the grown-ups did nothing to stop them. When Fawaz showed up with some of the iron poles after he had been tending the sheep, his father scrutinized them carefully and a little fearfully. He knocked them on a rock, knocked them one against the other and listened to them for a long time, then he said that they must not be brought near the fire.

And the water. Where was the water and how could they find it? Did the government know where they were and what they were doing? When Miteb al-Hathal asked him, Ibn Rashed said that they had a certificate from the emir and had been his guests for a week. When Miteb asked the two guides, they said that the emir had sent them and that was why they had come.

Miteb al-Hathal grew more pessimistic with every passing day; his fears mounted and his curses were more frequent. He came to talk about nothing else. If all the men joined him in discussing the problem, not all of them agreed with him, but because of his age and social standing they let him think and swear as he pleased.

He sensed that something terrible was about to happen. He did not know what it was or when it would happen, and he took no comfort in the explanations offered him from all sides. The very sight of the foreigners and their constant activity all day, the instruments they carried around, the bags of sand and stones they had amassed after writing in their notebooks and drawing symbols on them, the discussions that lasted from sundown until after supper and the writing that followed, the damned questions they asked about dialects, about tribes and their disputes, about religion and sects, about the routes, the winds and the rainy seasons—all these caused Miteb's fear to grow day by day that they meant harm to the wadi and the people. The wadi's inhabitants, who at first viewed the three foreigners with scorn and laughed when they saw them carrying bags of sand and rock, grew more surprised when they discovered that the three knew a lot about religion, the desert, the bedouin's life and the tribes. The profession of faith they repeated whenever asked, and their scriptural citations, moved many people of the wadi to wonder among themselves if these were jinn, because people like them who knew all those things and spoke Arabic yet never prayed were not Muslims and could not be normal humans.

Ibn Rashed, who had seemed a different person since the arrival of the foreigners, showing them lavish attention and hospitality in the most demonstrative way, as if he had been expecting them, or perhaps had prior orders from the emir given by their guides—Ibn Rashed inwardly believed that there was great gain to be had from these men. As a consequence, he overdid everything, his speech and his actions, which was more than the wadi could bear and more than the people could stand. If at first people tended to feel arrogant, as if they enjoyed ease and prosperity in the wadi and knew how to honor their guests, soon they were overtaken by doubt as to whether they could keep it up: the foreigners had been there quite a while and showed no signs of moving on.

Miteb al-Hathal was embarrassed and infuriated by Ibn Rashed's behavior. Although Miteb respected hospitality and was a generous man himself, giving his guests the best of whatever he had even if his family went hungry, he could not understand why Ibn Rashed seemed so fearful and servile before these men.

"Listen, Ibn Rashed," he told him a few days after the Americans had arrived. "We can eat dirt and offer our very children to our guests, but we cannot nod our heads like slaves at every word they say."

When Ibn Rashed smiled, in an attempt to soothe Miteb's anger, Miteb told him, "Even the way you smile and look at them is despised by the people of the wadi. They're only men like us, and if the emir hadn't sent them we'd send them right back where they came from. We have all the water we need in Wadi al-Uyoun and we don't need help from anyone."

Miteb paused a few moments, his face showing strain. He shook his head several times. "Talk to them like a man. Treat them like men, Ibn Rashed."

"God bless you, Abu Thweiny—why so harsh?"

"By God, from the first day they came you've been doing nothing but laughing like a hyena."

"Abu Thweiny, they're not like us. We have to treat them kindly so that they'll say we're Arabs," said Ibn Rashed slyly.

"We are Arabs, Ibn Rashed—we don't need a certificate from anyone," replied Miteb impatiently. Then in a milder tone he added, "So kill sheep for them, laugh, talk with them—but like a man."

Caravans still passed regularly through Wadi al-Uyoun, and Miteb al-Hathal loved to talk exclusively—after asking the travelers all the necessary and customary questions—about those dangerous, sneaky foreigners who had come, no one knew for what reasons, or what they wanted to do, or what would happen in the end. Not only that, he would insist that all the men of the caravan go to see the Americans and agree to help him find out the secrets behind their coming. The travelers who heard Miteb's story acted in a way that confirmed all his suspicions: "We saw some of them on the way to Wadi al-Uyoun. They looked like slaughtered sheep from the heat of the sun! When we stopped to rest and saw the emir five days ago he told us, 'Whoever causes them any trouble will be punished. They're brothers and have come to help us out.' " When Miteb asked what kind of help they could offer, and said that things were fine and their help was not needed, the men exchanged glances and said nothing.

Whenever the men of the caravans saw the three foreigners

and spoke to them, their fears and doubts increased. The foreigners spoke and inquired about places no one knew of or ever went to, so it was clear that they were not looking for water.

This is what happened at that time. As to why Miteb al-Hathal behaved as he did, why he viewed the foreigners with such anger and fear, a state of inspiration more like prophecy had filled his heart and life in recent years!

5

··

TO EVERYONE'S SURPRISE, HADIB AND SHAALAN
arrived with one of the caravans after a three-
year absence from the wadi. That day was
long remembered because the news of their arrival, brought by
the boys who first saw the caravan on the East Khabra road,
was all confused: some of the boys said that Khosh had come.
The youngsters had got the wrong name and wrong person, but
no sooner had the news reached the wadi than Umm Khosh
began to dance, laugh, cry and trill shrilly all at once. She did
not know whether to go and meet the caravan or to ready the
house for his reception. She raced in all directions and back again
like a madwoman. When the caravan finally arrived and it became clear that it was Hadib and Shaalan who had come, everything changed: silence, then a feeling of depression, and then
real sorrow prevailed as Umm Khosh's screams and sobs filled

the wadi. She had never been more miserable. Miteb al-Hathal tried to comfort her but failed; he too was overcome by grief and wished in his heart that the two travelers had never come.

That night Miteb told the men that he had not been expecting the travelers' return so soon; there were times when he thought they would never make it at all. Now that they were here he recalled how he and Hadib had struggled to save enough to buy three laden camels from a man in Wadi al-Uyoun who had left his caravan.

"Shaalan was just wandering around. He didn't see or hear anything, but when he saw his mother's brother getting ready to set out, he just went crazy and had to go with him." Miteb told the story looking at Shaalan, who listened quietly, as if the story had nothing to do with him. Miteb laughed loudly, remembering how he had not been able to dissuade Shaalan, and repeated the old story. "I told his mother, Umm Thweiny, that's your son and that's your brother. They have our money and other people's money as a trust, and if we end up starving or cursing this day, don't blame us—blame them!"

He motioned to Hadib and Shaalan and went on harshly. "I told her, if they're going to be like the people of Wadi al-Uyoun, planting a tree wherever they go and waiting for its fruit, then forget it. But if they're easy on us and come back after a year or two, then splendid—we won't worry about what people say."

He laughed happily, confidently, and told how after that Wadha took charge of everything, how she did all the packing for Hadib and Shaalan, and how with every step and movement she made she implored her son to come back, to come back quickly. Shaalan promised his mother he would, wanting his father to hear, as he busied himself preparing all the travel necessities according to what he imagined and what he had seen other travelers carrying. The last hours before his departure were filled with a crushing sadness. Words seemed fruitless and died away before they were heard, so Miteb decided to leave Zahra to go down to the wadi. He took care to go down early.

"The land needs its people," he told his wife before leaving Zahra. "Hadib and Shaalan are like Khosh—it might be years before they come back."

When she told him that her brother had promised to return quickly, that he would only be gone a short time, depending on how the journey went, he answered her sarcastically. "If you ever see Shaalan's children, Wadha, then praise the Lord."

Wadha cried silently. In her heart she conceded that her husband was right; perhaps she was even more anxious than he.

Now Hadib and Shaalan were back suddenly, bringing as much rejoicing as surprise. Wadha's smiles were mingled with tears as she went out to greet her son and brother, but she did not even know whether she was laughing or crying or dreaming.

Miteb was speaking with deliberation, looking at his son Fawaz as he spoke, as if he wanted him to learn a lesson, or at least to grasp what the lesson was about.

He skillfully steered the conversation toward his topic, as if driven by a hidden force, wanting as quickly as possible to ask the travelers about the devils which had recently come. He wanted to know anything they could tell him, and what people were saying about them elsewhere.

The relationship between Miteb and his brother-in-law Hadib al-Hamad was special, in the depth of its affection and its large degree of petulance and competition. Miteb believed that life alone educated a man; he viewed younger men with distrust and skepticism, and made no secret of this. Hadib al-Hamad saw travel, the change of locality and acquaintance with other peoples, as the thing that taught a man and developed his mind.

That night the conversation was once again about travel and

how it alone was the great teacher. Miteb did not comment but only laughed scornfully, because he remembered what Hadib had said.

"Life is the only thing that teaches whoever wants to learn, cousin."

After the laughter died down, he asked, "What do you think about al-Dreibi?"

"Al-Dreibi?"

"Yes, al-Dreibi, the one who says he's visited the four corners of the earth, and who speaks Egyptian like he was born in Egypt. You know him."

When Hadib nodded to show that he knew him, Miteb went on. "A few days ago he went to East Khabra with his friends and when they looked around they couldn't find him. Al-Dreibi was gone like salt in water. If it hadn't been for God's grace and the cleverness of one of the wadi's donkeys, he would have stayed lost and died."

Hadib smiled and shrugged.

"Do you know who got him back to Wadi al-Uyoun?" Miteb asked.

Hadib did not reply, and Miteb laughed.

"Ibn Madawwar's donkey—he's the one that led him and brought him back here!" He added in a different tone, "A boulder, cousin, doesn't teach or learn. It's people who teach and learn. The prophet Adam learned everything and got to the heart of a new thing every day."

Miteb al-Hathal was waiting for the opportunity to ask questions and find out how travel had changed the men who had just returned. Every little while he would steal a glance at his son Shaalan to read the effects of the long journey in his face and eyes. The two then began to talk about different places and people, about the misery and difficulties, the weather and the cold nights, about the caravans that got lost and were never heard from again. They told of the disease that afflicted Egypt and how they were held with hundreds of others in special areas bounded by wire fences; armed soldiers forbade them to go in or out until a certain period of time had passed. They had been perfectly healthy prior to this, but they'd left the quarantine weakened by discomfort, illness and hunger. Then they told about food and fruit, and about the cold water that gushed through the streets of Damascus at all times. Miteb al-Hathal listened attentively, often showing amazement and demanding further details; he repeated some of the facts and names and appeared shocked at the loss of so-and-so's caravan and deeply touched by the death of some other whom he knew and had traveled with years before. But he wanted to change the subject to the one that now occupied him the most. He wanted to know why the foreigners had come and what they were doing.

"Bad news, Abu Thweiny," said Hadib, who seemed to know more about it than Shaalan. "We met them everywhere. People say they'll dig into the earth and turn it all inside out. No one knows—" He paused a little to shake his head sadly. "A few days ago we saw ten or more of them on our way. They were in four tents and had some of our folk with them. When we asked if we could come in and rest with them, they told us, 'Drink and then go rest somewhere else.' So we drank and left, and when we visited the emir he told us, 'We know all about this—it's none of your affair.' "

"By God, they'll turn the whole wadi upside down on our heads if we let them," said Miteb angrily. Hadib's words had amazed and infuriated him. "Infidels! They have no mercy."

"It's the government's doing, Father," Shaalan said, looking at his father reprovingly. "As long as the government knows and the emir says it's none of your affair, it's useless to oppose it."

Miteb al-Hathal looked at his son as if surprised at his presence, as if he could not at first believe his ears. But when the words sank in he said mockingly: "My boy, your uncle says travel teaches, but I see you haven't learned anything!"

These words struck Shaalan like stones. Although he had long been used to talking to others cruelly or flippantly and even contemptuously, before his father he always felt terribly weak. At that moment he was utterly unable to respond or to endure his father's mockery, and as the silence grew heavier he felt as if he were suffocating and went out.

Miteb was so angry that he might have done something foolish—Hadib, who sensed this more than anyone else, spoke up in an effort to change the atmosphere. "Abu Thweiny, the devils will get here whether we want them or not. There's nothing you can do about it."

"The devils are already here, Hadib," replied Miteb. "They have arrived. They are here."

"So what do you propose, Abu Thweiny?"

"I say we see the emir, we talk about it there. As for the rest, God is great."

"I don't think there's much use in that, Abu Thweiny."

"So what will do any good?"

"The only good is in what God wills." Hadib stretched out and went on softly. "Abu Thweiny, cousin, people are not like you and me. The people are with the emir and Ibn Rashed— they are afraid and ambitious. You know better than I do: Ninety needles don't make one awl. Miteb, the government is ruthless."

"What have we to do with all this trouble? What have we to do with the government?"

"The government does not care, cousin," replied Hadib sadly.

"Listen, Hadib. The government doesn't belong to Ibn Rashed and his kind of people. The government knows better than anyone that Wadi al-Uyoun belongs to its people, and what kind of headaches have come out of this water nonsense. If that problem is settled and people go on as normal, Ibn Rashed will simmer down."

"Ibn Rashed is nothing, cousin. He just says what he hears."

"But these days he and the emir are like one man, and you know that when the shepherds become friends, the sheep are lost."

"Abu Thweiny, Ibn Rashed is nothing. That bunch over at the emir's are the root of the problem."

"It's all Ibn Rashed's fault. Every day or every other day he's at the emir's: 'Wadi al-Uyoun needs water; the bedouin used up all the water; Wadi al-Uyoun is dying of thirst, so you have to dig us new wells; no one passes through Wadi al-Uyoun any more; Wadi al-Uyoun, Wadi al-Uyoun.' If Ibn Rashed just picked up and left Wadi al-Uyoun we'd be a lot better off."

"Cousin, the emir has nothing to do with it and Ibn Rashed is just full of talk. The problem is bigger than the two of them."

"What do you say we send them a messenger?"

"Providers are always prey, Abu Thweiny. Over there they think they own Wadi al-Uyoun, and a thousand and one messengers wouldn't do any good. They'll have their way."

They talked of other things. All the men had their say, and Shaalan, who had quietly crept back looking wounded and ashamed, tried several times to clarify what he had said earlier. He did not address his father directly, but his tone and the things he said, his movements and the careful looks he aimed at him were intended to make the older man listen and understand. Meanwhile Miteb cursed vigorously and lost no chance to tell everyone exactly what kind of evil was in store for the wadi. He felt miserably sad and wished that Shaalan had never come, or ever said what he had said.

"Be patient, my friends," said one old man in an effort to soothe Miteb al-Hathal. When everyone looked at him he added,

"It's our village and we know it. We can deal with any devil."

The old man laughed hoarsely. "Shame on you for fighting and arguing before the devils even get here. If you fight among yourselves, the devils will destroy you and you'll be pretty uncomfortable then."

"We have to find a way to keep them from coming," said Miteb al-Hathal almost to himself. "If they come, we'll bury them—we'll burn them and curse their grandparents!"

6

....

SEVENTEEN DAYS LATER THE AMERICANS LEFT AND took their two guides with them, but this time they headed deeper into the interior rather than going back where they had come from. Miteb al-Hathal, who was not convinced by this departure, regarding it instead as an even greater cause for alarm, said in Ibn Rashed's encampment one night, before many of the men of Wadi al-Uyoun, "They're after something. The water is just an excuse." He laughed mockingly and added, "They're looking for jinn, or devils—who knows? But be assured of this, people of the wadi—if they find what they're after, none of us will be left alive."

This speech, so strange and angry, came as no surprise to the men, for the surprises of the first few days had been replaced by uneasy questions. Conversations between any two of the wadi's inhabitants, at any place or time, were bound to revolve around the Americans. No excuse or introduction of any sort was needed to start discussing them. The subject so dominated the wadi that one could begin discussing the Americans with one group of people and continue the same conversation with another group; every new detail known spread that quickly.

The Americans' behavior created endless suspicions. The coins of English and Arab gold they so liberally handed out, the inflated prices paid for the bags and wooden boxes they used to store sand and rocks, above all the sum they gave Ibn Rashed for two camels—these and other things utterly bewildered the people of Wadi al-Uyoun. Even those who had said, "Let's wait and see before we judge" no longer believed that the Americans had come for water.

For Wadi al-Uyoun, so accustomed to caravan traffic and the endless different sorts of people, the Americans were something completely new and strange—in their actions, their manners and the kind of questions they asked, not to mention their generosity, which surpassed that of all previous visitors.

At first Ibn Rashed had defended them, insisting that the emir had sent them and that they were friends who had come to help, but he no longer did so with any enthusiasm. More than that, he told anyone who asked about the foreigners' habits, how they slept and how they behaved among themselves, that they had some terribly odd habits and smelled peculiar.

Neither profuse use of perfumes nor incense burning could get rid of their smell. Ibn Rashed also said that they never went to bed at night without doing some writing—they might have been practicing witchcraft. Often they would stop writing, talk to each other and then go back to writing. The one who spoke no Arabic was the busiest one, always taking charge of the sand they had brought in. He wrote on the boxes and drew a variety of strange symbols on them. But nothing was stranger than their morning prayers: they began by kicking their legs and raising their arms in the air, moving their bodies to the left and right, and then touching their toes until they were panting and drenched with sweat.

"Look under their beds, under the sand, Abu Muhammad," one man counseled Ibn Rashed. "They may have left some of their sorcery things behind."

"Ibn Rashed should move his whole encampment," snapped Miteb al-Hathal, who had been listening and shaking his head. "The jinn took possession of the whole place from the day the infidels came—it's haunted." When he saw that his comment was heard with interest and approval, he added in a different tone, "Jinn or no jinn, their smell could kill birds!"

"Listen, all of you," said another man, hoisting himself up. "The open desert under the sky is better than this place."

Ibn Rashed seemed embarrassed, unable to defend the strangers as he once had just as he could not deny the hospitality he had shown them. To end the discussion he said, "Just as you say, the desert's better. God damn them and the hour of their coming. Thank God we're rid of them."

"The next time you turn around, Ibn Rashed, you might see them coming back," said Miteb al-Hathal, who had moved to Ibn Rashed's side.

"Talk to me of the devil, but not of them," replied Ibn Rashed testily.

Not ten days later the American who spoke no Arabic came back, with most of the cargo of rocks and sand they had seen before. He spent one night in Wadi al-Uyoun with his guide and moved on at dawn the following day. No one knew what had become of the other two.

Day by day, Wadi al-Uyoun returned to normal. The images of the Americans faded and were forgotten by everyone except

Miteb al-Hathal, who remained observant. If before it had been his habit not to ask too many questions, now he showed a new alertness, meeting every caravan from every direction. Vaguely he asked caravans coming from the direction of Syria and the sea if they had seen anything or anyone unusual. If they came from the interior he asked about two men possessed by jinn who had gone into the desert and lost contact with the world. He dearly wished to be told that they had died of thirst or been eaten by wolves. He craved any news of the two ghouls, and he was never satisfied with vague or confused details. Instead of asking just one person he would ask everyone, inquiring at the same time about a multitude of other subjects, and after hearing all there was to hear he would sink deep into contemplation.

Wadha had other things to worry about besides the hell Miteb was pursuing; tired of his questions and fed up with his neurotic behavior, she pleaded with him despairingly. "Leave it alone, man. The government knows better than all of us."

"Oh yes," began Miteb sarcastically, "the government knows better than—" He did not finish his sentence. Perhaps the government did not know, after all, what the devils were doing.

The summer passed, then the fall. The foreigners who had come through Wadi al-Uyoun long months before were forgotten; no one asked about them or remembered them. Miteb al-Hathal, still anxious and expectant, found that any mention of them redoubled his anxieties, especially since his friends had begun to show impatience at his notions and questions. They considered it bad luck even to mention the Americans, so Miteb kept the subject to himself. But nothing could save him from the dreams and fears that stalked him at night. Nighttime became a torment to him, and to avoid it he began napping for a few hours during daylight, though the broken sleep did him little good. Wadha and the others took notice and feared that his health would fail. They spoke to him gently to help him forget, treating him with tenderness and sympathy, but instead of soothing his fears this only made him more irascible.

When news of Miteb's painful condition reached Ibn Rashed, he observed sadly to the two or three men around him, "The Atoum have always been like that. If they do manage to reach old age they either go senile or go out and kill someone." He added, almost in a whisper, "He should be roaming about with the sheep or playing with children."

Most of the wadi took pity on Miteb and watched his actions closely; Hadib was uneasiest of all. He worried that unless Miteb found something to occupy himself with, Ibn Rashed's words would prove prophetic.

One fall evening, when gentle sundown breezes blew after a scorching day, Hadib told him, "It will be a good year, Abu Thweiny."

He turned to Miteb, who was gulping down the cool air. He turned away again and added, "If we get good rains, everything will change—the wadi will be a different place!"

"May God hear you, cousin."

"I've noticed that your house isn't in good repair, Abu Thweiny. I'm afraid the winds and rain will just carry it away!"

And so they repaired Miteb's house on Zahra, Hadib and the young men they recruited from among Shaalan's friends and relatives. The work was done with much joking and horseplay, and even Miteb himself joined in and worked tirelessly. They rebuilt the mud walls, reinforced the roof, walls and wooden columns, cleaned the gutters and sank new posts in the corral fence. In his enthusiasm Miteb decided to add a new room, since Wadha had hinted the night before that the time had come to think of arranging a marriage for Shaalan. The work was accompanied by many hints that a new and important change would soon be made in Miteb al-Hathal's household. It didn't take much intuition to guess what it would be, and the young men kneading the mud and carrying the stone blocks smiled and carried on in a way that showed they knew everything. Miteb took all this in with happiness and pride.

His decline reversed itself. He ate with renewed appetite and slept long and soundly. His strength and confidence returned. If his dreams did not cease entirely, at least in his absorption in a new activity he forgot everything.

Three or four days before the construction was finished, Wadha carried over her usual pitcher of tea "so the poor tired fellows could drink," and as Hadib busied himself with the pitcher and cups he told her, "Miteb is younger than he ever was."

"Those sons of bitches who came through just worried him to death—otherwise he'd be in better shape than any young fellow."

"I hope we've seen the last of them."

"Never again!"

On the last day, Miteb al-Hathal killed a sheep on the threshold of the new room and all the workers cheered and clapped, looking at Shaalan and his father and exchanging glances among themselves. One said, "The trough is ready—now for the horse!"

"Trust in God." Miteb laughed. "Not until the wedding."

"Shaalan's or his father's?" asked Hadib slyly.

"Shaalan and his father both, cousin!" answered Miteb. A wave of joy and festivity had come over everyone, and this feast was one of Wadi al-Uyoun's great nights.

The house was now capable of withstanding any rains, and Miteb lost no time in preparing his garden for planting. He threw himself into the work: hoed the earth twice, rooted out the weeds and thorns, mixed manure with the soil, opened up seed holes and cleared the northern irrigation ditch of dirt and sand for the heavy rains he predicted. As he dug he told himself, "This land is a treasure, but you never know what it contains until it rains. Heavy rains that come early bring wonders." He remembered the good years and smiled, lifting his head to breathe the sweet air deeply.

This season Miteb felt stronger than ever and chided himself for getting upset over the sons of bitches who had come through the wadi months before. "They came and went," he told himself. "The wadi has seen and heard more people come through than there are grains of sand here, and none of them ever left a trace. There's no trace or memory of them left." He felt more fervently than he ever had the ties that bound him to the earth, the date palms and fig trees, and to the people of the wadi as well. He spoke to his young son, who played around him and watched him. "That tree, the fourth on the left, is just your age, boy. You grow every day, and it grows with you. Tomorrow you'll plant a tree for your son, and he'll plant a tree for his son, and Wadi al-Uyoun will get greener every day. People will keep coming to drink the water and hope never to die, and when they sit in the shade of the tree they'll say, 'May God show mercy to whoever planted the trees and the green plants.' "

Mugbel kept running around his father like a small dog and jumping on his back whenever he leaned over. When the day ended in the enveloping twilight, Mugbel grasped his father's clothes so as not to lose him and they walked to the brook. The younger men had finished their watering chores and headed back to Zahra. Miteb rested and washed his face and hands in the brook, chanting and making happy and thankful sounds; then he continued up the hill, all the while talking to his son. He knew that the small boy didn't understand much of what he said, but he kept it up anyway.

"Praise the Lord—here he comes," Wadha told Hadib as they watched Miteb's shadow approach.

"Work does wonders, Umm Thweiny," replied Hadib quietly, almost inaudibly.

It seemed that everything in the wadi had returned to normal, but Miteb al-Hathal's fears and dreams continued.

7

··

I T WAS A COMMON THING, WHENEVER A CARAVAN CAME
through or letters from travelers arrived, for everyone to ask the same questions: Was there news of
Khosh? What had become of him?

These questions, so often asked of so many, were entirely
different from the dozens of similar questions put to travelers,
for Khosh was well known even to people who had never met
him. While descriptions of his traits varied from one person to
another, and his name left widely different impressions among
different people, no one lived in Wadi al-Uyoun or traveled
through it who didn't have some kind of connection with this
man.

Why? Was he a real man of flesh and blood or a creature of
fancy? If he were a real man, then why this aura of mystery and
flood of questions? Because he was away traveling? Because he

had not returned, and contact with him was lost? There were more travelers from Wadi al-Uyoun than there were actual residents, and no household in the wadi, Zahra or the surrounding area was without at least one family member on the road. Many stayed away long years and were completely out of touch for extended periods, but they always came back in the end. At the very least there would be news of them or letters, and the bolts of colored cloth that no traveler ever forgot to send.

So there was something that made Khosh different from the rest. Every person in Wadi al-Uyoun might have his say, and each might say something different, but all of it was true. Some said that Khosh was courageous—that his valor was proverbial—and they were right. Some said that he was fierce in battle, that he could stay on a wild camel even for a half-day's ride, that he had been seen hanging from a camel's tail as if he were a mere bit of cloth, or even altogether weightless, and they were right too. Whenever they talked about men's endurance, particularly of hunger and thirst, and told tales of tough men, most of the stories were about Khosh. Such oft-repeated and extravagant tales were an ordinary feature of life and had lost their magic and luster, except at emotional times or in front of strangers. But the tale of how Khosh disappeared never lost its fascination.

After he joined al-Salemi's caravan and traveled with it as far as al-Jouf, he was never seen again. He disappeared without warning and for no apparent reason. The travelers in the caravan swore that he went with them as far as al-Jouf, a seven days' journey from Wadi al-Uyoun, parting from them there. Had it not been for these firm testimonies, the people of the wadi would have said that the earth had swallowed him up or a wild animal eaten him. Naturally no one accepted the fact of his disappearance, even though the men who brought this news were known to be trustworthy and their account was repeated by many others. Some caravans from al-Jouf brought conflicting stories, deepening and multiplying the people's doubts, and travelers who were importuned to inquire about him and who promised to investigate never came up with a final answer or even any reassuring response.

The disappearance of Khosh and loss of contact with him would not have excited such a degree of concern and pity had it not been for his mother. He was her only son, and since his father's death long years ago Umm Khosh had taken on a great many masculine qualities and aspects of appearance. In addition to caring for some of the date palms, for this was all she possessed after her husband's death, she raised three or four goats and some chickens. She sold milk and eggs to travelers and did small jobs like rope weaving and mending of torn clothes, and what scraps the travelers left behind she would work with patiently and perseveringly to make something useful. In this difficult but obstinate way she raised Khosh, who at first because of his youth did not miss having a father; he had no sense of loss because many of his playmates had no fathers either—some were away traveling and some had died.

Life went on as usual in spite of the hardships, and Khosh grew to manhood. The mother who had been so patient and borne so much found consolation in this strong, courageous new man whom the whole wadi admired. Many of them, including Miteb al-Hathal, said that after Khosh grew up his mother seemed younger and happier, but when Umm Khosh heard this kind of talk, which meant nothing to her, she began to keep her distance; people were used to her and loved her, and the beautiful qualities she had attained through age and experience made her loved more than before, an object of respect and great affection.

All this, however, was a nearly forgotten episode in the wadi's history, because what followed was what left a deep impression in the people's hearts and minds, much as rushing water does in hillsides. With Khosh's mysterious disappearance, Umm

Khosh's happiness ended and was replaced by profound sorrow. The woman who at first would question all travelers and get no reply took to waiting at the entrance to the wadi all day long for a caravan that would bring news of Khosh. If she got used to showing determination and sternness when she asked, as if her question were about some very minor or routine matter, she became a new woman with every passing day: she asked more belligerently and was sure to ask every single member of the caravan. To those who did not know Khosh and had never heard his name she would tell stories about him; she delighted in talking about him for hours.

Those people of the wadi who knew Khosh and his mother were brokenhearted over the lack of any news. In the beginning they were as persistent as his mother in asking for him all over, and they persuaded travelers in their turn to make inquiries about him. They wrote letters to friends and relatives to glean the slightest news of him. But the days passed and there was no news of him—none. The people had nearly forgotten Khosh in the daily flood of adversity and hardship they endured, but with the old woman's face staring at them every day they were never allowed to forget. Khosh's presence was more felt than that of many of the wadi's actual living inhabitants, and it grew ever more palpable as the old woman wasted away with sorrow at first, then turned into a creature that no man knew how to talk to or handle. Her never-ending talk about Khosh, with its accompanying smiles and questions, evoked sadness because it was never long before she broke into sobs, speaking excitedly, quoting poetry and singing.

She did all this without the slightest fear or embarrassment, with the greatest enthusiasm and always in a loud voice, as if addressing a large number of people. Sometimes she would orate to the goats and chickens for hours at a time, as if telling a story that had no end.

Whoever heard Umm Khosh talk for the first time considered her a woman of unquestionable sanity; when she told the story of her son's journey it was as if she were talking of some other woman's problem. Even when she recounted the small details, deep in the shadows of the distant, forgotten wadi, which would suddenly emerge, it was as if she was speaking of something that had happened only the night before. But presently her voice would change, she would look about in terror, grasp the ground as if she were afraid it would open up and scream. "Listen, everyone in the wadi! Sleep does not lie. Three angels came to me—they were wearing white robes. And they told me, 'Khosh will be here on Thursday.' The big angel looked exactly like Khosh and laughed like him too. The small one was strong like Khosh, but I couldn't see the third one because he had his back to me."

When they asked her to be patient and wait, she answered derisively. "You people of Wadi al-Uyoun are unfair and cruel. You just leave your children the same way you leave animals. When the animal's time has come you take it and slaughter it, and the one that's no good for slaughtering you throw out in the stony desert to die. I don't want to get like any of you!"

She would keep repeating and singing, "Thursday, Thursday, this Thursday." People looked at each other and then at her, their kindly smiles mixed with curiosity. "Life has been hard on the old woman," they said to themselves, "and the worst of it is waiting for someone who will never come." No one could say such a thing to Umm Khosh herself because the words would kill her, so everyone let her go on waiting, and they waited themselves to see if anything would happen.

The letters, coins and colored cloth sent by travelers were like invisible ropes binding the wadi residents to their absent loved ones, rendering the travelers present with their voices and features, making life bearable for those who never grew tired of waiting in Wadi al-Uyoun. Umm Khosh wanted to be one of them. What she wanted was a letter or a bolt of colored cloth, and then Khosh could go and do whatever he liked. But to stay like this, knowing nothing and having no one tell her anything, this was harder than death. Nonetheless she was positive that he would come back, so she would show every extravagant kindness to new caravans and hover over the new arrivals from the moment they got there until the moment they left, hoping to hear that Khosh was still alive, that he was doing business somewhere, buying and selling, and had amassed uncounted camels and sheep.

Umm Khosh acted this way every time a caravan came. When they had left, she would wander around the wadi from dawn until sundown and sometimes later, in an endless patrol, speechifying to young and old alike, talking to the trees and animals. She asked anyone who came near her if they had seen or heard anything from Khosh. In some places people might have made fun of her, and boys might have ridiculed or even attacked her, but not in Wadi al-Uyoun. No one said anything bad about her, and she was the object of everyone's care and sympathy. She could walk into any house or tent in the wadi or on Mount Zahra as if it were her own and be treated as an honored guest. Men and women alike would listen to her and talk to her rationally and respectfully.

Such behavior was not the result of any prior agreement or contrivance—it was the way of life in the wadi, whose people were like one family. True, family relationships did link many people here, but even stronger relationships were born when husbands and brothers went away and their friends obligingly tended the date palms and planted seed. This is what happened with Umm Khosh's small walled garden. When she became obsessed with her son she was no longer able to look after the trees or plant the vegetables, so some men took charge of it for her. They did this without being told and without saying a word, as if doing it for themselves. When they gave Umm Khosh money from the sale to travelers of some of her produce, she looked happily at the coins they placed in her hand and asked with a child's sigh, "Did Khosh send this money?"

When they said nothing, from fear that a denial would wound her or make her cry, she became absolutely silent and pensive, then shouted, "With what I've aleady got, this money is enough for Khosh to get married!"

For a while she toyed with this thought, laughing and trilling, walking in circles and dreaming; then she burst into tears. At first she cried silently, trying to stifle her sobs, then her weeping began to sound more like a cry for help. The men could not bear to hear it and left, and the women and children looked at her in surprise and then in sorrow; some women even joined her in stifled lamentation. When she stopped, there was a heavy, aching silence. The bedouin, and those of Wadi al-Uyoun in particular, were not used to crying, did not like it and did not know how or why people cried; but when they saw this, they were perplexed and embarrassed and engrossed in their pessimism.

A mysterious connection, which no one could explain, formed between this state of affairs and the wadi's subsequent misfortunes. Miteb al-Hathal had arranged the meeting between Umm Khosh and the men who planted the garden and tended the palm trees, and amid the joy, laughter and tears that followed, more than one person heard him muttering to himself: "O Lord, Creator of the blue sky, You are almighty and know what is in the hearts of men. Protect the wadi and preserve it from calamity."

He and others remembered the previous time when the cross-eyed, gap-toothed bedouin came from the interior, from a far-off place. That bedouin brought Umm Khosh a sum of money, but though she asked for Khosh and showed radiant joy at this new event, he refused to say anything until more people were present. When a group collected, including Miteb al-Hathal, the bedouin said that he was Abdallah al-Maktoum. He said he had stabbed Khosh's father one day twenty years or more ago and had now come to pay off the blood money in cash; all present were witnesses.

This incident, and the joy and weeping that followed, was only a few weeks old when the wadi was struck by a strange plague that affected men and animals, and some say the trees as well.

Miteb al-Hathal was reminded of this incident and what followed when the three foreigners arrived; he said something terrible would happen. He was not sure of his ideas and notions, but a strong premonition filled him and took him over, and for a certain period he went around repeating, "If a cross-eyed, gap-toothed bedouin could bring all this trouble, then surely those blue-eyed, gap-toothed foreigners could cause Waḍi al-Uyoun and its people to be annihilated."

At first most people did not agree with Miteb's premonition and his notions did not fill their heads, but no one could convince him that he was wrong. If he were unable to prove or explain his convictions, he was also unable to agree to any others. The people of the wadi had received the foreigners rather warily but still expectantly, since their curiosity was greater than their suspicion, but Miteb was different from all of them, and that explained his strong emotions in this particular period.

No sooner had Miteb taken his stand, which so many found odd, than whispers began to make the rounds: "The man did not look like that." "Those devils who came will surely leave tomorrow or the day after, but no one knows when Miteb's melancholy will leave him." The people would be quiet for a while and then say, "He's got just like Umm Khosh—you can't reason with him."

Umm Khosh, more grief stricken than ever, wandered through the wadi from end to end with her hair disheveled, repeating words that made sense to no one: "Before the dawn of the year the upheaval will arise up and the wadi will burn."

The men were reminded of this incident when the three foreigners arrived, because Umm Khosh took up a position by Ibn Rashed's encampment and did not leave it for a moment the whole first day. She wanted to ask the foreigners about Khosh, if they had seen him or heard anything about him, but they paid her no attention. They asked about the rainy season and the hot season, about where water might be found, how the sands moved and in which direction, about the caravans, how often they came and how long they stayed, and other matters that concerned them. She meanwhile stared at them, following their every movement, and screamed out from time to time: "You men! Which of you can tell me how Khosh is?"

The men of the wadi had heard this question thousands of times and had no answer to give, had no idea what to say to Umm Khosh or how to handle her. The foreigners to whom the question was put every now and then ignored it since they did not know what the old woman was saying. They were not sure whether the question was being posed to them or to someone else, particularly since one look at the woman's face revealed such great fear.

"You crazy old hag, that's enough!" Ibn Rashed shouted in her face. "These men have never heard of Khosh and don't know where he is!"

Umm Khosh got up and started toward Ibn Rashed, looking at him contemptuously. She looked at the three guests, who instinctively began to back up, out of fear or perhaps a sense of self-defense. Her long stare at them was searching and accusatory, and a heavy silence had fallen over everyone. Ibn Rashed was afraid she would start trouble.

"Get this crazy woman out of our sight!" he shouted to one of his men.

Umm Khosh nervously swung one arm behind her, as if trying to slip free from the arm she imagined might encircle her, then looked to the right and the left. She took a few small steps backward, her eyes still fixed hatefully on Ibn Rashed. Before going much farther she spit on the ground and spoke. "This wadi will burn. Because of you."

"Take this woman away. Take her," said Ibn Rashed, laughing nervously in an attempt to maintain his self-control and suppress his agitation.

That is what happened, according to the men in the encampment. They remembered that Umm Khosh then began to plod through the wadi raging in a loud voice, and when she got tired of that she selected a spot near Ibn Rashed's encampment—not close enough to it to expose her to insults or the danger of being chased away—and sat there, planning to ask the foreigners if they had seen Khosh or heard any news of him. But Ibn Rashed, worried that she might cause his guests some annoyance and knowing that the foreigners themselves were now wary of her, having placed themselves as far away as possible from the "madwoman," forbade her to ask any questions.

For as long as the foreigners stayed the whole wadi was preoccupied with them, in a whirl of questions and theories like a desert sandstorm. Then shortly after they left life began to return to normal, and the townspeople looked in all directions for caravans, rain and travelers, but the accursed misgiving buried in the hearts of many at the foreigners' departure raised its head to harass two individuals: Umm Khosh and Miteb al-Hathal.

After the foreigners left, Umm Khosh insisted that they had come to inform the wadi of some important news relating to Khosh; that was why they had kept her far away, giving her no chance to ask them and find out; otherwise why did they show such fear when she got near them at Ibn Rashed's encampment, and why did they stay silent when she asked them? Had they killed him and come here to reach a settlement over his blood? There was no one to settle with after Abdallah al-Maktoum left except herself, but no one had even approached her or spoken to her. Even if they were not the killers, they at least knew a great deal about him. Also, wasn't it likely that Khosh had grown rich and had sent these men to inform the wadi of his circumstances and whereabouts? Didn't she have a right to hear whatever they had to say about his wealth? Wasn't she his mother, who had suckled him with her own breasts? Who knew and loved him as she did? Why were they dividing his goods while he was alive and she did not even know?

She was certain that some harm had come to Khosh. Ibn Rashed, al-Soheimi and Abdallah al-Mayouf had been making fun of her. They had told her, "Be patient. Patience is the key to victory. Tomorrow Khosh will come and marry, and you'll rejoice, and all Wadi al-Uyoun with you. Just trust in God!" They said that and more. At other times they joked and asked her if she planned to marry after Khosh returned, and when she curled her lip scornfully they assured her, "You'll put henna on your hands and feet and dance seven days and nights. If Khosh comes back married you'll make him get married again!" When she heard these words dreams and fantasies swirled in her head; she smiled and gazed far off. Then suddenly the rapture fell away and she trembled, looking at the faces that spoke to her; she looked at them yearningly, wanting to discover what was behind the words she heard, but the faces turned away, afraid to meet her eyes.

In Ibn Rashed's encampment now, al-Soheimi, al-Mayouf and the others, none of them budged when she tried to question the three foreigners. They let Ibn Rashed drive her out like a dog. They forgot the things they had told her. They had forgotten

the days when Abdallah al-Maktoum was alive, and they had
forgotten Khosh completely. No . . . they had forgotten nothing; the three devils had come to tell them that Khosh was dead,
or that he did not want to come back. If they had said anything
else they would have told her. Perhaps he had decided to stay
where he was and get married there. If he were still poor, his
father had been poor before him and there was no disgrace in
poverty. She had borne much but was still strong and could bear
yet more. If he had died, who had buried him? Why didn't she
know? Was it that these devils had killed him or knew who had
killed him? They had paid out English and Rashadi coins for
bits of cloth and boxes made from palm leaves. Were they madmen to pay all that money if they had not killed him?

"The old lady is gone," the people of the wadi said. "Once
she had hope, but now . . ."

One man put his hand to his mouth when he heard this and
flicked his thumb on his front teeth, meaning that there was no
hope left.

Many people now avoided Umm Khosh, turned their faces
away when she passed and kept silent when she sat nearby. Some
did not hesitate to ask the boys secretly to "spirit her away"!
Boys who had held back from mocking her in the past out of
fear of their elders' rebuke or punishment now eagerly did what
was asked of them. They became expert at making up dozens
of stories and pretexts for coaxing her away from the men, using
every means to excite her: "Khosh has come back! We saw him
at the brook." "A caravan has come and the men are asking for
Umm Khosh."

What happened provoked irrepressible laughter and endless
sorrows, for the old lady who raced off like a bitch dog at the
slightest word of Khosh believed everything she was told. In
her smiles and footraces she seemed like a little girl until she was
struck by the truth and the sight of the empty places. On seeing

nothing, she fell to the ground and began to cry. Her sobs were enough to break hearts or even crush them, and even the children who were the cause of it all, who egged her on and ran at her side whooping with laughter, even some of them were affected and felt guilty when they saw her collapse in a heap of sobs.

The only one, or one of the few, who kept his old feelings toward Umm Khosh or even grew more sympathetic to her was Miteb al-Hathal. He made sure to be near her most of the time to protect her from harm, to keep the children away and to save her from the collapse that overtook her when she fell down in a spasm of crying and lamentation.

He told her comforting things to restore her composure and sometimes patted her on the back and told her to try to stop this unseemly weeping. He said that Khosh himself would be angry if he saw her in this state. Slowly she calmed down, and having regained her lucidity she would start to talk like any reasonable person and listen to what she was told. Other thoughts and feelings came to her, and she did not hesitate to talk about them.

8

H ADIB'S PREDICTIONS PROVED CORRECT AND MI-
teb's hopes were fulfilled when heavy rains fell
early on Wadi al-Uyoun and the surrounding
area. People felt encouraged and expected that this would be one
of the good years, and their optimism grew when the caravans
arriving in the last days of autumn and thereafter reported that
rain had fallen steadily for days, filling the wadis and brooks.
Another source of joy was the fact that the goods the caravans
carried had not become more expensive, as they usually did at
this time every year. The air was cool and refreshing and full of
moisture, and the light winds that blew from the west and north
some nights were laden with a fertile smell, infusing the body
and soul with vigor. The happiness showed everywhere, in men
and animals and even in harsh, unmoving nature. Wadha remembered that Shaalan told her for the first time that he wanted

to marry, but he did not insist or nag, and although she did not give him a clear answer, she laughed with joy and said that as soon as she was through with Hadib, who was giving her trouble and had not made up his mind yet, she would choose him the most beautiful girl in Wadi al-Uyoun; if he didn't like any of them she would go to Ujra and enlist the aid of her relations there.

Miteb al-Hathal was a changed man. Since the heavy rains had come he spent the whole day in his small garden. He had nothing to do there and his presence or absence made no difference, but it gave him pleasure to watch the water drip into the earth to remain there. Then the earth began to do incredible, unfathomable things. A few days after the rains began—as Miteb himself said—there was a prolonged tremor within the earth, like a convulsion, and the insides of the earth began to spill out, he told Hadib excitedly. He had seen seedlings planted only a few weeks before pushing up forcibly through the soil, their small tips aloft, getting bigger by the moment. In an attempt to convince Hadib, and to convey what he had felt when the earth trembled, Miteb told him that it was like the moment of man and woman's mating—like a moment of rapture.

In spite of the fact that Miteb was telling the truth about what he felt, he was also using the incident and his descriptions in a sly attempt to warm Hadib to the idea of marriage, as he and Wadha had agreed should be done. When Wadha whispered in his ear that Shaalan wanted to marry as well and had told her as much, Miteb laughed loudly and said that building the new room was a good omen and had shown foresight.

An air of contentment now pervaded Wadi al-Uyoun; even Umm Khosh was more tranquil. The caravan traders were the first to notice it, before the townsfolk themselves. Ibn Rashed, who spared no one his criticisms or sharp tongue, and who often said that Miteb al-Hathal was finished and should go graze with the sheep, went to visit Miteb first in the garden and then on Mount Zahra. He seemed very cordial and did not utter a word that could be interpreted as anything but friendly; in fact most people said that the two men were on better terms than they had ever been—better than anyone could have imagined. When the subject of the Americans came up, Ibn Rashed seemed exasperated. "They are long gone, Abu Thweiny, and will never return."

Subsequently he hinted in several ways that Wadi al-Uyoun could live in peace and tranquillity if only left to itself to prosper as one of the caravans' most valued way stations.

It was at about this time that Hadib agreed to marry. He let this be known indirectly, telling Miteb and Wadha that he was not opposed to the idea of marriage and would marry tomorrow or the next day if he found a nice girl that suited him.

"Leave the nice girl to me," said Wadha, who considered his implied consent sufficient and wanted to finalize the matter.

The three of them laughed, and she began to review the likely candidates in her mind one by one. By nightfall she was still disqualifying some and hesitating over others, so she decided to leave it until the next day.

Even Miteb al-Hathal, who spent long afternoons gazing at the trees and fields, no longer tending to the caravans or going to Ibn Rashed's encampment, felt that he did not need news—if the latest news took a day or two longer to get to him, it did not make any difference. When Ibn Rashed scolded him and reminded him that he had visited Miteb twice, and that his absence from the encampment could not be explained or understood by anyone as friendly, Miteb and Shaalan replied that they were busy with planting and would visit when it was completed.

So it was from early autumn until mid-winter. It was clearer than ever that water would remain plentiful and fill the entire wadi. The northern canal was brimming with rainwater, and the desert was covered with growth. The animals grew fat, and many predicted that lambs would be born two by two. The dogs provided entertainment for young and old alike as they fought, wrangled, mated and then fought again! Fawaz reminded his father of his promise to allow him to travel soon.

"Wait until your brother gets married," Miteb told him one night, placidly roasting the coffee beans as the rain hammered down outside. "After we harvest the barley we'll see. God is good."

When Fawaz began to complain, or was about to, his father laughed and said, "The caravansary is full to the rafters and the travelers are sleeping on top of each other. They won't go now for fear of being carried off by floods, and you want to travel!"

In a hidden and wordless but eloquent signal to Fawaz, Hadib winked, a plea to stop nagging, to put off the discussion for now, to explain that he would arrange everything himself. The conversation took a new turn while the discussion of this and many other matters was postponed.

In the last days of that bitter winter, without warning, the American who had left them long months before returned with four others and some of the emir's men. Miteb had nicknamed him Nahs (Disaster) while others called him Ghorab (The Crow), but this time he had a new name: Abdallah. No one knew who had given him that name or why. It was what the emir's men called him, and when he spoke to anyone or asked them questions he pounded his chest once or twice and said, "Abdallah . . . Abdallah!"

Within days everything in the wadi changed—men, animals and nature—for no sooner had the American, his friends and their companions been settled in than a large number of other people arrived. No one had ever dreamed such people existed:

one was short and obese with red hair and another was tall enough to pick dates from the trees. Yet another was as black as night, and there were more—blond and redheaded. They had blue eyes and bodies fat as slaughtered sheep, and their faces inspired curiosity and fear. They came on camelback and horseback, dragging behind them numberless crates, bundles and tents, and before long they had unloaded the crates and bundles and pitched the tents a short distance from the brook. It happened as quickly as in a dream. Miteb al-Hathal did not immediately comprehend what had happened because he had been in the garden, but he paled and trembled when he heard what the others had to tell him, and quick as a flash he hurried over to Ibn Rashed's encampment to find out what had happened in Wadi al-Uyoun.

People long remembered the moment he arrived, shaking like a leaf and glancing about him like a wolf. When he caught sight of the newly built camp, he could not stop cursing. He wanted to destroy it utterly, but the people prevented him. Later on many of them would say, "Miteb al-Hathal was right . . . yes, he was right!"

As soon as the camp was erected, the men paced off the area, put up wire fencing and short white pickets, scattered some strange substance around the tents and sprayed the earth with water that had a penetrating smell. Then they opened up their crates and unloaded large pieces of black iron, and before long a sound like rolling thunder surged out of this machine, frightening men, animals and birds. After several minutes of the rumbling, one of the Americans raised his hand and signaled to another, who extinguished the sound, but it was a long time before it stopped ringing in the ears.

When that was over, as fast as a magic trick, the people still watched everything that went on in silence and fear. When the sun began to sink in the west, it seemed that Wadi al-Uyoun was about to experience a night such as it had never known before. As soon as the animals began to bark and bray at sunset, the machine started to roar again, frightening everyone, only this time the sound was accompanied by a blinding light. Within moments scores of small but brilliant suns began to blaze, filling the whole area with a light that no one could believe or stand. The men and boys retreated and looked at the lights again to make sure they still saw them, and they looked at each other in terror. The animals who drew near retreated in fright; the camels fled, and the sheep stirred uneasily. Miteb stood not far from the place and spoke loudly enough to command attention over the fear and the machine's noise. "Go back, people of Wadi al-Uyoun! If you don't go back you'll get burned and there'll be nothing left of you."

This marvelous incident, so crystal clear and yet impossible to believe at first, became with time a routine affair, for the men who for a certain period kept silent and watched everything in fear mixed with anticipation were soon used to it. Ibn Rashed went forward and asked Ghorab to explain how the lights and sound were produced, but in spite of a long and detailed explanation no one understood anything.

The people expected strange occurrences that first night, as one expects thunder to follow lightning, but nothing happened. That night and others passed, but their hearts were full of fear. The mysterious activity that went on everywhere left no chance to ask a real question, because every movement was followed by something else. These foreigners who strode around and shouted, raising their arms and behaving with unheard-of peculiarity, took no notice of the people around them or their astonishment. They were completely self-absorbed. During the few moments when they did bump into the wadi's men and children, while moving their equipment from one place to another, they reached out to pat their shoulders or smack their cheeks, as if playing with animals or unknown creatures.

Everyone who saw Miteb al-Hathal that first night remarked on his insistence that everybody keep far away from the camp and stay alert all night. Something was bound to happen before the next day dawned. He was particularly insistent that the women and children stay away and sent them to Zahra. He himself expected the place to explode at any moment: to see the foreigners streaming out, cutting off all escape routes, unsheathing their weapons to slaughter the townspeople.

Miteb saw strange doings inside the fences with his own eyes, and he called the men's attention to them. He stayed intensely watchful and cautious, because he saw a tall black man waiting for the right moment to attack, murder and annihilate. Miteb's sleepless eyes did not close for a moment, but they passed over the man to look at something else, and in the twilight before dawn he perceived that the man no longer stood there. Standing in his place, or just by it, was a pillar!

How did the men of Wadi al-Uyoun take this news? What fears and misgivings gripped them? Were the people of Mount Zahra more fortunate than those of the wadi?

These and dozens of other matters could not be recounted in words, because words would diminish or alter them. Fear grew by the moment; apprehension took over and paralyzed the people. Nothing but constant surprises could be taken for granted.

After a watchful vigil lasting three days and nights, with little real sleep and even less food and water, Miteb al-Hathal went back to Zahra a different man. He was utterly changed: after dismounting from his horse, haggard and wild eyed, extremely feeble or ill, he staggered to his house and fell in front of the door. Nothing his wife could do roused him, so she brought out a mattress and pillows for him to sleep where he lay. She could not convince him to wash his face or to take a cup or two of tea, for he was as spiritless and weak as he was insistent. He seemed to be in a state of crushing depression and frailty, as if the end of the world had come, but he was completely conscious, if despairing, when he finally spoke: "They talk about the resurrection day? Today is resurrection day. They say, when iron moves on iron? Today I saw iron move on iron!" He paused to think and went on in a more anguished tone: "We should have done something a long time ago, when they first came. I knew they would return. I knew they would do things men and jinn never dreamed of. They came. I saw them myself. In the wink of an eye they unleashed hundreds of demons and devils. These devils catch fire and roar night and day like a flour mill that turns and turns without tiring out and without anyone turning it. What will happen in this world? How can we kill them before they kill us?"

He seemed obstinate and imbecilic. He had forgotten his age and dignity. If it were a matter of strength, the people of Wadi al-Uyoun and Zahra were so renowned for their numbers and ferocity that no one thought of attacking or raiding them. If it were a question of intelligence and fair-mindedness, the encampments of the Atoum, the Soheimi, the Marzouq and the Rodhan were never empty of litigants who had come great distances, happily and voluntarily, to seek an arbitrator in Wadi al-Uyoun. If it were a question of those foreigners who had come to the wadi to pitch their tents and settle down, then some way would have to be found to get rid of them or to reach a compromise over the water, especially since they had some of the emir's men with them this time; it was not like the first time they had come.

In the last part of the night a nightmare woke Miteb and he started, terrified. Without speaking to anyone he picked up his rifle, mounted his horse quietly and rode down to the wadi.

9

....

No murder was committed that night or the next few nights; everything was deferred by the initial state of bewilderment and the subsequent state of expectation. Miteb al-Hathal, who was accustomed to bearing arms only on rare occasions, when preparing for travel, upon hearing the baying of a wolf near the sheep or in his rare angry moments, frightened Wadha badly when he took his gun and went out, not because guns scared her as they did many women, who prized safety over anything to be gained by fighting, but because Miteb's condition worried her.

"Follow him," she ordered Fawaz, who had wakened at his father's noise. "Don't leave him, and don't let him see you or even sense that you are there. He might need you," she added in a different tone.

Wadha was capable of making hard decisions at the right time.

She seemed a submissive woman, and some people who saw her thought her weak, but her brief but firm words in the last dark of night infused Fawaz with strength and a little nervousness, and without a moment's hesitation he followed his father.

Contrary to his usual habit, Miteb rode down to the wadi by the longest and most difficult paths, as if by taking that route he wanted to see the whole scene. After viewing the camp from the Zahra side, he examined the wadi and the surrounding hills and wanted to see it from the opposite side, or perhaps he feared something or sensed trouble. Fawaz said to himself, "If he opens fire he'll set the whole wadi ablaze; we won't be alone. The people of the wadi wouldn't let a man fight by himself; they'd fight with him to the end. *After* the battle they'd ask why he was fighting." Fawaz had heard of such things many times. Old and young men talked about them. Young men, who had never seen a war or experienced the turmoils that old men talked about, would be delighted to see a battle. When the boys and young men talked eagerly about these infidels and the need to kill them, the older men looked at them with surprise and disapproval and said that they were not afraid, but that they could not take up arms against friends, and as long as the emir had sent the foreigners they were friends. True, no one felt comfortable with their presence, and everyone had his doubts, but still no one had thought of taking up arms. Now that Miteb rode through the darkness with his rifle on his shoulder, something was bound to happen.

Miteb was not sure of anything; he felt trapped and hesitant and incredulous, for the first lesson a man learned in the desert was not to threaten with firearms or play with them, not because he was afraid of guns but because he loved them so much that he did not allow them to be used as a means of threat or horseplay. But Miteb had forgotten this lesson as if he never knew it. Like any man in the wadi, Miteb al-Hathal scolded his children when he saw them carrying guns or pointing them in all directions as a joke. One time he told Shaalan, "Never play with guns, because if you play with them once you play with them all the time. People who value guns, and men who kill, don't value or respect the man who plays with guns." Another time he told him, "If you pick up a gun, shoot . . . or don't pick it up at all."

In the shadows of dawn he moved forward with his gun, and after a long wait at the end of the wadi he lay in one place, his horse beside him, as his son lay in another not a hundred yards away. He raised the rifle every so often and aimed it at the camp, then lowered it. Lowering it, he seemed defeated and docile, and even after raising it again, perhaps with greater determination, he lowered it despondently. He kept raising and lowering his rifle, sitting then getting up, reaiming it . . . He did nothing, even when the sun rose to fill the air with light. Fawaz had stopped expecting his father to do anything. He was no longer able to stay hidden, and no sooner had he crept from his hiding place to shout for his father, then caught sight of him, than he jumped with fright and confusion. At that moment he wanted the earth to suck him in or swallow him; to die, to shoot himself or his horse or fire at the camp. He neared his father and saw his sallow face, wild eyes and his violently trembling lower lip. Miteb ran his hand rapidly, convulsively up and down the rifle barrel. He could not speak, even when Fawaz asked him if he had seen a wolf or an enemy. He wordlessly shook his head no, but his eyes conveyed more than censure or reproof. His eyes said, "The depths of the earth are better than its face. I don't want you to see my weakness . . . to see me like this."

After a long silence which hung heavy between the two, broken only by Miteb's nervous and despairing hand moving along the rifle barrel, a weary voice croaked: "Did you water the animals?" He did not look up as he spoke or as he listened to his son's reply.

"Today it's Shaalan's and Ibrahim's turn."

For the first time Miteb raised his sad eyes filled with mute questions: How long have you been watching me? Who asked you to come? Why at this hour?

He withdrew his gaze and lowered his head. He was tired and dazed; he longed to say so much, he longed to be quiet.

When a man feels as if he is naked, or as if he is committing a crime, and wants no one to see his nakedness or the criminal act, he can be irrational and cruel to himself and others.

"Take the rifle and go back to Zahra," Miteb ordered Fawaz harshly, even belligerently. He gruffly drew the bullet and clip, then threw him the rifle. It landed between his feet, and Fawaz left it there a moment before picking it up.

"Get going. Get out of my sight," said Miteb as he turned.

Fawaz felt that it was all over with his father, that he had fallen into a bottomless well, that he no longer wanted to see any person or hear any voice. Even his horse standing at his side in the shadows, who seemed beautiful and tame, as if she never wanted to leave him, appeared to annoy him. He no longer wanted her near him. No sooner had Fawaz picked up the rifle than his father told him irascibly, "Tie the horse under that tree."

He pointed to a distant date palm and turned on his side as if entering the kingdom of sleep or death or a trance.

Miteb al-Hathal did not return to Zahra that day or the next, and his absence caused Fawaz's feelings of error and injury to mount. Had Fawaz not seen him thus, weak and despairing, things would have turned out differently. Had he done what he had in mind, he might have set the whole wadi ablaze and things would have been very different, but now that he was gone, where or for how long no one knew, this was a wound in Miteb's spirit that would never heal.

Some said they had seen him twice, lurking near the camp. He had been extremely angry and bitter; he stood and shouted curses at the Americans to provoke them, but whoever heard him raised their heads for a moment, glanced at him fleetingly and went back to work. In the evening, in Ibn Rashed's encampment, he used every curse he knew. He said that the fire had started in Wadi al-Uyoun when the accursed Nahs first arrived. Something should have been done then, before the innocent got hung with the guilty. If they kept quiet and did nothing but sit and wait, all would be lost. He also told the men that if they did nothing he would act on his own. When one of the old men proposed that a delegation be sent to discuss the matter with the emir, Miteb shook his head sarcastically. " 'Pursue the scoundrel to the door of his house.' The emir is our kin but he's useless."

They had this exchange over and over, and most of the time nothing came of it. The activity in and around Wadi al-Uyoun never slowed or stopped. Ibn Rashed would stay in Wadi al-Uyoun for a few days and then mysteriously drop out of sight for long periods of time. If Miteb al-Hathal continued to curse, challenge and defame Ibn Rashed, he still feared Ibn Rashed's absences more than his presence and the old man's attempts to convince the people of the wadi to move. Miteb had no idea what Ibn Rashed was up to on these travels or what tragedies might befall the wadi as a result of his visits to the emir or others.

Feelings alternated between hope and despair, fear and optimism; when a messenger came from one direction, Miteb managed to speak to him alone to ask him what he had seen and heard, and, somewhat encouraged, he conveyed the news to the wadi himself in his own way. When a messenger came from the other direction bringing news of another kind, Miteb tried to find some hope in it. For days at a time he did not know what to do with himself or how to express his feelings to others. If Ibn Rashed returned thereafter, wanting to give the townspeople news of the devils who would begin working within a few days or weeks, Miteb al-Hathal would stand against him, not leaving Ibn Rashed alone until he had used up every curse and threat he could think of. Ibn Rashed always met Miteb with an air of jocularity and pleasantry, but it was not long before he was giving the people of the wadi his own thoughts and suggestions, hinting to them that they were wise and reasonable people who knew enough not to harm themselves. Surely they had listened enough to this senile old man. When Miteb was told what Ibn Rashed had said, he attacked him night and day, scorning all the flattery the wadi had been used to for long years. In this coarse and antagonistic way the duel between the two men began, with the people of the wadi following it closely.

Ibn Rashed maintained his silence, putting in only a word here and there to respond to what Miteb al-Hathal said. If Miteb passed certain boundaries, Ibn Rashed would get bolder, but in a mocking way, using implied threats. "Never fear, Ibn Hathal," he would tell him. "Trust in God and you'll get your rights. You know that what generous people give is never lost."

If Miteb refused to listen, or made fun of him, Ibn Rashed would change his tone. "Ibn Hathal, you are the sheikh of this wadi. You are its most intelligent man, so you must know that the government deals justly with people—but it knows how to use force as well."

"Are you threatening me, Ibn Rashed?"

"We have told you, Ibn Hathal: they make the decisions. We are obedient slaves. You are a troublemaker—I tell you we have no choice but to kneel and obey. We scarcely finish with one discussion, one problem, and you've found another one. Cousin, leave off the problems and let the government do its job."

"And if I don't, Ibn Rashed?"

"You'll cause anger, but then the regret will be your own, Ibn Hathal."

"This is our village, Ibn Rashed. We know it, we know its men and its heart and everything about it, and you know it better than anyone else. *They* had better learn . . . over there."

"Ibn Hathal, cousin, if you want to part ways, then just keep asking the impossible."

"By God, Ibn Rashed, every man has a hole in his ass. You know Ibn Hathal."

"A messenger only brings news—he deserves no blame," said Ibn Rashed, who wanted to put an end to the fruitless discussion with subtle mockery. "You know, Abu Thweiny, that you have to be patient, and we have to keep our promise."

Things were undecided and uneasy for several weeks after the camp had been built. The Americans had begun to spend the noon hours of each day in the sun, stretched out on their faces, with nothing covering their bodies but short trousers. They did this unmindful of the boys and men around them, as if they were in tents.

At first this daily occurrence was greeted with surprise, then anger and resentment. Even Ibn Rashed, who always defended Abdallah, tried to explain to him that the people would not accept the idea of having to look at men lying around like this. But he got nowhere. The men still passed by the camp, and the boys as well, but the women, whose habit was to pass it on their way to bring water from the brook, stopped completely, in real shock. Miteb al-Hathal was regarded as wiser and more knowledgeable than they had given him credit for being.

First there were whispers, then complaints, then serious thought of sending a delegation to tell the emir: "Your Excellency, we have no objection to their taking water from the brook, but we'll die before we let them take it over. Our womenfolk, Your Excellency, our honor, Your Excellency . . . If you want to solve the problem, solve it. And if you don't want to solve it, we will ourselves."

This was the kind of talk making the rounds in the encampments and social councils. Some men who felt deeply insulted and even afraid, and had premonitions of evil, forbade their women to go to the brook at all. They had the children bring the water, telling them not to stop and not to look in the direction of the camp.

Miteb al-Hathal was in Zahra, far from the brook, but even had he lived near it he would not have changed his mind or taken back the things he said. The other men, who lived near the brook, in the heart of the wadi and amid the gardens, felt that the question was far more serious than they had at first imagined, and that there could be no delay or hesitation. The emir's men with the foreigners were unable to do anything; all they could do was tell the translator what the people were saying, and the translator was tougher and more arrogant than the Americans themselves.

Fear gripped the wadi. The men grew more rash and nervous, and Miteb was considered indispensable—if he absented himself from the wadi a single day to sleep in Zahra the people missed him acutely; only he was capable of saying everything, of expressing their innermost thoughts.

Confusion reigned in an atmosphere of ambiguity and disruption. Despite their bold words and challenges each night, their agreements and pledges, the day brought new fears; with each dawn came a tacit agreement among the men to postpone the visit to the emir one more day; perhaps something would happen that day to relieve the anxiety that enshrouded the wadi.

A caravan came, bringing other news and subjects of concern, and they were absorbed in buying, selling and bartering, but when evening came with its social councils to discuss the news and latest events, talk of the foreigners pushed aside all other subjects, inspiring interest, fear and unease. Although the travelers usually did most of the talking, for it was they who had been places and seen things to tell others of, the men of Wadi al-Uyoun had a very great deal to say about these devils who had suddenly come to stay, no one knew why or for how long! The travelers paid close attention, for they would pass on everything they were told to people in other places who had not yet heard of the devils.

The discussion of the band of devils, at first very general and neutral, soon grew harsh and vehement, with most of the men joining in. Most of the foreigners, based on their physical qualities, were assigned nicknames. It was the custom in Wadi al-Uyoun to give everyone a nickname after long acquaintance, often unintentionally or without realizing it, but the giving of nicknames was now an essential part of confronting the new situation and distinguishing between these creatures who had appeared so similar in the early days that one could not be told from the other. Constant surveillance and untiring scrutiny made the name giving extremely easy. Ghorab (Crow) or Ibn al-Mal'ouna (Whoreson) was the name assigned to the first foreigner to arrive. Others became al-Ak'hal (Blackie), Bateen (Fatso), Jarbou' (Kangaroo Rat), Moghzel (Spindle), Dajaja (Hen), Aboul Hseyin (Pony) and al-Afsah. All the people of the wadi took part in choosing the names; even the names which did not exactly fit soon became highly appropriate, so that there was no need to know the devils' real names!

Thus the group that had come was discussed and stories told about it, although most of its members, after resting for a time, spent most of their days in strange projects too far off for the men's surveillance. In the tents they were engrossed in drawing and writing, every so often carrying large sheets of paper from one tent to another, sometimes placing them on the ground to examine them for hours and measuring them with a small stick. They did all these things completely oblivious to the people watching their every movement from behind the fence. Most of their audience were children and young men; with every movement the watchers shouted and gesticulated, expecting something to happen.

Tales of what went on traveled quickly from house to house and from tent to tent. The travelers and caravans listened carefully and were consumed by eagerness to see what all the wadi was talking about. When night closed in and the next day had come, the travelers approached the foreign camp and started their vigil. If they did not recall the stories they had been told the previous night, they grew impatient to know which one was al-Afsah and which one Jarbou' and were overjoyed when one of the men pointed out in confident but awestruck tones, "That one's Bateen" or "This is al-Afsah—cut off my hand if it isn't!" Whenever he had located the right foreigner, the man looked at the others with a pride that had reached the limits of childish satisfaction and stood up or shouted. If their voices were loud or a wager had been made on knowing which name to give to a particular foreigner and he looked up curiously, then the joy reached unimaginable heights and the shouts reached new levels accompanied by the arm waving of old and young, giving of congratulations, and other unlikely behavior.

This is some of what the people did to try to allay their fears and apprehensions and to forget the anxiety that grew each day. When the caravan had gone and the people of Wadi al-Uyoun went back to confronting the cruel reality, so full of fear and worry, they began to look for some means of averting the catastrophe that had encircled them and was closing in.

10

THE DAYS PASSED SLOWLY. AS THE HEAT GREW
more oppressive, new numbers of the bedouin who had left the wadi in early winter to
seek grazing land were forced back to the water, for the desert
became a less endurable hell with each passing day of early spring.
It was their habit to follow the clouds and stop wherever they
found water to keep the animals alive; they knew where to go
at all times of the year, when to leave these places and where to
head next. The people of Wadi al-Uyoun knew all of the routes
and the seasons, and knew that the end of the spring, the summer, and part of the fall were the times when people crowded
into the wadi. Even the caravan travelers whom urgency or
homesickness forced to resume their journey after one or two
days' rest in Wadi al-Uyoun during winter or spring, stayed

longer than at other times and waited for the moon to grow full, thus making it possible to travel at night rather than during the fiery day. Prolonged stays in Wadi al-Uyoun at this time of year meant double the number of animals drinking at the brook and the wells, severe overcrowding at the water holes all day and all kinds of ensuing arguments and difficulties. Despite the townsfolk's natural good nature, this season made them noticeably more peevish, and they did not hide their annoyance at certain things. The smiles vanished from their faces, and they lost the desire to socialize for long or even at all.

So these were days of waiting for the summer to assail them with its burning heat and torment, and the waiting was harder than at any time in the past because of the devils who had come and set up camp near the brook. No one knew what the foreigners had in mind to do, or what the state of the water supply would be if they continued fetching large quantities of water dozens of times a day and using it wastefully as if it were some plentiful commodity of little importance.

After a few days the first of those who had moved into the desert arrived. The time for the emir's traditional visit came and went without any news of his intended arrival, causing great unease among the wadi's elders. Miteb al-Hathal's mania reappeared, and when he began to appeal daily for a delegation to go to the emir there was little resistance; then he won general acceptance of the idea. In Ibn Rashed's encampment the men agreed to dispatch some of their number to go see the emir and tell him everything.

The area where the emir resided was three days' journey from Wadi al-Uyoun. Since it was the emir's custom to go hunting at this time of year, passing through the wadi on his way out and on the return trip, some of the elders thought of waiting until this opportunity presented itself; if they went to him, the emir would not have the chance to see for himself the things that worried and frightened them. The camp was in plain view, and the bare-bodied foreigners came and went shamelessly at all hours. He could see the godless machines that roared ceaselessly and often stirred up and scattered the camels, causing their owners the tremendous inconvenience of rounding them up again. These were things that could not be expressed in words or imagined by anyone who had not seen them. The emir had to see it all for himself to appreciate their hardship and anxiety. Even so, they decided to send a delegation.

The men emphasized to each other that the presentation to the emir should be calm and reasonable, and that Ibn Rashed should do most of the talking, since he was an elder and the best speaker. Besides, he was on excellent personal terms with the emir and knew the most about the Americans. They hoped that this strategy would serve to restrict Miteb al-Hathal's chances to make himself heard. His excitability, the curses he heaped on the Americans day and night and his constant provocation of the wadi's people to do something about them—including bearing arms or going to the capital to meet the sultan—made the men think twice about even allowing him to go along. They thought of asking him to stay behind until the emir came, although the elders hesitated to say so, but they all felt that Miteb would not be able to keep a cool head. He might cause trouble or provoke the Americans or even insult them if he stayed behind. Then again, what if he went and reasoned with the emir? In spite of his other qualities, he did possess great composure and good manners. He knew majlises, and what could be said and what could not be said; and so despite the men's overwhelming doubt and strong reservations, they decided to include him in the delegation. It was a thousand times better for him to be part of it than not, and for him to speak to the emir rather than be compelled not to say anything. As to their last recommendations, before they reached the emir's residence, perhaps they would prove useful or perhaps not.

The emir began talking before Ibn Rashed spoke, as if he knew why they had come and what it was they wanted. After general remarks about hunting, the weather and Wadi al-Uyoun, he came to the point: "People of Wadi al-Uyoun, you will be among the richest and happiest of all mankind, as if God saw none but you."

He went on in a different tone. "You have been patient and endured much. God is your witness, but you will be living as if in a dream. You will talk about times past as if they belonged to some old legend."

He resumed his original tone. "And once blessings come, my friends—they have come."

Ibn Rashed had been preparing the words he planned to speak, how he would begin and lead the discussion to the sensitive points. If he could not convince the emir, he at least wanted to create doubts in his mind. He wanted to persuade him to visit them—soon—to see for himself and verify everything they were telling him now. But when the emir began speaking, giving the conversation this direction, Ibn Rashed was disconcerted and did not know how to begin.

"As you know, Your Excellency," he ventured desperately, "money is not everything in this world. More important are honor, ethics and our traditions."

He wanted to continue in this vein, but the emir's ringing laugh changed the atmosphere once again and utterly confused the men. Ibn Rashed spoke in embarrassment. "Whatever we say, Your Excellency, the ear is not the eye. Hearing a tale is not the same as seeing and believing."

The emir shifted in his seat, decisively harsh lines drawn on his face. "If, Ibn Rashed, you speak of ethics, then know we are the most covetous of ethics, and if you want religion, religion is ours and no one else's."

"But you should come and see everything for yourself."

"Don't be afraid. We want you to help them in every possible way. They have come from the ends of earth to help us."

"God damn them," said Miteb al-Hathal angrily. "We don't want them and we don't want their help."

"But we do want their help," said the emir mockingly, looking at Miteb. "And if *you* don't—then know that the earth is wide."

"Yes, by God . . . the earth is wide."

"But Your Excellency, what do they want?" asked Ibn Rashed hastily, to calm the situation.

"They don't want anything," said the emir with the same sarcasm. "We invited them, and they have come to help us."

"What kind of help, Your Excellency?" Ibn Rashed asked innocently.

"Under our feet, Ibn Rashed, there are oceans of oil, oceans of gold," replied the emir. "Our friends have come to extract the oil and the gold."

Ibn Rashed looked at the emir and nodded in surprise and trust, then looked at the men to see the effect of the emir's words on them. He addressed the emir with the same innocence: "How did you know, Your Excellency?"

"How would we ever have known without their help?" replied the emir testily and self-confidently. "They told us, 'There are oceans of blessings under this soil,' and because they love blessings, because they are our friends, they agreed to come here and help us out."

"Is the gold in Wadi al-Uyoun, Your Excellency?"

"In Wadi al-Uyoun, and here, and in every part of this blessed land. When His Majesty liberated this land with the edge of his sword, fighting enemies and infidels, he knew what he was fighting for."

Miteb al-Hathal spoke coldly and firmly. "We're the ones who fought. With our own swords we took this land, inch by inch."

The emir appeared deeply angry at being challenged in that tone, but he ignored Miteb. "Since God bestowed grace upon us we must thank him, not create problems."

He changed his tone and went on. "You are the oldest and wisest of Wadi al-Uyoun's people, and your job is to make things easy for our friends and serve them in every way possible. By the end of the new year, God willing, you'll have money up to your ears."

"By God, Your Excellency, we were as happy as we could be before those devils came along," said Miteb. "But from the first day they came to our village life has been camel piss. Every day it gets worse."

The emir answered him sharply. "Listen, Ibn Hathal, I am speaking to you and to all others, and let him who is present convey it to him who is absent. We have only one medicine for troublemakers: that."

He pointed to the sword hanging against the wall and shook his finger in warning. "What do you say, Ibn Hathal?"

Miteb al-Hathal laughed briefly as if wanting to show that he was not finished yet. A heavy silence echoed through the room.

"Hah . . . so what do you say, Ibn Hathal?"

"You are the government, you have the soldiers and the guns, and you'll get what you want, maybe even tomorrow. After the Christians fetch the gold for you from under the ground you'll be even stronger. But know, Your Excellency, that the Americans aren't doing it for God."

He wanted to continue but the emir interrupted him angrily. "Leave that talk aside and answer my question. Did you understand what I told you, or not?"

Miteb replied sharply. "Listen, Abu Radwan, I'm as old as your father. Don't raise your voice, I can hear you fine. If you want to redden your eye, remember that not everyone is afraid of a red eye. We have come to tell you what our own eyes have seen."

These words had a powerful effect not only on the emir and his men but on Ibn Hathal himself, who felt so strong that he feared nothing and no one. He was repared to say what he wanted, at whatever cost. This kind of talk found its target quickly and never erred. He went on. "Our village is small, Abu Radwan, and we know each other. We are generous to whoever treats us generously and have nothing to offer the wicked but a beating. These infidels have come to our village and before them there were three others who came in the winter. Since then we have had nothing but trouble.

"Now it is late spring," he said more softly. "The bedouin have left the desert and are starting to arrive in Wadi al-Uyoun, and the wells won't provide enough water for all. How do you expect us to let the infidels take a hundred and one buckets of water from the wells every day and throw it on the ground, and not say a word about it?"

The emir laughed in an attempt to reassert his control over the situation, and rubbed his nose. "Listen, Ibn Hathal. If it's water that's bothering you, don't worry. We'll dig you one hundred wells to take the place of those three, if not there then somewhere else, just as you like. That's a minor matter. Don't worry—after today no one will be thirsty. We don't want Wadi al-Uyoun to remain a stable for camels and livestock forever. The friends want to dig in Wadi al-Uyoun, and you'll all benefit."

Ibn Rashed spoke. "By God, Your Excellency, it was the water that was worrying us."

Miteb spoke quickly to cut off this drift toward capitulation. "Listen, Ibn Rashed, it's the water and other things, and you know it. I live on Zahra and my women can't go down to fetch water, and all I have is one small garden—I could leave it and walk away. But the people in the wadi are worried about the water and other things as well—they're thinking of honor and morals. We don't want anyone telling us what to do. We don't want those infidels, those pigs. We don't know what to expect from one day to the next."

Perceiving Miteb's strong and weak points, the emir spoke. "My friends, the government knows better than you and is stronger. As I told you, as to morals and faith, we're the ones who safeguard morals and faith for you. And don't worry about the water."

Miteb al-Hathal spoke slowly. "The problem, Your Excellency, the whole problem is that we cannot live with them. If it were a question of a day or two it wouldn't matter, but to live all together—no, we can't. Until now we have never carried arms against one another, but no one knows what tomorrow will bring."

The emir spoke with new hostility. "We have allowed you to say everything you wanted, Ibn Hathal—now let us hear what the others have to say."

Ibn Rashed spoke up, as if reciting a lesson he had memorized. "We are with the government, Your Excellency. Whatever the government chooses to do has God's blessing and we accept it. If you can guarantee our water supply, dig wells and see that there is enough for the bedouin, the caravans and the gardens, then we can close our eyes to the Christians and have nothing to do with them."

"It's a simple matter, Your Excellency," said Salem al-Maktoum. "When we saw that you delayed in coming and didn't want to go hunting, we decided to go to the emir to see about it and reassure ourselves, and, Your Excellency, you have said enough and more."

Obaid al-Suweylemi said, "If the gold is under Wadi al-Uyoun then the depths of the earth are better than its face. We must ask God to bless His Majesty with long life."

"Yes, by God, the depths of the earth are better than its face," said Miteb mockingly. "So we in the wadi must choose between water and gold."

He was silent a moment, then said, "And it seems the people of Wadi al-Uyoun have chosen the gold."

Suweylemi's and Ibn Hathal's words, and this curious equivocation, seemed to indicate that a tacit agreement had been reached. The men had told the emir what they had come to say, but Miteb al-Hathal felt a profound bitterness: he would long remember this day and deride the men and the emir for agreeing to what he heartily opposed.

"Tonight you shall all dine with us," said the emir, taking advantage of the friendly atmosphere created by the last words.

This announcement ended the meeting, and the invitation to dinner was intended to communicate the emir's happiness with its results. In order to soothe any bitterness Miteb al-Hathal still harbored, the emir told him laughingly: "If you have anything more to say about the friends, Ibn Hathal, please postpone it until dinner."

"What I have to say would not please you, Your Excellency," said Miteb sarcastically. "But what you and they have is enough for you and more, so forget it."

"More of this, Ibn Hathal?"

"You're the one who brought it up, and if you don't want to discuss it I'll leave. Then we'll both be happy."

"I am happy—I just want you to be happy."

"We have forgotten what happiness is, Your Excellency. We

only want to be left in peace and safety. I think we lost our peace
the day your friends came, and only our safety is left. You know
that a man never knows when he'll die or what land he'll die
in."

"Trust in God, man."

"In Him I trust and to Him I pray."

This conversation might have gone on and developed had the
emir not pronounced the polite formulas, usually repeated unnecessarily and meaninglessly, to signal that it was ended. He
then dismissed the men, who went out.

Feelings of shame, surprise, joy and apprehension overwhelmed all of the men but not Miteb al-Hathal, who saw the
world darken and close in on him; in spite of the clamor of voices
around him, he was filled with silence and felt surrounded by it
on every side. For the first time in his life he felt alone, like a
meaningless grain of sand no one cared about. His comments
had angered the others, particularly the emir, and even Miteb
himself, who felt paltry and useless. He wanted to speak as he
usually did, to shout at them, to say everything he had on his
mind. He had been struck by fear and then dumbness. He had
said nothing important—only made blind sounds. Otherwise
why had Maktoum and Suweylemi spoken to the emir that way?
Why had he come with them? What did he have in common
with them now? The gold? He did not want an atom of it. Was
it possible that the infidels would give over the gold for free? If
they demanded compensation, what would it be?

These and other questions, thoughts and sensations passed
through Miteb al-Hathal's mind. Some of the men with him
maintained a shamed silence and others preferred to discuss trivial subjects, but he did not see them or hear a word they were
saying. He was distant and preoccupied, tired and lost, and when
Ibn Rashed suggested they go to the market and visit some
friends, Miteb replied angrily, as if still making his speech: "I

don't want you and I won't go with you. I'm getting on my camel and riding back to Wadi al-Uyoun."

He paid no attention to the men's stares and their pleas for him to stay, since his sudden departure and rejection of the dinner invitation would insult and anger the emir. Things had gone peacefully until now, and the meeting had ended with everyone happy or at least trying to look happy, but Miteb's leaving in this manner, with no apology or explanation, would complicate things all over again. Miteb, however, did not want to discuss it. He climbed onto his white Omani she-camel and galloped off without looking back, without hearing the men's cries.

11

WHAT SORROWS POSSESSED MITEB AL-HATHAL in the accursed desert during the two days and nights of his ride back to Wadi al-Uyoun? What grief-stricken impulses made him sing or weep? No one knew; Miteb al-Hathal took his secrets with him and departed. He spoke about the trip with no one and told no one his thoughts, even after arriving back in Wadi al-Uyoun. He was possessed by a silence more like a stupor. He showed an even greater capacity for silence than he had ever shown for speech. He was surrounded by talking, questioning men but was totally oblivious to their voices and gestures; he neither heard nor responded. Even the expressions that can be read in men's faces no matter how they try to hide them, or pretend they do not understand, were absent from Miteb's face. He was a stone, or like a stone: stiff, haggard and expressionless. Had it not been for the occasional glimmer in his eyes, they would have thought they were looking at the face of a dead man. No one, not even Wadha, could induce him to speak. He quietly withdrew and behaved as if none of them existed. He slept or passed the time away by himself.

Wadi al-Uyoun awaited the return of the men to find out what had happened. After Miteb al-Hathal had come back alone, wrapped in unbroken silence, everyone in the wadi was affected by feelings of bitterness and fear. If they faced their expected troubles by looking for any glimmer of hope however frail or false since they could not avert these troubles, the sight of Ibn Hathal's face crushed this hope and extinguished every glimmer. No sooner had the idea of waiting for the other men to return— an idea that obsessed many—disappeared than a state of depression more like despair took its place: "What could Ibn Hathal's words add, even if he did speak? His face and eyes are more eloquent than words, and crueler." "When he speaks, his words will be deadly; he has seen much in this life, but this malady will kill him." "If the other men tell a story different from the one in Ibn Hathal's eyes, they will be lying. Miteb does not lie because he does not know what fear is . . . but they do."

After Miteb al-Hathal returned, after his dreadful immersion in silence, everyone in the wadi was convinced that an accursed, catastrophic end awaited them all and could come at any moment. They could only wait helplessly before such a fate; at times they felt incapable even of the sorrow which often had seemed so copious and effusive, and which they actually desired; for a terrible, tenacious despair had settled over their senses and paralyzed them, making action impossible and the passage of time sheer torture.

Wadha threw a thick blanket over Miteb, in spite of the heat that filled the air.

"If this fever doesn't kill him, he'll live to be a hundred," she said, but shook her head in doubt and fear.

When Hadib and her children asked her what had happened, she shook her head to say she did not know a thing and did not care, but after a moment of silence she murmured as if talking to herself: "A devil entered him the first day the three bastards came. Instead of getting rid of the devil he nursed it the way a hen nurses her eggs, and now the fever's killing him. It's the devils' fever."

No one clearly understood what Wadha meant, and no one asked her any more questions. She was nervous and jumpy, rushing from one place to another, the mark of fear visible in all her actions. People began to be intimidated by the vehemence with which she repeated her reply to anyone who asked about Abu Thweiny: "It's all over with him. He's finished, unless Almighty God wants to make a new Job of him."

When the men returned five days later, clamor filled the wadi and the fever began to kill Miteb. None of the townsfolk who crowded into Ibn Rashed's encampment could believe a single word of the many long stories they heard. The words *rich* and *gold* hung in the air like smoke, and like a black banner the big question arose: Had they come to stay? Ibn Maktoum's, Suweylemi's and Ibn Rashed's words and actions had turned blind and false: "Gold? How on earth could we find gold unless we toiled to find it and ran all over the place? Oil? The naphtha we find is enough to light these lamps of ours that choke you with fumes before they shed light."

12

THE DETAILS WILTED, SHRANK AND WERE FOR-
gotten, down to the very last one prompted
in the memory by an act of will or a persistent
ghost. Any attempt to recall the image of things and places that
had been encountered an oblivion that spread like warm air and
made them all dreamlike.

It was a special kind of tragedy, like amnesia followed by
long-belated remembrance in which the chaotic confusion and
curse of things were made apparent. Even if Miteb al-Hathal's
life mattered, even if Wadi al-Uyoun had once existed and then
vanished under the soil of another time, only the final moments
survived, and perhaps only they had truly occurred after all.

Very late one night, in the late summer or early fall, a mad
roaring suddenly filled the wadi. It was like distant thunder or

the sound of huge numbers of filled waterskins falling on swamp-land; it shook the air and pained the ears so much that it was hard to tell where it was coming from. Miteb al-Hathal had decided to stay up in Zahra until the late summer, categorically refusing all attempts to induce him down to the wadi, but after his refusal and isolation, and as a result of the illness that did not leave him for a single day, a sort of tacit agreement took effect: he would be forgotten, considered dead or absent, and life in the wadi would go on as before. True, there were some difficulties that summer, but they were dealt with; now, how-ever, it seemed that the group of men in search of oil, after completing the requirements of their first phase, had decided to begin.

It was not important how they began, because the thunder that filled the wadi that late summer night was the best-remem-bered beginning; it alone moved Miteb al-Hathal to end his isolation and go down to the wadi.

There may have been some other kinds of details that preceded that beginning, important in their own way, but they had not seemed so to Miteb al-Hathal. The many attempts, in which friends and relatives had played a part, to sell the small garden he owned in Wadi al-Uyoun at a price that seemed high for those times had failed.

All Miteb did was shake his head in refusal, and when his relatives resorted to pressuring him, he only laughed mockingly and walked away. As to what the emir was supposed to have said, that Ibn Hathal would sell like it or not, it was heard with head shaking, as if to say let's wait and see. So the thunder that Miteb heard that night excited him very much; he must have thought or hoped that an explosion in the camp had destroyed everything. He may have imagined that something momentous had just happened and that he had to see it for himself; or perhaps other thoughts occurred to him. How else could one explain the enthusiasm that made him forget his isolation and rush to the wadi?

With the first light of dawn, huge iron machines began to move. Their deafening noise filled the whole wadi. So gigantic and strange were these iron machines that no one had ever imagined such things even existed; the lights that shone from them were like shooting stars. They moved on the same open track the caravans used, and within a short time the noise grew louder, and the machines arrived in the wadi.

No one could describe the moment in which the machines moved into the wadi or know the feelings that gripped the people as they watched the huge yellow hulks move along and roar, then stop at the border of the camp. No one could describe or imagine it. Miteb al-Hathal, who had reached the wadi with the stealth of a cat, watched everything carefully, keeping far away from the strange creatures with whose evil he could not contend, not approaching for fear they would do something he could not stop. Deep inside him he knew, when the thunder stopped, that the world had ended.

When the machines stopped, small windows and doors opened up in them and dusty men came out and looked around them. A bewildered silence reigned: Where had these men been? How had they entered and come out of these machines? Were they men or devils? Why were they there, and what would they do? These yellow iron hulks—could a man approach them without injury? What were they for and how did they behave—did they eat like animals, or not?

The boys were the first to run over to the machines and did not hesitate to touch them. At first they stretched out wary fingers in order to touch, and upon feeling the hardness of the iron, they put their palms against it and struck it lightly as if gently knocking on a door that must open. Slightly reassured, they circled the machines, probing in various places with hands or small sticks, and one boy dared to throw a stone at one of them. The men of the wadi, who had been watching the boys with annoyance, fearing that some harm would come to them from this game, soon decided to do what the boys were doing, because that way they might learn what the machines were for and what they might do.

These were moments of serious scrutiny, of fear and surprise. When some of the workers came out of the camp with those who had been in the machines to have a look, the men and boys of Wadi al-Uyoun retreated a few steps and stood waiting and fearful. Filled with pride and confidence, the new men walked around the machines, opening the doors and lifting the covers, while the others watched raptly. Suddenly one man jumped up and disappeared inside a machine, and instantly it roared and then moved. The machine began to run in diabolical circles, up and down, roaring and whirring. The people of Wadi al-Uyoun, who had retreated far off, looked on with fearful eyes in utter silence, not knowing when the gates of Hell would open up and swallow everything.

For the first time in long months, the people of Wadi al-Uyoun heard the voice of Miteb al-Hathal. "The devils are here and we must fight them. If we do nothing, they'll eat us up and we'll leave no trace behind!"

He may have wanted to say more, but the silence that fell after the machines stopped and the questioning and fearful gazes appealing to him from those around him made him feel useless. No one understood him or stood by him, and nothing he could say would do any good. Nervously, shaking his head in pain and despair, he turned back as if in regret, for his words had slipped out in spite of himself. When some of the men held him back and asked him to explain the nature of the strange creatures and what they would do, he pushed their hands away roughly as if he could not bear to be touched or to hear another word. Men who were used to Miteb al-Hathal were not surprised by this kind of behavior and did not expect him to talk to them, so they went away. Miteb set out for a nearby hill and sat there. In a tense squat, nearby and yet distant, he monitored everything from his post and meditated, as if witnessing the end of an age.

It was the end of the world, or perhaps the end of one of the long ages in the life of this distant, forgotten desert. Only Miteb al-Hathal said so out loud; the others in and around Wadi al-Uyoun sensed it but did not articulate the feeling in thoughts or words. They were possessed by rancor and recklessness and fear and looked around questioningly but could not clearly imagine or guess what might happen next. Or perhaps they were hoping that something would happen at the last minute to reverse all that had been planned and devised, so that everything would go back to normal in the wadi, ending this long bad dream.

Although long hours had passed and the people waited, the Americans remained squatting silently inside the camp. During this time a group of men came out of the other tent, shouting and singing, but not for long. Once more the camp fell silent. People sat clustered in small groups outside the camp, in the shade of the palm and fig trees, as if watching something. Each one of them felt certain that something was about to happen. Some sent their children to bring food and others made coffee in the open air, far from their homes and camps; the desire not to miss a single thing was overwhelming, and they knew the chance might never repeat itself.

Sitting atop the high hill, Miteb took everything in and meditated quietly. He ignored the cries calling him to come down and eat, to share the morning coffee and then noon coffee. He was still silent and preoccupied; his senses were aroused and expectant, more so than any of theirs. When they sent him up some figs, dates and bread, he put them aside as if he were not hungry or did not want to eat, though something did not allow him to refuse the food, for the vigil was a long one and he had no intention of leaving.

This was one of the rare times in which all of the townsfolk were like this. From the time the devils first came a few months before, they had grown ever more mysterious and their intentions harder to divine. They spent the whole day in tents, especially the big tent in the middle, or in the wooden cabins they had skillfully built, writing and drawing with the same air of secrecy that enshrouded all the other aspects of their life. The people of the wadi had long used their knowledge and intuition to figure people out; this scrutiny played a major part in the many wagers they made among themselves over what travelers might be bringing or what caravans might be carrying, but these travelers stumped them. The people were afraid to make bets; all they knew was that the Americans would extract gold and oil from the earth, though they could not even guess how that could be done. Sometimes Ibn Rashed used his friendship with Ghorab and the translator to try to find out more. But he got only general answers, and when he tried to clarify matters with his own information, he could only invent words that added more mystery to the one that already baffled them.

Now that the hellish yellow machines had come on the scene, they all assumed that an ending of some sort was at hand, and everyone wanted to see the ending for himself, to find out all the details, even the smallest and most obscure.

The hours passed slowly. The afternoon hours that day were the longest the wadi had ever known. Even the chores the men were used to doing, like tying up the camels and making coffee by themselves so as to achieve just the right taste, even these were postponed or performed laggingly. The young men were assigned chores they had never done before and did them enthusiastically.

The men waited for something to happen, but everything was as normal in the daylight hours, and it seemed as though the day would pass, like all others, without surprises. As the sun sank, the animals came and filled the wadi with their din, and the shepherds and the bedouin came to the water, making their own noise, shouting and gesticulating; then the Americans came, adding to the rest of the clamor with the machines they had brought earlier, which emitted light and noise and frightened the others. As a result, the wadi rang as if with the howling of lost wolves and the screams of hungry jackals seeking prey or companionship.

Dusk fell. Most men were dazed with boredom and depression, reckoning that another weary night would pass as they had for three months or more, when suddenly a procession of all the men from the camp moved out. Ghorab led the way, and it seemed that they had had a long talk prior to this, for as soon as they exited through the camp gate Ghorab made hand signals to the left and then to the right, talking all the while and looking first in this direction and then in that. When the Americans began to march, the whole wadi was struck with fear, and there was a loud racket as the children and young men who were watching while they watered the animals and helped with the irrigation began to shout and run chaotically. The older men acted more calmly; after watching, they moved back a little out of the Americans' path, and when the foreigners had passed, first stopping at the brook and the wells, then continuing on to the wadi, the men followed them with their eyes and then got up and moved slowly after them. Miteb al-Hathal had leaped up at the very moment the Americans left the camp. He stood on the hill like a wolf ready to spring, moving only when the Americans moved, keeping the same distance and pace, but his eyes observed every movement and his ears took in every sound and he looked as if he did not want to miss a thing. He noticed and interpreted every motion, and when Ghorab spoke, pointing at the sand dunes, the brook and the trees, Ibn Hathal's hatred rose so much that he began to shake and the color drained from his face. The boys were able to make out a few of the words he kept repeating and later said they'd heard him say, "You sons of whores, you horned stones, I'll get my revenge before the great Avenger judges you." They also said that he cursed the government, the sultan, the emir and everyone who had helped the infidels.

Miteb missed nothing. He moved and stopped and cursed and gazed at everything as though he would never see the place again, and although none of the Americans looked at him he flinched every time they pointed back in his direction, thinking at first that they were pointing at him. Then he realized that they were pointing instead to the land he was walking on; that he was no more than a landmark to them. Had it not been for Ghorab's movement in his direction, though without looking at him or noticing his presence, leaving a footprint on the soil, then measuring the distance halfway through the wadi, had it not been for that movement Miteb would have thought that they were motioning to him. He almost did something stupid. What could they want from him as long as he followed only ten feet or a little more from them? Couldn't he go to his own garden on the other side of the wadi if he wanted to, to sing, think or curse as he pleased? Couldn't he do what he liked as long as he harmed no one, just as in the past?

These were Miteb's thoughts as he watched Ghorab hurry along, pointing and raising his voice. He was genuinely frightened by the others, who asked questions and made several comments, and he felt sure that this evening would end badly. He did not know why he decided to return to the water before the Americans. He hurried to the brook, rolled up his sleeves, scooped up the water and splashed it on his face, snuffing it in and letting it drip through his beard; then he scooped up more water and drank. He took off his cloak and dunked his head, shaking it, with his eyes open. He felt coolness and pleasure and fear and stayed that way for a moment, then pulled out his head when he felt his breath bursting in his chest. Water streamed down copiously and then ran out; once again he breathed deeply and drank from his hands, and tranquilly, as if he were alone in the world, he headed back to his hill and sat in a spot directly overlooking the water. Perhaps he guessed that the wadi would be nothing if the water stopped; perhaps he guessed that his garden and the land before and beyond it, to the end of the wadi, would be nothing if the Americans wanted to stop the water; but he also knew that the lands in the wadi were all so alike that his own was hardly any different or more valuable than any other. If he thought differently he would have stayed in the garden and slept under one of the palm trees. If he wanted to defend only his own garden and trees he would not have chosen this open spot where he could be seen by all. Something made him choose this place, and when the Americans came back, when their faces and shadows appeared in the strong light, he lay flat against the hill and decided to stay watchful, to wait for the long overdue miracle.

....

13

S HORTLY AFTER DAWN, WHEN THE FIRST LIGHT OF
day appeared distinct from the shadows and
shone gently above, the wadi was still wrapped
in the light mist left by the night, the moisture wrung from the
air, trees and brook water, and from the breath of people then
quietly waking up to begin another day. Miteb al-Hathal's wide,
sorrowful eyes, which had not closed for a moment, watched
and listened and thought and followed the movements of life in
its new phase that long-ago autumn day. People and places and
life had, until that moment, existed uneasily in sad, serene silence, as if nothing would ever change, but a loud shout rang
out in the camp, and with this sudden shout, which alerted Miteb
al-Hathal, life began to change. It was only a few moments before
the Americans got moving and came out.

They poured out like a band of devils. In a flash they headed for the machines with a speed and excitement that finally signaled that the end had come. No one told Miteb al-Hathal, but he was overcome by a strong premonition; although he did not know what was going to happen, that measured, solemn instinct told him. He got up slowly, inhaling the wadi's air into his lungs and whole body. He looked all around him as if in farewell. A flock of sand grouse glided by. He looked at the men in the camp, filled with a strong sense of finality, and when the mad machines went into action he screamed in a harsh but pained voice: "I'm sorry, Wadi al-Uyoun . . . I'm sorry!"

This was the final, insane, accursed proclamation that everything had come to an end. For anyone who remembers those long-ago days, when a place called Wadi al-Uyoun used to exist, and a man named Miteb al-Hathal, and a brook, and trees, and a community of people used to exist, the three things that still break his heart in recalling those days are the tractors which attacked the orchards like ravenous wolves, tearing up the trees and throwing them to the earth one after another, and leveled all the orchards between the brook and the fields. After destroying the first grove of trees, the tractors turned to the next with the same bestial voracity and uprooted them. The trees shook violently and groaned before falling, cried for help, wailed, panicked, called out in helpless pain and then fell entreatingly to the ground, as if trying to snuggle into the earth to grow and spring forth alive again.

The butchery of Wadi al-Uyoun had begun, and it continued until everything was gone. Miteb al-Hathal witnessed the beginning of the butchery but not the end, for the men who came when they heard the sounds of the maddened machines and stood watching what was taking place before them, after they recovered from the daze that possessed them, looked around and saw Ibn Hathal and made many sad comments. They said it was the first time in their lives they had ever seen a man like Miteb al-Hathal cry. He could not stop crying, but he did so silently. He was perfectly silent. He did not say one word. He did not curse. Not a single sound or word escaped his lips; he shed his tears, unashamed and unafraid, but not proud either. He looked quietly through his tears at the whole wadi and shook his head.

At some point, no one knows exactly when, as the men ran out and got to work, as fathers called their sons to help them gather the pieces of wood, Miteb al-Hathal withdrew quietly and left the hill, heading in the direction of Mount Zahra. Within a short time, although Wadha pleaded and fell to the ground to kiss his feet, and despite his cousins' arguments, he made his decision. He worked calmly, readying everything he needed, without looking at anyone, without hearing a single word they said. He still had tearstains on his face but he did not cry, and when he had finished preparing everything he gathered up his rifle and waterskin and mounted his Omani camel. He looked at them all, at each of their faces in turn as if memorizing them, and when he had scrutinized them all he kicked the camel's sides, and she trembled as she reared up and stood. Miteb al-Hathal rose on her back like a huge tent, and then he looked like a cloud, and when he sped off he looked like a white bird. He faded from sight and grew smaller, dwindled and then disappeared.

14

O NLY A FEW PEOPLE SAW HIM LEAVE. THEY WERE busy and afraid, watching the maddened machines uproot the trees and level the earth and topple everything on it, and when they grew weary of watching, having seen everything demolished and finished, they looked at each other in shock. When they asked about Miteb al-Hathal, someone said he had gone. This seemed strange and unnatural and even eerie. "Miteb al-Hathal? How could he go and leave the wadi . . . Where could he possibly go?"

Nothing seemed real anymore.

"Miteb would never leave the wadi," one man said. "He would die first."

"He left a long time back, when they cut the first tree."

"Miteb would never leave. I'll make a bet."

"Zahra is right there, and you can see what's happened to the wadi. Nothing's left!"

"My camel against your camel."

"But he left three days ago. Shaalan said he had left. I saw him on his camel with my own eyes—heading east."

"I prefer to lose my head and my camel. Miteb would not go."

"Trust in God, my friend, keep your camel, leave your head where it is, and listen to me! Miteb is gone!"

Miteb had gone off the way he often did, many people said; he was feeling melancholy, so he would be away for a day or two and then come back; no matter how far he wandered he would surely return.

The townsfolk were all absolutely positive that Miteb would never leave the wadi, that unlike so many others he could never just pack his bags and disappear. If he had headed into the desert angry and hunted like his father and grandfather before him, he would do as they had done. They had been the wadi's fiercest warriors against the Turks; they had never slept in the same place twice and had turned the entire Sultan's Road into a Hell on earth. The Turks had offered a reward of one hundred pieces of silver to anyone who could kill Jazi al-Hathal or bring him in alive. Before Jazi was his father, Miteb, whom the Turks had once arrested. But before morning he had escaped. Some said that he had put some sort of drug in the guards' coffee, and others said that he had bribed them to let him escape. All the men at the garrison in Wadi al-Uyoun were punished because they had been unable to hold Miteb al-Hathal and send him to the garrison at Kerak.

The people recalled these stories and expected that Miteb al-Hathal would come back again. Some were afraid and said that these times were different from those of the Turks—Miteb would not be able to carry a rifle or kill anyone. The more courageous and optimistic among them agreed that Miteb would come back but said that if he did so he would set the world on fire—he would kill and destroy and maybe even burn everything down. It was unthinkable that Miteb would leave the Americans alone after what they had done to Wadi al-Uyoun.

"The Atoum are like winter snakes," said Nizar al-Ma'aani as he looked off into the distance. "They hide and sleep, but when they surface . . . God help us."

Muhammad al-Medawwar shook his head and smiled. "What will happen to you—where will you go, Ibn Rashed?"

"By God, people of Wadi al-Uyoun, all you do is talk." Abdallah al-Masoud, who had been listening but did not want to join in the discussion, laughed. "The man picked up and left the wadi to get something out of his system; that's all there is to it. And you go on about him like you had nothing to talk about but Ibn Hathal."

The men looked at each other's faces and shook their heads sadly.

It seemed to everyone that Ibn Hathal's journey, no matter how long it lasted, would have to end; he would have to come back.

They all looked at the strange scene before them as if it were a dream or a hallucination, but the line of neatly parked tractors, and the deadly silence that reigned over the new land—for the wadi now looked like part of the desert beyond, except for the hills and the heaps of ruined trees—convinced them that it was real: a cruel, wicked sight that resembled death.

Beside the ruins on the broad plain they sat, determined to stay and wait. They moved slowly and mournfully, like windblown scarecrows made of rags and palm branches, moving and then settling down gradually to become part of the boundless, dusty, motionless expanse, now rising again and now reposing.

Ibn Rashed had done all he could, in the last days, to cooperate with the Desert Forces' efforts to relocate the people of Wadi al-Uyoun. He had selected twenty men to work in the camp, but he was deeply troubled and afraid that some would prove stubborn and refuse to move. On the afternoon of the third day, after the razing of the last trees, he stood stern faced and decisive and shouted at the clustered people: "My friends! Leave of your free will like the ones who went before you. It's better than being driven out. Every one of you will get his rightful compensation. The emir has said good riddance to anyone who wants their desert and tribe, but for those who want a place to live, the government is arranging everything."

After that no one saw Ibn Rashed, and he never came back. He moved into the American camp and was replaced by some men of the bedouin police.

The bedouin police informed those remaining in Wadi al-Uyoun that they would have to leave. There was to be no discussion. They summoned them and grouped them near the camp, and one of the soldiers looked at the ground and spoke: "You can have tonight, but by sundown tomorrow you have to be out of here. We will see to that."

Despite the rage, sorrow, humiliation and scores of other emotions that filled the people of the wadi, Umm Khosh was the only person who refused to follow the orders and ignored the entire proceedings. After they had gathered her belongings in a small pile and put it with their own things, some of them donated a few items and then tied up the bundle. Its meagerness and incongruity inspired laughter and pity at the same time: old clothes, mismatched tin pots and plates, pieces of wood, some ropes and a curved-headed bamboo cane. While this was going on Umm Khosh sat near Mount Zahra, as was her habit every day, waiting for a new caravan to bring news. When she came and saw her bundle and was told that she had to leave with everyone else, she gave them a silly look, smiling more than usual, calmly fished her bundle out of the huge heaps of baggage piled in a circle and untied it. She carried it off a good distance from the travelers and their things. She undid the belt carefully and took out some of Khosh's clothes, shook them in the air and smelled them, held them out as if admiring their beauty, then drew them near her face to examine them carefully for the soundness of the cloth and quality of the needlework. She smelled them again, deeply this time, and refolded them one on top of the other. She caressed them and talked to them, saying things that made her sad and cheered her up, made her laugh and then cry. She did all these things as if she were alone in the desert, and the men and women who watched her as if seeing her for the first time saw their faces in her face and felt that their lives were hopelessly tragic and fragmented. They watched her in silence, and many did not even notice the tears that streamed from their eyes; they tasted the bitter salinity and looked at the ground, not one daring to look in the face of another. When they went to sleep that night, which they did early, like cats on winter nights, on top of their bags and bundles, sinking into torpor and then slumber, they heard the voice of Umm Khosh. Some who were still awake or were awakened by the sound thought it had come from a dream or another world, for it was tremulous, high pitched and anguished. "My dear friends. People of the wadi—I forgot to ask you about Miteb, Abu Thweiny. Where is Miteb?"

No one dared to reply. The silence grew heavier and more oppressive, and she asked again. "My friends—let whoever knows about Abu Thweiny tell me what happened to him."

Silence, with the tension that borders on fear because the next moment could bring an outburst. A rough voice, whether a man's or an old woman's no one could tell, spoke up. "Get some sleep, girl—everything will be fine in the morning."

There was a dry, strangled laugh and then Umm Khosh's voice: "Don't worry, my friends—let whoever knows about Abu Thweiny tell me what has happened to him."

When the oppressive silence reigned again, more sadly than before, the voice rang out mockingly: "Everything will be fine in the morning? You'll tell me about Abu Thweiny tomorrow?"

The monotonous, fear-laden silence reasserted itself. She spoke again in the same mocking tone. "My friends! Yesterday . . . no, two or three days ago . . . I saw him. We had a talk and he told me, 'Don't worry, Khosh is coming back.' You all know. For years I've been pleading for Khosh to come back, and now I'm begging you for news of Abu Thweiny and nobody's answering me, and nobody's listening!"

She waited a few moments and went on bitterly. "God help you all!"

Then she was silent.

Some of the wakeful ones heard her talking to herself. They couldn't understand a word. She no longer asked questions or waited for answers. Those who had entered the kingdom of sleep or approached it heard a continual droning, which sometimes grew slightly louder and other times waned but did not stop; it was like the whisper of a stiff breeze or a faraway cry for help, and when it began to sound incoherent and wavering, almost dying out, only to rise again sounding tormented, those who had woken up or never been asleep felt in the voice a drawn-out cry from the heart like a prick behind the eye. They closed their eyes for the long sleepy journey with sad memories, as if the pained monotony of the voice gave things the strange fragrance and burning taste of an open wound.

Some time in the night, as the light and darkness wrestled, the old woman's voice died away, though not all at once; it diminished gradually, becoming a sound like slowly dripping fat, and when it died out completely, the nonsleepers looking at the stars said, "There's nothing like sleep. The old woman is asleep."

When the morning star faded the piles of people began to stir. At first hesitant and indolent, with the spreading of the sky and the appearance of the line between earth and endless space, the bodies moved more clearly and with more strength. They got up with the first rays of sunlight as if a hidden hand had shaken and woken them, and opened their eyes. Fear and disbelief followed immediately, as if sleep had robbed them and made them forget where they were and why, but the first moments helped them to grasp what had happened. They shook their heads repeatedly to dismiss the sleep and looked again to make sure, and when it came back to them they reclosed their eyes in an attempt to forget, but it was impossible. It was too late.

They were all up before the sun rose, all except Umm Khosh. She was asleep with her head against the pile of clothes, almost in a praying position, half kneeling, in a semicircle. No one wanted to wake her, since she had missed so much sleep the night before. They walked carefully and spoke softly so as not to disturb her. She stayed asleep or continued her prayer even when the dogs barked at two of the soldiers heading back to the camp, and when the boys began playing and one of them ran near Umm Khosh, Abdallah al-Masoud threw a pebble at them and pointed angrily at Umm Khosh and told them to play farther away. Some people nearby heard him say in a low voice, "The old woman didn't sleep until dawn." He added, shaking his head sadly, "God help her, and help us."

By the time the sun had risen a forearm's length everything was bustling. The baggage was roped up again, a fire was kindled, and the men strode about supervising, but unlike on previous days, the women moved slowly, as if they did not know what to do or how. The boys played more roughly and shouted louder than before, running wherever they pleased. Even Abdallah al-Masoud, who had not taken his eyes from Umm Khosh, guessed that enough time had gone by since throwing the pebble at the boys, and he no longer scolded them or bothered to speak softly himself.

Umm Khosh lay as she was, unmindful of all that was happening around her, and did not hear or stir. She was serene and quite still in her slumber, even when two of the desert police came over from the American camp and stood near her. One of them spoke in a very friendly tone. "My friends, you'd better set off early, otherwise the sun is going to massacre you."

"Don't worry, we're going, we're going," Abdallah al-Masoud answered him sarcastically. "Trust in God, my good man."

"If you had left at dawn you'd be in East Khabra or even farther than that by now."

The two men walked away. The boys looked at their fathers to see if it was time to go yet. Muhammad al-Medawwar spoke loudly to no one in particular. "If we get going now we can rest in Khabra, and continue on in the afternoon."

Abdallah al-Masoud pointed at Umm Khosh. "What about the old woman?" he asked.

"She's coming with us."

Several people repeated these words approvingly.

"And if she doesn't want to come?"

"Whether she wants to or not," said Muhammad al-Medawwar. "We'll take her with us and go."

"Fine. See for yourself. Ask her."

Muhammad al-Medawwar strode over and put his hand gently on her shoulder. "Umm Khosh . . . Umm Khosh."

She did not reply or move.

"It's nearly noon . . . Umm Khosh."

She did not reply.

Muhammad al-Medawwar shook her by the shoulder. "Umm Khosh."

She moved slightly but made no answer. He shook her a little harder. She leaned to the left but otherwise stayed stubborn and sleepy, or perhaps she was not finished praying. He raised her shoulder a little, with difficulty, and her face rose an inch as her body changed position. When he let go she fell back as she was: reclining on the pile of clothes as if kissing them or pausing to sort them out.

"Hurry up!" said a man standing far off.

Abdallah al-Masoud moved closer and knelt by Umm Khosh. He put his hand on her shoulder and looked at Muhammad al-Medawwar and then at the people standing around, and whispered kindly, "Umm Khosh . . . Umm Khosh."

She did not reply or change her position.

"We'll carry her along," said Muhammad al-Medawwar, his patience exhausted. "Whether she agrees, or doesn't agree—there it is."

"Fear God, my friend, what do you mean, carry her?" said Abdallah al-Masoud. "Like a sheep? She is not a sheep!"

"Hurry up!" said a man standing far off, perhaps the same man who had shouted out before.

Muhammad al-Medawwar moved closer than before, directly over Umm Khosh; he cradled and lifted her up like a pile of clothes. In his arms she seemed to be a big child. He shook her vigorously to wake her from her deep sleep. The boys gawked at them curiously and shouted with laughter, and the men and women smiled. Still kneeling, Abdallah al-Masoud looked up to see the game Umm Khosh was playing in the last moments of their departure. When he saw her face, he jumped up like a man springing out of a nightmare and felt his heart nearly burst from his chest. He screamed in pain. "Shame on you all!"

He took Umm Khosh and laid her down gently. She rolled

on her face as she had been before, and he trembled fearfully as he knelt. He held her face and looked at it carefully, then turned to the others who drew near. Her face was dry, yellow and cold. There was no life. When he was sure of that he replaced her on the pile of clothes.

He got up slowly in resignation and took a few small weary steps to the last group of men.

"God, Almighty God, may He be praised, has given her rest. She is dead."

No one believed it, but when Wadha came near and touched her, she pulled back in terror and screamed like an angry child. "Where are you, Abu Thweiny—where are your eyes to see this?"

In less than an hour a grave was dug and Umm Khosh was buried. No one wanted to touch her belongings, so the wind scattered them and the sand buried all that she had left behind.

It had been decided that the caravan would leave before noon, but the death of Umm Khosh was reason enough to delay it for one more day. Everyone hoped that in the space of the day something would happen to change that decision and make it possible to reconsider the whole move. The soldiers of the bedouin police stayed far off and refused to get into a discussion with them or to answer any of their questions. The police pretended to have seen nothing but resolved that there would be no staying behind after that day.

15

I
N THE FADING BLUE SHADOW, AMID LIGHT, REFRESH-
ing gusts of wind, the townsfolk silently completed
the preparations for their departure. When they left
Wadi al-Uyoun, or more precisely when they were forced to
leave it, shortly after the sun rose, the family of Miteb al-Hathal
was among them. Fawaz, the eldest, was with his brothers. Only
Shaalan stayed in the wadi, to see about obtaining the compensation due his family: the price of the small garden that had been
theirs and the land where their house had been.

Hadib had gone before them to Ujra, the main way station
on the Sultan's Road, leaving to Fawaz the responsibilities of the
journey and many other matters, for ever since Miteb al-Hathal
had left Wadi al-Uyoun so mysteriously, leaving much dust and
even more speculation behind him, the emir's men had begun
to regard Miteb's family with special spite and suspicion. There

were rumors that the family would receive no compensation of any kind, that they would be driven out by force if they did not choose to leave and that once they reached Ujra they would have to fend for themselves. These and other matters obliged Hadib to forgo the compensation collected by so many others who waited in Wadi al-Uyoun, leaving Shaalan to pursue it. He hurried to Ujra to await the family and to prepare for a journey inland to relatives on both his mother's and his father's sides who might be able to protect them or offer some stability in their lives until Miteb al-Hathal came back.

Fawaz was the "biggest" of the brothers, and this description caused a great deal of laughter at his expense, for he was barely fourteen years old. He was as slender as a bamboo stalk but as strong as a whip, or at least so he appeared and so he wished to be. He used to creep up on their camel like an insect to mount her and hang on to her tail when she galloped to prove to everyone that he had attained manhood. These images seemed so distant to them now, so blurred, that the people were not even sure they were real, for everything after Wadi al-Uyoun seemed so confused. The wadi itself was, however, still fresh and intact in their memories, with its features and smells—even the whispered conversations and the uneasy questions of those preparing to leave, about ropes and water and flour, still rang loudly in the ears of those who stayed and those who left.

"I was afraid you had run into trouble, or given up on the way," said Hadib when the caravan arrived in Ujra. He said this with an admiration he could not hide and addressed his sister as Fawaz began to unload the luggage from the camels.

"I had thought more than once of going back to Wadi al-Uyoun, or going out to meet you on the road."

"We saw plenty of wolves," said Radiya.

"Wolves are nothing to fear," Hadib replied. He paused and then added, "If you have men with you."

Was Fawaz as brave as his uncle imagined and as his sister assumed? Had he been frightened or shown fear at any point during the three-day journey? He had been extremely cautious, since they had been left in a caravan of only five households after many travelers had stopped in Khabra or traveled by other routes, but Wadha al-Hamad was so strong that she had inspired most of the courage and common sense he had shown. Her eyes had shone with sublime sorrow since Miteb's disappearance. She could think of no rational motive for his agitation and misery or for his departure. She pressed her lips firmly together and refused to offer any explanation for what he had done. Deep inside she realized that some dark resolve had possessed his heart and mind and compelled him to make the decision. She was familiar with the fits of nerves that drove him to isolation, sudden departures and long absences, but this time she was not convinced that he would come back as he had before. She had been positive that something would happen at the last moment that would change everything, for Miteb would not change his mind of his own accord, especially now that Wadi al-Uyoun was gone forever. He would not leave without doing something—killing, burning or destroying. When she perceived his firm surprise decision, followed by his departure, she waited hour after hour for him to reappear, to circle the wadi once or twice until he grew tired, then return full of spent anger and regret. But when the days passed and he neither returned nor sent word, and they were all forced to leave, she felt depressed to the point of utter despair. Was it possible for them to depart and leave everything behind? Could they survive the move to another place after losing their homes, land and livelihoods . . . having already lost the dearest thing in their lives, Miteb al-Hathal?

No one dared ask these questions, but the unflinching strength of Wadha's will, her silence through most of the journey and the depthless sorrow in her eyes which touched all the others, made matters final and inevitable.

In spite of all this, it was this magnificent woman, Wadha al-Hamad, who led the caravan, who helped to rope the packs on the animals and to unload them. Fawaz was filled with caution all during the journey and expected trouble at every moment, and this feeling made him nervous; he slept little and ate like a frightened bird, but he did not want Wadha to notice. She tried to influence and inspire him through her silence and strength until they reached Ujra. When they met up with Hadib, he wanted to soothe their trouble and create a pleasant atmosphere, but he ran up against Wadha's silence, along with her sorrow, which he soon shared.

They would never forget the four days they spent with relatives in Ujra. Nothing out of the ordinary happened, and there was no news from or about Miteb al-Hathal despite the procession of hajj caravans that never let up for a single day.

For those four days all of the refugees felt the departure from Wadi al-Uyoun like a hard, unexpected punch. From the first night in Ujra they had an overpowering feeling that they were totally alone and that they would not be able to face the new life. In the dead silence that enveloped them after going to bed, broken only by the barking of dogs and disjointed shouts far away, Fawaz heard for the first time in many long years the sound of his mother, Wadha al-Hamad, crying. It was stifled and intermittent crying, which she did not want anyone to notice. She cried like a small girl hiding from the others. She bit the blanket and buried her face in the pillow, and cried.

Fawaz knew, that night, that what had happened was not just the loss of a place called Wadi al-Uyoun, nor any loss that a man could describe or grow accustomed to. He realized that it was a breaking off, like death, that nothing and no one could ever heal. Despite the anger they felt toward their father, who had left them to deal with the tragedy alone, Miteb's angry words mingled with Wadha's weeping that night, and he seemed easier to understand and perhaps less cruel.

After that night and for a long time to come, Fawaz, who had left boyhood to become a man before his time, could not sleep. He was haunted by the spirits that filled that night, and many after it, with a painful expectancy.

16

IN UJRA, WHICH HAD BEEN A CARAVAN STOP FOR
thousands of years, linking the Sultan's Road with
many other routes, they met up with other caravans, and during the four days they spent there they bought
supplies to last them through the first phase of living in their
new homes in al-Hadra. In the process they spent all the money
they had. For the first time they discovered that other people
and other places were very different from Wadi al-Uyoun. The
merchants' words were rapid, short and sharp. Their glances
were full of suspicion. Hadib's attempts to get lower prices for
flour and sugar, and his visits to several different merchants to
check on the prices and to haggle, ended in despairing resignation.

"If it were any other time of year we would have got more

flour and at better prices," he told Wadha. The bags of flour were stacked in the shade of the wall.

Wadha nodded in agreement and said bitterly, "They say that 'religion is conduct,' but merchants are only interested in money—that's their only religion."

Silent and disappointed, they roped up the luggage again at dawn on the fifth day and left.

The caravan grew smaller when they left the Sultan's Road and headed north. They had prepared themselves for a long journey and were determined to reach Rawdhat al-Mashti quickly in order to catch up with a caravan said to have arrived there a few days earlier. It was said that this caravan would wait awhile for two or three caravans more before pushing on to al-Hadra and beyond.

For the first time in their lives, places seemed hostile; they were so awfully cruel. The family felt a surge of confidence in Ujra when they met their uncle, who took all their problems, including leading the caravan, upon himself. But people's faces seemed unfeeling to them wherever they passed through, and the water they drank tasted brackish and almost bitter. The places they stopped seemed unnatural, and they could not understand how anyone could get used to living in them. Wadha, who had been strong and composed all the way from Wadi al-Uyoun to Ujra, now seemed like an old camel. She gazed at everything slowly but not contemplatively. She never spoke; even when her brother asked her questions about the journey, she contented herself with nodding to agree or to indicate that she did not know. When they sat down to eat she moved her hand, lean from the trip, from her mouth to the platter of food and chewed each morsel as if she wanted it to last or did not want to swallow it, or as if she were not capable of swallowing. The rest of them usually finished eating first and left her what remained. They avoided looking at her or asking her to eat more, because the one time Radiya, visibly upset, did ask her to eat to regain her strength, she saw her mother slip into that state of silent grief and gloomy illness. The look she gave her chilled Radiya completely and inhibited any of the others from trying to nag her again.

The journey was full of quiet sorrow. The camels plodded on monotonously, and shortly after dawn the sun became an unbearable torture. Attempts to converse or joke when they stopped to gather kindling for cooking fires were a clumsy substitute for the kind of talk they were used to. Each of them in his own way tried to respect their mother's silence or to share in her suffocating sorrow. The few times they tried to talk, to say something, their words were brief and obscure and at other times completely meaningless, but they were always faint, almost inaudible, and they trailed off, leaving each speaker with a strong sense of having committed a misdeed. Even though their uncle had been addicted to joking, singing and exaggerated joy and anger for as long as they had known him now he was an entirely different man. Ibrahim tried to get him to sing or chant, and to tell stories of his travels, but he had no success, even though Wadha was usually not listening or not even present.

They arrived in Rawdhat al-Mashti, but the caravan they had wanted to join had already left, so they would have to wait several days, which stretched into weeks. The route that led inland was traveled by caravans only infrequently, and almost never in summertime.

It would be impossible to describe that journey or those days in all their details, for silent Wadha al-Hamad, filled with a rare kind of pride, seemed, especially in Rawdhat al-Mashti, even crazier and more fanatic than Miteb al-Hathal.

Was this the same kind of fever that had saved Miteb al-Hathal, that had changed his children's perception of him and embodied in him an absolute innocence? Was it the fever that spoke, that chattered endlessly? At least some of her words were still strong, stronger than any others, for when Wadha al-Hamad fell prey to the illness and that dreadful fever that made her rave one evening, she said many things, the clearest of which was: "Abu Thweiny, you are the best and most constant of men in the world. You are the best man, the ornament of Wadi al-Uyoun. You spoke the truth but they didn't believe you. Wadi al-Uyoun is gone, Abu Thweiny. After you went nothing was left but dates and stories. Don't come back until the children grow up. When you come back you'll all be successful and they'll be all broken and consumed with regret. Your children, they're the ones we can count on, Abu Thweiny, and may you know it well!"

17

AFTER TWO WEEKS OF TORMENT, WAITING AND illness they prepared to depart again, this time from Rawdhat al-Mashti to al-Hadra. It was a hard journey, and a silent one.

They were at the end of the caravan; this was Wadha's wish. She did not utter a word from the time the fever left her until they arrived in al-Hadra, but her every look and movement was full of curt orders only too clear to all of them. Her brother, like a big child, ran in all directions to do what he thought might be his sister's bidding, or perhaps he was only happy.

After her several days of acute illness in Rawdhat al-Mashti they had all reckoned that this was the end, for their mother would neither eat nor drink and took refuge from the world in her delirium. Hadib's anxious looks and utter confusion gave him away; he almost gave up the idea of continuing the journey, especially since there was no news of caravans. Once again he proposed going back to Ujra; there, he could think and make the appropriate decisions. Wadha's sudden awakening, however, and her gradual return to lucidity, followed by the arrival of a small caravan bound for al-Hadra, changed everything and helped Wadha overcome her illness; after all, she did not want to die in this place. Without much being said, without discussion of any kind, she nodded in approval when Hadib proposed to her that they continue the journey; she made her preparations to be part of the shabby caravan, and they left.

It was a small caravan, made up of three herds of camels with their own camel, the family of Sulayim al-Hazaa' and that of Miteb al-Hathal. They expected to make it from Rawdhat al-Mashti to al-Hadra in five days.

When they were nearing the outskirts of al-Hadra, Fawaz and one of the shepherds were sent ahead to announce their arrival to the townspeople. Three of the Atoum, relatives of Miteb al-Hathal, were sent out to meet the caravan and help them along; two of them knew Miteb's family personally, having visited Wadi al-Uyoun and stayed for a while a year or two before. No sooner had they reached the caravan and greeted the travelers than they showed their surprise that Miteb al-Hathal was not there. They asked about him, when he would join them and where they had left him, and when these questions were put to the family as they all rested at al-Hadra's east well, the family discovered that Wadha had gone into a new phase, for the silence that had begun in Wadi al-Uyoun as a result of her sorrow and perhaps because of her own wish had now given way to something else entirely, something greater than sorrow and more powerful than wish or will.

When Suleiman al-Hadib, one of Miteb's maternal uncles, moved his eyes about the small, mournful caravan and asked about their journey, when they had left Wadi al-Uyoun and where they had left Miteb, Wadha burst into tears. The question itself did not call for crying, especially from a woman of Wadha's strength and power. At first shocked and a little frightened, Suleiman al-Hadib looked at their faces in alarm, finally settling on Hadib, whom he wished to speak, but Hadib's embarrassed look and confused words only complicated things.

"My friends!" shouted Suleiman sternly. "We know that the world is life and death. If Miteb is alive, say so, and if he is dead, then say so!"

"Trust in God, man," said Hadib. "Miteb is alive and there is nothing to worry about."

"What do you say, Umm Thweiny?" Suleiman asked harshly, looking at Wadha.

Wadha nodded in agreement, confirming what her brother had said, but Suleiman al-Hadib was not convinced, guessing that there was more to the affair than he was presently capable of grasping, so he shouted: "If the man is alive, there is no need to cry!"

Again Umm Thweiny nodded in agreement and Suleiman al-Hadib spoke lightly. "And you, Umm Thweiny, are this man's sister."

Again she nodded, and worn out by her inscrutability he said impatiently, "God rest your parents."

Once more, tears rolled down her cheeks.

That morning in late spring or early summer at the Masbala well, a short distance from al-Hadra, that long-ago day unlike any other since, when the men rode out happily from al-Hadra to greet the family of Miteb al-Hathal, they looked in the faces of this tribe that had suddenly come from so far away. It was not known whether Miteb al-Hathal himself, the head of the family, was alive or dead; the response to any question about him was these indistinct words and tears. What sorrow was bred in their hearts? What confusion was this? Why this bleak and complicated spectacle?

This is what each man asked himself. Despite her black sorrow, Wadha al-Hamad tried once more to speak, to explain, to say something, but the sounds that came from her mouth were more like animal sounds or the groans of mourning, exactly like the clash of branches or the echo in a narrow valley.

Like a strangled cat, she tried to talk. Like a small child, she tried to talk. Then she was silent for quite a while. She gathered all her strength, gathered in her throat all the words she wanted to say. Several times she shifted in her seat. Suleiman al-Hadib gazed curiously but welcomingly at the members of this lost tribe and smiled faintly upon detecting some sort of resemblance between the tribe and Miteb al-Hathal and Wadha al-Hamad, that ancient blood kinship that represented some extension of this tribe that spread out in all directions, lost in all places. He felt the comforting feeling that blood could never change and that for those who drank from Wadi al-Uyoun and from the waters of al-Hadra and from other brooks no matter where, there were hidden waters. The waters of the Atoum supplied all the other brooks with this extraordinary power to rush away and be lost and then come back; life in this desert, however it changed and varied, had, like death, to end somewhere, but to some purpose.

In this atmosphere, redolent of sorrow and heat and expectation of the next moment, after the sudden flood of tears, Radiya and Da'ija moved closer to their mother to find out why she was crying. But Wadha's features tightened sternly, almost angrily. When she made one more attempt to whisper, to say something, it suddenly seemed to her and to everyone else that she was unable to speak a single word, that the sounds she had learned more than fifty years ago had left her forever. She had

lost the power of speech, the sounds and words that the others
knew, and sank into silence.

In the first days, the old women of al-Hadra who hovered around
Wadha said that the fever had tied her tongue, but that it was a
temporary condition that could end at any time. Months later
they said that a black devil had entered her body between her
stomach and the upper chest through the water of Rawdhat al-
Mashti. By winter he would certainly leave her, because he
would have to return to his post by the wells of Rawdhat al-
Mashti to lie in wait for future caravans. When winter and the
year ended and spring came with Wadha's condition unchanged,
Suleiman al-Hadib's wife said that Wadha's depression had mixed
with fear; she could not get well until Miteb came back or until
the occurrence of some catastrophe greater than his absence, but
she said no more than that.

Everyone around Wadha heard some of what was said, but
she heard everything. They were filled with fear and uncertainty,
but she grew more bitter and more mocking at the same time.
She looked at the women's faces and heard them talk, followed
everything that went on, and when the old women suggested
some sort of remedy she shook her head in refusal. Sometimes
she simply got up angrily to go walk in the desert, leaving the
women who had come to help her.

Najma al-Mithqal, al-Hadra's fortune-teller, said when asked
about Miteb al-Hathal that he would certainly come back. She
said that he was wandering in the desert, moving from one place
to another, and that he slept far away in a place near the sea. He
would be there for years but would eventually come back, and
his return would be sweeping and violent like the simoom, the
hot sandstorm: no one would be able to stand against it.

That is what Najma al-Mithqal said. Everyone had despaired

of Miteb al-Hathal's returning, for there had been no news of him at all, and no one in al-Hadra asked about him anymore, so what was this family waiting for, and what would they do next? Hadib had lingered for a while and then gone traveling in midsummer, even though everyone except Wadha had appealed to him to stay—she had nodded vigorously when he'd asked her if he might travel. Would he come back soon, or stay away like Miteb, for years, as the people of this region were used to doing? Was Shaalan still in Wadi al-Uyoun, or had he gone off to look for his father? And Ibn Rashed—was he still content, as before, with mockery, or had he found an opportunity to revenge himself on Miteb al-Hathal and all his family?

It was up to Fawaz, as the eldest of Miteb al-Hathal's sons, to listen and think and finally to run the family. He translated his mother's looks and gestures and felt the torment that flooded from those eyes, and did not know what to do.

The relatives who had welcomed Miteb al-Hathal's family and showed profound solicitude after learning what had happened in Wadi al-Uyoun regarded the family with sympathy and an uncertain sorrow. They thought that Miteb's children were still very young and should only eat, drink and wait to see what might happen next. They did not accept Wadha's sorrow or fully approve of her silence. They did not understand the wariness that possessed her children, especially Fawaz; they regarded it with perplexity and wonder.

18

SHAALAN STAYED IN WADI AL-UYOUN. NO ONE really knew whether he stayed there for the compensation or to work in the company, as Ibn Rashed had promised in an attempt to appease Miteb al-Hathal's family and win them over. The two matters were intermingled to the point where Shaalan, when asked about it years later, could not remember which had come first: the collection of the compensation or his job in the company. Because he stayed in Wadi al-Uyoun, a wadi that bore no resemblance to the one that had been there before, except in name, he was compelled, in the absence of his father, to establish a new tribe to replace the old one. And because each of the two worked in his own way, the new tribe Shaalan founded, which flourished and of which traces still remain today, also began in Wadi al-Uyoun but spread far afield and worked somewhat differently. It kept going around in the orbit that made everything, however far from its center, part of it ruled by the same unbending laws . . . This new tribe was a doomed extension of Miteb al-Hathal, of the Atoum and of the life that had been.

Shaalan planted himself in Wadi al-Uyoun not like the palm trees that had filled the wadi in times gone by but like one of the iron columns that now stood everywhere, and within a short time he changed very much indeed. Even his name changed in this new era: he was "Company Shaalan" or "American Shaalan" instead of Shaalan bin Miteb al-Hathal, to distinguish him from Shaalan Abu Tabikh who was contracted to supply food to Wadi al-Uyoun and Shaalan al-'Aouer who guarded the rear gate of the camp. Shaalan bin Miteb learned English better and much more quickly than the others. For a long time they laughed at his new names, considering them a sort of joke that would end just as it had begun, but as the days passed and Shaalan stayed with the company, moving from one place to another, from one department to another, the name Miteb al-Hathal virtually disappeared except in official records, and the new name took its place. The new name surprised people who heard it for the first time, and sometimes it even bothered Shaalan himself and Miteb al-Hathal's other children and relatives, but he soon got used to it and so did the others, except when it was used to provoke or make fun of him.

How is it possible for people and places to change so entirely that they lose any connection with what they used to be? Can a man adapt to new things and new places without losing a part of himself?

Shaalan sent a message by word of mouth to al-Hadra in which he asked Fawaz, along with any other relatives, to come to Wadi al-Uyoun, "because you are assured to find work in the company." This message caused a storm to break out in the heads of two of the Atoum and filled them with an urge they could not control or resist.

Fawaz, who had spent a year and a few months in al-Hadra, had no sooner received Shaalan's message than his head began to spin with the old magic: travel. When he thought of Wadi al-Uyoun he could not bear to wait. He made his decision quickly: to travel with the first available caravan. Suweyleh, the middle son of Suleiman al-Hadib, did not take long in deciding to accompany him. Wadha accepted the idea more quickly than most people expected her to, but she made Suleiman al-Hadib take pity on this youngster who "might be lost like his father"; he tried to persuade Fawaz to postpone his journey so that Suweyleh might go before him and send for him if there was work to be had. But in the face of Fawaz's insistence—he had never been more stubborn—and in a murky attempt to set an example to this family that had begun to disintegrate, he gave in . . . and thus the two young men prepared for a journey from which they would return "as soon as possible" and in which they would go "no farther than Wadi al-Uyoun," as Suleiman al-Hadib made them promise several times.

When they reached Wadi al-Uyoun, it seemed to Fawaz a place he had never seen before. There was no trace of the wadi he had left behind; none of the old things remained. Even the fresh breezes that used to blow at this time of year had become hot and searing in daytime, and a bitter cold penetrated his bones late at night. The men who had gathered there, he did not know from where, in their tents and wooden houses, were a bizarre mixture of humanity; they bore no resemblance to anything a man would recognize. Even the caravans Fawaz had encountered in Ujra on his first and second journeys, whose looks were so odd, now seemed to him kindred creatures in their features and smells. Now in Wadi al-Uyoun he saw strange and disgusting creatures filled with silence and sorrow. One of the workers seemed to resemble a bird who had strayed from the flock and lost his way, unable to stay where he was and powerless to resume the journey.

Fawaz almost turned back in the few hours after he arrived. He had been sitting like a dog by the barbed wire, waiting for Shaalan to return, he did not know from where, and he and the others who had come with and after him had been asked to keep away from the gate to the camp, without any explanation or look of understanding or sympathy. They were pushed away several times when they came near. Sand blew on them where they sat, and they were covered with dust whenever the huge, maddened machines rolled in or out of the camp.

These hours of torment and suffering were worse than the hardships of the whole trip, which had been different from the first one; even the water in Rawdhat al-Mashti had tasted better this time and the people had been readier to talk with them. But here, in the hours between noon and sundown, they felt that the Wadi al-Uyoun that had been, that had existed for long years and given shelter to caravans and men and birds, was no longer. Shaalan, who had arrived at sundown, looked as strange as his clothes: the black line like light down on his upper lip was now nearly a full-grown mustache; he had a beard composed of ir-regularly scattered but strong stubble; and his face, comically smeared with oil and dust, looked out from the shade of the white tin drinking bowl he had put on his head.

After they embraced, talked and fell silent before the gate of the camp, Shaalan was able with difficulty to get the two into the tent he lived in. He used his friendship with the guard at the gate, resorting to jokes and cajoling and other diabolical tricks. He put the drinking bowl on Suweyleh's head, over his ghotra, and in an air of laughter and hilarity ushered them into the big tent.

There were several men in the tent, some of them sleeping, some eating and others playing cards and shouting. Fawaz looked at them in utter amazement; the tent was huger than any tent he had ever seen, bigger than Ibn Rashed's or Ibn Hadib's; even so, it seemed too small to contain new guests. None of the men moved when the newcomers entered; they only glanced up briefly and vacantly even though Shaalan in his noisy entrance had tried to create a lighter atmosphere. No one moved even when Shaalan whispered in Fawaz's ear that one of the three men playing cards was a relative of theirs.

At no place and at no time in his life had Fawaz ever been gripped by fear as he was now, in this place. How did these men sleep, and where? How did they eat? Why were they so different from the sort of people who used to live in Wadi al-Uyoun, who lived in Ujra and al-Mashti and al-Hadra? It seemed to him that each of these men lived by himself, without any connection to the others around him.

Fawaz wanted to discuss everything with Shaalan, but the words he had been preparing for the whole of the journey, which included the details of all their experiences since leaving Wadi al-Uyoun, vanished from his memory. He was not able or eager to talk. He smiled whenever his eyes met Shaalan's, and when Shaalan asked about their mother and brothers and al-Hadra, and if it were anything like Wadi al-Uyoun, Fawaz mumbled his answers. But when he thought of Miteb al-Hathal he said that they had heard nothing of him since leaving the wadi. He wanted to ask Shaalan about it but only when they were alone or in some other place.

"Come on—let's wash our hands and get our supper ready," said Shaalan to change their mood.

They left quietly and headed for the water drums. The ground around the drums was slippery with stagnant water and mud, and the place smelled disgusting. When the water touched their faces they sensed its unpalatable taste, perhaps because of the rust or some foreign substance added to it. Suweyleh asked whether this was drinking water. When Shaalan nodded yes, he looked at Fawaz.

"The water in Wadi al-Uyoun was better," he said sadly.

"If our father were here now, he would not drink this water," said Fawaz, as if he wanted to say something brilliant or start trouble.

Shaalan looked at him with uncertain bitterness; perhaps he was stifling his reaction. After a few moments of sad silence he spoke, as if talking to himself. "Thank God that at least we have water."

"What news of our father, Shaalan?"

Skillfully, spontaneously, Shaalan shouted to one of the men passing by the water barrels on his way to the tent far away, and when the man turned around he asked about things Suweyleh and Fawaz did not understand in the least. When he was done, Shaalan said enthusiastically, "We'll finish talking about that later, but now we have to prepare our supper."

So they hurried off to prepare their meal.

19

THE THREE SAT FAR FROM THE TENT, IN AN OPEN
space in the middle of the desert. The moon
was small and had appeared early that eve-
ning, without anyone noticing. They were like frightened children or conspirators, looking around them when they heard any
sound or saw a shadow. They did not raise their heads or feel
the coolness that began to fill the night air, for they were possessed by a strange conversation about Wadi al-Uyoun, how it
had been and what it was now. The diabolical Americans, who
had come looking for water, why did they continually dig into
the earth, never stopping but never taking anything out? The
water from the wadi, from Sabha and from the many wells they
dug was pumped back into a hole in the ground—why wasn't
it given to people? Did the ground hold such ghastly hordes of
thirsty jinn, whose screams day and night could be heard only

by the foreigners, who had come to quench their thirst? Were the jinn burning in the depths of the earth, and were the Americans pumping the water down to extinguish the flames? Was there another world underground, with gardens, trees and men, all clamoring for water?

This was how the three young men reasoned, and they asked each other questions they knew none of them could answer; the questions multiplied quickly and with them the three men's fears and anxieties. Shaalan considered himself the most knowing and most experienced of them all, but he was also the most afraid. His fear had emerged suddenly a few weeks back when his father began to appear to him. He had appeared suddenly at the fringes of the camp one night. No one told Shaalan that; he saw it himself. He could not divulge this secret to anyone, so he had kept it to himself and stayed waiting and watchful from that night until now.

He saw his father the first time near the camp gate, but when he ran toward him to make sure, Miteb mounted his camel and galloped off. He shouted, but Miteb hurried away and disappeared. He saw him several times after that but was never able to overtake him; Miteb would gallop away and disappear, and this made Shaalan more afraid than ever; he could no longer conceal or tolerate this fear. He was positive that this was his father who went riding around the camp, sometimes entering it. He never doubted it. The man was Miteb al-Hathal's height and moved as Miteb did. The camel was the same white Omani mare his father rode; Shaalan could never be wrong about that.

After seeing him near the gate the first time, Shaalan decided to go to the same place at the same time, but Miteb did not come. A few days later Shaalan saw him near the water drums, very late at night; he was directly under the light; his face was illuminated and he seemed animated; he was making happy sounds like the whinnying of a horse, but when Shaalan took a few

steps in his direction—for he was still far from the drums—
Miteb turned slightly, then leaped up and vanished completely.
Subsequently Shaalan saw him in different places: once near the
rear guard post, in the shadow of the big tent, and he was sure
of it when he found the camel's hoofprints.

From the first sighting, Shaalan became almost ill. He was
besieged by his fear and imagination, for he knew his father was
there; he had seen him. True, he had not been able to speak with
him, to stop him or question him, perhaps because his father
was still angry at him, but even so he harbored no doubt; he
knew he was not imagining it. If his father was still roaming the
area around Wadi al-Uyoun, refusing to return or talk to anyone,
Fawaz would be able somehow, at some point, to convince him
to come back.

Now that Shaalan had chosen this place, with two of his close
relations, he would be able to express what was tormenting him,
what was on his mind; he could ask them, without fear, if what
he had seen was Miteb al-Hathal himself, his own father, or
someone else; if it was a vision or a real thing. When he sent for
his brother Fawaz he wanted Miteb to reappear, right there in
Wadi al-Uyoun. He was burning to confirm what he had seen,
for some close relatives to join him, to find out whether his
father had come back, if there was any news of him or if anyone
had seen him.

Darkness spread and thickened until it was like a dark wall.
The voices of workers laughing in the tent floated to the three
youths, distant and intermittent. The flashlight that the guard
used now and then cast a long pallid beam that passed quickly
over the sands near the barbed-wire fence, illuminating nothing.
The guard swung the light every so often more to relieve his
boredom and solitude than to help him see anything.

In choosing this particular spot and beginning to talk about
Wadi al-Uyoun and the jinn, Shaalan was preparing the two

others for the right moment. His father might show up; they might see his father, no matter how far off or fleetingly . . . even if it was a phantom, they would not let him get away; they must cry out or chase him, to tell him that Fawaz was there too. At any rate, something would happen that would convince Shaalan and perhaps the others as well.

Shaalan's gaze moved around in a broad arc. Suweyleh thought this strange, and turned to Shaalan.

"Are you waiting for someone?" he asked.

Shaalan shook his head in such a way that they did not know whether to take it as a yes or a no and made a frightened movement. After a long silence he spoke in an almost raving tone of voice. "God damn the times we live in. God only knows what is happening in Wadi al-Uyoun."

"Wadi al-Uyoun used to be a thousand times better," said Fawaz firmly.

"If people had only listened to the old man, Wadi al-Uyoun would still be as it was, but I don't know what's come over people," said Shaalan, still looking around.

The moon had begun to set. The three had much to say, but Shaalan's fear had infected the other two. In this place, inside the barbed wire, they felt so foreign that they could not imagine that it had once been their home, or indeed that they had had a home anywhere. Endless fears and desires and thoughts filled their minds.

"God curse Satan, who divides people," said Shaalan despairingly. He was silent for a moment and then sighed, "Haven't you heard news of our father, Fawaz?"

Fawaz looked at him sadly and curiously. He had told Shaalan urgently, a few moments after they'd arrived, that there had been no news of his father since before they had left Wadi al-Uyoun.

"Where could he have gone?" asked Shaalan almost angrily.

"He may be gone for a year, or two years, but he has to come back."

"Trust in God," said Suweyleh, who felt the depression that possessed the others. "He knows his own news, and he has to come back."

"I saw my father the day before yesterday!" said Shaalan suddenly.

The two looked at him in joy and amazement. Fawaz was astonished and wanted him to say more, but Shaalan turned his head away as if he did not want them to look at him. When silence fell again, without Shaalan explaining what he had said or adding a single word, Fawaz spoke. His words were rapid but shaky. "When did he come back? Where is he?"

"At just this hour," said Shaalan, turning back to look directly into Fawaz's eyes. "And be sure of it, be sure of this—you will see him!"

They looked all around them to see him coming but saw nothing.

"Where is he?" sighed Fawaz. "When did you leave him?"

Shaalan began to tell them how he had seen Miteb and where, how when he tried to speak with him, Miteb had disappeared instantly, like lightning that flashed and vanished; he had not wanted anyone to approach or bother him. He had circled the camp all night, once on camelback and once on foot; he had drunk and washed his hands in a barrel of water.

Shaalan told the tale excitedly but fearfully, turning between words as if he saw Miteb al-Hathal coming, and when he had finished he told them expectantly: "Listen, my friends, if he comes tonight we will not leave him even if the sky falls on the earth!"

20

LONG DAYS OF HARD, UNEASY WAITING. THE THREE hardly slept except as wolves do: they knew no comfort and could not rest at night or during the day. They waited beside the water barrels, by the camp gate, by the barbed wire, by the rear guard station. They waited in the late hours of dusk, and in the dead of night. They waited as the moon grew, when it was full, as it rose ever later and then ceased appearing altogether . . . but Miteb al-Hathal did not come!

Even during the daylight hours, when Shaalan went to work, where and to do what they did not know, Fawaz, Suweyleh and some of the night shift workers waited. Fawaz would go out and have a long, unhurried look through the whole camp. He would scrutinize the faces and look searchingly into the shadowy corners near the tent and the wooden cabins to find him, but he did not appear.

Once, when they had stopped speculating to have some supper and were reclining on the sand, Shaalan let out a shriek. "That's him, that's him—look closely!"

They looked at where he was pointing, held their breath and could not utter a sound from fear. They looked carefully in all directions. The light shadows of twilight had fallen; visibility was poor but still sufficient to make out the contours. They strained to see. They looked in the direction of Shaalan's outstretched hand, and when they looked at him his face was marked by shock and fear. He shook his head two or three times as if to shake a veil from his eyes. He grabbed Fawaz's upper arm tightly and spoke through his teeth. "He went by that way— he was on his camel and was moving fast as a bird."

Shaalan exhaled angrily until he was nearly purple and looked at the other two in pain and exasperation. He wanted them to be quicker, to pay closer attention.

When they looked over once again to where Shaalan had indicated, they saw two men moving far away. They had just come out of the tent in front of them. These two were perfectly visible as they walked out, and now they were headed for the camp gate. Had Shaalan seen a specter or only imagined something? Could a man move so quickly and secretly that no one could see him?

They did not speak for a long time, and the silence reigned heavy. It was like an iron tent over their heads. The soft breezes that blew were scented with humidity and perhaps rain.

"That is the farthest away and the fastest he's ever been," explained Shaalan.

"Maybe you saw someone else, cousin," said Suweyleh uncertainly.

Shaalan shot him a wounded look. In his eyes was an urgency more like entreaty; he wanted to agree, to believe Suweyleh. He moved closer to Fawaz, at whom he gazed with a sad intensity. His look asked, "You . . . did you see him as I did?" Fawaz said nothing; he was subdued by fear. Shaalan got up despairingly and headed toward the tent.

Fawaz and Suweyleh did not move for a long time. They were silent as stones, as devoid of will as water running down a hill. They did not know what to do and had no desire to talk or move. Fawaz may have been convinced that Shaalan had seen something, a specter or a ghost, or perhaps even their father, but Suweyleh had his doubts and they showed on his face.

"I don't know what's wrong with Shaalan," said Suweyleh almost to himself. He paused and then asked, "Might he be ill?"

"Nothing is wrong with him," replied Fawaz firmly. He added somewhat resignedly as he got up, "We have to see him."

For more than two weeks and several days—that is, that night and many before and after it—they neither slept nor rested. Even though Suweyleh never left them during these nights, they, the two sons of Miteb al-Hathal, were in a different situation and were enduring a different experience.

Did Suweyleh tell anyone anything? Did he ever discuss the matter in any form?

Something like that must have happened, for within two days Ibn Rashed showed up. When he saw the two brothers in the corner of the tent at sundown, he registered surprise that drew the attention of everyone present.

"Hah!" he said sarcastically. "So it looks like we're still not done with Miteb al-Hathal and his calamities?"

When Shaalan showed his surprise and gave him a hostile look, Ibn Rashed pointed at Fawaz and spoke again. "You . . . whose son are you?"

Shaalan replied with a firm, brief answer. "I see you've forgotten the people, Abu Muhammad."

Again Ibn Rashed directed his intense stare at Fawaz and shook his head.

"The sons of Miteb al-Hathal, Abu Muhammad, have nothing to do with calamities."

Ibn Rashed laughed to hide his vexation, feeling that there was no need for the attack upon him. Shaalan continued. "The esteemed Miteb al-Hathal has an echo."

Ibn Rashed looked the other way and addressed a man who was listening carefully to the conversation. " 'If you want your friend to work, pay him his reckoning every day.' "

"If there is any reckoning between us, Abu Muhammad, we're more than ready to settle it—you're a hundred times welcome, we're ready!" said Shaalan hotly.

Ibn Rashed laughed loudly and came nearer Shaalan. When he had stopped laughing he spoke in a friendlier tone. "Nephew, you Atoum have some qualities you will never give us a rest from!" He said this glancing from one to the other. Silence had fallen since no one knew what to say.

"What quality are you referring to, Abu Muhammad?" asked Shaalan angrily.

"Wrath!" Ibn Rashed guffawed. "You all get so furious over a single word!"

Ibn Rashed sat near them on the ground and began to talk to them in a fatherly tone. "God bless your father, Shaalan. We told him, be patient. He said no. We said, at least keep an open mind, he said no. We told him, today the world is as you see it, but tomorrow it will be different. He said no. And he left." He paused. He was not making his point. "The Atoum only know one way of doing things. They make no distinction between what harms them and what can benefit them. They make no distinction between friends and enemies."

"If there is anything between you and him, you should discuss it with him when he comes back," said Shaalan impatiently.

"My boy, there is nothing amiss between us, and if he comes back we will talk, never fear."

They waited several more long, difficult days. They waited for Miteb al-Hathal and for work. Miteb al-Hathal did not appear again. Shaalan did not see him after that night. He seemed silent and almost ill the next day and for the following few days, but he seemed to improve gradually after that. His gloom departed and he began to sleep deeply and normally. Fawaz was still frightened and attentive to every small movement, every sound, and was unable to sleep for very long. Shaalan had become used to going out into the desert some nights, perhaps to wait for his father or to look for him. Fawaz would toss and turn on his bed and feel for his brother, still floating between sleep and consciousness but ready to go out with him for the mysterious vigil, and yet hesitating to tell him, not ready to bring up the subject directly, perhaps avoiding it out of fear of being misunderstood.

Twenty days later Ibn Rashed arrived and had a short tour of the camp. Before leaving he told Fawaz and Suweyleh that the company had not agreed to hire them; they would have to leave. He was in a hurry, as if he had many things awaiting him. He said that Fawaz was still young and would have to wait a year or two before applying for work again, and that Suweyleh was practically blind and would not do for work in the company. He said all this quickly, then turned his back and walked away.

When Shaalan came home from work and they told him what Ibn Rashed had said, he shook his head and spoke very slowly. "I knew it." He spat on the ground. "God's grace, not Ibn Rashed's."

He looked at them sadly, as if in apology. He shook his head several times and then said to himself, "When I told him, he said, 'Priority goes to the people of Wadi al-Uyoun.'"

He looked in the other direction and said bitterly, "A few days ago one of his bunch told me, 'Ibn Rashed says, "One of the Atoum has already darkened our door, that pestiferous Shaalan bin Miteb, and that's quite enough!"' "

Silence fell.

That same night, with secret but resigned urgency, Fawaz and Suweyleh left Wadi al-Uyoun for Ujra once again, on their way to al-Hadra.

21

···

H AD THE WATER OF RAWDHAT AL-MASHTI PUT ITS
curse on one more of the Hathal clan, or was
there some mysterious hidden force, cruel and
intense in its ferocity, that would stalk them one after another
until it destroyed them all, sparing nothing and no one?

On the way to al-Hadra from Wadi al-Uyoun after the few
weeks with Shaalan, they spent ten days in Rawdhat al-Mashti.
The weather went mad their third day in Rawdhat: within a few
hours there was not a drop of water in the sky or anyplace else,
from Wadi al-Jenah to al-Dalle', that did not fall on Rawdhat
al-Mashti. The wadis filled up with torrents of rainwater. Rawdhat al-Mashti had been ambushed; it was soaked, and full of
fear and joy at the same time. Its astonished people looked at
the sky, at the maddened rains that pounded down, as if this
had never happened before, but they quickly focused on the

wadi, which was filling with water every moment. The children clung to the old men, and the women stayed close at hand. They were all dumbfounded. The old men were the happiest. Their faces, tormented by the long years, filled with creases and memories, were seeing something they had not seen before. They raised their voices as they moved their hands and limbs, as if each drop of rain and every new rivulet than ran into the wadi gave them new life.

Could they ever forget those sparkling, festive hours? Could those sudden, strange, supplicating voices, like hymns rising in a roar from the wadi's mouth, from the mouths of the waterskins that opened from the sky, ever be effaced? The voices they heard, especially the voices of the old men and children, this melody like the sound of the wind, were they human voices or heavenly ones emanating from the sky or from within the depths of the water? The cries of "There is no god but God, there is no god but God, there is no god but God" erupting in every direction evoked awe and caused fear and trembling. The children were excited, full of awe and desire. Their wonderment was reflected quickly and clearly in the men's actions and prayers. Even the women who were far off at first came closer and closer and crowded in among the men to have a better look at the rushing water in the wadi. They grew happier and almost rapturous, singing and praying without the least fear or hesitation.

This memory might have faded and grown dim had Miteb al-Hathal not appeared.

Rain filled the earth and sky. The narrow wadi at the end of Rawdhat al-Mashti gushed crazily with water, and the people stood and watched in bewilderment.

When the great moment came and the men stood by in fear as the violent waves rose, they backed up a few steps and asked everyone to move back, out of instinctive caution. Men and women, young and old, repeated with one voice, perhaps without even realizing it, "There is no god but God . . . there is no god but God," and at that very moment, as a brilliant flash of lightning rent the sky, creating fear upon fear, Miteb al-Hathal appeared. He seemed enormously tall and rather white skinned. He had his staff in his right hand and pointed it at them from the other side of the wadi. His physical form was so clearly discernible and so extremely powerful that he appeared to be closer than the opposite bank—as if he were directly over the water. His voice was clearer and stronger than the thunder, the rushing water and the screams of the women and children.

"Don't be afraid," he told all those who had gathered in Rawdhat al-Mashti. "Don't be afraid of what you see."

When silence fell, and the people were filled with fear and anticipation, he spoke again. "This is the last of your happiness."

He moved back and seemed to stand squarely on the opposite bank of the wadi. He struck the earth with his staff, looked at them all sternly and shook his head three times. Before he turned away his voice rumbled again. "Fear is from things to come."

Once again the people shrank back from the dark torrent, and when a huge wave rumbled through the wadi with the strength of an enraged camel, Fawaz sprang forward like an arrow or a bullet to reach his father.

As he addressed the people and moved back, and as he struck the earth with his staff, Miteb looked at Fawaz. As he looked he did not smile once; he seemed almost angry, and Fawaz was afraid of his anger. At that moment he wanted to please him, to be wrapped in his cloak. He wanted to grasp the staff and shake it and tell him, "After you left, Father, we left Wadi al-Uyoun—they made us leave. Only Shaalan stayed. We went to al-Hadra, Father. You know al-Hadra and the people there. My mother no longer speaks. She has not spoken since we left, and we, all of us, are ill. We are waiting for you to come back; every day we say it will be today. We haven't slept one night the way people in other places sleep. Why don't you come back, Father, why don't you visit us? Don't you love us, Father? Don't you want to see us? Who has made you so angry, Father? The older ones may have sinned, but we are young and have not sinned. I have grown up, Father, now I'm bigger than you knew me. I visited Shaalan, Father. We waited for you in Wadi al-Uyoun. We waited by the barrels and by the fence."

He wanted to say a great many other things as well, but Miteb al-Hathal's powerful words, his stern face and the fear of the retreating people, and the voice that roared when darkness fell over everything frightened and inhibited Fawaz. When Miteb al-Hathal turned away from the opposite bank of the wadi, when he moved farther away, Fawaz felt a force pushing him forward, and had it not been for Suweyleh and three men standing by him he would have leaped across the wadi and reached his father. But as soon as he felt impelled forward shouting, "Father, father," Suweyleh grabbed him and restrained him as a camel is restrained and checked him as a horse is checked. He tried to break loose; he shouted at the top of his lungs, he kicked and cursed and tried to break loose again from their tight grip, but he suddenly found himself on the ground with Suweyleh standing over his chest.

Miteb al-Hathal was there. First he was upon the water, above the wadi, and after calling out with a voice more powerful than a muezzin's, he moved back a few steps, but his features were still strong and visible, and his eyes looked around at every face. He had struck his staff three times on the hard earth, and Fawaz heard the loud rapping and felt the staff piercing his side. When Suweyleh grabbed him the way a lamb is grabbed, and jerked his head the way a lamb's head is jerked back before the slaughter, · his eyes met his father's. He was sure of that. Miteb's eyes were more kindly this time, and he even smiled. When Fawaz tried to get up and lunge forward again to follow him, Suweyleh grabbed his feet and held him down and pressed his face to the ground, and when he fell he could no longer hear the voices or see anything but the muddy, bitter ground. When he got up again he saw all the people of Rawdhat al–Mashti looking at him. They were all above or beside him like a surrounding wall of flames and appeared to be terrified. Even when they cleared a broad path they still surrounded him, and he looked across at the far bank of the wadi before looking at them. The bank was empty; his father had gone away. He looked up and down the wadi but could not see him. He looked at the faces around him; perhaps they had come to help him, to save him, to push away the others who wanted to prevent him from getting to his father. He gazed carefully into their faces, at every face, but he did not see him.

He looked at Suweyleh, who looked at him, upset and afraid. He hated these looks. He felt alone, utterly alone. He kneeled on the ground and looked at Suweyleh sadly.

"Didn't you see him? Where is he? He was there . . . he was there."

Suweyleh looked at him, and Fawaz looked at the men, women and children. When he saw them all looking at him he got up quickly and ran away.

While Fawaz was far off with Suweyleh running after him, an angry flash of lightning lit the whole sky and drowned the people's voices with its rolling thunder. Fawaz looked at the sky, his tears rolling down as the rain fell steadily, and a deep voice reached him: "There is no god but God . . . there is no god but God."

The rain fell more heavily than ever.

22

WHEN THE DELUGE CEASED AND THE SUN ROSE, the desert looked like a sand grouse: gleaming, fresh and wet, as if it had not swallowed all that rain with such insatiable gluttony. The brilliant happiness that shone in the people's faces affected even the animals, expressing the new energy they felt inside. Very different from this joy was the depression mixed with fear that spread through the bodies of the two young men of the small caravan which was bound through the desert from Rawdhat al-Mashti to al-Hadra. Shepherds and other travelers rushed out chaotically but nimbly to look for early green plants after the heavy rains of the preceding days, but the two young men were deep in mournful contemplation. While it was true that common concerns united them, each had his private concerns as well. Fawaz was the son of Miteb al-Hathal and had to pay a certain price for that, because

Ibn Rashed would not forget. Young or not, revenge was revenge. He may have been young when he applied for work, but when the time came for revenge he would be old enough to be killed, to pay the price. Ibn Rashed did as he liked; he was the master now and gave orders, and no one could force him to do anything. Miteb al-Hathal had told Ibn Rashed and the others what they needed to hear; he was strong as a horse, he was not hesitant or afraid. Miteb was now in the shadows, appearing and disappearing, but without anyone taking notice, as if he were no longer there at all, or no longer alive. In a word, he no longer feared anyone.

Suweyleh al-Hadib's sorrow was an entirely different matter; even his silence was different. When he had left al-Hadra he had been confident of finding work, as Shaalan had assured him in his brief verbal message. Suweyleh had told his father, Najma al-Mithqal and others who had been present that he would be in Wadi al-Uyoun for a year or two. He would then return home and marry at once. If he went wandering, as so many from al-Hadra and al-Dalle' did, years might pass before he came back. He could not stand to do that for years, or to wait, because in that time Watfa might marry someone else. Besides, Wadi al-Uyoun was nearby—a stone's throw, as they said. He would return quickly, as soon as he had a large sum of money. Many of his friends and relatives had done the same, and everyone talked of doing it. He was like them but stronger than they; even the eyes that Ibn Rashed had called blind saw more than most, saw everything; Najma al-Mithqal had said of the white spot in the iris that it was "an envy spot that will disappear with time." So what difference did the point make to Ibn Rashed or anyone else? He worked with his hands and his whole body, not with his eyes. Some of the boys in al-Hadra had gone to the mosque and spent years learning the Koran with Abdulaziz al-Hawqalli, but he had not done so; since his boyhood he had refused to learn and his father had not pressed him, and so he did not think, as others did, of bothering himself with reading letters from travelers or writing to the people of al-Hadra!

Ibn Rashed had told him that there was no work for him in the company because he had poor eyes; he had slain him by saying so; anything else he could have said would have been easier to understand and accept. He should have answered him back and discussed it, but the surprise of the announcement, and Ibn Rashed's hasty departure from the tent, did not give him the chance to utter a single word. He told himself sadly: "Shaalan did not miss a chance to tell Ibn Rashed exactly what he thought of him, and had I done the same he would not have dared to say what he said."

In the splendid winter weather, as the caravan made good time one day and slower progress the next, the two young men were full of dejected thoughts and feelings. In spite of their restlessness, determination and desire to talk, some other force pushed them back. They felt weighted down with sins they could not bear, as if this experience had proved them unworthy of the confidence others had placed in them. Here they were returning to al-Hadra, not as they had left it but abject and disappointed. What would people ask them? How would they meet their eyes? Some things could be told and understood, but other things could not be told, even if the others knew of or guessed at them. What would Fawaz say when questioned? Wasn't he the man of the family, after Shaalan, since Miteb al-Hathal had left? Didn't the others see him that way? Could he say that he had been rejected because he was too young? Some of the people knew Ibn Rashed and would understand, but some others would not understand why he had been rejected.

And Suweyleh, the strongest of all the youths of al-Hadra, who shouted the loudest on holidays and moon nights, the most daring of them all, could anyone believe he could be rejected, especially for that reason? What would Watfa say? In other places didn't they make a distinction between envy and a blank eye? Was it possible to deny a man work for such a stupid reason as that?

They said little to each other for five days, and their words were not clear but more like the sound of the wind or the rush of the water. Fawaz worried that the water of Rawdhat al-Mashti had cursed him with a muteness like his mother's. He wondered if a demon had lodged in his body and deprived him of the power of speech. In an attempt to combat that fear he moved his tongue and talked to himself and sometimes shouted at his camel for no reason. He did that several times, and each time Suweyleh looked at him curiously. His voice seemed strange to him, as if it were coming from someone else, and so he sank back into his silence.

Even the empty desert, which had been full of Suweyleh's singing and shouting on their way to Wadi al-Uyoun, was sunk in a leaden silence. At night the sky seemed far distant and the stars lusterless. Suweyleh, who had been full of life and energy on the way to Wadi al-Uyoun, had become another person on the return journey. He spent most of his time at the rear of the caravan, far off and alone, and seemed emaciated to the point of illness. On the last day in Rawdhat al-Mashti, he almost turned back to Ujra to wander, but he changed his mind at the last moment.

One day before the journey ended, before they reached al-Hadra, they exchanged a certain look: it seemed that they had agreed to conspire.

"Listen, Fawaz," said Suweyleh in total despair, "if we get to al-Hadra we'll tell our families that we're going back to Wadi al-Uyoun in one month, that Ibn Rashed told us to wait another month and then come back again.''

Fawaz remembered that a sudden, powerful sound like a flash of lightning and a thunderclap filled the desert when al-Hadra came into view. When Suweyleh began to sing, everyone in the caravan was surprised, and they looked curiously at the two young men of the Atoum.

23

THEIR ARRIVAL IN AL-HADRA WAS JUST LIKE THE arrival of a caravan in Wadi al-Uyoun: everyone, especially the men and children, even the ones who lived far away, gathered around in the village square, near the wells, and the arriving travelers and the residents alike shouted in excitement. Everyone asked the travelers the same questions, about the rain, vegetation, the brooks and caravans, to make perfectly sure of everything time and again. They asked about the prices of flour, sugar and cloth in Rawdhat al-Mashti and Ujra, and whether the people there expected the prices to stay the same or go up. Once they found out all they needed to know, the questioning took a different turn: about relatives and friends and others who lived in far-off places like Wadi al-Uyoun and beyond.

That night, in Ibn Hadib's encampment, Suweyleh told his

father and everyone, decisively, that he and Fawaz would go back to Wadi al-Uyoun before long, to do the same kind of work that Shaalan was doing, and when they asked him about Shaalan's work he could not say anything very clear; he said that he dug holes in the ground, nothing else but that! He did not want to tell them that the devils were draining the waters of Wadi al-Uyoun, of Sabha and other wadis through iron sheaths and pumping the waters into holes they had dug in the ground, why and for how long it was impossible to tell. That whirlpool of jinn and the depths of the earth began to whirl in his head.

Suweyleh wanted to tell about everything he had seen and heard, but he was still pained by hearing Ibn Rashed say what he had said, and he had returned thus defeated and disappointed only to discover that Najma al-Mithqal had become troubled by hallucinations and that his mother and sister and some of his other female relatives were looking after her. Consequently Watfa was now in a situation which made him unable to think of or pursue the dream that had pushed him from one place to another. He appeared deeply pessimistic and unwilling to say anything; he limited himself to short, obscure replies and sought refuge in silence.

The people of this immense, harsh desert were born, lived and died in a grim natural cycle, like the alternation of day and night or the succession of seasons, but the deaths of some people, especially those who held off death for others and those who revealed the secrets of the future, had an unnatural impact upon the memory, since they seemed to challenge the cycle and yet confirm it. When a death involved a wasting disease, a splendidly lucid mind and supernatural prophecies, people tended to remember it for a long time or perhaps never to forget it at all, passing it on to coming generations.

Had they left Wadha al-Hamad alone to do as she liked, Najma al-Mithqal would have lived on for years and years. Had they left Najma alone with no one to disturb her she would not have died so quickly. If they had kept Sabiha—Umm Homeidi, the wife of Abdulaziz al-Hawqalli—from going near her, Najma would have continued creeping on the ground smacking the chickens and dogs with her cane and then turning to wave the cane threateningly in the faces of the young men to warn them of the days to come! But the strong, overbearing Umm Homeidi allowed no one but herself to approach Najma. She decided to keep Najma al-Mithqal's treatment in her own hands, and she refused all offers of assistance.

The cure had two phases. In the first, Umm Homeidi gave the sick woman bitter herbs she said she had prepared herself. She did not say which herbs they were, but assured her that they were time tested and fast acting. Tormented by the pains that tore at her insides, Najma agreed to take next the medicinal powders that Umm Homeidi prepared and to drink the bitter fluids forced upon her; she would have done anything to get rid of the pains. The second phase of treatment, which began two days after her last consciousness, took her over completely.

Wadha al-Hamad wandered through Shatiui al-Azem's house looking for some of the herbs she had hidden and could not find, mumbling vaguely and perhaps cursing; she too refused any offers of assistance and seemed upset and almost angry. When she saw Fawaz, instead of looking happy her face and eyes knitted up questioningly as if to ask rebukingly, "Why did you come back!" When he told her that Ibn Rashed had asked him to go back to begin work in a month or two, she shook her head somewhat bitterly, perhaps recalling what Ibn Rashed was like. She remembered bygone days in Wadi al-Uyoun, especially the final days. When Fawaz finished explaining she nodded her approval and motioned Radiya to go with her to do something for Najma al-Mithqal.

When Wadha al-Hamad arrived, Umm Homeidi had just finished massaging Najma's stomach and back with warm oil, and both women were dripping with sweat and very tired. Najma seemed fairly comfortable or perhaps she was slightly drugged, for her eyes were half closed. She might have dropped off to sleep had she not jumped like a cat when anything frightened her or a pain tore her insides.

Radiya said that in recent days Najma had been saying things no human had ever said, not only about past events but many things about the days to come. She asked some of the women to come near her, laughed in their faces, then sang and wept but suddenly burst out laughing, like a small girl at first, as if someone was tickling her, then she cackled and no one could make her stop. She cackled for a long time, and the women around her were dumbfounded, but they soon joined her in smiling and laughing, without even realizing it. At first they looked at her lamentingly, but when she began to laugh they laughed too. Wadha al-Hamad, who looked on in surprise that reached the very limits of disapproval, could not put a stop to it. She was decidedly stern, turned her head away at first, then looked at Najma so unfeelingly she seemed angry. She shook some of the women and shouted at them but then found herself smiling and joined in the fits of tears and laughter. Her tears were quicker than her voice and stronger, and she went out into the garden, and when the voices pursued her she walked out into the desert followed by Radiya. She was laughing and sobbing at the same time, and she smeared handfuls of sand on her head.

No one in al-Hadra or its environs could ever forget this, for many women insisted that what had killed Najma al-Mithqal was not Umm Homeidi's liquid and powder medicaments, as Watfa strongly tried to affirm. Nor had she died from the warm oil Umm Homeidi had rubbed into her stomach and back, kneading more vigorously than any baker or wool dyer; what killed her was the fits of cackling, because each one of the women who had been laughing with her that day later complained of an illness that not only afflicted the palate and neck with severe pain but spread to the shoulders and internal organs. These pains were surely lethal for an ailing woman of Najma al-Mithqal's advanced years.

Najma died after Suweyleh and Fawaz arrived back in al-Hadra. Her hope in this period was always followed by despair, and she was always sarcastic when lucid. The day she died began with hysterical laughter followed by her last hot tears, and then death came.

A pall of mourning and pessimism descended over everyone, made darker by the things Najma al-Mithqal had said only days before she died, before the severest pains which had moved Umm Homeidi to try the last remedy.

Many people remembered everything Najma had said and passed it on to others, and although some distortions came into it, most remembered her as saying: "From Wadi al-Jenah to al-Dalle' and from al-Sariha to al-Mataleq, fire will consume fire and the young will die before the old. Count the beginning and prolong the end. The child will not know his father and brother will not know brother.

"From Wadi al-Jenah to al-Dalle' and from al-Sariha to al-Mataleq, every day a year from now. First all the land will be blessed, and then worshipers followed by locusts. First rains and floods and then an ignorant ruler. First wheat and silk brocade and then weeds and swirling dust. People will go and multiply, led by gold and silver, and some will find repose and others sin. The rich will consume the poor and the great will oppress the small, and all this will come to pass, O my soul!

"From Wadi al-Jenah to al-Dalle' and from al-Sariha to al-Mataleq, the world will not be the world. In the desert people will look for the stars but the stars will not rise. They will look for a caravan but the caravan will not come back. They will cry out but no one will answer them or hear them. That is how you will know the hour, and the hour is not distant. The appearance will crumble into the depths, and the base will rule over the noble. Roads will be as hard as hearts, feeling and knowing nothing.

"From Wadi al-Jenah to al-Dalle' and from al-Sariha to al-Mataleq, and beyond and beyond, people's faces will be perplexed, not knowing whether they are asleep or awake. First sultans as numerous as the sand, but in the end they will be destroyed. First the lash and then Sodom. First the chosen prophet and then the blind deceiver and people with drums and horns and swords and banners, but you don't know where they are going or whence they come. Aliens will rule trueborn sons and an outsider will rule the tribesmen.

"From Wadi al-Jenah to al-Dalle' and from al-Sariha to al-Mataleq and far beyond, the honorable man will be weak and lose his rights and the bastard will eat his portion and those of others but not out of hunger. The fool will speak the truth, and there will be many depraved, and the liar's voice will fill the roads and travel from town to town and say: My time has come. Antar bin Shaddad will wander with the sheep and remorse will consume his fingers, because he said I know the sword's blow and my heart knows no fear.

"At the end of that time the people will arise, and oppression will not last, and there will be tales and tales that people will tell their children's children."

24

I N AL-HADRA, SO REMOTE THAT IT SEEMED THE VERY
end of the earth, people did not wait for rain because
they did not want to see their hopes dashed; they
were resigned. When rain did come every year or two, it did
not last long or make much of a difference. It ran into Wadi al-
Basheq from the desert, but the rain, or the smell of rain, changed
their lives and behavior.

That is how it was in the first days after their return to al-
Hadra, after their unsuccessful journey, for the townsfolk never
stopped talking about the rain or the deluge in Rawdhat al-
Mashti, the grazing land two days from al-Hadra, and the brimming ponds, but all this was not enough, for a sudden depression
attacked them like an enemy after all they had said. They stopped
talking, full of expectation, as if a catastrophe were about to
strike al-Hadra at any moment.

Winters had been different in Wadi al-Uyoun, where the wait for rain brought a unique happiness. Even when the rainfall was late, no one gave up waiting for a single day. They consulted the caravans and the shepherds and looked at the sky, filling their lungs with the rain-scented air, and when the rain came their faces and eyes shone and they looked at each other in the knowledge that the promise had been fulfilled. Huge tracts of desert around Wadi al-Uyoun turned green, the nearby ponds filled up, and the brooks flooded, spilling water over large distances. The rain changed not only the pace of life but the people themselves.

Nights—especially winter nights—in Wadi al-Uyoun were very different from those in al-Hadra, where dusk came early, bringing in its shadows a harsh cold that cast a certain gloom. Because there was little wood in this area, the people used it sparingly, allowing for the days to come and for unexpected emergencies like a caravan's arrival or a death. Because of this, the people were accustomed to going to bed early and speaking little, showing nothing of that wit that sparked the imagination and roused the emotions, as in Wadi al-Uyoun.

Al-Hadra's was a very different winter. The winter past had brought deep gloom and pessimism, especially to the family of Miteb al-Hathal. This year it brought in addition to the gloom a black melancholy stemming from Najma al-Mithqal's unusual death and what the women retold of the old woman's last words and prophecies. Those prophecies had instilled fear or more precisely a certain watchfulness; they were narrated differently from woman to woman and interpreted in endless different ways. When the men heard them they laughed mockingly and said that it was all madness and could not be taken seriously or even considered worthy of any attention, but nevertheless the women continued to retell what Najma al-Mithqal had said, with new additions every day, for in the past Najma al-Mithqal had said things which came true. The men racked their brains to try to extract the likeliest or most convincing explanations, and because they could not arrive at any conclusion they pretended to forget it all for a time, but their hearts grew anxious and uneasy.

Al-Hadra and its surrounding areas a few days' ride in every direction had not changed since God created the earth. Since the life of the people was marked by extraordinary difficulty and harshness because of the lack of rain, the scarcity of caravans and the consequently high prices they paid for flour, sugar and cloth, they were used to it and never expected anything better. If the earth became too crowded, something had to give. It was usually death that solved that problem, in the form of raids and feuds, frequently the results of disputes over grazing and water, or as the result of diseases that struck men and animals. Death was the regulator that made them capable of living and enduring, and when the men got tired of death and were no longer able or willing to continue killing one another, or when caravans arrived, they felt the powerful lure of travel, unprepared as they were and having given it no previous thought. When they did leave, there was more room for the others, who kept on living.

What Najma al-Mithqal had said, and what had been attributed to her by the women, excited even more curiosity than fear, but curiosity was the beginning of fear, and so the gloom inspired by some of the words and prophecies of that wise and powerful old woman, who had seen so much that no others had seen, roused even more turmoil than her unusual death had done.

Suleiman al-Hadib lost patience when he saw his son nagging his mother to do something to assure him of Watfa's hand in marriage.

"My boy, after what the old woman Najma al-Mithqal said, we should all prepare ourselves for the Judgment Day," he told him.

He felt that he was getting into trouble with these words, for until recently he had been ridiculing Najma's words whenever anyone brought them up, but now he was quoting them himself, and he wondered if they had settled in his inner mind as a hidden conviction, and if he had made a mistake.

"Be patient, my boy," he said in an attempt to rectify his error. "The old woman has just died." He paused a moment and added in a different tone: "Everything will come in time."

Suweyleh put the matter aside for the time being, but his old lust for travel flickered again. "I'm going with the first caravan," he told his mother, "but as soon as you know it I'll be back and getting married."

"Don't worry, my boy," she said smilingly. "Trust in God."

Once again Suweyleh and Fawaz entertained the idea of leaving and began to prepare. Suweyleh burned with enthusiasm to travel as soon as possible, to make sure that he had enough money to last him. Najma al-Mithqal's death had unsettled him; it had given rise to circumstances that called for canceling and postponing weddings. One of Watfa's male relations had visited and asked for her hand in marriage, but after she moved to her aunt's house she told Suweyleh's mother, "Aunt, I have no one in this world but God and you!" This was taken as an unconditional acceptance, only after a decent interval passed and Suweyleh came back from his trip; at that time al-Hadra would celebrate the match it had awaited for so long.

The two of them had invented the lie together and had to stand by it together. While it was true that Fawaz was deeply unhappy in al-Hadra and wanted to leave as soon as he humanly could, after the frustration of his visit to Wadi al-Uyoun he felt that he was powerless to do anything to confront this cruel world; he had better wait a year or two before packing up again and going to Wadi al-Uyoun, to Shaalan, to work with him as Ibn Rashed had promised. Suweyleh, however, insisted and painted glowing pictures of the world beyond Wadi al-Uyoun, new places and big cities, not to mention the money they could earn, and Fawaz grew more confused as his resistance weakened.

Suweyleh never stopped retelling the tales for a single day. Fawaz listened without responding and looked at him as his mind wandered. If he was convinced deep down that he should leave, it was largely because of Miteb al-Hathal himself. The disease he had seen in Shaalan's eyes, and the fear that had pursued him since his first night in Wadi al-Uyoun, the sight of Miteb in the flesh in Rawdhat al-Mashti which had deprived him of sleep and peace for days and nights at a time, all induced in him the defiant urge to follow and catch his father. He could tell no one of this; even his mother and Radiya would not listen to a single word from him about his father.

Could he and Shaalan both be wrong? He told himself, "I might make a mistake, and he might make a mistake, but can we both be mistaken? No!" Miteb al-Hathal had become more than a father to them, and he could not be absent forever. Had it been merely a question of absence, a man might have found some explanation and put his mind at ease, but this was bigger and more complicated than that.

All Suweyleh's efforts would have done no good had Fawaz not seen Miteb al-Hathal in Rawdhat al-Mashti, but he was still afraid, not knowing where to go or what to do.

He was silent and undecided whenever Suweyleh asked for his approval, and he might well have remained undecided or not traveled at all had Khosh not appeared.

When Fawaz looked back now at those moments, he felt that a hidden force shaped men's destinies and pushed them from place to place and defined their life and death.

This man, absent for long years, with no message or news of any kind, who had brought on his old mother's madness and then death on her last day in Wadi al-Uyoun, was assumed to have perished in some nameless place. Scarcely anyone even remembered what this Khosh had looked like; he had become a mere memory, his features fading and waning as each day passed. This man who had been gone all these years now returned unexpectedly with Ibn al-A'sar's caravan, which came to al-Hadra at this time every year for a month or so to sell merchandise brought from far-off places—flour, sugar, tea, textiles and uncounted other things—bringing back on its return trip butter, wool and a few horses.

Time had much changed the seventeen-year-old who had gone off with al-Salemi's caravan. He was a grown man approaching middle age, or at least so he looked.

Fine wrinkles showed clearly when he smiled or was immersed in thought or remembrance. A weather-beaten tan covered all the exposed parts of his body, and when he turned up his garments or took off his ghotra the people wondered at the contrasting colors of his skin, but his facial features had stayed the same or perhaps changed only slightly.

Khosh's coming was greeted with surprise more like disbelief and excited as much endless nostalgia and sadness as it did joy. The people's past life flashed before them without their willing it, and there was an uninterrupted stream of tales and memories: how he had been so set on traveling that his mother had interceded with the men, among them Miteb al-Hathal, to let him go; how he was the best of Wadi al-Uyoun's youth; and the night he had left, how his mother had packed him enough provisions—as Miteb al-Hathal said—to see him to Egypt and back!

When Wadi al-Uyoun was mentioned he said that he had passed through there and not recognized anything; had it not been for Shaalan and Ibn Rashed he would not have known that it was Wadi al-Uyoun at all. When the old woman was mentioned he bowed his head and went completely silent, as if he did not want to remember or to say one word. He seemed sad, dead or like another person altogether; he wished he had come earlier to see his mother before she died. Shaalan had urged him to stay in Wadi al-Uyoun and work with him in the company but was unable to convince him to stay after Khosh heard about his mother's death just prior to the leaving of Wadi al-Uyoun and how Miteb al-Hathal had fled, no one knew where to or for how long.

Delight at the return of Khosh increased day by day. Even Wadha, who had maintained her silence since Rawdhat al-Mashti, was a different woman: she could be heard making sounds like those produced by children who are learning to speak; her eyes lit up with happiness and she became more active. When Khosh drew from within his dusty old clothes the leather wallet that hung around his neck on a stout thong, stuck against the flesh by his heart, Wadha, just opposite him, watched closely, not knowing what he was going to do. He opened the wallet calmly and spread out all its contents in his lap with both hands. She began to cry copiously. It was the first time she had cried out of joy, sorrow and pain all at once, and this was very different from the crying she had done on their first night in Ujra after coming from Wadi al-Uyoun.

Khosh had done this with exaggerated calm, and when he saw her tears he bowed his head but without sorrow, and stayed that way for a while. When he raised his head again there was a faint smile playing around the corners of her mouth and eyes, and without a word being spoken the two understood each other.

Fawaz followed this scene silent and perplexed. Radiya had gone in and out more than once looking irritated and upset; her woman's intuition told her that something important was happening then, and that something she had been waiting for over long years, and dreamed of more than anything else, had just quietly taken place.

Two weeks later Khosh married Radiya.

"If you can find us a caravan before Ibn al-A'sar's leaves, we'll go with it," Fawaz told Suweyleh one week after the wedding. "Otherwise we'll have to wait until he travels."

When he told his mother that he was planning to return to Wadi al-Uyoun to see Shaalan and work in the company, that the search for his father would not let up for a single day and that he would come back with Miteb, she seemed happy and sad at the same time. Her heart filled up with hopes and fears and her face looked stern, but she got up quickly and began to prepare some things for his journey. She questioned him with her eyes and stammered incomprehensibly, apparently asking when he intended to leave and what he would need to take with him.

"I'll be going with Ibn al-A'sar," he said smiling.

Wadha had prepared him ample supplies of food by the time Ibn al-A'sar's caravan was ready to go, and Khosh laughed when he saw her, repeating what Miteb al-Hathal had told her long years before. "All this will see him to Egypt and back!"

25

AL-HADRA SEEMED OLDER AND SADDER AS THEY left. Even the children looked sad and entreating as they crowded around the caravan and were less boisterous than usual. The men showed all their sagacity and overdid their advice on how to tie up the luggage properly, but others paid no attention. As usual, the women did not come near, but they did not miss a single word or movement. Wadha al-Hamad, who displayed superb detachment, prepared everything with such exaggerated care that everyone noticed her. She knew deep inside that this time her son would be gone a long time. She did things for him that she had not done when he'd first left, and she monitored his every movement, never taking her eyes off him. This discomfited and embarrassed him a little, and when he bid his brothers and sisters farewell and came near her she hugged his shoulders tightly and shook him as if testing his strength, entrusting to his body the strength that remained in hers. When she saw his features hard and expressionless, she shook her head with the detachment of a mare and buried her face in his chest. She did so with all her strength and did not move for several moments, and when she raised her face to his, two tears showed in her eyes but did not fall. The tears grew larger and at the last moment rolled onto her chest. She took one step backward to tell him wordlessly, "You may go now."

Khosh was full of energy and enthusiasm and stayed with Fawaz and Suweyleh until the caravan was ready to move. He told them many things that seemed irrelevant and out of context, as if he were passing on to them all the acquired knowledge of his personal experience, wanting them to understand and fully grasp more than his gestures and head shaking could convey.

On the trip to Rawdhat al-Mashti, which took them seven days since a strong head wind forced them to take the northern route to al-Rawdha, their memories returned, and with them the last moments: Fawaz, who exercised his self-control and insisted on being tougher than a boulder, especially against the old woman he had left behind in al-Hadra, felt a deep sorrow, which confused Suweyleh, whose eyes continually asked if he were afraid or possessed by the same worries that had bothered him when they were on the return journey from Wadi al-Uyoun to al-Hadra. No matter how Suweyleh tried to put him at ease, to interest him in other things, Fawaz did not cheer up. When Suweyleh began to sing, as he did several times, to the delight of the other travelers in the caravan, he felt that this time his song was sad or even anguished.

Did he sing of his permanent separation from places he would never see again or people he would never have the chance to meet again? Did he sing of his separation from Watfa and of this unknown journey which would lead him to he knew not where, or when or if he would return? Did he sing of the life and memories that were already fading as the caravan moved out of al-Hadra?

A certain finality fluttered over their heads and cried out in the shadows of night and dawn. There was no saving them from the unknown into which they rushed with each step from al-Hadra, and from which they would not emerge until the end.

The strong gusts of wind dusted the men's faces and made the camels skittish, ruined visibility and slowed the pace. Their faces reflected the violent inner strength which drove them along, forgetful of their weariness.

"We'll rest in al-Rawdha for one day and then go on to Ujra," said Suweyleh when Rawdhat al-Mashti came into view.

He said this looking straight into Fawaz's eyes, as if testing the strong intentions he had shown on their previous trip. Fawaz said nothing.

"You know that from Ujra we can go on to wherever we want," Suweyleh continued. "We could go to Baghdad or Damascus, or to Oman. If we want, we can go to Egypt."

Fawaz's mistake was in agreeing with Suweyleh to spend a short time in Rawdhat al-Mashti, then to proceed to Ujra.

Suweyleh was very much afraid that Fawaz would not want to leave Rawdhat al-Mashti, that he would wander around looking for his father, especially since they were crossing the wadi. And after that the sudden harsh voice sprang spontaneously from Fawaz's lips: "Here—here, Suweyleh." He jumped off his moving camel with the lightness of a cat and pointed his bamboo cane.

Suweyleh patiently nodded to show he understood and agreed, or perhaps he was hatching some other idea, but he quickly slid down, seized his camel and made her kneel. Then he did the

same with Fawaz's camel and asked abruptly, almost offensively:
"What do you say, Fawaz, to spending the whole day here?"

Was he challenging him? Telling him indirectly that what they
had seen on their previous trip had been nothing but his imagination? Did he want to prove to him that his father, whom he
had seen here on the assumption that he had really been present
had gone somewhere else and that therefore it would be useless
to stay here and look for him?

Suweyleh must have reached some final decision, and now
wanted to compel Fawaz to go along with him where he wanted.
Fawaz was upset and afraid, and perhaps needed someone to
think it over and decide for him: no sooner had Suweyleh made
his suggestion to leave the caravan and spend the day there than
Fawaz felt he was being mocked.

"I told you I saw him here," snapped Fawaz. "He was here.
I didn't say let's stay here."

"It's a fine spot, and convenient. There's nothing wrong with
staying."

"No. We'll stay with the rest of them, near the wells."

"You said it, not me, cousin. Whatever you want."

This was the first mistake of the journey; had Suweyleh not
given in as he did they would have spent the day here, the place
where Miteb al-Hathal had appeared and spoken to the men,
women and children of Rawdhat al-Mashti, where his voice had
drowned out the thunder and rushing water. If he did not come
in the daytime he would surely come at night. If he did not
come here he would surely be somewhere nearby. But Suweyleh
had agreed to continue the journey, so they crossed the wadi
and made it to the eastern edge of Rawdhat al-Mashti, by the
wells on the road to Ujra, and the mistake was made.

Fawaz was a changed man in Rawdhat al-Mashti. The accursed
water had entered his body and paralyzed him. It was decided
that Ibn al-A'sar's caravan would stay for three or four days,

but one day had scarcely passed when Suweyleh pulled Fawaz aside. "They want to buy and sell, but we have nothing to sell or buy. What do you say to leaving?"

In the same deadly, occult way, and perhaps from fear of the accursed waters, Fawaz agreed that they should continue on to Ujra the next day.

The same measure of joy that motivated Suweyleh to continue the journey quickly in a small caravan to Ujra filled Fawaz with the dread and fear that paralyzed his thinking and immersed him in silence.

Suweyleh feared that some sort of illness would prevent Fawaz from continuing the journey and create problems they were not prepared for, so he did his best to put Fawaz in a healthy state of mind. He spoke of the world that the Sultan's Road was leading them to, far from the harsh, deadly desert; there they would find everything men dreamed of. Their travels would not last long, but they would return rich. He recited all the stories he knew about poor men who had taken the Sultan's Road to faraway places and returned before long with proverbial wealth and power; some had gone away again and others had stayed away until now. They married and had children, divorced and married two or three wives, sent money and clothes to their families in al-Hadra, al-Rahba and Ujra, and would someday come back themselves.

Suweyleh had hardly finished the story about the men who had traveled to faraway places and gone back to them when he noticed that Fawaz was still completely silent and preoccupied, so he began to sing.

Suweyleh tore his heart out when he sang. Fawaz had heard him sing before, but this time, on their way from Rawdhat al-Mashti to Ujra, he sang as never before. His voice rose and fell like a dove and a falcon conversing. It would almost fade away, only to burst out and soar to the sky.

They had just reached the Sultan's Road, one or two hours from Ujra, when they saw a tent, and a little farther on they saw a group of men. In their midst was Ibn Rashed.

When Ibn Rashed saw them he would not leave them and did not let them proceed to Ujra until they had spent three days with him. Then he only let them go to buy some provisions they needed, because "work begins today, and you get paid starting from today; we cannot wait."

Thus it was, though no one could have foreseen it, that Ibn Rashed recruited Fawaz and Suweyleh and they went all together on to Harran.

26

I BN RASHED TOOK CHARGE OF THEM AS SOON AS THEY
met just outside Ujra. "You have come, and God
sent you. You are my family, and all a man has are
his family and his friends. If he doesn't look after his friends
he'll come to no good. You must come with me to Harran."
He had forgotten everything he had said in Wadi al-Uyoun two
months ago, and when Fawaz tried to bring it up Ibn Rashed
dispensed with the topic. "God curse the Devil. A man has to
act."

He went on to tell them that the work in Wadi al-Uyoun was
arduous and below them, whereas in Harran "a man could make
piles of gold" in the space of a year or two. He used diabolical
arguments to convince them, and in spite of the deep mistrust
and bitterness they felt on account of his previous refusal and
Fawaz's inclination to turn him down, Suweyleh was hesitant

to deny him. Then Suweyleh wavered and finally agreed to go as long as Fawaz came too. At this Ibn Rashed began to entice and intimidate Fawaz and made many promises until he consented.

After a few days in Ujra, during which Ibn Rashed gathered the men he required, they set off for Harran, that unknown place which only a very few had heard of and which none of them had ever visited before. They stopped several times on the way and asked the shepherds and old men they found near one of the ponds to make sure they were headed in the right direction. After five days they reached the sea.

They stopped and looked in disbelief: water . . . endless water, as far as the eye could see. It was the sea! The sea, like the desert in its breadth and volume, the very sight of whose fabulous expanse of water flooded a man with joy and terror.

No one could ever dream or imagine that any part of the world held such a stupendous amount of water. Where had it come from? Had it rained down or sprung from within the earth? Did the townsfolk of al-Hadra, al-Rawdha and the dozens of other places behind the hills know that all this water was here? How long would it be here—where was it going?

None of the twenty men had ever seen the sea before. Wonder and amazement showed on their faces. From this spot they could also see a small village that their eyes could not identify at this distance. Ibn Rashed pointed, and everyone looked in the direction he was pointing. "From what the old man we saw yesterday said, that must be Harran," he said. They could see a cluster of low mud houses with long ranges of hills rising to the right and left of them. There were a few trees, but no one could tell which kind from this distance.

In a silence that suggested secrecy or conspiracy they started down the hill, headed to where Ibn Rashed had been pointing. The men had heard the name of Harran mentioned for the first time in Ujra, and now that they had arrived they saw Harran and knew what it was.

"Is this the Damascus you've been telling me about, cousin?" Fawaz asked Suweyleh scornfully as they made their camels kneel.

"Shut up." Suweyleh laughed. "All places are the same." He added, as if talking to himself, "And this place is a lot closer than Damascus."

The people of Harran showed no surprise at the caravan's arrival; they knew in advance that it was coming because two of Ibn Rashed's men had preceded them, and perhaps there had been other visits as well before their arrival. The townsfolk of Harran were like those of Wadi al-Uyoun, kind and helpful; they did everything they were asked to do. The only difference was the people of Harran were very quiet: they spoke little, and then only when they were spoken to.

Ibn Rashed gathered the men of Harran around and addressed them, just as he had done in Wadi al-Uyoun. "Have no fear, my friends, for blessings have come. Almighty God has opened the gates of Heaven to you and now, God willing, after all your toil and hardship, you will rest. His Excellency has spoken of you to say there are no men like the men of Harran—strong, brave and generous. This company is your company. It has come in your interest to serve you. It is here to help you so you must help it, and with regard to the compensation due to each one of you, have no fear. God willing, none of you will be anything but satisfied; every man will get his due and then some."

He paused a moment, examined their faces carefully and then went on. "The friends are arriving in a few days and we want you to do your utmost for them, to work hard and obey them as if you were their servants."

After that there were questions and comments, but Ibn Rashed, who had talked and joked paternally in Wadi al-Uyoun, dealing patiently with every man's opinions, was a different man in Harran. He was extremely self-confident and made no jokes; he was serious and even harsh. He gave curt orders and spoke in such a way that no one knew whether it was out of hostility or distrust. When one of the old men said that they were happy with the life they had, that they did not want to change it and did not want anything else, Ibn Rashed scanned their faces carefully as if looking for the son of Miteb al-Hathal, and after looking into each man's eyes for a fleeting moment he addressed the old man. "Old man, in a few short years you're going to say to yourself, 'If only I were younger and stronger,' because the happiness to come will flood the world, and everyone will have his share."

The old man blinked and said despairingly, "We've had our share of this world, cousin, and God willing it will end well!"

Decisively, in a way that admitted of no further discussion, Ibn Rashed told them it was absolutely necessary to cooperate with the company and help them out. He said that the houses they were living in would be demolished because the whole area had to be changed; then he plunged into detailed questions about the surrounding areas, their names, the distances between them and the roads and how much water was available in each place.

A few days later a group of Americans arrived by the sea road and it appeared that they had been here several times before, since they clearly knew the old man and some of Harran's other people: they joked with the men and slapped them on the back. Then they went away, absorbed themselves in the papers they took from their boxes and began to write and make plans. They told Ibn Rashed, through their translator, that a ship would arrive in a few days and that he should get the laborers ready to help unload the many things that the ship would bring.

27

THE DEMOLITION OF THE HOUSES IN HARRAN began only a few days after the hellish machines arrived by sea. If the people of Wadi al-Uyoun had shown shock and bewilderment in watching those machines arrive and get to work, the people of Harran were less affected. True, the ship that had dropped anchor far off the shore frightened everyone, even Ibn Rashed, whose unease was obvious. He was clearly alarmed when asked what this "calamity" was that drifted toward Harran, and he mumbled a reply that no one understood. He seemed placated after a whispered conversation with the translator, which involved a great many signs and gestures, but he still looked surprised. His men were plainly nervous and afraid and kept as far as they could from the shore, leaving the unloading of the machines from the smaller boat that was dropped from the ship's side to the Harranis. When Ibn

Rashed tried to spur them on, emphasizing in his own way the importance of going in and helping, the men responded by telling him, "We'll do everything except go near the water. The water's dangerous." He understood them and did not insist after that, keeping himself occupied as the frightened supervisor.

Most of the men felt pangs of pity as they destroyed the small, poor houses. Until compensation could be arranged later, tents and money were distributed to the townspeople, who gathered on the western hills to watch.

"If we hadn't come, Ibn Rashed would just have found some-one else to do the same thing," said Suweyleh that evening, after Harran had been reduced to rubble.

He showed considerable skill, attempting to convince himself before trying to convince the others, in arguing that work was work, whether it involved flattening houses, mining salt or any-thing else. There was no difference at all. When Fawaz com-plained about Harran's humidity, which he found unbearable, Suweyleh answered wistfully. "Men adapt, cousin. Be patient for a month or two and you'll get used to it."

In the first days a number of the workers thought of leaving Harran, of going back where they had come from as soon as they were paid, but the first salary Ibn Rashed distributed changed their minds. No one had ever dreamed of getting that much money, and none had ever possessed that amount before. They received their pay in a silent, solemn, almost majestic rite.

On the afternoon of the third Thursday, Ibn Rashed suddenly asked them all to stand in a line. Daham al-Muzil stood haughtily at his side, and when the men stood waiting he called their names one by one and took a handful of silver coins from a canvas bag, and after pouring them from one hand to the other in a regulated, ringing stream, he counted them quickly and expertly and handed them out, asking each man to count them again. He turned away to motion the man where to go, then looked at Daham to have him cross off the name. When Daham nodded his head to indicate that he had done so, Ibn Rashed had him read out the next name, and so on until the end.

When Ibn Rashed had finished distributing the salaries and made sure that everyone had counted them, he said that the salaries would go up in coming months since the allowance now subtracted for food would be reviewed: each man would have the option of taking company food or preparing his own after buying what he liked from the shops that would be established soon.

Ibn Rashed explained all this in several different ways, and then looked at their faces. "There's one more matter, my friends." He looked at them carefully. "The camels. From today onward they are of no use here."

He gave them a choice between selling the camels directly or assigning one of themselves to take the camels to Ujra, where they could be sold at the market, but he assured the men that they would never get as much in Ujra or anywhere else as he was ready to pay.

For the first time the men felt that they were confronting an agonizing situation and a decisive choice; they were being asked to give up the most precious things they owned. Each had exhausted himself and made sacrifices in order to buy his camel and knew that if he sold it today he might never have the chance to buy another; in doing so he was committing himself to this place, to staying a long time, perhaps forever.

Fawaz had fought long and hard to get from his father that camel which had accompanied him everywhere for the past two years; she was extremely wise, obedient and understanding, and he had invested great hopes in her. He could not let her go to an unknown place or person, and he was ready to leave his job and go back whence he had come in order to keep this camel. Suweyleh knew it without being told, without Fawaz alluding to it; he looked sad and lost, and late that night, after most of the laborers were asleep, he asked Fawaz to go out to the desert with him, because he could not sleep and wanted to talk with him.

In the still of the night, in this place that no longer had a name since the houses had been destroyed and all the landmarks obliterated, Suweyleh wanted to tell Fawaz so many things, to talk without stopping, but he was troubled and hesitant and substituted a song for the words that filled his breast.

He sang a sad song more like a whispered monologue. He sang of Watfa. He wanted to fly to her, to see her even for a single instant, to hear her speak one word. For her sake he could stand anything, he could suffer or travel, to work anywhere. When he had earned the money he needed, nothing and no one would hold him back: he would return to al-Hadra.

After singing he spoke, as if talking to himself. "My insides are burning, God help me. Cousin, you have to help me!"

He was pleading. He wanted Fawaz to stay, to put up with everything, even though they were able to leave immediately if they wanted to. A man could not tie his fate to a camel; they had to take up Ibn Rashed's offer and sell the camels, and when the time came to go back to al-Hadra they could buy new animals anywhere.

When Suweyleh talked this way Fawaz felt that he was very far from home. He knew that Suweyleh would do anything for Watfa, for the sake of getting the money he needed. He spoke in a moment of anger. "I hate this place. I want to leave."

Was Suweyleh looking at him in the dark? Did he sigh? Was he trying to say that he would abandon or kill any man to get what he wanted? Perhaps so, for Fawaz suddenly felt ready to stand by him. He did not say so aloud and made no move to suggest that his decision was made, but he felt dejected and defeated, and utterly alone in this bleak place. Even his closest friend, Suweyleh, thought of nothing but getting the money to go home and marry. This being the case, Ibn Rashed could do anything he liked.

The next day they turned their camels over to Ibn Rashed with no discussion, and he gave them some money.

"Now you have nothing to worry about. We'll take care of the animals and you won't have to worry about them."

No one said a word. They were all thinking of the safest ways to store their money so that it would not get lost or stolen, and after long deliberation most of them decided that the best and securest way to safeguard it was to have Ibn Rashed keep it for them.

28

Wadi al-Uyoun, Ujra, al-Rahba, Rawdhat al-Mashti and most other towns and villages had roads from which caravans and news arrived. People knew the routes and watched them for newcomers; even when Umm Khosh used to wait, having tired of begging and searching, she did so in Zahra, always on the same dune because it commanded a good view of the road and the horizon. In Rawdhat al-Mashti the wells were on high ground; this was where caravans arrived and the people waited and kept a lookout even to Ujra, where, though numerous roads from all directions converged, the Sultan's Road was viewed by everyone as *the* road; all the others were tributaries.

And so it is throughout most of the world. The idea that eyes might turn instead toward the raging water, to gaze unceasingly at the sea—that men and caravans and news could come from that quarter too—never occurred to most of them; but this is how it was in Harran.

The desert on the other side was, most of the time, flat, hard and desolate; nothing and no one came from its depths except rarely. Even the food Ibn Rashed provided for the workers, instead of coming from Ujra, arrived on ships from various foreign lands. The bedouin who had at first refused to go near the sea or take part in unloading cargoes from the small boats were soon won over. It seemed to them curious, arousing and somewhat risky, and before long they went closer to the sea. They did so hesitantly, in stages, with a sense of experimentation and secrecy. One of them approached slowly and cautiously in measured steps parallel to the shoreline; he stepped quickly and lightly as a cat, tracing a broken line near the water, then just as quickly jumped back. They all tried this numberless times. They sat on the beach and contemplated the water carefully, lost in thought, completely dumbfounded at the sight of the Harranis, young and old, diving into the water, riding it with such ease that they seemed to be walking on solid ground. They envied them for being able to do this and secretly wished they, too, could swim, but their fear never left them, for "water is treacherous, a swallower who never is satisfied."

Later on they waded into the shallow water. It was enticing, caressing their feet with its coolness and density, and with the passing of time they did not hesitate to bathe in the sea; they squatted right on the beach, where the water immersed their feet and swelled up to the middle of their calves. They scooped up water in their hands and with metal cups to pour over their heads and bodies, but the waves alarmed them: they got up and ran away, looking all around, afraid that these wild beasts would attack them.

Among the bedouin two brothers, Mizban and Hajem, were the only ones who knew how to swim; they had learned in a well in their village. They enjoyed the water the most and did not hesitate to help the people of Harran, going into the water as soon as Ibn Rashed asked them, though they spent much of the time in childish playing and racing. They were ready and eager to teach the others to swim, insisting that swimming was easy and could be learned in one day, but no one was convinced.

The others listened and watched, their wonder apparent, and though they seemed to approve none of them was ready to undertake the perilous experiment: the sea before them was endless. The way it carried and moved the boats despite their hugeness, and the stories circulating about how it swallowed up great ships with hundreds of men aboard, leaving not a trace of them behind, filled their hearts with a nameless dread that reached the outermost limits of terror.

The new things—appearances and places—instilled in the men a desire to explore and presented a challenge that could not be resisted for long, but the sea, especially for those who had never seen it before, excited undying wonderment and fear, though the tales they knew and the others they made up did not satisfy their curiosity. So in spite of the long hours each of them spent submerged in endless contemplation, the mystery grew with every passing day: Where had all this water come from? Why was it here instead of in other places where people needed it? The rainwater and well water were sweet and drinkable, if at times a little brackish, but how had the seawater become so salty and bitter that no one could possibly drink it?

Those who had come from the interior, from the depths of the desert, were lost in a whirlpool of thought and bewilderment. They were deeply troubled and afraid, and their fears increased when Ibn Rashed bought all the camels. They felt afflicted by total paralysis; in this isolated place, which had lost even its name, they were only a band of men besieged, not knowing what to do or what their lives would be like in the days to come. They were prey to anxiety and whispers, and they no longer wanted to eat. Some ascribed their loss of appetite to the nature of the food Ibn Rashed supplied; others said that the smell of the sea, which filled the men with anxiety, also made them incapable of eating. Still others explained it by saying that the smell of the Americans and the boats they arrived on would choke a dog and made them unable even to go near food.

When the men reached this point Ibn Rashed was no longer able to stall or avoid them, for some of them were ill and others had demanded their camels to go back where they had come from. At first he was angry and upset, but soon he asked them all to be patient and tolerant, to give him a little more time, at least enough time to travel to Ujra and back again. After that he would grant what they asked: allow them to do their own cooking. He only wanted time, enough to go and come back, "just for the road," as he said, and in the meantime he ordered that the men be served more meat and rice.

The traffic of ships never slowed or stopped. Some were small and others were as huge as mountains, and from these ships came endless new things—no one could imagine what they were or what they were for. With the cargoes that mounted and piled up came men from no one knew where, to do God only knew what. All day they unloaded the heavy cargoes, tied them with strong ropes and hoisted them higher than the ships themselves. Who was pulling them up? How were they raised? Everyone was possessed by numb fear as they watched the huge crates rising in the sky, with no one pulling them up. Even the man on the deck of the ship who pushed the tremendous crates with one hand, moving them from one side to the other, seemed to the watchers on shore more a demon than a man. When Daham al-Muzil called him the Demon, everyone agreed that that name suited him. Their eyes followed him everywhere, monitoring his every move, and when he came ashore their eyes never left him for a moment: how he behaved, how he moved his hands, how he looked at the people around him. When he took off his clothes, leaving only a small garment covering his nakedness, and leaped into the water, everyone retreated. They were afraid that he had the same power to jump that he had to move the crates on the ship; they were sure of it when he raised one arm and beat the water—surely the water would rise and rise until it submerged the whole shore. They thanked God loudly when he headed from the beach out to sea; otherwise there would have been a disaster. When he neared the ship he had come from, Daham al-Muzil spoke. "The son of a bitch will move the whole ship. He'll turn it over."

He floated near the ship for a while, and when he began heading back to the beach Daham asked everyone to move back and be extremely careful, "because how can you confront someone who can move a ship as big as a mountain?" When he reached the beach and stretched out on the sand everyone watched cautiously from afar, for this beast could get up at any moment and might behave like a beast if he didn't like being watched or didn't like the looks of the people. Naim Sh'eira, the translator, went near him and they began to talk and laugh, then Naim waded into the sea and scooped up water in his hands and poured it over the Demon, who shouted, then got upset and chased Naim until he was four or five yards out in the water and fell down. He got up again and tried to catch Naim, who managed to stay away. Everyone watched, waiting with bated breath until the two men disappeared around the other side of the ship.

Everything was strange in this desolate place. The ships brought tons of things that kept everyone busy, and Daham, who supervised the workers, was not content with shouting and bossing: he swore and cursed, especially at the poorest and youngest workers, and the ones who had come a long way from the interior, in his attempts to force them to work without stopping or even pausing.

Despite the arrival of more ships and the interest and curiosity they provoked, as well as the exhausting work they provided, depriving the men of any ability to rest or even talk, everyone was in low spirits by the time night fell. Their depression grew when the work ended and the sound of the sea grew louder and the wind suddenly began to blow. The men were silent and bitter. Questions that could be answered in other places had no answers here; they did not know how long they would be here or what their lives would be like in the desolate place where they found themselves.

In this hollow in the earth, where poor mud houses nestled by the sea, nature took shape in a fashion unknown anywhere else: on one side a long rocky cape jutted into the sea, and on the other the shoreline was shallow and sinuous; further on the sea was broader and deeper. Instead of large boulders there was sand, and behind the range of hills of varying height the desert began.

In this depression, like a mother's enfolded arms, where the water met the shore, far enough from the sea to avoid the distance and the islands or nature's wrath, which flared up without warning, the small village was created in one day, the village which named itself, or was named by some passing stranger, Harran. It was hotter and more humid than anyplace else, perhaps because the east winds, which often reached other places, did not reach Harran with the same strength: the winds broke when they hit the projecting cape or swirled around it. The desert winds, which were fresh and sweet at times of the year, blew high over Harran without stopping. When the sandstorms raged, Harran disappeared in the dust and the surrounding hills were buried under huge quantities of sand, and before reaching the sea to smite the water most of the blowing dust fell on the shores of the gulf.

Harran was Hell itself in summer: the wind died and the sky hung low like a leaden dome. The air was saturated with humidity. Breathing was difficult and bodies were heavy and slick from constant sweating. Clothing, damp and reeking with perspiration, became a hindrance. Men were overcome by apathy and exhaustion, and each limb of their bodies felt disconnected from the others, as if randomly assembled without flesh to bind them together.

Other hot places were bearable at night, but Harran's nights were no different from its days; when the sun went down the sky filled with a light haze, which limited visibility and made breathing a chore. The coolness that accompanied sundown here was like a thick damp blanket which a man did not know whether to throw off or burrow into, and the salty heat hung in the air until an hour or two before dawn; only then could a man fill his lungs with good air and rest, in anticipation of another dreadful day.

This was the weather through most of the year, except for winter, which lasted about three months. Then nature softened, became hidden and secretive, almost spectral, and man hardly felt the heat or the coolness. The humidity disappeared; the air was clear except for the days of intense rain, but even those rains lasted just a few hours, after which Harran was swept by sweetness-laden desert winds redolent of soil and rare vegetation, which imparted feelings of well-being and nostalgia.

A forgotten human community lived and waited for such days; they survived by fishing and receiving assistance from travelers, depending also on the trade of the small ships that plied the coast. Harran had little contact with the world, but it remained strange and volatile though the town had but two or three roads for the rare, brief journeys necessary to secure her few requirements. Men were often seduced by the calls of the mysterious, arousing sea and set off in their small boats for the port of Manal, only two days away. If the wind or the powerful waves were against them, they would be a day or two late in getting there, but if the wind were far too strong for them, they would have to turn back and wait for the next time. When favorable winds brought them to Manal, they behaved like madmen: most sold their boats and continued their long journeys into the unknown on one of the large ships usually at anchor in the harbor. They lived, worked, sang songs and reminisced on these journeys, and years passed before most of them returned home to Harran richer in faraway places, stories and memories than in money and possessions but able to live on their earnings for a year or two. They went back to fishing and the life of Harran. Some got bored or wearied of town life and sailed off again. Many men did that, to the sorrow of their wives and children, but the old men did not object; something about Harran made men act that way; even the old settled men, whom the sea no longer seduced or drove to make mad decisions, had in their time been prey to the urge to travel to Manal and beyond.

Just as the call of the sea was powerfully arousing, carrying so many men to Manal, the lure of the land behind Harran held fascination for others; some of the men who went into the desert and reached Ujra, then took the Sultan's Road to far distant places, were not heard from for long periods, and at times they came home close on the heels of news of their travels. The travelers at sea usually returned with tales, but those who took the Sultan's Road had fewer and more commonplace stories and exchanged them for the many things they brought with them. The Sultan's Road seemed better and luckier for those who set off upon it. Those who didn't return or stayed out for long periods never forgot Harran; they sent all they could to those who had stayed behind—gifts, money, letters and constant assurances that they would come back soon.

So Harran lived and waited, bearing up under the pain of waiting for winter. The people there who had known past winters seemed stronger and more optimistic, and some of the village elders went so far as to say Harran's climate was better than that of many other places!

The humidity thickened and the heat, carried by winds from the west, oppressed the air with a heavy layer of dust. The people felt they could take it no longer. Surely it was only the images of their traveling sons that allowed them to survive in this desolate part of the world and enabled them to be patient and endure and wait.

29

So Harran had been since the beginning of time, and so it was when Ibn Rashed and his men arrived. The company men, who had visited many places before Harran, chose it as a port and headquarters of the company, as well as a city of finality and damnation.

The ships docked one after the other, and no sooner were the huge crates mounted up in ever higher hills with every new ship, than another large plot of land was sealed off behind barbed wire. This land began in the middle of the gulf coastline and stretched northward and eastward as far as the far-off hills. Ibn Rashed and his men were asked to move to the other side of Harran, no less than a thousand yards from the fence. Soon after the arrival of a new group of foreign men in a ship different from the others, a phase of work began that never slowed or stopped. It was like madness or magic. Men raced back and forth with the raging yellow machines that created new hills racing behind them. They filled the sea and leveled the land; they did all this without pausing and without reflection. Ibn Rashed's men were called together within a few days of their arrival and divided into small groups of three or four. What with the crazed racing to and fro and the rumbling machines that swerved like untamed camels, the men were utterly frightened and confused; they had no idea how to make themselves useful. They carried the wooden planks, steel posts and precast concrete sections with so much fear and misgiving that they fell down often, made the crates collide with one another and dropped things.

The Americans gazed at them with a neutral curiosity when Naim gave them instructions, but this neutrality turned to amazement when they saw the Arabs carrying the lumber and steel posts from one place to another, and then the amazement turned to hilarity as they pointed at the workers bumping into the crates and falling down. The loud peals of laughter and pointing fingers made the men nervous and bitter and they made more mistakes, and one of the Americans moving among the work crews and supervising them asked Naim to dismiss the Arab workers early.

The workers trudged in a herd back to the area designated as theirs on the western side of the site, and in spite of the sun that bore down from the sky like a raging cataract, darkness enveloped their eyes and hearts. Their throats were parched and filled with a bitterness that gave everything the taste of colocynth. They took short steps in complete silence, overcome by fatigue. They wanted to get to their tents as quickly as possible, to fling themselves on the ground, to flee in deep sleep from the imbecile manners and mocking smiles and sneers that pursued them every moment of the day.

Daham, who strutted like a rooster among the workers in the early morning, busy and energetic, could not understand why he'd been asked to take the workers and go back at this particular time.

Now he was marching toward the tents on the western side like the rest of them: silent, confused and defeated. He said to himself that had Ibn Rashed been here when the Americans spoke to him that way, they would never have gotten away with it.

It was Daham's nature to make everything his own business, to talk too much and swear, and he wanted to get back before the rest of the men, to vanish from sight, for if there had been a mistake he would be held responsible for it. Had he been able to give the men precise orders, to make them understand what they were to do, things would have gone more smoothly. Why, he wondered, was Naim's voice so soft, like a woman's? Why didn't he talk like everybody else? He hated him. He was to blame for all the mistakes; he told them things only at the last moment and always so that they could hardly hear.

Hajem and Mizban made it to the tent before Suweyleh and Fawaz, though the latter two could see nothing at first. There was unbroken silence. When their eyes grew accustomed to the comparative darkness after the brilliant sunlight outside, Mizban spoke aloud to himself. "God gave me a new life today." He was silent a moment. "If that black hadn't held the blasted thing back it would have crushed my bones."

Most of the workers had seen the hellish yellow machine nearly pulverize Mizban, since the black man driving it had let out a yell and drawn everyone's attention. Now Mizban told the story to all the workers to remind them how the terrible incident had come about and why.

Mizban told the tale in a weary, subdued voice; he seemed sad and happy at the same time; he could not really explain what had happened. He had been at quite a distance from the "blasted thing." He was carrying a wooden plank and suddenly found himself face to face with the machine. Why hadn't he heard the deafening roar of its engine? Why hadn't he seen it moving nearer?—for none of them had ever seen anything so huge in their lives.

Angrily, cursing, Suweyleh's snarling voice began. "The bastards run like devils. One of them flies by, and you have no idea where it came from or where it's going. They race and butt each other, and rear up over each other, and the roar is enough to deafen you."

He sighed tormentedly and went on in a sad voice. "Where did these things come from? What can we possibly do against them?"

"God curse the day Ibn Rashed brought us to Harran," said Hajem bitterly. He laughed, looking at their faces, and spoke in a different tone: "If those machines don't kill us today, they'll kill us tomorrow."

Silence fell again. The men felt overcome with despair. The hard days, the black days, were not the ones past but the ones that were still to come. They felt that Ibn Rashed had not only deceived them but had placed them in a desperate and irreversible situation. They had lost the freedom to act while he went off and abandoned them in this accursed place with people who did not understand them and did not even know how to behave.

When Hamidi called them to gather for lunch, Suweyleh said wryly, "Who can get a crust in this world might as well eat it."

Fawaz did not move from his place; he had no appetite.

"God damn the Americans and their fathers," Suweyleh told the other men loudly. "They've come and brought all the evil in the world with them."

Naim came to them unexpectedly that day, between mid-afternoon and sundown, and some instinct in the men told them that something was happening.

The men were sitting in the tents or in their shade that afternoon, thinking or walking back and forth, looking at the sea and the nearby hills, sipping tea after it cooled off, contrary to their usual habit.

He appeared far away like a black specter, but no one noticed. He was one of the other camp, and those of the other camp were up to all their strange doings, as usual: rushing around like madmen, swimming, moving in packs like dogs, quarreling like children, in a word, doing things it would never enter a man's mind to do. His shadow stretched behind him as he came step by step closer to the workers' camp. As always, they laid bets on who it could be. Most of them guessed it was Naim Sh'eira, the translator.

Naim did not raise his head as he drew near; he walked with his eyes on the ground, as if thinking or avoiding looking at the men's faces, not wishing to know that they were watching him and following his every step.

He looked up just once, to find Daham's tent, and headed directly toward it.

Daham had selected the first tent for himself so that he would be the first, the nearest to the other camp and the nearest to the path that led from the hilly western side to the Ujra road. The men said to themselves: "Something's up; that's why he's coming here." Everyone began thinking, trying to guess what had brought Naim here unexpectedly; surely it had something to do with the day's work. He had only come to this camp two or three times before, only after Ibn Rashed had pestered him with several messengers insisting that he had something very important to tell him.

Now he hurried along, pensive, his head bowed, after a tense day: he must have some message. No sooner had the men told Daham who was coming than Daham came out from his tent to greet Naim loudly and ostentatiously, so the men's fear and curiosity grew. Naim swept into the tent without stopping or looking at them, and they all concluded that something was wrong.

"Fawaz! Fawaz!" shouted Daham from the flap of his tent.

For a fleeting moment Fawaz was afraid, but then resentment displaced his fear. This was so clear to Suweyleh, who was sitting by him facing the sea and turned suddenly on hearing Daham's call, that he told Fawaz in a fatherly tone, "Be careful. Don't make trouble, even if they try to make trouble for you."

Fawaz was ready for anything at that moment, despite his youth. He was able to assert himself, to command the respect of others, and Daham treated him differently from the others. Perhaps Ibn Rashed had told Daham to avoid him, or perhaps the avoidance had to do with the distance Fawaz had kept from him from Ujra until the present. He had rarely spoken to Daham in the past weeks except to say hello or ask a question. But what did Daham want from him now that the translator had come? Why had he chosen him out of all the others? Had he made some mistake, or did it have to do with Mizban's accident?

It made him uncomfortable, but he was ready for a fight, ready to face any man. He ignored Suweyleh's words and did not look at the faces of the men sitting by the tents. He had barely arrived at Daham's tent and greeted him when Daham spoke to him softly, as if he did not want Naim to hear. "The translator wants us to talk with the men, to tell them how to work."

Naim was seated when Fawaz entered and did not return his greeting. He nodded briefly and gave Fawaz an almost hostile look, as if he did not trust him. He spoke after a short silence. "Do you know how to read and write?"

Fawaz nodded yes. Naim did not look convinced.

"Where did you learn?"

"In Wadi al-Uyoun."

"Is there a school in Wadi al-Uyoun?"

"I learned from the sheikh."

Naim scrutinized the lad's face and watched his movements appraisingly. One of the lessons Fawaz had learned from his father, which he had put into practice earnestly in Wadi al-Uyoun, was to look into the face of whomever he was talking to, for when a man's tongue was silent his eyes spoke. He stared directly at Naim with equal hostility, or at least without the submission expected of him.

"What sheikh?" asked Naim sarcastically. "What did you learn?"

"Sheikh Manawar, the imam of the mosque in Wadi al-Uyoun, taught all the children reading, writing and arithmetic."

Fawaz did not know why Naim was so hostile. His questions were unfriendly, full of mistrust and sarcasm. His manner and arrogant gaze, and the kind of man he was—slightly built, speaking from between his teeth, as if the words were coming from somewhere else—made Fawaz hate Naim.

"Fawaz writes letters for everybody," said Daham, to end the pointless discussion.

Naim gestured with his hand, as if to dismiss this remark as unimportant or untrue, and spoke brusquely. "In any case, you two are responsible. We've written out the instructions for the workers to follow, and you have to explain them to those people."

Naim held out a large printed sheet, which Daham took anxiously and respectfully. He looked at it and nodded gravely.

"It begins with conditions and ends with bye-bye."

Naim said this almost inaudibly and looked at them questioningly. They were silent. He laughed.

"They don't report to work tomorrow. Tomorrow you read them these instructions. Read them once, or a hundred times, until they understand, and we'll start work the day after tomorrow with no misunderstandings." He added, sternly, "Tomorrow morning send us over three men to receive the new clothes the workers will wear instead of the filthy rags they have."

He struck the cushion beside him to signal that business was concluded and asked, "Understood?"

Daham expressed his perfect understanding and unconditional readiness to carry out his instructions to the letter with all the servility of an abject, hungry animal; he expressed these attitudes in words and excited, exaggerated movements, as his eyes alternated between the piece of paper and the translator's face.

Fawaz felt depressed and deeply hostile to this short man, to Daham for humbling himself, and to the mission imposed on him. Daham tried to make Naim stay for dinner, but Naim replied with a smile that spoke more of rejection than apology. He shook his coffee cup as a sign that he had had enough and stood in the opening of the tent looking at them appraisingly.

"We'll see after tomorrow," he said as he walked away.

30
....

WITHIN LESS THAN A MONTH TWO CITIES BEGAN to rise: Arab Harran and American Harran. The bewildered and frightened workers, who had in the beginning inspired American contempt and laughter, built the two cities. They lifted the white lumber on a winch, carried the heavy steel girders, and placed them over the wood and screwed them together; they installed the glass windows and the shutters, and they did all the painting. Every few hours they put their tools down to step back and look at another completed house. The American engineer who watched and supervised came over at this point to test the walls and ceilings with his hands and with instruments, and if they seemed sound he looked at the men's brown faces with surprise and some wonderment, and repeated the same word: "OK."

This happened again and again in American Harran, and in

less than a month the nucleus of a large and well-ordered city had appeared and sped toward completion: hard streets, some wide and others narrow, all perfectly straight, rolled smooth by the accursed heavy machines and coated with a gleaming black substance. Houses like the geese who flew over Wadi al-Uyoun in winter, small houses and others so tall and huge that no one could imagine who would inhabit them. Many swimming pools, on several scattered sites, near them houses made of straw and palm branches, and a long street linking the northeastern hill to the sea. Hundreds of pipes lay by this roadside, but no one knew what their secret might be.

An endless line of ships arrived, carrying cargoes whose use no one could guess: even after they were unpacked from the crates and emerged from the crude wrappings and boxes to be carried away by one or two Americans to stand in shining heaps of steel, no one had the slightest idea what these new terrors were.

The Arab workers, who stood like dummies in the first days, their muscular bodies straining the overalls and stiff new white caps on their heads, were divided into small groups and sent to different areas all over the work site, and within a few weeks they had become different creatures. Words of praise and slaps on the shoulder meant approval and appreciation. They never hesitated to accept any work or to offer any assistance asked of them. They were not motivated enough to take anything on; after the fear and anxiety of their first days, especially when they were read those deadly instructions, they had felt intimidated to the point of despair, but doggedly, and independently of each other, they saw things take a new turn: their hands moved more quickly, oft-repeated foreign words and names somehow found their way into their vocabularies, and relationships were formed as they smiled and gestured more. Their fears vanished, or at least retreated.

The ships that brought all the new "calamities" also brought men in ever-larger numbers, men who came from God knew where for purposes no one could guess at. They poured off the ships like locusts and swarmed to every part of the camp. Their housing was completed in a single day; even the food served in that long hall whose use no one could guess at while it was under construction, was ready for all of them.

Every finished building pushed the Arabs one step backward, for after the walls were completed the roof was put up, and after the windows and shutters were installed the Americans started to do strange jobs, hanging strong black ropes inside the walls. They filled the windows with iron blocks that emitted a cold breeze. The men who had come by ship were each given complete sets of clothes, blankets and furniture, and their very own places to sleep. After a day or two they all had become one group, as if they had always known each other, and were equally driven to work without stopping. Some worked in the sea, others moved the pieces of pipe from one place to another, while still others assembled the machines which had arrived in pieces in crates. They ran back and forth like frightened cats, naked except for short drawers and white hats; most of the time they wore nothing else. Their faces and bodies were covered with spots; they had small scars on their fingers and elsewhere on their bodies, and sweat ran like rain over their chests and faces. Clownish people like these had never been seen here before, but they became such a common sight that no one even noticed anymore.

Less than a month later, Ibn Rashed came back with several more men. Seven of them were from this region, from Ujra and al-Rawdha, but the rest were from far-off places that no one had heard of.

Ibn Rashed had left Harran when it was a wilderness, without a single house or even any marks on the ground except for a few tents and packing crates on the western side. Now he could not hide his amazement at the miraculous things constructed in his absence; he loudly voiced his astonishment to the group of men. When he arrived and saw the men returning from American Harran in overalls and caps, he threw his hands in the air and shouted with fear, "God help us! What of your souls, you poor men?"

At first most of the men did not notice how shocked Ibn Rashed really was; they looked at each other and then at Ibn Rashed, who spoke again, only laughing harshly this time. "I said to myself, the Americans could never change the sons of Arabs—never!"

He went over to Daham, who looked silly in his tight clothes, with his round belly and bulging rear end, and patted him on the shoulder. "Man grows a new heart every day."

Ibn Rashed had not got over his shock, but he loudly and exaggeratedly praised everything he saw. He praised Daham and the other men, he praised the beautiful houses the Americans had built and said that the Arabs should try to emulate them; then he somewhat shyly asked to have everything explained to him: when the buildings were put up, who had built them and how long it had taken, and when they had been given the overalls. He reached out to finger one of the caps admiringly and asked if all the men had got clothes and caps and if there were any left. He was very excited, asking a new question before they had finished answering his last one, and in his passion to know everything he missed many of the details that Daham told him.

In his excitement Ibn Rashed forgot to introduce the men he had brought. They were deeply impressed, too, but stood quietly off to one side with their camels, and when he began asking his questions they made the camels kneel and began to unload them, until they realized that they were still far away. In an attempt to show equal awe when he saw what the men were doing, he moved quickly and called out to the others for help in unloading the camels and putting their supplies in his tent.

They made short work of this task in their enthusiasm and eagerness to cooperate, joking and asking more questions; they looked at each other, and then Ibn Rashed spoke up as if he had suddenly remembered something. "Don't worry, my friends, everything is going to be just perfect."

The men gathered together and sat down in the clearing between the tents which faced the sea; most of the workers had taken off their close-fitting work clothes, undoing the buttons that made the overalls as tight as molds, and left their caps in the tents or on the ground beside them. In a moment of silence, Ibn Rashed announced that one of the men he had brought would work as a butcher, like his father and grandfather before him, and sell meat to everyone who wanted it. He pointed to a short, very dark man and said that he would sell goods to everyone in Harran—all kinds of goods, just as in Ujra and other towns. Then he looked around until his eyes met with those of a very small, skinny man. He laughed, showing his gappy teeth. "I know the bedouin—they like their own kind of bread and won't touch anything else, and he knows how to make it!" He laughed loudly. "Never fear, Arabs—trust in His Highness!"

No one knew who was meant by "His Highness"—the baker, Ibn Rashed himself or some third person. The shamefaced young man, who was wearing trousers and a jacket, who sat silently at a distance as if dreaming or watching some strange play was—Ibn Rashed said—the "engineerist" who would build houses for the Arabs like those the Americans had.

That is what Ibn Rashed told the men. He was visibly tired from his long journey but was still animated. He wanted to see everything and hear about everything that had transpired in his absence: the number of ships that had come in and what they had brought, and the new people who had arrived. Daham answered the questions as fast as he could, but Ibn Rashed was interested in too many different things, and eventually he stood up and asked Daham to accompany him to Arab Harran.

Ibn Rashed was a different man among the townspeople of Harran. He was extremely gracious and talked to everyone. He inquired about their health and asked if they were happy in their new houses or needed anything. He was especially polite to the "aged gentleman," as he called Ibn Naffeh out of respect. When he was through with his first question, he asked about the land in Harran, if it was mostly public property or divided up, and if it was divided up, who owned it. Then he asked about the lands adjoining Harran, whether they were wilderness or privately owned. He was very precise in his questions and asked Daham to make notes of everything he was told. On their way back he told him to "take good care of all this, because it's important," but he said nothing more.

Ibn Rashed thought and made decisions by himself; he consulted no one and let no one in on his secret. He had gone to Ujra very suddenly, as if involved in some conspiracy; the only people who knew he was traveling were the ones who saw him ride off. He had asked the men several times to allow him plenty of time on the road, as he put it. He had been gone a month and now he was back—instead of solving the problems they had had, he had brought with him new men and new problems.

These were his own secrets. On arriving he had asked about Naim before asking about anyone else, and when Daham al-Muzil told him that "there are a lot of new men and Naim is busy with them," Ibn Rashed had one of his men go to the American compound and tell Naim that he had arrived and wanted to see him on matters of importance. But the man came back and said that he had not been able to see Naim.

"You have to see him tomorrow. It's urgent," Ibn Rashed told Daham. He smiled and said softly, "He is the key . . . we have to get him."

Daham nodded vigorously but had no idea what Ibn Rashed was talking about.

....

31

AMERICAN HARRAN GREW TALLER, MORE SPA-
cious and more alien with every passing day,
until one afternoon the workers were sent
away early and not allowed to reenter certain sectors, even though
their work was incomplete. The large pool, for instance, was
not finished. That afternoon there was an uncanny feeling in
American Harran, as if something were about to happen. Ibn
Rashed decided to declare a holiday for the next day and a half,
to celebrate the opening of the three shops—the bakery, the
butcher's and the general store—but it was a huge ship appearing
on the horizon that changed everything in both Arab Harran
and American Harran, and a great deal more besides.

When the huge ship dropped anchor at sundown, it astonished
everyone. It was nothing like the other ships they had seen: it
glittered with colored lights that set the sea ablaze. Its immensity,

as it loomed over the shore, was terrifying. Neither the citizens of Harran nor the workers, who streamed from the interior to look, had ever seen anything like it. How could such a massive thing float and move on the water?

Voices, songs and drums were heard as soon as the ship neared the shore; they came from the shore as well as the ship, as all the Americans in the compound flooded outdoors. Music blared as small boats began ferrying the passengers from the now motionless ship. There were dozens, hundreds of people, and with the men were a great many women. The women were perfumed, shining and laughing, like horses after a long race. Each was strong and clean, as if fresh from a hot bath, and each body was uncovered except for a small piece of colored cloth. Their legs were proud and bare, and stronger than rocks. Their faces, hands, breasts, bellies—everything, yes, everything glistened, danced, flew. Men and women embraced on the deck of the large ship and in the small boats, but no one could believe what was happening on the shore.

It was an unforgettable sight, one that would never be seen again. The people had become one solid mass, like the body of a giant camel, all hugging and pressing against one another.

The astonished people of Harran approached imperceptibly, step by step, like sleepwalkers. They could not believe their eyes and ears. Had there ever been anything like this ship, this huge and magnificent? Where else in the world were there women like these, who resembled both milk and figs in their tanned whiteness? Was it possible that men could shamelessly walk around with women, with no fear of others? Were these their wives, or sweethearts, or something else?

The men of Harran stared, panting. Whenever they saw something particularly incredible they looked at each other and laughed, and looked back again yearningly. They clicked their teeth sharply and stamped their feet. The children raced ahead of them and arrived first to sit by the water, and some even dove into the water to swim toward the ship, but most of the people preferred to stay behind on the shore, where they could move around more easily. Even the women watched everything from afar, though none of them dared to come near.

This day gave Harran a birth date, recording when and how it was built, for most people have no memory of Harran before that day. Even its own natives, who had lived there since the arrival of the first frightening group of Americans and watched with terror the realignment of the town's shoreline and hills— the Harranis, born and bred there, saddened by the destruction of their houses, recalling the old sorrows of lost travelers and the dead—remembered the day the ship came better than any other day, with fear, awe and surprise. It was practically the only date they remembered.

The workers who marched down in groups to see everything with their own eyes were far more tormented and depressed than cheered by what they saw. For the first time, they were overcome by the agonizing feeling that they had made a bad mistake in coming here and must not stay long. Ibn Rashed did not seem interested at first, but he sent a couple of men to have a look at the "new calamity" and report back to him. He was busy planning for the men to resume building Harran, but even he could not stay away long. When the ship came in and its whistle blew twice and the men and women crowded its decks, waving and dancing amid the lights and the music, he started and said to Daham: "If your whole tribe loses its mind, what use is there in reasoning?" He laughed loudly. "No one I've sent over has come back or even sent word. Let's go and see for ourselves what's happening."

They started off slowly, but as the ship came into view and he saw more of the scene, something impelled Ibn Rashed to walk faster. He sat with the workers on the beach and saw the women and heard their laughter. After one of the men let out a loud groan, there was silence.

"Brothers—this is the court of King Solomon you've heard about!" shouted Ibn Rashed giddily.

They laughed and began to talk and comment on what they saw, and even some of the boys made rude remarks and were not rebuked by their elders.

Arab Harran was silent, and the men sitting on the beach were rapt in their longing surveillance, but the festivities on the ship and in American Harran grew noisier. The Arab workers had not noticed that the first Americans to arrive had brought musical instruments with them, so they were astonished to see the drums and trumpets and other instruments now piled on the American beach. After the ship emptied and its music stopped, the music from the beach grew louder, especially the sounds of the big drums, which set the beat for the singing and dancing of the partygoers, creating a new atmosphere.

"The American sons of bitches!" said one man angrily. "They don't even mind if we watch—we're no better than animals to them."

"They eat like sheikhs, Mubarak," Hajem told him. "And why shouldn't they do just as they please in their own colony?"

Most of the men had something to say, but the blaring music and dancing and the bizarre scenes that followed prevented them from speaking; others were immersed in contemplating this impossible dream. At first they pointed in fear or shame at some of the goings-on. They nudged each other to look at some new scene, but as the party spread and grew wilder and the naked or seemingly naked men and women appeared on the ship and in the small boats striking dramatic poses—the men stroked the women and then attacked suddenly for hugs and kisses, and carried the women around on their backs, and made them sit on their laps—the Arabs shouted and pointed more boisterously. The climax was when the last boat came ashore with one man and seven women. The women were reclining around the bushy-bearded, hairy-chested man, who fondled, smacked and leaned over them one by one and put his arms around two at a time. He shrieked with laughter and jumped up, rocking the boat in time with the drumbeat, and helped one woman stand up with him. They danced three or four turns to the drums, which grew louder as they neared the beach; then the man jumped into the water and pushed the boat in, singing.

"The jinns of Eden, underneath which rivers flow," said Abdullah al-Zamel, "with lads and maidens there to serve."

"By God, it's just what Abu Muhammad said," replied Hammad al-Zaban. "Solomon and a thousand Queens of Sheba. 'Die in your lust, you poor bastards, you Arabs!'"

No one could believe his eyes: it was indescribable. Words failed them; it could not be happening. Even the boys and small children, constantly laughing and making remarks in their high voices, eventually fell silent, utterly spellbound by what they saw. The men changed their positions and craned their necks to look, more fascinated than the children, at the procession of celebrants entering American Harran. The men were mostly quiet now and slightly dizzy, feeling sharp pains throbbing in certain parts of their bodies. Some cried out, and most of them wished that they had never come to see what was transpiring before them.

The gates of American Harran swung shut behind the ship's passengers, and Juma, the black man, stood by the gates with an elephant-tail whip in his hand, like the king of Death. The voices and din intermingled and grew fainter but never faded away completely. Music and singing could be heard from scattered places all night long. When for a moment it died away, the men squatting on the beach expected something to happen, for whenever there was silence and the minutes passed slowly, violent screams of laughter burst out suddenly, followed by music louder yet than before, and because of this game their waiting was sweet and cruel at the same time.

None of the men felt the cold that filled the night, and none of them felt like talking. The ship had arrived and the Americans had filed into their compound hours ago, but time passed tonight in a way it never had before. Although the people of Harran usually went to bed early, except for a few workers who stayed up to play cards, tonight none of them felt the time passing or wanted to leave the beach. The children, fascinated by what they had seen, could not stay still. They chased each other and called out words their parents never imagined they knew! Some of them ran back to the tents, perhaps to tell the women exactly what they had seen, for it turned out that the women who had kept far off when the ship landed and disgorged the Americans knew everything that had gone on, as if they'd seen it all themselves. They even knew all about the Billy Goat, as they had named the bearded man who came ashore in the last boat, and could describe in the greatest detail how he danced, how many women were with him and how he had jumped into the water. They told the story with shame at first, then with more spirit. They reminded the children to have their fathers come home for supper, but they must have done so unclearly or not very insistently, because in their excitement the children forgot to relay the message.

Had it been a summer night, a night with a moon filling the sky or a night that saw the triumphant return of long-absent travelers, this long evening in Harran would have been one endless succession of stories about the old days and far-off places interrupted by peals of delighted laughter and persistent questions about other travelers and foreign lands, about rain and vegetation; but tonight the men were silent except for anxious questions with no answers. They were overcome by endless worries and uncertainties.

Every one of them had much to say, and even the habitually quiet men may have wanted to speak. Some of them sang, as if to deny that their hearts were as leaden as they seemed, but depression overcame all their senses and paralyzed their power of speech. A feeling of bitterness spread from their dry throats to their stiff joints, and silence reigned completely: even Ibn Zamel, who had been active and talkative, strolling more than once to the gate to stand by the barbed wire and reporting back to the men whatever he heard, had now quieted down. He had not managed to find anything out, so he got up abruptly.

"Good night, my friends," he said weakly. He paused for a moment until they took notice, then said, "These American sons of bitches are nothing but trouble and bad news. We'll never see any good from them. They'll get the meat, and we'll get whatever bones they care to throw us."

He walked a few more steps, then turned and spoke again. "Leave them be—have nothing to do with them. God curse them and the day they came here."

Someone had to do something, because the mood of wariness born of silence and expectation that now enveloped everyone, and the departure to shadowy places near and far, and the phantasm that suddenly blazed up permitted no one to think or act. Ibn Zamel, who had dodged like a hungry wolf from one spot to another and urged the boys to jump over the barbed wire on the eastern side to have a look and report to the others in spite of his own failed attempts, now instinctively knew that their stay here would only mean more pain and problems for them all. When he made up his mind to go and had said his piece, they began to move around, to curse and sigh.

Ibn Rashed stood up and cleared his throat. "Like you said, Ibn Zamel. We have enough to worry about."

"Happy days are short," said one of the men from Harran.

"And nights shorter yet," said Ibn Zamel, now some distance away.

"Say what you want, but I'm afraid we've lost our world and our faith," said one of the men from the darkness. "We'll never touch the meat they have—we'll be lucky to get gravy!"

They all laughed because they knew what he meant. The Harrani—whose pride was inflamed by what he had seen, well traveled enough to know how people lived in lands far distant from this desolate, unknown part of the world—did not want to come back like this. As the laughter died down, he said, "You'll know by the end of this night."

No one in American Harran slept that night. The American singing and shouting never let up, and some of the men later said that the singing was louder at sunup than it had been the evening before. Others said that the ship's whistle let out a loud blast at sunrise, which only provoked louder singing.

Nor did Arab Harran sleep. After the men went home, the boys stayed out to wander along the beach in front of the ship and near the barbed wire. When they got tired of that, they moved closer to the tents to sing, shout and tell obscene jokes. Hammad al-Zaban shouted at the boys and dogs to be quiet— "There are people trying to sleep!"—but they paid no attention.

The men who headed home felt hungry but had no appetite for food. Abdullah al-Zamel told them that his father had always quoted a saying of the Prophet that said fasting was the only way to conquer sin and temptation and suggested that they go to bed without supper. Some men thought this a good idea, and others just did not have the energy, at this late hour, to prepare food, so they decided to have only tea. They sat in the clearing between the tents and sipped at the small glasses in silence.

They were no less bitter there than they had been on the beach, and the stories they tried to tell trailed off as the desert rang with the sound of loud music and shrill laughter. It happened again and again. Even Hajem's and Hammad's ribald jokes, which at any other time would have raised loud laughter, were met with wan, forced smiles.

It was the same in the homes of Harran, where some men had light meals and went straight to bed, though it took them a long time to fall asleep.

Sorrow, desires, fears and phantoms reigned that night. Every man's head was a hurricane of images, for each knew that a new era had begun. Harran had been a desolate, forgotten village, which received only the kind of visitors who came to sell or barter goods and then promptly rode away—and then only rarely. The only exceptions were the foreigners who came to bring news, presents and money from Harran's own traveling sons.

It would have seemed unthinkable for Harran ever to change as it now had, this quickly, for ships to bring such immense numbers of people, for its eastern quarter to be covered with buildings. This was unimaginable. The people had got used to the new buildings and even to the new faces, but nothing had prepared them for the arrival of this last ship. Ibn Rashed had called it the ship of King Solomon, because the women it brought resembled the Queen of Sheba, or were even more beautiful. No one in Harran had the powers to describe to others what he had seen.

What new era had begun—what could they expect of the future? For how long could the men stand it? This night had passed, but what about the nights to come?

No one asked these questions aloud, but they obsessed everyone and visited the uneasy sleep of men in the form of phantoms; their repressed desires swarmed over them as the night wore on. Those men who went to bed wide awake, whose sleep came to them in uneasy fits, woke in vivid terror only to be filled with desire and warmth, fear and expectation.

32

···

THE ARRIVAL OF KING SOLOMON'S SHIP—OR SA-
tan's ship, as Ibn Naffeh called it—which sailed
off after sundown the following day, was not
the only thing that prevented the Arabs from resuming work
on the new city. Ibn Rashed, who thought more than once of
asking the men to return to work, held back and finally put it
off, because the frame of mind the men were in made discussion
impossible. Whoever didn't complain about the previous night
pleaded sickness or exhaustion, and the more honest or daring
among them did not hesitate to say that they had simply wanted
to stay at the beach to gawk at the American sluts! In Harran
those who knew where the stone quarry was and had the proper
tools for stonecutting considered their Friday prayers excuse
enough not to comply with any requests. So Ibn Rashed preferred to close the subject, especially after noticing, the next

morning and afternoon, the clearly fragile state of the men's nerves. They were pale and excitable, and though they were still mostly quiet, Ibn Rashed told himself somewhat resignedly, "Men are men. The workers left their families long ago and have been patient since then, and the sights they saw yesterday must have turned them into animals. I'll wait until they cool off."

Most of the men usually said their Friday prayers in the mosque, the only building that had not been changed; Ibn Rashed had asked the Americans, through the translator, to leave it alone after the earthmovers had flattened the ground. They seemed deeply ashamed this morning, torn by doubts, sins and suffering. The ones who had to go to the sea to wash themselves were embarrassed, because the partygoers had been spread all over the beach since early morning. Some of the men watched the ship and others walked nervously, over a long circuit, though if they strayed too far they hurried back, afraid of missing something; still others were so sunk in their own thoughts that they noticed nothing.

"Don't worry about it now, Ibn Muzil," said Ibn Rashed when Daham asked him if the time was right to order the men back to work. "The Arabs' minds are not right just now."

When Daham made a face, Ibn Rashed laughed.

"Ibn Muzil, you know that there's a time for praying and a time for singing." He paused a moment and looked Daham in the face without seeing him. "Yesterday the fellows sang their hearts out."

Daham understood and pressed him no more.

Harran may not have slept well the previous night, but it had not been still for a single moment since dawn. People were everywhere. Even the women, so reticent yesterday, were struck with sudden daring: they wandered closer to the beach to see everything for themselves. The young men who had slept late this morning jumped out of bed when they saw the rising sun and raced like scared birds to the beach to see what had happened in the last few hours. The men, who were so deeply affected and disturbed by the events of the night, whose heads were so confused and desires so aroused by them, hesitated to go directly to the beach, but they soon found sufficient pretexts for going and set off.

The whole population of Harran was on the beach—all except for the very old and infirm and the very religious, who stayed in the mosque. They did not gather all in one spot as they had the night before, but they were all there, for it was easy enough to be in one place without any invitation or excuse, to see everything for themselves. Ibn Rashed and Daham were busy, deep in thoughtful conversation, when they heard the sound of distant voices, and when the ship's whistle blew Ibn Rashed looked attentive and stood up.

"So they're leaving," he said to Daham.

They both started over to the shore, slowly, just as they had the day before, even though something inside them urged more speed. When they arrived the ship was still in its place, like a white mountain, and sailors were moving back and forth polishing the steel.

"Hah. So they're still here," Ibn Rashed said to Ibn Zamel and several others. "Do you think the party is over, or not yet?"

"The sons of bitches' party is never over. They party all the time, day and night. We've had as much as we can take."

"As our friend said yesterday, happy days are short."

"All our days are short, Abu Muhammad, and you know it."

"You seem full of trouble."

"Who wouldn't be, after what we saw last night?"

Ibn Zamel paused, sighed, smiled sadly and went on as if talking to himself. "The men's balls are ready to burst after what they've seen, Abu Muhammad. These women might as well be nymphs of paradise. Their thighs are like fire. Bring us some manacles. Get us some rope to tie up the men, Abu Muhammad; we'll need it after today." Ibn Rashed and Daham laughed loudly, as if they'd had the same thought but didn't dare say so out loud.

"To think they aren't even wearing jewels," said Ibn Rashed, trying to provoke Ibn Zamel into saying more. "These women are like sheep—white and soft and naked, and nothing else."

"Abu Muhammad, my friend, give me a sheep and you can keep your paradise."

"Sheep don't grow on trees, Ibn Zamel. If they did, our troubles would be over."

"If I got one, it wouldn't be to teach her to say, 'There is no god but God,' " said Daham between his teeth.

When noon came only a few men went to the mosque to pray—fewer than had ever gone before—and those who stayed away had their reasons! When the ship sailed away at sundown, its departure marked by events that could not be described, that none of them would ever forget, most of the men went to bed early. But before going to sleep they traveled far, traveled to horizons they had never known before, and their dreams were full of women, bejeweled white women with firm bodies, and slave girls whose appetites knew no bounds. The men were strong and happy in their dreams, and the women happy and full of desire, and so it was until daybreak, when the men woke to find their throats parched and their limbs stiff, crushed by an extraordinary weariness. When they remembered what had happened the night and day before, and the dreams that had filled their sleep, and looked around them now, they were filled with misery.

33

AMONG THE TENTS THE NEXT MORNING, THERE was an uncommon clamor of hurried movement, of cries and shouted questions, and when the workers came out to see what was happening they knew something was wrong. They learned, from barked questions and answers, and Daham's racing to and fro and his accusing looks, that three workers, two of them brothers, had fled the camp. The third was a distant relative. What made Ibn Rashed angry was that they had stolen four camels; this had been discovered only long after they had left. What proved that they had left in the first part of the night, as soon as the men went to their tents, was the discovery of their torn work clothes, scattered by the wind, at the beginning of the Ujra road. They had sent a message to the company and to Ibn Rashed personally by shitting in the caps, though one of the men, whose bowels had not obliged him, had filled his cap with camel droppings.

After much discussion and examination of the traces left behind, it was discovered that they had left Harran early, after choosing the best and fastest camels, so it was impractical to try to follow them; but Ibn Rashed refused to give up. He chose Daham and three others to accompany him, and they set off in pursuit.

The men were shocked and surprised, but the thought of the three who had left inspired admiration. The three, especially the two brothers, had enjoyed great respect; they'd never thought twice about lending a helping hand to anyone; they were handsome and friendly and universally well liked. One of them was a brilliant talker with a repertoire of memorized stories that he retold magically, and the men often sought him out and followed wherever he went in order to hear his stories and thoughts.

Now that they had left this way, the men recalled their behavior in the two or three days before they'd left, and though they could not remember all the details, they did remember that Muhaisen had played some practical jokes the day the ship arrived and also when it left; he had even been behind some of the children's practical jokes. Hazzah al-Majoul, Harran's nine-year-old orphan boy, had thrown a cat into a boat as the Americans left, creating a panic among the women. One of the Americans tried to throw the cat over the side of the boat, but it hid under the seats, and in the ensuing commotion, as the drums beat, they forgot about the cat and it rode with them to the ship. It later leaped from the deck and fell into the sea but did not drown, to the hilarity of everyone watching.

At Muhaisen's urging, Hazzah had pinched the buttocks of an American woman when she was clambering onto one of the smaller boats. Juma the gatekeeper grabbed him by the ear and squeezed it until Hazzah felt it had been torn off, and he screamed and cursed all the Americans. When he got away he shouted obscenities at the top of his lungs and threw rocks.

Hazzah and other boys gathered stones to pelt the Americans and their boats, and ignored Hammad al-Zaban's shouts to stop it at once, so Hammad ran after Hazzah and almost caught him but then stumbled and fell down and everyone laughed. This episode was remembered for a long time, and Hammad claimed not to recall it even though the fall had broken the little finger on his left hand, which was bandaged for three weeks afterward.

Muhaisen was behind all this. At the time everyone had thought of them only as spontaneous jokes, but now they saw them as something different, especially after his insult to the company and Ibn Rashed. His escape and that of the two brothers had a special meaning, though no one had noticed anything strange and though they had not said a word to anyone, and it appeared premeditated to everyone; surely the three had been planning it for a long time. All the men hoped that they would cover their tracks so that Ibn Rashed would never find them; if he caught up with them there would be a battle. Ibn Rashed was proud of his British rifle, which he constantly shifted from his shoulder to his camel's back, to show it off, on the ride from Ujra to Harran. He had used it twice, once after asking a man to set up a target at the outset of the journey as they had left Ujra. The second time he had drawn it in irritation and taken aim at a fox but missed; the fox had disappeared immediately. Both times he had used it to scare the men and teach them a lesson. Now the three men surely knew that he would try to use it again to assert his authority, especially since they would never surrender or come back to work.

The men remembered their faces clearly and felt that tragedy was in store for everyone; they knew that the arrival of Satan's ship, and the temptations it had brought, marked the beginning of an era of hard times, otherwise why had those three fled? Had they been forced to steal camels and expose themselves to dangers the others could only imagine? Ibn Rashed had said, when he took their camels after buying them, that he was ready to return any camel to its owner if the owner wanted, so why had the three men put their lives in danger by stealing? And their flight— why had they bothered to flee? All they would have had to do was pack their belongings and tell Ibn Rashed that they did not want to stay. Try as he might, Ibn Rashed could not force anyone to stay or work against his will. He had been very flexible when he left on the trip to Ujra; he had told them to take it easy until he came back and said that things would change when he re- turned. True, he had not kept his promise and had been back for quite a while, but things would surely change, as he had said they would.

These were the thoughts and questions that filled the men's heads, but there was one real, unanimous conviction on the part of the men: the ship, the women on the ship, were the sole cause for the three men's flight. They just could not stand it any longer, and had chosen that solution, having no prospect of any other.

When the men went to the other camp, American Harran, they saw everything differently. They wanted to find some trace of that night and the day that had followed it. What had the Americans done, and how were they now that they had acted out their pent-up desires? The accursed ship, and the women it had brought—had they all left, or had some of them stayed behind?

The Americans appeared much more cheerful and energetic this morning; they smiled and behaved as never before, but when they asked for the other workers and could not find them they were surprised. Naim came to explain and interpret, but he looked half-asleep and his eyes were bloodshot. His exhaustion was apparent, and his lips hardly moved when he asked for

Daham and Ibn Rashed. The workers gave him vague answers.

"These bedouin don't understand any language but a beating," shouted Naim. After conferring with the Americans—no one knew what they were saying—he turned to the workers again and shouted angrily. "We thought you were human beings, and we thought you knew that work was work, but that wasn't your mistake. We made the mistake by trying to trust people like you!"

The workers said nothing.

"Where's this shit Ibn Rashed, and the shit Daham?" Naim asked sharply. "Where are they?"

The workers said nothing, possibly because they did not know what to say, or possibly out of protest at his language and manner toward them, and he changed his tone. "Fine, fine . . . if they show up we'll settle it then."

He muttered a few words no one understood, then divided the men up into different groups and sent them to work. They were seething with a rage that bordered on despair, for while they saw themselves as guiltless, they regarded Ibn Rashed and Nusayis, as they now called Naim, with hatred and contempt—and their self-hatred increased, for they had chosen to come here. They were possessed by an urge to leave, to destroy things and to kill Ibn Rashed, who had embroiled them in this predicament in the first place.

Ibn Rashed returned unsuccessful at sundown the next day. Muhaisen and the two brothers were continuing their journey, no one knew where.

34

IBN RASHED CAME BACK A DIFFERENT MAN; HE EVEN looked different. His happiness was gone, and his talkativeness and willingness to listen of two days before were replaced by scowls and silence. He got angry at the slightest thing, was easily provoked to shout and even curse, and grew suspicious of everyone. He kept his eye on everything and asked about the smallest details, but when they told him what Naim had said, quoting the very words, he nodded and said nothing. The men expected him to get angry, to threaten and curse, but he heard it all in silence. Most said that his fury at failing to find the men and bring them back, or even to recover the camels, would be unleashed on Nusayis. He would return every curse with a viler one, put an end to that effeminate dwarf's meddling and see that the men were treated with more respect.

As the men were preparing to go to work the next day, Daham

seemed irritable and fearful. He did not stand up straight and his gaze wandered; he seemed confused. The work clothes he wore every day looked funnier on him than ever before, as if he was wearing them for the first time, and when it was time to go to the site he ran over to Ibn Rashed and talked with him, and from their speech it was clear that they were both uneasy and afraid.

All the men were waiting for Daham and Naim to meet; they would stand facing each other like roosters: one would speak, then the other, then they would start pounding each other, and everyone in the camp would see; everyone would stand breathless as Daham grabbed Naim's neck and threw him to the ground; if the other workers did not take part in the fight, they would at least form a human barrier to protect Daham from any Americans who tried to help Naim; they would stay by Daham and give him encouragement. What would the Americans do? What would they think? Oh, if only one of them would get into the fight! They would soon learn that these Arabs they ridiculed were stronger and tougher than their slim bodies seemed to indicate. They would turn the camp upside-down. This was a chance to settle things once and for all, to make themselves understood. It would not be easy; if the Americans tried to fetch their weapons, that would be that. Perhaps it would be best not to take sides, for Nusayis would have to pay the price for what he had said yesterday, and the time of reckoning had come if he was man enough for it.

These thoughts and images filled the men's minds as they walked to the compound, and they wanted to talk to Daham and shake his hand to encourage him, but for the first time he was walking at the tail end of the group. This and his apprehensive silence made the men hold back.

Daham saw Naim from afar, standing near the mess hall and talking to an American; as soon as the workmen entered American Harran, he headed directly for him. He ran clumsily and almost fell down. When Daham came near and tried to talk to him, Naim motioned him to be quiet and wait, and so like a child he waited two or three steps away. Naim kept conversing with the American until they suddenly burst out laughing and the American slapped him on the shoulder then walked away waving. Naim turned to Daham and they exchanged a few words. Naim nodded and moved nearer to him, and after talking a short while longer he walked off in the direction of Administration.

What did Daham say? Why was Naim calm after yesterday's threats? Had he heard about the men who deserted, and how Daham and Ibn Rashed gave chase, though they came back empty-handed? Did Naim consider the men's taking the camels a serious theft?

Naim must have heard some important news; the men gathered that from his frequent nods and the fact that he went to Administration. Most mornings he supervised the counting of the men and divided them up into work groups, with his usual scowl of contempt and mistrust. But he did not do so now, even though all the men were present except for the three who had left, and their absence should have required a recount. These facts, plus Daham's face, which had changed in these few minutes, made the men surer than ever that something was seriously wrong. When Naim stepped out of Administration and signaled for Daham to follow him, the men were positive that things were much worse than they had first imagined.

Ibn Rashed showed up at the compound shortly before noon. He could have come earlier but chose noon because the men had been at work all morning and the lunch hour was a much more congenial time in which to explain everything to Naim. And his anger had ebbed considerably too.

Daham used gestures more than words to explain everything to Ibn Rashed; it was clear that what he told him was important, because Ibn Rashed nodded many times to show he understood and took it seriously. When the two men met—for Naim showed up suddenly—Ibn Rashed spread open his hands and welcomed Naim loudly in a warm and friendly voice as if they had not met in a long time. The men, who saw what was going on and heard what he said, smiled and looked at each other disgustedly when they recalled Naim's words of the day before.

Immediately after lunch the workers were photographed, much to their surprise and suspicion, and they talked about it for a long time afterward. They were even more afraid when their fingerprints were taken, and though they submitted to the process with an air of resignation, they could think of no satisfactory reason for it. They told the people of Harran about it and discussed it with the more recent arrivals, but no one could come up with a clear or reassuring explanation, and two or more of the workers talked of leaving the company and going back to Ujra, because "Satan's work has begun, and once started it never stops." Daham tried, through persuasion and sarcasm, and the occasional threat, to make them stay; he hinted that leaving the company now would reflect badly on him. They all agreed to stay for the time being, but their fears and doubts were still very real, and for this they all blamed Ibn Rashed. He had acted in a way that would harm all of them, had become a different, underhanded person and put up a wall between himself and the rest of them.

"I told you, 'Let's stay in our own village,' " Hajem said to his brother before they went to sleep that night. "You said, 'No, let's go,' and we went and here we are. Now look. If you think today was bad, who knows what might happen tomorrow."

"Go to sleep," said Mizban, pulling a blanket over his head. "Go to sleep, and maybe you'll have a dream about an American girl."

"The American girls have all left, and now it's the Americans' turn. If you weren't as ugly as a horse, they'd grab you and fuck your ass."

Fawaz laughed. "My friends, I think today was better than tomorrow, and tomorrow will be better than the day after."

"Ibn Rashed is just what Nusayis said he is: shit," said Hajem bitterly. He paused, then added, "That Nusayis is a bastard. He knows people. You saw Ibn Rashed today."

"Be patient," said Suweyleh. "Patience is all."

It took the men a long time to fall asleep, and when they finally slipped into deep sleep they saw many things, but none of them dared to tell the others what he saw.

35

THE WEEK AFTER SATAN'S SHIP ARRIVED AND THE three men fled, construction began on Arab Harran. After the confused and fearful anger that had possessed the men, and the events that had followed their refusal to eat the food Ibn Rashed gave them, especially since the presence of the men who had been brought to sell bread, meat and other necessities created an atmosphere of provocation, an agreement was reached; the people of Harran would do the stonecutting during the week, Ibn Rashed's camels would transport the stone and construction was to be completed by Thursday afternoon or Friday, even if the Harranis did not join in. And so this is what happened.

The first shops in Arab Harran were built from the remnants of the big wooden crates, sheets of zinc and rough stones collected at the last minute. The roofs were a mixture of zinc, junk from the storehouses, cartons and what branches were left over after the demolition of the orchards that had once set Harran apart from other towns. The shops were built hurriedly, and all the workers took part in the building because they wanted a bakery and butcher's shop from which they might buy meat directly, so that they could cook their own food, and though they did not say so to anyone else, they also longed to build something of their own, after building the American city from the eastern hills to the sea.

The workers finished their task on Friday afternoon, and Ibn Rashed ordered two sheep slaughtered to celebrate. Abu Shayeh slaughtered them, and while doing so he gobbled up a large piece of one of the livers. He carefully excised the fatty posterior and offered it to the others after tasting it himself. When he had finished preparing the two sheep, he turned triumphantly to Abu Kamel and said, "This is Arab-style slaughter. Tomorrow let's see how the city people do it!" Ibn Rashed, who was busy socializing here and there, his robe drawn up and tucked into his drawers so that he could walk more easily, was giving everyone construction advice, telling them how and where to place the stones. He inspected the wooden planks himself to see that they were sound, and when he was content that everything was in order, he stepped back for one last appraising glance. Looking satisfied, he slapped the dust from his hands and readjusted his robe.

"Thanks be to God!" he told the men around him.

When the meal was finished, the men discussed methods of building houses over their glasses of tea and coffee and described the cities they had seen. Muflih had been to Egypt and seen buildings so tall that even jinn could not get to the top of them. He said that the Egyptians were the best builders in the world; he had never seen anything like their buildings in any other country he had visited. Ibn Rashed—who, unusually for him, was in high spirits—was very talkative and gave advice to the men who would work in the shops: how to care for them, and to keep him informed of everything. He promised to help them out in every way he could, and when he stood to signal them that the celebration was over, he told the men to go to bed early so that they would wake up refreshed.

"One year from now, the people of Harran won't recognize their own city!"

....

36

ABDU MUHAMMAD, HARRAN'S EXPERT BAKER, sang as he slid loaves into the stone oven, and sang louder as he drew them out. In addition to baking bread, he prepared grilled meat and pastries and cooked other dishes that he invented himself with whatever scraps were left over. He loved life and singing, and rumor had it that he was fond of "the stuff." After working hours he was a different man: when people saw him in his immaculate street clothes, looking like a barber, they could hardly believe this was the same man who wore a blue loincloth over his middle from dawn until evening in the sweltering bakery. His brief and at times sharp conversation at work was replaced at sundown or early evening by chatty eloquence, songs and jokes; but not for long. His excuse was always ready: "Dawn waits for no man!" They said he went home early to indulge in his passion, because his eyes were always bloodshot. Despite his gentle behavior and loyalty to his friends, he could be irritable. One word was sometimes enough to change his world and turn him into a different man. Abdullah al-Abyad, the owner of Harran's second bakery, opened seven months after Abdu's, said that Abdu had killed two people; it had happened in Tihama or Sumatra, and that was why he had not gone home to visit his family for years. When they asked Abdu when he would go back to his own country to see his family he evaded the question, and so their doubts grew; but his relations with the people did not change.

When Ibn Rashed opened the bakery, Abdu was only an employee, and so he remained for the first year, but as Ibn Rashed conceived more and grander projects he was advised to form partnerships with others, for "the more working people there are, the greater the profits." Ibn Rashed thought this advice sound, particularly since "Daham doesn't know how to keep books, and Ibn Hathal is too young and will mess things up. Men are only human: they forget, and they mix things up, because the mind is not a ledger." So Abdu Muhammad became a one-third partner.

From his first day on the job Abdu adorned the bakery with pictures he had torn out of the foreign magazines other workers brought from American Harran. He selected them carefully, chose the right spots to display them in and used flour paste to stick them up.

Most of the people who saw his pictures were shocked: they stared at them and commented on each one. The townspeople of Harran, especially some of the religious ones, objected, because the children, some of them young girls, often went to get bread from the bakery, and the pictures might corrupt them. Ibn Rashed asked Abdu to be content with "pictures of horses, castles and suchlike modest scenes," and for a while Abdu complied, but only formally and craftily, by hanging new pictures over the ones people objected to, and then only high up, so that by blowing hard or waving one hand he could make the front picture float up and reveal what was underneath. The diabolical idea came to him because he had just come upon a magazine of nearly naked women to arrange and stick up. He slowly but excitedly raised the front picture, which revealed bare legs, and mumbled and moaned at each small, slow revelation. He did this whenever he was alone, but as time passed he grew careless and let some of the people he knew and trusted look at the pictures. This he did after carefully closing the bakery door and checking to see that no one was looking.

Abdu subsequently elaborated on this process by placing pictures of men and women together in such a way as to suggest obvious activities, and this obsessed him; but not satisfied, he touched up some of the pictures with a piece of charcoal and assigned names both to the women and to some of the positions. Finally he cut up some of the pictures, juxtaposing them to suit his fancy, and was delighted with the results.

Every day brought more work, and more people came in. The Harranis began to build a neighborhood of their own as far as possible to the west, near the hills. The original three shops doubled in size and expanded every month, and the old road to Ujra, which had nearly disappeared in places, was now so broad and passable that one or two caravans came through on it every week. No one knew whether to consider Ibn Rashed a resident or a visitor, because he was always traveling but never told anyone what he was doing. He reappeared after every absence with a new group of men, all so different that no one could guess where they had come from or what they would do here. In addition to men who would work in the company were others who spent their time surveying the land from the sea to the hills, measuring the distance from one place to another with their feet or with ropes, placing stones here and there to mark out the places. Having done that they thought a long while and sometimes measured it all out again. The people of Harran were relieved when these mysterious, closemouthed characters finally left—their behavior smacked of witchcraft. But a month or two later they were back creating havoc, and within a short time there was a profusion of new shops: a restaurant, a warehouse, a shop for cloth, rope and other merchandise, and an office for Ibn Rashed and his new workers, where he received businessmen and job applicants and paid out salaries.

Abdu, who found time to sing and joke with his friends at work and finished with his doughs and batters early, had more and more mouths to feed, so instead of the one large sack of meal that had once sufficed for all Harran, the amount required multiplied week after week. As to the preserved meats and pies he had become proficient in making, he complained that he couldn't even start on them until he had prepared the last of the dough and taken the last loaves from the oven. His relations with Abu Kamel, the butcher, which had been friendly at first, had turned cool and tense: behind the many requests he had from people to prepare meat and vegetable lunches or meat dumplings in the bakery was Abu Kamel's wish to get rid of the last of his meat and take the rest of the day off.

At first people accepted Abdu's firm refusal, but they knew his weak points and asked about "the love animal," "the sword rider" and "the blonde." They began to blow, and the thighs flew, and the buttocks billowed, and as Abdu felt his mind wandering and his resistance weakening, and they repeated some story or joke, he became more willing to talk and listen, so he retreated bit by bit, and after his categorical refusal the favor was granted "not now, but in an hour or two, after I finish up with this dough." When he met with persistent nagging and privately decided to give in, he finally spoke up sharply. "I know, you're all thinking that Abdu is like a bridegroom's donkey: he has a strong back, he can take it. But one of these days I'll get enough of this, and then God help you all!"

In the sincerest voices they could manage, they told him that he was the greatest man in Harran and the most generous, and that was why they loved him and craved any cooking that came from his hands; an hour with him was like a visit to paradise: the rivers and streams and mountains and his virgins of paradise were what made life bearable in Harran. Their rough hands reached out for the pictures to turn them over, and when he saw their playfulness and lack of comprehension in turning over the pictures he shouted, "Fire! Fire!"

When they looked at him in fright he said sarcastically: "You jackasses, you and him. Treat him with some respect, some manners and grace. Otherwise forget it." He stopped a moment to look at them and shook his head. "Like you're hitching up a camel or cutting stone. Put your faith in God. Say 'Thank You, Lord God, we worship You alone because You gave us such goodness. You are beautiful and love beauty.'"

Sometimes he responded to their flattery and quoted poetry or sang, which calmed him down, and sometimes he ignored them.

This was Abdu Muhammad, and so he was for a long time.

Harran was hot and suffocating to its longtime residents, but it was far worse for the later settlers; it filled their chests with a strangling oppression from the very time of their arrival there, unless they came in winter, and it got worse every day, aggravating their weariness and distress and sometimes the restlessness that could turn to violence.

Abdu worked and slept in the bakery despite the blazing heat of the oven in summer and winter, all day and much of the night. No one else could have stood it, especially when the cool winds ceased and the air grew heavy over Harran, but he passed most of his time there, even when he was not working or sleep-

ing. People explained this by saying that Abdu was using narcotics all the time and did not want anyone to see him or know
what he was doing. He always locked up carefully and never
responded to the knocking of late shoppers who wanted bread.
When his friends, or those who considered themselves his friends,
came and knocked for a very long time his voice sounded from
within as if from the depths of a deep well. "We're closed. The
door is locked."

If they kept knocking even after that or asked him to open
up, he came near the door to shout: "Keep faith in God, ye
faithful! Leave people to their cares and miseries. Leave us alone."

This kept happening, and Abdu's responses and firm stand
did not change, so many people were even more positive that
he was using narcotics, but no one said so out loud or with any
intention of hurting or slandering him, because they liked him;
they knew they could not live without him. He had become a
regular feature of the new life in Harran.

"There's no sense in foolish talk like that," still others said.
"Abdu worships those pictures, he turns them over and looks
at them and finds one to doze over, and falls asleep."

No one knew precisely why Abdu was like that. When he
was asked he gave answers they did not understand.

"I have to find out who the scratcher is, who bangs at my
door and doesn't let me sleep . . ." He looked accusingly at
whoever asked him, as if that person had been the one to knock
at his door the night before, but no one confessed, so he shook
his head. "Maybe someone gave him a few coins and told him
to go disturb someone and wake him up!"

Then slowly, almost to himself: "Whoever the sons of bitches
are, they'll be found out. Dig a hole for your brother and you'll
fall into it yourself."

They agreed with him to calm him down and changed the
subject by asking to see his latest pictures, and how he had

arranged them and about the names he had given the new beau-
ties. Sometimes this worked, but most of the time it didn't. To
cut off questions he did not want to answer he said sarcastically,
"Leave the Devil alone" and looking in their faces asked, "Don't
you have work to do? Hmm? . . . Say something!"

Without waiting for an answer, he laughed. "Like they say:
People who have nothing to do play with their balls." After
relaxing and clearing his throat, he wandered far away with his
many confused thoughts and memories and said, as if addressing
invisible persons: "Listen . . . let people work. In an hour you'll
all be hungry. 'Abdu, where's the bread!' "

But when he was in a good mood it was because of new
pictures. When he saw an opportunity he pulled a new sheaf of
pictures from his hiding place. "Look, by the Prophet . . . look!
Hair like a horse's mane, a radiant forehead, a gazelle's eyes and
a perfect mouth, no, better than perfect, pink cheeks—an apple,
by the Prophet! Swelling breasts. Hail, Lord Elijah, a thousand
greetings to you, Prophet Jonah, who was in the belly of the
whale. The belly, the belly, look! Oh!" And he paused and
looked at those around him, looked without seeing them, and
when his ecstasy passed he looked at the picture again and said,
"If you pressed her waist hard it would snap," and he beat his
stomach where he rolled the dough and answered himself: "You'd
choke, you'd lose your breath before it happened. You'd die
before doing the filthy thing . . ."

When they asked him to go on describing the picture, to go
deeper and lower, he looked sad and said, "At the waist, Sche-
herazade perceived the coming of dawn and spoke no more."

On rare occasions, with a few very close friends, he would
go on to say intensely beautiful and tender things and breathe
hot sighs, hotter than the air from his oven. The men dreamed,
and when they finished they felt sharp pains in several parts of
their bodies, and weariness as well.

So it was for long months. Harran grew and more people poured in. Abdullah al-Abyad opened a new bakery with Dabbasi. The competition between the two bakeries intensified, and with it came rumors and slanders, but Abdu did not care what people said. He heard and forgot. The war between Ibn Rashed and Dabassi heated up, and the bakery was only one of the reasons, and perhaps one of the least important ones. Harran sank in the heat, humidity and flood of new faces and surprises. Abdu was pleasant one day and irritable the next. People were used to him and learned how to deal with him more nicely. Baking bread was his only responsibility now; he no longer had to deal with making meals, for several different kinds of restaurants had opened in Harran: some small, with limited menus, for the workers, and others large and more expensive. And the shops sold canned goods, fruits, vegetables and sweets.

In the beginning Abdu had been on everyone's mind, with everybody keeping track of him and his pictures, but now they all occupied themselves with their own business, hardly remembering Abdu except when they saw him or went in to buy bread. In those few minutes—if the atmosphere seemed right—they asked the same questions: "Any new pictures? When will we see them?" Abdu, absorbed in his work, usually did not reply, for he knew when to show his pictures and when to hide them, and most important he knew who to show them to.

In the daily routine of ever increasing and ever more complicated affairs, people turned in on themselves. In spite of the crowds and the endless influx of new people, each man became a world unto himself. Dealings between people from different and perhaps mutually hostile places were wary and full of apprehensions. In the rush of everyday life few felt the changes taking place around them, for they happened slowly, one by one, but had they come to pass all at once it would have been a shock.

Abdu went on with his work in the bakery, and few of the customers noticed the changes drawn on his face as they took bread from his hand. His eyes had changed, and his body, and his behavior. His pale, almost emaciated face, his sunken eyes and his trembling hands, which grew shakier with every passing day, and his almost dazed silences, were the gradual changes which no one noticed all at once and which he himself barely understood. True, his shaky hands bothered him, especially when he was with other people, but he ascribed them to tiredness and overwork. The clothes he wore in the afternoon and evening, once always clean and neat, were somewhat less so.

Later, perhaps due to a mistake on his own part, or a trap laid for him by the others, the enigma that had been so mysterious early on began to clear up: after long hesitation he confessed to a few trusted friends that he was in love. He said nothing more. Who was she? How and where had he met her? No one knew a thing.

Day after day Abdu sank into passion and torment, into silence and seclusion. Those who had said from the beginning that he used narcotics, that he did nothing in his small retreat but cloud his head, were now surer than ever that they were right. The rumors started by Ibn Rashed and Dabbasi, and spread by Abdullah al-Abyad, went a long way to explain his isolation to many: he was afraid of revenge after the two murders he had committed; some of the victims' relatives might come to get him one way or another, so he took care to stay hidden most of the time.

Those who assumed that Abdu worshiped the pictures and was infatuated with them had nothing good to say about him; they took particular note of his shaky hands. They said that he was addicted to masturbation, that he did it several times each day and that it was ruining his health.

Abdu heard some but not all of the stories, but he was in

another world, engrossed in a problem few others knew existed. For a long time he was silent and patient, but he finally confessed, just as he had the first time, either by mistake or because of a trap set for him by others.

After much hesitation, in a moment of weakness, he took a picture from his pocket and showed it to the people with him, and confessed with a humility more like despair, in an almost tearful voice, "That's her."

The men expressed their surprise and disapproval and then began to make fun of him, and he spoke in a tremulous voice. "She was on the ship that came to Harran that day."

They understood that he meant Satan's ship that had docked so long ago, and when he saw that they knew which ship he meant he went on. "As soon as she landed she looked at me. She left all the rest of them and looked at me. She did not leave me!" He paused and then went on as if talking to himself. "She was smiling happily, she was laughing. The day the ship left she left the others and kept looking at me and smiling. Even when the ship was sailing away she kept waving and smiling."

The men listened but said nothing.

They all were touched with pity and concern to see him in such pain, and after a long silence he went on. "I found her picture in a magazine, and if someone comes along who can read and write, he'll read her address and write me a letter I can send to her. Then she'll come."

37

SOME UNEXPLAINED KINSHIP BETWEEN DABBASI and the townspeople of Harran made them call him "uncle." Even men of his age or a little older called him that as a mark of respect. He had come to Harran in the very early days, two or three weeks after the arrival of Satan's ship. Ibn Rashed said that the Harranis were idiots: "Whoever doesn't have a big shot to protect him has to look for one or go and buy one. They'll send a messenger to go and find them an ancestor or a tent peg, and he'll bring them a devil. He'll bring them a plow."

It was clear that the people were deeply worried by the waves upon waves of foreigners. They had seen the Americans, and the ship—the curse that had changed so many of their lives—and before that the tractors that had torn up the earth, smashed houses and filled in the sea. When Ibn Rashed began to recruit young men to send to American Harran, the townspeople were so afraid that they did not know what to do. They wanted to find some eminent, powerful man to protect them and confront the flood that came nearer every day. Then Dabbasi came.

No one knew what Dabbasi had been told or what had prompted him to move so quickly. He had lived in Ujra a long time, or more precisely had had a store in Ujra and spent much of the year there, for he traveled a great deal along the Sultan's Road. He had visited Harran long ago: the first time in his youth and the second time just five years ago. It may have been by force of his travels or the shop he had in Ujra, which gave him links to the people of Harran because of delivering letters, especially letters from their travelers and the money they sent, but he also sent two or three caravans to Harran each year to buy supplies. Because of blood kinship, or perhaps for other reasons, they regarded him as generous, but he was still difficult to deal with in buying and selling. Harran's residents and travelers alike were used to him. They entrusted their money to him and he arranged credit for them, and whenever one of them went to Ujra, the first person he asked about and visited was Dabbasi.

So the people of Harran were not surprised by Dabbasi's coming; in fact they were overjoyed. But Ibn Rashed did not like it; he thought it an ill omen. Only a few days after Dabbasi settled in Harran and began mixing with the people, the two men started a silent feud. Although they treated each other with outward friendliness and respect, it was clear to everyone that each of the two was preparing himself for the coming battle.

The Harranis who had chosen the western side of town, and begun to build their houses there, ignored most of what Ibn Rashed told them; they stalled and put off building. Some who had decided to sell their land now turned down any offer to buy. Even the land American Harran was built on was, they said, grazing land for their animals, and now that it had been taken from them they wanted compensation. They hinted vaguely that they had contacted the officials to find a solution before matters got much worse.

Dabbasi, who had spent a month or more in Harran and personally supervised the building of some of the houses in the west, went back to Ujra, to return, he said, as soon as possible. He promised to ask all the Harranis he met, or communicated with, to return to Harran as soon as possible. He told them to "hold fast to the land at any cost, for it is your only capital." So much for Ibn Rashed's efforts and the preliminary agreements he had reached with them in the new and complicated series of negotiations and stalling. Instead of giving in, Ibn Rashed initiated a new war by having some of his people inform the Harranis that "all the land belongs to the government; it is the government's privilege to take and give out land" and that "they couldn't eat or drink land, so they had better take what was being offered them now, because someday the land might be taken from them, and then they would be no better than refugees."

The Harranis listened to Dabbasi and nodded, and heard what Ibn Rashed had conveyed to them, and nodded, and were profoundly bewildered. They did not know whether to sell or not to sell. If they sold the land, would Ibn Rashed pay a fair price? Would anyone else buy if he did not? Who had the money to buy land no one had ever before thought worth buying or selling? Was it really theirs to do with it as they pleased without being punished by the government?

Ibn Rashed often went on long visits to American Harran, and sometimes he spent the whole evening or brought Americans back to his home to spend the evening there. Before going into his tent, his visitors walked along the beach as far as the western hills, looking closely into the Arabs' faces and not hesitating to talk to old and young alike. Some of them knew Arabic, but their pronunciation was ridiculous. Having finished their stroll, with all its little incidents which the townspeople regarded as being of the deepest significance, they headed for Ibn Rashed's tent, and he slaughtered an animal and gave them a banquet. When it was over he sent a messenger or two to the Harranis, offering to buy their land and to help them if they depended on him and trusted him, but his generous promises were accompanied by indirect threats.

Their confusion and fear mounted. What could they do? How long could they wait? Dabbasi had gone to Ujra and tarried there, and no one even knew if he planned to come back. Even if he did come back, was he strong enough to confront Ibn Rashed?

Their doubts and fears increased with the profusion of people and the commotion. When they did not respond directly to Ibn Rashed's offers, he sent them a new messenger.

"Iban Rashed didn't send me. I came on my own."

They said nothing, but waited for him to speak.

"You must have heard about what happened in Wadi al-Uyoun. There isn't a single house or person left there—everyone had to leave. They were all scattered under the stars, some in the east and some in the west. Here, in Harran, some of the workers are originally from Wadi al-Uyoun."

He paused so that they might all see his point, and register it in their hearts and minds, and remember their traveling loved ones, and then he continued. "Common sense is the best thing a man has, and sensible people know what to do: they give and take, and buy and sell. Stubborn people lose everything they've got."

They thought this over after he left, and a new messenger came the next day who asked them, in a tone somewhere between wheedling and bullying, "So what have you good men decided?"

Their eyes said nothing.

"Ibn Rashed says: The land from the graveyard to the last hill in the west belongs to the people of Harran, to them and no one else, and from the graveyard to the market is for sale to whomever will buy, at market price. If you sell it to him he'll pay well above the market price."

Some of the Harranis sold, and Ibn Rashed bought from several persons. As the buying and selling were consummated he knew that they were waiting, so he generously opened his sack of money as he wrote out the contracts with the help of Daham and Ibn Hathal and took the sellers' fingerprints, and the transactions were witnessed by several of the people present. The Harranis were surprised at this method of selling—they were not used to signing papers, and some of them were afraid to leave their fingerprints. One of them refused to put his thumbprints on paper and said that he had a seal that had been wrought for him in Damascus years before; Ibn Rashed was satisfied with the seal, the fingerprints and the witnesses.

"My friends, the man has sold and I have bought. This paper is worthless, because a man's word is worth more than any paper or money, but this world is life and death. The land he has sold goes from east of the graveyard up to the mosque. You are the witnesses."

The land that Ibn Rashed had bought was marked off in a primitive but deliberate way, by placing stones in the corners after the distances were measured out with rope. On part of it he built a storehouse for the lumber he had brought from American Harran, and on another large site he piled heaps of rock which his camels had carried from the quarries west of the city. He moved the camel stand from the Ujra road to a spot near the market.

Ibn Rashed acted with a speed and confidence that excited

quite as much envy as admiration, particularly since the Americans who came to Arab Harran to visit Ibn Rashed spent an increasing amount of time among the people, and more time with Ibn Rashed himself, but Nusayis no longer came with them, as he had before. They did nothing but talk to the people and ask them all kinds of questions.

Many said that the ones who spoke Arabic were all old and could not work. Others said that they were infidels and wanted to make everyone else like them. Like devils they moved from one place to another, and Ibn Rashed was the devils' confidant.

Three months and a few days later Dabbasi came back, bringing two of his sons and three other relatives. This time he stayed, settling for good, leaving his middle son in Ujra. With his coming a new era began in Harran.

Dabbasi was, in spite of his long delay, very confident when he arrived. That was plain from the first night, and everything he did subsequently confirmed it. His travels had taken him to many far-off places, such as Egypt, and he had crossed the sea three times, once from the port of Alexandria to Haifa during the war, and twice from Beirut to Gaza and Port Said a few years after the war; he traveled the Sultan's Road two or three times each year to Iraq, Damascus, east of the Jordan and Palestine. His spirit of adventure showed even in buying and selling. His travels and his energy made him decide, without a second thought, to choose Harran as his new home; and he came prepared, with his sons and relatives.

Deep in his heart he had already decided to work without any regard for Ibn Rashed or anyone else, for "the earth is wide, there is room enough for everyone, the clever and the stupid, and everyone in between!" That was what he told Majbal al-

Khursa, his partner in Ujra, who had refused to extend their partnership to "that graveyard that even ghosts try to avoid." Al-Khursa thought that his partner was embarking on an unnecessary adventure, and a very risky one. Dabbasi's other adventures had paid off—once he had bought a flock of sheep, without even the price of a single head of them in his pocket, and sold them all the next day at an unheard-of profit; he had bought sugar, flour and textiles from a large supply caravan, spending all the money he had, but the prices had plunged in Ujra after the arrival of several other caravans. He had refused to sell at a loss and been able to wait, fearing only that the flour would get weevily. A sudden flood detained the other caravans and led to a rise in prices, with the result that Dabbasi made huge profits that year. These and other stories said much about his personality and his constant readiness to embark on adventures and begin anew, but the fact that so many of his adventures had succeeded did not mean that the opportunity available to him now would succeed. So as a token of the confidence and commitment between him and his partners, Dabbasi left his son Jasser in Ujra and took his other two sons, big Saleh and little Hmeidi, with him.

They arrived with no great fanfare and settled in Arab Harran as he had done before. Dabbasi learned, his first night, all that had taken place since he had left. He was disappointed that some of the people of Harran had sold their land, but he did not discuss it long or dwell on the point. What had happened was done with, and there was no good in regret or recriminations.

"The people of Harran got some benefit from the deal," he said at the end of the evening, "and if the foreigners have opened their mouths and bellies and come here, like Ibn Rashed and the others, then we must be greedier than ants and more cunning than foxes!"

He did not wait, but began the next day.

His specialties were real estate and trading. On his third day he invited Ibn Rashed to a meal.

"We are the sons of the Sultan's Road," he told him, "and we know nothing but business. We buy and sell, we lose once and profit the next two times, and so on. You know how it goes."

Ibn Rashed had no quarrel with these sentiments but did not know what he was getting at. What could Dabbasi do? What was he doing? He seemed humble and friendly, but how long would that last? Was Harran big enough for two men like himself and Dabbasi?

"My friends," Dabbasi told the Harranis, "you are the nerve center, you are the backbone. Have no fear."

When the Harranis were quiet, as was their habit, he went on hastily. "You don't need these people; they need you. You may be poor today, but everyone says that there's gold under your feet. Just be patient."

They said nothing. They looked at him calmly but did not speak.

"The problem is easy and difficult, but not like before," he said paternally. "Hold fast to the land—hang on to it with your teeth and pretend that nothing has changed. Don't sell even if the sky falls. Stay where you are."

After much explanation the Harranis understood that Dabbasi wanted them to be patient, to wait and, most important, to let him do as he pleased, but still they said nothing. They sensed that they were entering a battle of unknown duration. They had only these two men, Ibn Rashed and Dabbasi. They had known Dabbasi for a long time, though only by way of business deals and the letters and caravans that came each year, but for several months, until the present, they had seen only Ibn Rashed. They knew how he talked, how he sent messengers, and they knew best of all how he meant for them to give him whatever he wanted. Now they heard Dabbasi speaking this way and they did not know what he wanted of them. True, they had left their previous homes and started anew here; they saw how life changed and rolled like the sea, how the foreigners increased by the day; nothing was as it had been before, but they did not know what to do, or what Dabbasi was asking of them.

"We are patient people, uncle," one of the old men told him. "Our children are gone traveling—they left years ago. We say it's a good thing to keep moving, and they do come back, if not this year then next year. Praise God, we are more patient than camels, but from the day those devils came nothing has been the same. Since the ship came even our children have changed on us. You can see for yourself that everyone on earth is coming here. What will we do today and tomorrow? The world is all ruin."

The old man had spoken, and the others spoke their minds. Dabbasi listened, nodding his head in agreement. When they had finished, he stroked his small beard.

"The old Harran you knew is gone. It has been obliterated. Nothing is left of it but the mosque and the cemetery, and maybe tomorrow or the next day Ibn Rashed or someone else will come and build a cinema in its place. They may build a whorehouse over the graveyard. To someone not of this land and this town, all land is the same—it's just land. Men are all the same, and a native of this town is like a stranger, and a Muslim is like a Jew."

They followed all this, listening attentively. They did not understand all the words he used. He sensed that he had gone too far and shifted his sitting posture.

"Right now the most important thing is the people of this town. Everyone must get his rights and his share. Those people have eaten their fill and increased their numbers, but the people of Harran are the most generous people you will ever meet. So welcome, Ibn Rashed and all the rest."

That night the Harranis understood that a relentless war was at hand, and that the enemy was Ibn Rashed. They did not exactly understand whether he was their enemy or Dabbasi's, and they slept uneasily that night.

38

ONE OF THE FIRST UNDERTAKINGS DABBASI EM-
barked upon—unhesitatingly, for he must have
decided to do so during his previous stay in
Harran—was to marry a Harrani woman.

By the time the first week had come to an end—full, as usual,
of upsets and changes in their lives—Dabbasi had pretty firmly
established himself between the two Harrans. One night he had
most of the men over to visit and in a carefully chosen moment
said—half seriously, half jokingly, as a way of creating greater
warmth and trust between the natives and himself, a new-
comer—"Listen, my friends . . ."

They listened and looked his way. His round face and small
beard showed strength and confidence. He was smiling broadly
and pulling at his beard, and when he was sure they were paying
attention he went on. "If you want us, hitch us up!"

None of the Harranis understood. He laughed loudly—guffawed, really.

"From the time of Adam, men have bound themselves together by way of women. When a man gets married he binds himself to the land and the tribe. He becomes one with the land and the tribe."

The men looked at each other and then at Dabbasi. Things were clear now, or at least getting clearer, but no one said anything.

"What do you say?" he asked when he saw them silent. "Do you want us or shall we leave—shall we go back to our own folk?"

The men's laughter and the eager looks they gave each other made it plain that they were in agreement with him, but who would be Dabbasi's in-law? How would it be done?

"You're one of us, Abu Saleh," said an old man. "As for going back to your own folk—put that idea out of your head!"

"The prompt giver gives twice," Dabbasi said, laughing

The men shouted with laughter and looked at each other questioningly—who would put himself forward? And which girl would be the most suitable?

Until that moment, when the men realized what Dabbasi was driving at, it was not clear whether the girl was to be married to Saleh or to one of the three other men who had come with Dabbasi—they were all fairly young, except for one who was forty or fifty. Dabbasi, as their boss and decision maker, was making a proposal on their behalf that none of them could undertake directly.

"Uncle, Abu Saleh, your son is my son," said one of the men, looking at Saleh and smiling. "And his brother will be my other son!"

Dabbasi shifted in his seat. His face changed completely. He was surprised. To clear up the misunderstanding he shifted around a few more times and moved forward with his hand raised. This salute surprised everyone, and some of them thought they had made a mistake in thinking this had anything to do with marriage. The man who had spoken up cringed.

"Listen, cousin," said Dabbasi, "Saleh's time will come, if not today then tomorrow, but for now it is *Abu* Saleh who wants to marry!"

Shouts of laughter filled the air; not one of them had guessed that it was the older Dabbasi who wanted to get married. They had thought he wanted a wife for his son Saleh, and some had thought he had come to see a betrothal for one of the three men who had accompanied him to Harran. But him? He was fifty-five years old or more, so it seemed somewhat strange, or at least unexpected.

Exactly two weeks later, a Thursday evening, Dabbasi was married. He married the daughter of Muhammad al-Zamal, the man who had cringed that night after offering his daughter to Dabbasi's son Saleh.

It was the first wedding in the new Harran and was obviously of great interest to the Americans who visited Arab Harran frequently, for as soon as they heard that a wedding was to take place on Thursday, they were in touch asking to attend, and they wanted to come early.

Dabbasi's joy at being married was equaled by his joy at the presence of the Americans. He did his utmost to welcome and honor them and made sure that his son Saleh did not leave their side for a minute. He asked the Harranis to treat the Americans with deference and to see that all their wishes were satisfied. The Americans, who looked and behaved like small children, showed endless, unimaginable surprise and admiration. They asked about everything, about words, clothing and food, about the names of the bridegroom and his bride and whether they had known each other before, and if they had ever met. They asked people

how old they were and how many children they had and looked
shocked when an old man told them that the fellow who sat
near and talked with them all night was the son of Ibrahim al-
Dabbasi. They asked Dabbasi's permission to take some photographs and hoped he would allow them to photograph him
with his bride, and the rest of the women, but these suggestions,
which they did not press, were only their way of finding out
whether or not such things were acceptable to their hosts.

It was a great night for Harran. So many sheep were slaughtered that several guests disagreed on how many there were and
made bets. Five sheeps' heads were laid before the five Americans, and one before Ibn Rashed. Among the workers, Harranis
and other guests, heads were jumbled together with other pieces
of the animals. The men made an extravagant show of carving
the meat in front of the Americans and extracting the internal
organs, especially the brain, and of making the rice into balls
with one hand, which they tossed into their mouths without a
single grain of rice sticking to their palms.

Every small thing excited the Americans' amazement. They
took a great many photographs during the meal and tried to
conquer their embarrassment at their inability to eat like the
others, despite all the help offered them; or perhaps they did not
like the food. They tried to overcome this awkwardness by
constantly asking questions, speaking among themselves and
taking photographs.

Dabbasi, who wore an elegant suit in the early part of the
evening, much too hot for that time of day and that weather,
took off some of his clothing; he did so theatrically, before
summoning his guests to eat and to encourage them. Ibn Rashed,
doing his best to smile and talk naturally, began to fail at this
and went nearly silent. Visibly disturbed, he spoke only to the
people immediately beside him, and then only in a whisper.

"Your house is built and your glory assured, Abu Saleh," said

Mizban loudly, and perhaps deliberately, when the meal was finished.

Dabbasi nodded but did not look anyone in the face, out of embarrassment or modesty, but when Suleiman al-Zamel said, "Food for the men, Abu Saleh. Men have faith and the wretched have charity," Dabbasi understood these words as a token of support, perhaps even against Ibn Rashed himself! This was how the people of Harran understood the words, or explained them. They smiled broadly and some of them looked at Ibn Rashed, no doubt remembering the party he had given not too long before, to celebrate the completion of the shops.

Dabbasi was not the only one who wished this evening never to be forgotten—so did all the people of Harran, and the workers as well. The disjointed chatter of the early evening, the jokes and stories, the murmurs and conversations, grew louder and more orderly, then flared up and began to sound more like a battle. That was before dinner; afterward, after the cups of coffee and glasses of tea, some of the people looked like they were ready to leave. Ibn Rashed laughed and shifted around to look at the men.

"Abu Saleh says, in his heart, 'You've had your dinner, you've drunk your coffee, and God bless my guests this night.' "

Abu Saleh trembled like a wolf on hearing these words and said with menacing friendliness, "We understand what you mean, Abu Muhammad. There are two feast days a year, and today is the third!"

Harran was mad with excitement that night, as much from brilliant planning as from their spontaneity. Everyone sang, even the old men. Despite everyone's happiness, the songs were sad ones, as if Harran was singing of its bygone days, of a life that was coming to an end. When Suweyleh began to sing, which no one had expected him to do, he did so with piercing sweetness. Silence fell; even some of the women came near. The children, who had been romping around from one place to another and shouting, sat quietly in the middle as if dazed. Suweyleh sang as much to himself as to his audience. So faint was his voice at times that people craned their necks to catch the subdued melody they could barely hear; then his voice rang out again in a roar, like the crash of sea waves, and they followed closely the climax and resolution of the song, joining in and crying out; in spite of themselves several women shouted out loud. In the songs which demanded repetition and participation, the people were gripped by an enthusiasm that left no one untouched. Even Ibn Rashed, who felt compelled to stay, had never expected to see such an evening in Harran; he had never imagined that Suweyleh, this half-blind boy he had expelled from Wadi al-Uyoun as unfit for work in the company but allowed to come to Harran because he needed anyone he could get, had such a voice or could sing songs like this.

What longings filled the hearts of men in this desolate corner of the earth? What joys were detonated by song? And this coarse, overpowering sorrow—where did it come from?

Every shout shook the night and spread out endlessly, only to contract again like a black coal, and with the rising and the falling of the melody their hearts trembled and almost stopped, flying faster than lightning to distant places and then returning. The men, who had mastered sorrow to the point of addiction, had mastered silence with the same perfection. If a breath sounded, coarse and grief stricken, to break the silence, it lent the silence an earthy, murky color and seemed improper, and the man who had breathed might look searchingly at the others, anxious and apologetic, speaking without words. Pain reached the point of agony, and sorrow prevailed over everything.

Had the men been in any other place, or been fewer in number, or not had to deal with the foreigners, they would have known how to express all their sorrow and anguish, but something held them back. Only their eyes roamed in the distance to encounter the distress in the eyes around them, exactly like those of a prisoner in his cell or an animal tied to a post. Only their eyes spoke, and at times vented pained screams. When they faded or dwindled away, or suddenly shone in a prolonged appeal for help, blazing, the pain flamed out and called others near, to extend a hand or rope to save them. Suweyleh, singing to himself and the others, intensified their pain; the men were immersed in far more sorrow than they had felt at the start of the evening.

Dabbasi, gripped by a rapture that transported him to faraway places, looked like a slow-witted child, confused and intensely affected. He repeated a few syllables, sang and asked his neighbors to join in and sing. At one point, as Suweyleh prepared to split the silent Harrani night, Dabbasi's loud, rasping voice roared like the voice of an enraged camel, provoking waves of raucous laughter, and he himself laughed hardest of all.

Just as Suweyleh's singing came as a surprise, so did Abdu Muhammad's. No sooner had a weary Suweyleh stopped singing, drenched with droplets of sweat which he at first wiped away with his sleeve then with the palms of both his hands, than Abdu Muhammad began to sing. He sang in his own way, varying his melodies and creating a sudden change in mood—more festive.

It was the singers who set the mood and won all the admiration that night, but the Americans were no less excited: they were fascinated by the singing, by these people who had suddenly become creatures of a different species. At the start of the evening they asked careful, detailed questions about things and names, and wrote all the answers down in the small notebooks they carried, but they were overtaken by the air of excitement that had seized the Arabs and asked fewer questions. They did not ask what the song was about, or of which region it was characteristic, and suspended their questioning until Abdu Muhammad sang. As a result of the happy mood that prevailed after Suweyleh had stopped singing, and because the men were now laughing loudly, they guessed that the man did not confine himself to performing the song but was throwing in his own jokes, ambiguous allusions and other such pleasantries; in any case they understood very few of the lyrics.

Sinclair whispered to one of his friends, "You can't explain the sadness of these people's lives unless you've known the desert and lived in it. This damned desert breeds nothing but this kind of people and the kind of animals we saw on our way here."

When the other American nodded in understanding, Sinclair went on. "Weeping relieves them, but they're hard people, and stubborn. They weep inside—their tears fall inside them and are extinguished again by the shouting and lamentations they call song—they do it in their weddings, when they're celebrating!"

A moment later he added sarcastically, "They call this music!"

The other American pursed his lips, looking at the faces around him, and said, "These people are strange—they seem so mysterious. You never know whether they're sad or happy. Everything about them is wrapped up, layers upon layers, just like the desert under their feet!"

When Suweyleh resumed his singing, to the accompaniment of general murmuring and the rhythmical movement of the men's heads and bodies, Sinclair poked his companion and spoke rapidly. "Look, look—now they're expressing their happiness!" After listening for a while he added, "They're like animals—jostling each other and moving around in this primitive way to express their happiness. Imagine!"

The Americans were utterly enthralled and could not stop taking pictures.

For a long time afterward the people of Harran remembered that night, the night of Dabbasi's wedding.

39

G HAFEL AL-SUWEYD, EMIR OF HARRAN FOR LONGER
than anyone could remember, was a prince unlike others. He bothered no one and wanted
no one to bother him. Very few people had seen him, and even
fewer had known him from close up. He liked neither his position of authority nor Harran itself, nor even the desert. He
memorized poetry, recited and sometimes sang it. He would go
to the remotest corner of the desert to hear an ode, to see its
author and hear it from a reliable narrator. One old man in
Harran remembered that when Ghafel al-Suweyd was named
emir of Harran and the adjacent area of desert and first arrived
there one summer day about noon, he was utterly speechless.
The men who had come to greet him thought he was a deaf-
mute. When he began to speak—this was a few days later—he
found nothing to say to "these idiots who sit in front of the sea

brooding and doing nothing else!" He asked them several questions but found nothing interesting about them. He recited them part of his favorite ode, but no one responded, so he left his black servant, Maimoun, to rule over "these deficient wretches, to pick fights with them—who cares if he kills them, or they him." He went back whence he had come, taking a number of his men with him.

The stories told about him were few and somewhat contradictory. According to one, he traveled deep in the desert, moving from one place to another, to hear poetry. Another alleged that he was searching for a huge white bird that had kidnapped his beautiful bride the night before their wedding. She had been stolen away at night, when the moon was full. Ghafel al-Suweyd had seen with his own eyes how the bird tucked her beneath his left wing. Other stories said that the emir had loved and desired a woman, but his cousin, on learning of the emir's wish and intentions, carried her off into the desert one pitch-dark night. She was never heard from again, and the emir went off on these long, mysterious travels in the desert solely to find her.

These were the stories told about the emir, and what inclined the people to believe them was that the prince, though he was past forty, had not married or even thought of marriage. On one of his visits to Harran, Ibn Nafeh, who was trying to be friendly and hoping to form a bond with the emir, asked him if he was considering marriage. The emir smiled ironically at the question, not replying, and slowly shook his head for a minute or two.

His habit was to come to Harran every two or three months and ask Maimoun out of the corners of his mouth if anything had happened in his absence—if any caravans or travelers had come through. He asked if the people of Harran were the same idiots he remembered, or had they come to their senses? When he had asked all his questions he called for coffee and a stringed instrument and began to recite. The men shook their heads as he performed, not concealing their admiration; he felt refreshed and played with delight, his mind far away. They said that on moonlit nights he was terribly sad and at times even wept.

He was not happy to see the townspeople of Harran when they came to pay their respects and remained silent most of the time; he regarded them as his enemies. Why had he come to this place "that even birds avoid"? The Harranis, who could find nothing to say to the emir and had no requests or complaints to make, only drank coffee, rubbed their hands and smiled two or three times, then asked leave to be excused, which the emir quickly granted, and as soon as their footfalls died away he asked for the instrument to be brought and sometimes for the musician to sit and play upon it directly in front of him so that he could appreciate every beautiful and tender note.

So it went with Ghafel al-Suweyd for years. In the course of the years he spent only a few months in Harran; had it been any longer than that he would have appointed Maimoun emir and gone off into the desert for good; but when the Americans came he was traveling, and when he came back and saw how changed things were he was shocked and became very upset. After two Americans came to visit him, with Naim to translate for them, he made an important decision: to leave and never come back.

"We used to have one problem," he told some of the men from Harran. "Now there's no problem we don't have." He turned to Maimoun and laughed. "Have you actually seen them? Have you seen their faces? They look like kangaroo rats, or like bread dough. They're speckled and have beady eyes. They might make it through the winter, but I doubt they'll be able to take the summer."

He was silent a minute amid the quiet and confusion, then said to himself, but wanting the others to hear, "Tomorrow they'll be out of here. They'll be farting from fear!"

Several days later the camels were saddled up and loaded with the big tent and the smaller ones which had been erected a long time ago, and the emir and his friends, including Maimoun, left with no one knowing if they would ever come back. After a few weeks passed, a new emir came, and no one ever heard from Ghafel al-Suweyd again.

After Ghafel al-Suweyd came Khaled al-Mishari, the new emir of Harran.

Emir Khaled was middle aged, heavyset and dark skinned— almost black. He arrived to a boisterous welcome and noisy reception, having sent some of his men ahead of him to inform the people that Emir Khaled, Harran's new emir, would come any day now, and they took care to describe the emir to the people with a combination of sternness and menace. They told how he ordered executions for the slightest of crimes and would take pity on no one, not even his own brother; his mission in Harran was to make the town as peaceful as a graveyard, since already people spoke of its fights, misunderstandings and general chaos; left to themselves, it was said, the people of Harran would end up killing each other off. This terrified many of the towns-people, and those who were not terrified were shaken by the waiting and anticipation. Harran, which for long years neither had nor needed an emir, and saw Ghafel al-Suweyd half asleep most of the time he spent in Harran, thought itself unable to stand an emir. What would he want—what would they do with him? Would life in Harran continue to change with the coming of the Americans and all the other foreigners, plus Ibn Rashed and Dabbasi—let alone who might come along tomorrow? And as Harran was changing, would an emir make things better or only create more problems, making things much worse?

The Americans sent Naim to help welcome the emir. This

move might have come about with Ibn Rashed's connivance, since no sooner was the day of the emir's arrival announced than Ibn Rashed and Daham made their preparations and went with several men, including Naim, to the Ujra road. They set off in the early morning, and when the emir arrived just before sundown they went with him to Harran.

The emir was entirely different from his predecessor in his looks, his manner and the number of men in his party. The people of Harran, whose caution had reached the point of outright fright, for they had committed an unintentional error in failing to meet the emir on his arrival, as Ibn Rashed had done, felt that some new evil would befall them; but that night Dabbasi spoke to them in a way that soothed them considerably. "He is the emir of Harran," he said, "and we are the people of Harran, and have been since God first created the world. The emir knows that everyone chasing around him now is saying, 'I'm so-and-so,' but tomorrow when he has a chance to relax he'll get to know everyone equally well."

Furthermore, Dabbasi agreed with the men that he and some of them would go to the emir the next day to pay their respects. He would be with them, but since he did not think he'd ever seen the emir before or heard anything about him, he hesitated to make any prediction about the future. Nevertheless he was confident that this small battle that Ibn Rashed had won would not change anything—he would know what to do next.

When the Harranis went along the next day, Ibn Rashed was just leaving the emir, and in the brief moments they stood with him chatting, the man seemed supremely self-confident, almost haughty, as if he had some favored position with the emir or wished to convey to the people of Harran that he had come first, and that this was significant. Dabbasi, laughing, could not let this opportunity pass.

"Very impressive, Abu Muhammad—are you living with the emir?"

Ibn Rashed laughed and nodded, so as to avoid making any explanation, but Dabbasi went on. "Don't forget, a week of familiarity breeds a week of contempt."

"One day at a time, Abu Saleh!"

The people of Harran took an immediate dislike to the emir, for after some pleasantries about the journey and the road, he told them that he had come to Harran to enforce the law and put an end to fighting and theft. He asked, suddenly, if any of them knew the three men who had stolen the camels, and if any of them had any complaints or requests to make.

The conversation might have gone on in this vein, with the result that their relations would have remained chilly, but Dabbasi caught sight of one of the emir's men holding and stroking a falcon and guessed that the emir was a huntsman; skillfully, full of cunning, he turned to one of the elders of Harran and asked about the bustards—whether they had come to the area, and when. Suddenly, unexpectedly, the emir's face showed keen interest. The men of Harran mentioned some of the areas, but Dabbasi brought out some of the hunting information he had accumulated over long years: the right places and the right seasons; how in Egypt he had seen uncounted birds filling the sky like black clouds; how on one of his trips to Gaza he'd seen birds massing near the shore; all of the sand grouse, gazelles and bustards he had seen. The vast amount of information he was able to discuss absolutely amazed everybody.

The people of Harran recall that Dabbasi was a devil in human guise, because from the minute he began discussing hunting the emir underwent a complete transformation—he was like a small child listening raptly to Dabbasi's tales. After the coldness and antipathy of his words and looks during the first part of the visit, he softened and asked Dabbasi to come nearer; Dabbasi, for his part, asked him if by chance they had met before, and where. In an attempt to excuse himself from the ordeal of trying to remember any such meeting, the emir said that he traveled a great deal and saw so many faces that he could not remember clearly, though all the same "I never forget a face—I just can't recall when and where." The emir, delighted with Dabbasi's remarks, looked him in the face carefully, as if perhaps he might remember, and help determine the time and place, but they did not continue this game long, because they could not.

Next, the people of Harran described how they had left their homes and built new ones on the western side of the town, to help the company and in accordance with government orders; how they feared the future, especially after seeing the ship with the naked women; how the young men, since that day, had become unsociable and hot tempered. The emir smiled several times and asked detailed questions about the ship that had come to Harran and about the number of women on board, what they had done and how long they had stayed. He promised the people that this would not happen again: the preservation of religion and morals was his chief mission here, and he would never hesitate to take whatever steps were necessary.

Once again Dabbasi spoke, asking the emir to "include the people of Harran among his concerns, for they had no one but God and himself." He said that some of the foreigners who had arrived in recent days had used threats to force them to sell their land, and that the foreigners had appropriated everything, leaving the Harranis with nothing. He did not mention Ibn Rashed once, or refer to him by name, but the people of Harran understood his words perfectly. The emir repeated that he had come to safeguard religion and morals: "Truth is truth, and natives come before strangers." Before the visit came to an end, Dabbasi asked the emir, in the name of the people of Harran, to name a date on which the people might celebrate his coming. The emir laughed, not setting a date or promising anything. He stood in the middle of his huge tent to bid the visitors good-bye and addressed Dabbasi and the two men by his side. "When the winter comes, the coldest part of the winter, we'll go bustard hunting in the places you mentioned."

40

....

T HE EMIR AND THE AMERICANS OFTEN EX-
changed visits during the first weeks.
During the emir's visit to American Harran,
which came off in an atmosphere of immense ceremony and
splendor, there was a shooting contest between three Americans.
The emir was delighted with everything he saw and told them
so in words that Naim could not translate with much precision
because he did not understand them perfectly. After the shooting
was over the emir asked to see the hunting rifles, and they brought
them before him, and in a joking and congenial mood Ibn Rashed
suggested he try one of them out. At first he was hesitant, but
when Daham set up one of the empty shells as a target at about
ten or fifteen yards distance, the emir sent away the hunting
rifles and asked his companion Mubrid al-Huweizi to hand him
his own Mauser rifle. He aimed carefully, and with consummate

skill scored a direct hit on the shell to loud applause and shouts of admiration, then without a pause pulled the empty shell from his rifle and handed it to Mubrid, asking him to put it for a target in the place of the first one. Then with the same care, and a certain unhurried skill, he raised his head a few times to check the shell's position, aimed and fired, and blew it away. The Americans and others did not content themselves with mere applause or repeating their admiring shouts but whistled loudly, and two of them stepped forward to pat the emir on the back. Then, in an atmosphere of mirth and good feeling, the emir was invited to the Americans' clubhouse to eat.

It was the first time the Arabs had ever set foot there, and only a few of them went in. Daham told the workers to "keep a good distance and be well mannered for the sake of the emir and the foreigners . . . food will be brought to you where you are." The luncheon party was only for the emir, his men, Ibn Rashed, Daham and Saleh Dabbasi; box lunches were prepared for the others, full of foods that none of the men recognized or could name. The emir marveled at everything he saw and every-thing that was put before him. When he remarked on the im-mensity of the dining hall, its orderliness and cleanliness, Ibn Rashed told him that the workers who had helped to build it could scarcely believe its size and could not imagine how it would be used—and that went for himself too, for though he had walked by many times, he had never imagined it to be this spacious or beautiful. After lunch the emir and his group were given a tour of the compound: the swimming pools, the rec-reation club and the offices. The Americans consented to the emir's request to inspect one of the houses. He was awed to the point of incredulity by everything he saw and told them so in his own way, forcing Naim to consult Ibn Rashed for the mean-ing of certain words and expressions.

The emir was visibly hesitant to take up the Americans' offer of a boat ride. He said he had never sailed before and was very much afraid of the water and could not swim. When the Americans assured him that it was easy and completely safe, since "the boats were designed with great care and could sail to any part of the world without danger of any kind of accident, and were in any case equipped with lifeboats and other devices," and after Naim translated all the compound manager's assurances, the emir consented so as not to look like a coward, on the condition that "the ride be short, and we do not go far from shore," to which the Americans agreed.

It was the first time that any of the men had traveled on water. Their hearts beat violently, Ibn Rashed's face turned yellow, and the emir wished that he had never embarked on this experiment. Daham resisted slightly in boarding the boat, but Ibn Rashed laughed and gave him a shove, telling him nervously that "if we have to die, Ibn Muzil, you be our model," and when they sat on the wide, comfortable seats they did not say a word or even look around them. Even the few wan smiles they exchanged did more to frighten each other than to instill confidence. When the engine roared and the boat took off, everyone heard Ibn Rashed saying, "In the name of God, in the name of God . . . thou shalt not be afflicted except by what God hath decreed," and although the Americans moved back and forth, showing no sign of fear, the rest of them were obliged to stay rooted to their places like parts of the chairs. They made even the slightest movements with the greatest economy and caution, and when the emir looked toward the shore and saw it moving away, he asked softly, "What do you say, Ibn Rashed, shall we go back and die on dry land? What more could you want?" Ibn Rashed nodded and said nothing. When the boat swerved and sped across the gulf toward the open water, the men could stand it no more.

"Tell your friends we've had enough," the emir instructed Naim firmly. "We would like to go back."

The Americans looked surprised when Naim told them what the emir had said, thinking that there was some misunderstanding, and when Naim asked him to explain, the emir reiterated the necessity of returning at once, and so the boat returned.

With the same ceremony and splendor with which they had welcomed the emir, the Americans saw him off as the sun began to set.

For a while all Harran talked of nothing but this visit. With the passage of time and the retelling of the story and comments upon it, however, it got greatly distorted. Some of the workers swore that the target the emir had hit was a small needle set so far off as to be scarcely visible, whereas the American marksmen had been unable to hit a large glass bottle! In the restaurant and around the swimming pool were naked women, at whom the emir had leered and smiled! The sea voyage was said to have been fraught with countless perils, and save for the emir's valor the boat would have been lost.

This is what many people said, how they recounted the events. When, the day after his visit, a hunting rifle was delivered to the emir by Naim and Ibn Rashed, Dabbasi was disgusted.

"The game is won at the end, not the beginning," he declared in front of several Harranis, "as Ibn Rashed will soon find out."

When the emir made preparations for a reception in honor of the Americans, he asked Ibn Rashed and Dabbasi to help him. He asked each of them separately and then met with them together. The men showed every willingness to cooperate but were in stiff competition when they all met, and within a short time all the preparations were final. It was decided that the reception would be held at sundown, followed by dinner.

The emir decided on Thursday, and he and his men did everything in their power to make the party magnificent and the event memorable; Ibn Rashed and Dabbasi helped prepare with indescribable zeal, and each of them held something back until the last minute.

All the Americans came but three—the chief of their camp said he could not bring them because some urgent matters required their presence there. They arrived in Arab Harran, some of them for the first time, in a cloud of dust early on Thursday afternoon, although they were not expected until sundown. Everyone was waiting for them, though a heavy silence more like fear hung over the people of Harran as they saw the Americans coming in armies—armies. They marched in disarray, waving their arms, and their voices could be heard as they approached. The eyes of the Harranis and workers took in every step of these guests. Even the women came out, though it was unusual for them, to have a look at those whom the men talked about so much every day, to see what kind of men they were. The teenagers and children waited nearby, then walked along with the Americans, but at a distance. The Americans tried vainly to speak Arabic with them but could not get into a conversation with the youngsters or induce them to come any closer.

When the Americans approached the huge tent erected for the emir, roughly halfway between residential Harran and the market, he came out to greet them. He took several steps toward them, surrounded by a crowd of men, and when the Americans came closer, leaving only a few steps between them, he welcomed them warmly and shook all their hands. Naim at first busied himself with introductions and interpreting, but he could not keep these up for long because of the noise and confusion, and some of the words he heard, perhaps for the first time, whose meanings he could not even guess at.

After the coffee cups made the rounds and the emir chatted with the chief of the camp and some of the Americans who spoke Arabic, he said that he had arranged a camel race for them and asked them all to proceed to the open space behind the tents, for there Ibn Rashed and the emir's men had readied the best and handsomest camels. Ibn Rashed was pacing nimbly and excitedly between the large tents and the clearing, waiting for the emir's signal. Then the guests arrived.

It was a huge surprise for the Americans. They had imagined that camels were created only as pack animals and that, should they run, they would be able to do so only very slowly and for short distances. But when the Americans saw them racing they were astonished; they took photographs, applauded and exchanged wondering looks. When the race was over they insisted on going nearer the camels to have their pictures taken beside them. Two of them expressed their wish to ride on the camels, which they did with enthusiasm, and all their wishes were granted.

Dabbasi had arranged the next surprise, shrewdly and in secret, with Sakhr, who tended the emir's falcons.

As soon as the camel race was over—Sakhr had done his utmost, in collusion with some of the jockeys, to try to end it early—Dabbasi went to the emir and whispered something in his ear, which changed the atmosphere at once. The emir, looking surprised and excited, told Naim to ask the Americans for complete quiet, because they would now see something that would amaze them; then he again asked for silence. With the dexterity of a magician Sakhr and two of the emir's men came forward and presented the falcons with such an air of sublimity that several of the guests thought that this was all they would see. But then the pigeons were set loose—no one knew where Dabbasi had got them—and the falcons dispatched behind them, and the battle in the air took place, and everyone—including Ibn Rashed, who had never expected this surprise—was gripped with astonishment and a little fear. When he learned that it was

Dabbasi's doing, he felt that he had lost face in front of this enemy—where in the name of Hell and earth had he come from? The Americans were no less amazed than Ibn Rashed, and they took dozens of pictures of Sakhr and got too close to the falcons. An American tried to stroke one of the birds, and several accidents would have occurred but for Sakhr and his men, who took the falcons far away and did everything they could to calm them down.

Emir Khaled al-Mishari presented the Americans with his surprise at dinner; a camel's head placed in front of the camp chief among the other dishes, with the sheep's heads, for one sheep had been killed for each guest. Since three had not shown up, the extra sheep's heads were put in front of other guests.

After dinner the emir had planned a sword dance for his guests, and it was performed magnificently by his men. At one point the emir himself got enthusiastic and got up to join in the dance; this had an electrifying effect on the party: several of the Americans asked permission to join in. The emir's men consented and offered to teach them, but the Americans ruined everything. Taking photographs was the only thing they cared about, and instead of enlivening the dance, their behavior and the remarks they made weakened it and slowed it down, and when the dance was over it was clear that the party had ended. In an attempt to create a better mood and to get back at Dabbasi, Ibn Rashed proposed to the emir that some of the men sing, as they had done at Dabbasi's wedding, but the emir's anger and the things he said settled everything. "After we've become their acrobats, Ibn Rashed?" said the emir sharply. When Ibn Rashed tried to explain himself, the emir snapped at him angrily. "If we sing for them today, then tomorrow they'll want us to dance for them, like monkeys; that's all I'm worried about, Ibn Rashed."

The coffee cups were passed around again, and the Americans who spoke Arabic talked to most of the people and asked about many things. The chief of their camp said that it was a long walk back to the compound, so they would have to leave. The men crowded out to see them off with exaggerated compliments, and the Americans' voices were audible from afar long after they had set off with some of the emir's men.

The people long remembered this night in Harran.

41

THE AMERICANS WHO SPOKE ARABIC NO LONGER visited only Ibn Rashed. They began to visit Dabbasi, Ibn Surour, al-Salaami and others, and whenever they came they brought others who had not come before. The newcomers took charge of the conversations and set forth many topics of discussion with those accompanying them, then translated everything.

All Harran talked about these visits, which were as a rule very lengthy but full of long-remembered novel occurrences. At first the visits were spontaneous: the Americans had barely reached the houses in Harran, or by the camp, before the Harranis or workers saw them and invited them in for a cup of coffee or glass of tea, which was always accepted. In the course of the hour or so these visits lasted all talked companionably, even the youngsters, who generally did not speak in the presence of their elders. They were not afraid to speak, and in any case were forced to speak in order to answer the questions that were put to them. The Americans listened carefully, scrutinized their hosts' faces and everything else around them, and thought nothing of touching things, whether textiles or skins, and one time they stood for an hour or more, watching an old man dye a skin and taking pictures. Another time they stood and watched the shoeing of a donkey and shot a whole roll of film. They took pictures of an American holding up one of the donkey's hooves and then another, as if he were shoeing the beast.

This is what the visits were like in the beginning—very chaotic, with all the children running behind the Americans and large groups of people crowding around to look.

Later on the Americans began to come directly from their compound to some of the houses in Harran, to Ibn Rashed's or Dabbasi's or someone else's. They brought books and vast quantities of paper with them. Some of the paper was colored cardboard of various sizes, tiny, medium sized and large. Young and old were fascinated by the cardboard; the older men felt the sheets and turned them over, and the children never stopped trying to get some of it for themselves. Sometimes the Americans gave them some, telling them to take it and go away, and as soon as calm had reasserted itself they opened up their books, flipped the pages and started asking questions.

What astonished the people of Harran was that there was so much in these books that was familiar to them—names, places, tribes, the seasons for rainy weather, wind and the migration of birds—and they felt an indescribable sense of importance when the Americans started to write down everything they were told. The men stopped when they said certain names, which the Americans asked them to repeat several times before writing them down on the colored paper.

The Americans' books inspired puzzlement and a little fear.

Books of every color and size—some of them carried several books and others only one or two. The people of Harran, who were baffled and frightened by the books, paid careful attention to see if the Americans carried the same books on successive visits or changed them for different ones, and when they saw that some of the books came and went several times while others were brought only once, the old men said: "They are magical books, and each of those men has a jinn of his own. Those Americans are trying out book after book to gain control of Harran and its people!" On several occasions the men managed to get hold of some of the books and examined them, but they could not understand a thing. Ibn Naffeh once said, after his youngest son came down with fever the day after the Americans visited the house of his neighbor al-Salaami, that "the jinn had infiltrated his house." He was sure of it, because he found a sheet of yellow cardboard beneath his son's pillow, and the boy was not cured of the fever until the cardboard was burned.

Others said that Abdu Muhammad had learned magic from the Americans, and that he practiced witchcraft in his long periods of seclusion, which led some of the Harranis to switch to Abdullah al-Abyad's bakery. Perhaps they were the ones who made Dabbasi decide to open a new bakery, for "bewitched bread cures no one—it kills."

The men asked the Americans about the books—what they contained, and why they always carried them around—but the muddled and contradictory answers only fueled the Harranis' worries and doubts. No two Americans gave the same answer, and no one American ever gave the same answer twice.

"History books," the Americans said, but each time they said "history" they had a different book than the last time. Some of the books were black as night and others blood red; and some were blue or green. They were all bound in tough leather like the amulets Sheikh Salem al-Oteibi had written years before when he had visited Harran and stayed for two months; during his stay he had made several kinds of amulets to protect the children from worms and other vermin, and from fear, and encased each amulet in leather. These books were like those amulets, though of course the Americans were using infidel magic, which sooner or later would work its evil on everyone.

At other times, when they asked about the names of the books and what was inside them, the Americans said things besides "history." They said "geography" and went on to say that they were looking for desert formations, and studying the wind patterns and caravan routes. Still later, they said that they were researching ancient ruins; they asked serious questions about some of the sites and asked if any of the Harranis had visited the areas or could give directions to them.

These books and questions provoked quite as much worry as surprise and wonderment. What did these devils want? Precisely why had they come? They said that they had come to help the people and to search for water, that there was gold underneath the sands and that they would extract it and distribute it among the people, but what did any of that have to do with their books or the questions they asked? Was there gold only in Harran or in other places as well? So the gold was there and they were going to extract it; but what had made them go there to look for evidence of it in the first place?

Many such questions began to make the rounds among the people, together with the other questions of those who had direct contact with the Americans. The people of Harran began to ask others, who had come from Ujra, Rawdhat al-Mashti and elsewhere, whether the Americans had reached there, which books they had brought with them and whether they were books of witchcraft or books of blasphemy.

One day the group that usually visited was accompanied by an American with a beard as red as if it had been treated with henna and notable for its sheen and thickness. No one in Harran had ever seen such a beard before. This American carried a big book and sat down in Ibn Rashed's camp, with Ibn Naffeh present, and after a list of questions about the wind, the sands and distances, this man began to ask very strange questions. He asked if the people of Harran practiced any kind of magic, and if they had any other beliefs besides Islam, and whether they had heard of nearby communities that worshiped trees and the wind and the sun. The men were deeply shocked by these questions and looked at each other. The man opened up his big book and pointed to some of the pictures. Some of the men came closer to inspect the strange figures—idols and animals they had never seen before—but, frightened, they drew their hands away from the book and fell silent.

Once again the man began asking questions, and one of the Americans interpreted. Seeing them silent, the interpreter said that "his friend was studying the beliefs of various peoples and the evolution of religion" and wanted to know all the current beliefs.

Ibn Naffeh was excited and enraged.

"Now we know for sure," he shouted. "They are infidels—all of them are infidels, and anyone who sits with them is an infidel!"

When the townspeople of Harran went to visit the emir, Ibn Naffeh was outspoken and angry. He said that the Americans had come to turn the people away from Islam, that they practiced sorcery and that if they were allowed to stay they would lay Harran waste; there would be catastrophes. The emir listened carefully to what Ibn Naffeh and others had to say and nodded several times, though no one knew exactly what was meant by these nods, for he muttered only a few vague, general remarks. When they asked his leave to depart, he excused them. Only Dabbasi remained, and no one knows what the two talked about together, but the Americans changed. They visited Arab Harran less frequently and no longer carried their books around, though they did usually have the colored paper with them and wrote down what they heard. The questions they asked had little to do with religion or magic. Later, they stopped writing altogether and started carrying around small black boxes, which they pressed whenever they got into a conversation. "Devils are inside them," Ibn Naffeh said when he heard about the boxes, "and sooner or later they'll come out and settle in our houses in the form of cats or snakes." He asked the people not to allow these boxes into their homes and failing that to refuse to speak in front of them, because "all the devils had to do was to hear a voice once in order to follow its owner to the ends of the earth; they could follow you even if you crossed the sea to Egypt."

The Americans made fewer visits to Arab Harran in this period, but Ibn Rashed, Saleh Dabbasi, al-Salaami and others went more often than ever to the American compound, and some of the workers said that one night they saw Ibn al-Zayan going home from the American compound.

42

THE SEVEN TENTS IBN RASHED HAD ERECTED LONG
ago, in which the workers had lived for six
months, were maintained as a receiving sta-
tion for new workers. A new city, near the American compound
but closed off behind a barbed-wire fence, was built for the
workers who had lived in the tents. This was done after their
numbers swelled and it became clear that the workers should
live nearer the compound while the seafront was dredged and
the harbor built.

The new city, by the hills between Arab Harran and American
Harran, facing the sea, started out as three large barracks hastily
constructed with wood and sheet metal. The earth was paved
with cement. Daham and Naim, who supervised the workers'
move to the new quarters and assignment to the different structures, assured them that "these are temporary—in a short while

the Arabs will have houses built for them just like the ones the Americans have."

The workers moved into the barracks with completely different feelings. As a result of several quarrels over who would fetch water from the wells, or sweep the tents' packed-dirt floors, in addition to the shouting of the cardplayers, which made it hard for many of the others to sleep because the tents were so close together, some of the workers thought that "the barracks were a clean place with good water just two steps away; and a barracks is better than a tent." Others held that the mere move from the tent, from that tomb, even if it meant living in the desert, under the stars, would save them from the depression that affected them all, creating tension and short tempers. They needed a change and did not care where it was to. Still others thought that the site chosen by the Americans for the barracks was the worst possible place, "because a man doesn't know if he's in Heaven or Hell, if he's with his people and among his own kind or isolated in the desert." Despite the depression they all suffered, the return to Arab Harran each night, passing between the houses and the shops, talking to the people, and the sight of the children, dogs, donkeys and camels, provided a respite from the torment and silence that reigned the whole eight hours they spent in the devils' compound. That was not all, for "the sight of Abdu Muhammad strolling down the beach muttering his gibberish and counting his sweethearts is better than a vacation!" as Abdullah al-Zamel used to say. When they sat with Ibn Naffeh he looked them right in the face and asked whether or not they had seen the Americans conjuring that day or what exactly they had been doing; then while they answered he repeated, "I seek refuge in God from the accursed Satan; I seek refuge in God from the accursed Satan; I seek refuge in God from the accursed Satan." He trembled at anything they said that he did not like, rose to move closer to his interlocutor and glare in his face, then resumed, more excitedly and more rapidly: "I seek refuge in God, I seek refuge in God from the accursed Satan."

For most of the workers, the sight of Abdu or a chat with Ibn Naffeh, listening to the latest news of the world from travelers recently arrived from Ujra or other places, was as good as the kingdom the Americans had, especially since this desolate, fenced-in place made everyone inside feel like a genuine prisoner. Why had the barbed wire been strung around them? Why were they always to enter and leave by that same gate, each showing his yellow identification card as if it were the only thing that proved a man's existence?

These were the men's thoughts and feelings as they moved their few belongings into their new "homes." Ibn Rashed, who had not been seen in three days and may have been away on business, showed up on the fourth day, and after inspecting the barracks he praised their cleanliness and the wisdom of dividing the men up in them.

"Beautiful and lasting residences," pronounced Ibn Rashed, standing amid a group of workers. He shook his head and laughed. "God shame him, this Ibn Muzil, I'm sure he didn't slaughter . . ."

After a moment he went on in a chuckling tone, "That's the way he is. Thinks it would look conceited."

He palpated the wall with his hand and knocked hard to test it, then grasped the barracks door and opened and closed it a few times, and when he was through continued talking. "If we've stinted you this time, brothers, we'll compensate you many times over, God willing."

43

T HE NEW CITY THAT STARTED OUT WITH THREE barracks and thirty-five workers, a source of joy to some workers and a source of anguish to others, certainly a change for most of them, grew wider and higher. In less than a month a new barracks was built, and before the end of the year there were seventeen of them. The barracks that originally housed fifteen men was later to hold twenty or twenty-five. The men who had rejoiced at the move were badly disappointed, for the atmosphere of the tents, pleasant and agreeable late at night and at dawn, did not exist in these tin cans that became suffocating ovens reeking of heat, sweat and sleep. Within a few weeks the white wooden walls were an unrecognizable color, a mixture of smoke, sweaty hands and dust. Hardest of all for the workers to deal with, and a cause of distress they could do nothing about, was the metal roofing. These roofs had become their worst enemy, for they not only radiated heat but shed melted leaden death constantly from the earliest hours of daylight until late at night. The lead was harsher and more hostile than the faces and behavior of the Americans; for a long time the workers were not content with glaring hatefully at these ceilings but actually spat at them, and some even hurled sandals or anything else that came to hand at them. A sandal party happened at least once a week in all the barracks, for as soon as it started up in one barracks the next one over would join the competition, and within minutes sandals were piled on the beds and scattered between them after their flights between the hands and ceilings, and some flew into the barracks, by way of the windows or participants outdoors.

Every past source of disturbances or quarrels had just the opposite effect now. The men who had complained about the cardplayers and fought with them late at night when they had lived in the tents now slept peacefully among the noisy cardplayers. When the players went out into the open air, the others did not hesitate to stretch out beside them to seek the sleep that had deserted them indoors.

Those who had quarreled over keeping the ground clean discovered in the barracks that they were even readier to argue and fight in spite of the fact that they now had cleaners and were themselves exempted from that chore.

The same may have been said of the water, and the hours for sleep and the time to wake up, and the question of who slept where.

Everywhere there was potential for endless quarreling, and many of the men felt, vaguely, that the fistfights and constant cursing were not always the result of mistakes or ill intentions and had little to do with the actual words spoken; they felt this even more since depression and homesickness and other damned "things" were still within them and tore them apart before the quarrels and curses and the rest. Had it not been for the exhaustion that crushed their bodies and helped to break up their quarrels, compelling them to sleep, there would have been ominous incidents, but as it was every day brought new problems. It was true that a secret desire was more powerful than the will that ruled their men's behavior and their relations with one another, and this desire was visible in their antagonism and extraordinary actions. Despite their remorse, unforced faith and firm resolutions not to fight or lose their tempers, the quarrels continued and incidents did not cease.

The depression was never deeper than when the workers looked around them to see, in the east, American Harran: lit up, shining and noisy, covered with budding vegetation; from afar they could hear the voices of the Americans splashing in the swimming pools, rising in song or laughter. On some nights they filled the sky with colored fireworks, particularly when new groups of Americans arrived. To the west were the houses of Harran, from which smoke rose at sundown and the sounds of human and animal life came. Last of all they saw the barracks they lived in and this dry, harsh, remote life, at which point memories flooded back and their hearts ached with longing, and they found endless pretexts for quarrels and sorrow, and sometimes tears.

The evening gatherings the workers held, to sing, tell jokes and spring surprises on one another, to cheer themselves up, usually ended with new wounds. Instead of cheering them up, the songs filled the men with intense gloom. The stories that made them laugh loudly when first heard went stale, and many of the men were surprised that they had ever laughed at them at all. The practical jokes some of them played, instead of producing gaiety and lightening the atmosphere, often led to fistfights, especially when the "victims" were not chosen with great care.

Suweyleh—the "neighborhood singer," as Ibn Zamel called him, with no objection from Suweyleh—who had enthralled everyone at Dabbasi's wedding, had not changed. His voice was still strong, but he could no longer produce the splendor and radiance he had created in their hearts that night, even though every time he sang his emotion reached the point of tears and collapse.

One night in early summer, Ibn Zamel spoke up in a voice that trembled with anger. "My friends, if we keep quiet we'll die like prison mice, and as long as death is the beginning and end for us all, death among friends is better than death among the blue devils." He was silent a moment, then went on. "If I leave, who'll go with me?"

He looked at their faces questioningly, almost pleading. He wanted to hear a voice, an assent, and when he saw the men silent and confused, he spoke as if to himself. "You'll be sorry tomorrow, but then it will be too late."

What dissuaded him from leaving was Ibn Rashed's promise to find a way to "fix these roofs and keep them from spreading death."

Using means of terror and persuasion, and with promises galore, a number of the emir's men were placed among the workers. They were called observers, and they set wooden planks between the crossbeams and the roof and put a layer of dirt on top of the planks. They cut new windows in the southern walls of the four old barracks, and when the decision was made to put in the windows, Ibn Rashed said, "Fresh air will sport like a stallion in these spacious residences!" The new barracks were built by the company itself, not subcontracted to Ibn Rashed as the first four had been. The new barracks were smaller and built of several different materials: cement, earth and stone. They were cooler than the others, which led to more fights: who would move to the new barracks, and who would stay in the old ones?

The first workers had some power due to their seniority as well as to the clan relationships that bound most of them together, but the Americans began to use new criteria in classifying the workers; the first arrivals were better aware than the others, or better able to get their way. They spoke up and made demands, and drew rude and hostile stares. The more peaceable or docile among them were treated with special care; Abdullah al-Zamel, for example, who rarely stopped making jokes or criticisms and had created a fuss over the housing, did not have to wait long to be sent to Station 4. That station was so far away that workers were able to come home only once every three days, and the work there was notoriously dirty and difficult. Ibn Zamel agreed to work at that station after being compelled to do so by a threat from the emir, but he still made no secret of his desire to escape someday—though only, he said, after he had "killed two or three Americans, and Ibn Rashed, and their little dog Daham." Mizban, who had once punched Daham, was not allowed to forget the affront: he, his brother Hajem and twelve other workers who had been relative latecomers were selected, on the pretext that they knew how to swim, to help cut sea rock in the port expansion project. The brothers and the other workers with them did not protest the assignment; they seemed eager for a new adventure, but subsequent events made all the men view the matter differently from the way Ibn Rashed and others did.

Mizban and Hajem, who had never given up trying to teach the workers to swim and had always spent long intervals in the water—Ibn Zamel called them "the two fishes"—had finally, after much perseverance, convinced several of the workers to go near the water, for a start, and later to step into it; much later on many of them plunged into the shoals where the water reached their waists. Carefully and gently they immersed their bodies until only their heads showed. They did this very warily and only on rare occasions, especially after Salman al-Jaraf nearly drowned while trying to learn how to swim. The brothers had been by his side, laughing delightedly as they watched him dunk and heave in the water, gulping it down. They laughed because the water they were swimming in barely reached their chests, but when they saw that he was in danger they hauled him out more dead than alive. For a long time afterward the men were hesitant about swimming, and newly wary.

Being chosen suited the brothers' own wishes, but the job they were given was so dangerous that the accident took place.

After the start of the project to expand and deepen the seaside adjacent to the American compound, the men went back and forth every day and took on a dark tan color. They seemed different from the other workers; they told all kinds of stories about the boat that took them out to work and the tools they used, and, later, about the explosives that shook the sea and made gigantic waves collide. They saw what the Americans ate and what their table manners were like. The stories that the sea workers told the land workers made Harran's nights easier to bear that summer.

They remembered a night with a full moon. Suweyleh was singing in a soft but impassioned voice more like a sorrowful confession, having refused all requests to raise his voice or change his tone, and in spite of the first notes the workers tried to stimulate him with, most of the men remembered that Mizban was silent and pensive, and that he had only spoken once in the course of the long evening, to say, "My friends, I'd trade this whole sea for the well in our town. Tonight Ibn Hadib is opening wounds in me that won't ever heal." He said this during a lull, in a moment of anxiety, but the men would not have remembered his words had it not been for the accident.

At dawn the next day, when the port workers were accustomed to leave before the others, they had left the camp to board the boat, and three of the workers were asked to dive in and tie a rope to a boulder to pull it out. Mizban was one of the three who dove down to the seabed, but though the other two resurfaced within a few moments, Mizban did not. Ibrahim al-Saffar and Saad al-Rajeh came back, but Mizban did not. When two or three minutes passed and he did not surface, several workers plunged in to find him, but they returned and he did not.

They found Mizban after a long search: his foot was stuck in the crevice of a boulder. The crevice was like a necklace with Mizban hanging up from it. It appeared that he had fought hard to free himself, for his body was covered with bruises, but he had been unable to.

It was a black and sinister day, the day they brought Mizban back as a stiff corpse. The news spread quickly through the camp, American Harran and Arab Harran.

Mizban was buried at noon that same day, in anger and sorrow. Not a soul was left in Harran; everyone followed his body to the grave. For a long time to come they remembered the ringing laugh of the big fish, as Abdullah al-Zamel called him.

44

WORK ON EXPANDING AND DEEPENING THE PORT never let up for a single day, and Hajem, who was not asked to report to work the next day or for the next several days, was a different man from the very hour Mizban was lowered into his grave and the dirt heaped over him. He stared aimlessly, his jaw drooped, and he seemed feebleminded. He had not shed a tear or uttered one word; he was dazed. He looked in the men's faces as if searching for someone, and having confirmed that the person he wanted was not there, he smiled and then screeched with laughter, slapping his palm against his thigh. He did this unconsciously, involuntarily. The workers, who averted their gaze so as not to look at him in the beginning, were grief stricken, and some of them felt weak, almost dizzy. Mizban had not been just another worker. He was loved and respected, like a father or a big brother, and had been given many different names: the camel and the horse, and Abdullah al-Zamel called him the big fish. This last name was the best known and most widely used. Men used to seek him out when they felt depressed or lonesome. He looked like a big child but was very strong, and at times even rough. He used to grasp the forearm of whoever spoke to him and pull him in the direction of the sea in order to hear him better, and they would return looking different, like two brothers. When two men had a disagreement, Mizban was generally the mediator whose judgment was accepted.

Now that they had buried him, they had to believe that he was dead. When they saw Hajem's face as he peered around, looking bewilderedly into people's faces, smiling his imbecilic smile, they knew that they had lost a dear friend. When they remembered what Ibn Naffeh had said over the grave, they found different meanings in his words. He had shouted, "The man didn't die—they killed him with witchcraft before they killed him with the sea."

Why were they outcasts, pushed closer to death every minute? They had come to work but here they worked and were killed at the same time. The money they were given did not compensate for a single night under the roofs that dripped melted lead over their heads. And Ibn Rashed's words? Daham? Naim? The Americans' cruel faces? At first the Americans had laughed and slapped them on the shoulders. Now they did not look at them or if they did, spat out words that could only be curses. This was a guess but they were sure of it, for "you can't hide curses in any language," as Ibn Zamel said. Even the Americans knew it when the children of Harran came near them to raise their hands in greeting and said something like "you son of a bitch"—they shook their fingers in warning, and one American even kicked a boy, knocking him down. The Americans had changed; and that was not all, for the relationship between the two sides was curtailed and handled only through the "personnel office." The personnel office now meant Naim, young Dabbasi, Daham and two of the emir's men.

Ibn Rashed came on the afternoon of the day Mizban died. He seemed more solemn than he ever had before. He was wearing his new black cloak, which he generally wore only when visiting the emir or the American compound. He walked slowly. They saw him entering the gate of the camp with two of his men. The workers stayed at their posts, silent. They knew he had come to have a word with Hajem, to express his condolences, and at this moment they sensed that Ibn Rashed was their true enemy. He had brought them to this place and given them over like sheep to those people. They hated him and considered him responsible not for Mizban's death but for his murder.

Hajem was sitting with a group of workers in the shade of one of the barracks on the east side. When Ibn Rashed began to approach he cleared his throat, but no one heard him or looked up, even when his firm footsteps brought him right beside them.

"Peace upon you, men."

Some of the workers came near him; they shook his hand and walked with him. Hajem looked at their faces, then turned in all directions and smiled. Ibn Rashed approached until he stood above him, and Hajem looked at him and smiled.

"God bless you, my boy. I hope your sorrows are over."

He bent down to kiss Hajem's shoulders, then sat beside him. Hajem looked at him again and then again, and smiled. Ibn Rashed looked at the silent men's faces and shook his head, sensing what they felt. He spoke to change the mood. "Death is foreordained for every man from the day God creates him. Just as he is born, he must die. That is the law of life. A man never knows where he was born or where he will die. God is truth and death is truth, and no one is immortal but the Everlasting, the Eternal."

Ibn Rashed spoke by himself, to himself. His words seemed dry and meaningless, and when he saw the men's cold stares and felt the silence surrounding him, he asked, "Who was with the deceased?"

When a few names were mentioned and some of the men moved spontaneously because they had been with Mizban, Ibn Rashed addressed one of the men. "Come here, come here, my boy. Come near and tell me how it happened."

Even though Ibn Rashed and all of the men had heard how it happened several times, from several different people, silence fell and the man animatedly retold the whole story in detail, from the time they left the camp at dawn until the accident happened.

The only one to listen raptly to the story, as if hearing it for the first time, was Hajem. He stared into the man's face. He moved nearer to him and smiled, and when he finished, Hajem slapped his thigh with the palm of his hand, and raised his head excitedly to look in several directions, as if searching for someone. Ibn Rashed held him and made him sit down, and spoke to him in a sad voice. "Be patient, my boy. There is no power or strength save in God. We must all return to Him."

When silence fell again in a heavily charged atmosphere, Ibn Rashed spoke testily. "The man's blood must be compensated." He shifted in his sitting position and said in a different tone: "There is no question that it happened at work. For some time the workers have been under the company's protection. The company is responsible—they pay the wages and everything else, and they provide housing."

"The personnel office should pay compensation," said Daham, who had been silent until then.

Ibn Rashed was badly in need of some help, of someone to stand by him just then, and as soon as Daham spoke Ibn Rashed replied decisively. "Listen, Daham. You and Ibn Hathal, today, yes, this very day, you two write out a petition to the company, and tell them everything. Yes, everything: how the accident happened. When. And ask for compensation. Are you listening, Daham?"

Daham nodded his understanding and compliance. When he lifted his head to look for Ibn Hathal to assist him in the job, he saw Hajem's eyes. Hajem had turned to look at the men's faces, and when his eyes met Daham's he smiled. Ibn Rashed bent over to kiss Hajem's shoulders again and got up.

"God bless you, men. We belong to God and to Him we all must return."

When he left, some of the men went with him part of the way, but Daham accompanied him to Arab Harran.

When darkness fell that night the men felt intensely depressed, and not one of them remembered seeing the moon that filled the sky.

45

I N THE LATE AUTUMN HARRAN WAS BUSY WITH THE
construction of the emirate building and the emir's
residence. Heaps of rock and sand, steel rods and
lumber were piled up near the tents and on the north central hill
between Arab Harran and American Harran, west of the American compound. There was unusual bustle in anticipation of the
start-up of construction. In this period the emir, accompanied
by Naim, visited several of the Americans. They showed him
the plans and drawings, and it took the emir three days to give
his approval, for he asked Ibn Rashed, Dabbasi and others about
the proposed site and the number of rooms; he showed them
the plans and drawings, which meant nothing to them. They
merely suggested, in general words, that "the building be as
sound as the Americans' houses, and spacious." When the Americans came with Naim to see the emir a few days later, to present

the plans and drawings again, Khaled al-Mishari told them in a soft but firm voice, "We approve . . . with God's blessing."

When the emir was asked which set of plans he had approved, he replied, "We have given our approval. Trust in God."

Naim was confused and said nothing. He looked at the emir and then at the Americans, and the emir spoke to end the matter. "Tell them to use plenty of steel, and to put in windows on the southern side."

Naim explained to the Americans that the emir left the choice of the most suitable plans to them and indicated that there should be large windows facing south. The emir asked how long the construction would take, and the Americans said two or three months.

When the jackhammers set to work the emir went nearly deaf from their blasting, and when the earthmovers started piling the dirt he told Dabbasi, "Now keep your promise, Abu Saleh."

Dabbasi grinned and nodded, and pointed his finger at his eye: "By my eye, Your Excellency!"

The emir smiled and then laughed loudly, and Dabbasi smiled too.

"I thought it had slipped your mind, Abu Saleh, or that you'd forgotten."

With some effort, and after a great deal of sarcasm and evasion, Dabbasi understood that the promise the emir was referring to was the hunting trip, especially since "these damned machines are enough to take your head off or blind you!" Dabbasi seemed eager to accompany the emir on the trip and promised to take with him some of the men who knew where the best hunting places were, but he asked for a few days in which to complete some urgent business that could not be postponed. The emir consented and told him to choose their companions carefully.

When the emir asked Ibn Rashed to come along on the excursion, he rubbed his hands, seemed unable to accept or refuse and said nothing. When he was asked to explain he laughed. "Your Excellency, so many responsibilities . . ."

The emir understood that he wanted to stay in Harran.

"Don't worry, Ibn Rashed. Harran isn't going anywhere, and we're not coming back until it is even more beautiful!"

"Harran is for the Harranis," replied Ibn Rashed, raising his hands. "For Dabbasi and the others, and you, Your Excellency, you know that a man without his family gets no son, and Ibn Rashed longs for a son."

Ibn Rashed might have cited the example of the emir himself, who had brought his family with him, being unable to live without them, but he preferred to mention Dabbasi, to refer to his marriage to a Harrani girl within a few days of his arrival.

"You are right, Ibn Rashed," said the emir playfully. "Money makes men blind."

"I didn't mean that, Your Excellency, but people need money to live."

"If we come back and find you still in this town, we'll marry you off or get rid of you."

"Just as you say, Your Excellency."

Within a few days the emir's excursion was prepared—he was to be accompanied by several of his own men as well as Dabbasi and two Harranis, one of them an old man who could hardly talk and the other a smiling young man who seemed well traveled, intelligent and quick on his feet.

Emir Khaled ordered his deputy to keep an eye on the construction and to supervise all its stages personally. He reiterated his wish for large windows facing south and said that although he would not be gone long, he did not know exactly when he would return, because "everything depends on the hunting. We might be back in a few days or we might take our time." He added paternally, "God bless you. We are depending on God, and on you."

Ibn Rashed stayed in Harran for three weeks after the emir left. He had to procure the rock and sand for the emirate and the emir's residence, and recruit a crew of workmen. He had to reach an agreement with the Americans to guarantee supplies for the workers' cafeteria, especially since the rivalry between himself and Saleh Dabbasi had almost reached the point of outright warfare. He had these responsibilities, as well as a secret and anxious decision, still to be made, over whether to build himself a house in Harran now or put it off until later.

These were Ibn Rashed's ostensible reasons for staying behind in Harran, but there was another, known only to himself and Daham: he had to get rid of Hajem. Ibn Rashed had put all his genius into wording the petition presented three weeks after Mizban's death. He made several additions and emendations to the text and decided to have Fawaz al-Hathal write it out, because "his script is straight as a sword on the line and his words are clear and legible, unlike Daham who writes crookedly, with one word big and the next one small." Ibn Rashed filled the petition with all the flattering and imploring words he knew or could remember, and it took a long time to arrive at a version that satisfied him.

The petition was presented to the personnel office, and it went from there to the main office and from the main office to the legal committee so that it might be decided whether or not Ibn Rashed was responsible for the compensation, since steps to formalize the transfer of the workers to the company's responsibility had not been taken until ten days after the accident. The issue was further complicated by Hajem's condition: he was in a daze, incapacitated by visions, which led to his termination from employment after referrals to several doctors, one of whom was Indian. This doctor's opinion contradicted all the others, and the disagreement delayed the doctors' report and consequently Hajem's termination from service; there was a good deal of interference and rumormongering in the process, as Ibn Rashed and Saleh al-Dabbasi noted, aimed at "weakening him in front of the Americans and inciting the workers against him."

Ibn Rashed wanted the matter closed before he took any action, especially since the emir did not seem eager to get involved. When Ibn Rashed had asked him to, the emir had replied, "The people are our concern, Ibn Rashed. You had better look after your own, and win them over as best you can, and give us a rest from these complaints." Ibn Rashed reckoned that unless the problem was settled at once, it was bound to get far more complicated, particularly since Dabbasi was now traveling with the prince "and talks about nothing but Ibn Rashed these days—Ibn Rashed did this, and Ibn Rashed did that, and the emir will be like a woman or a small boy—he'll listen to all that and believe it, and the next time I have any business with him he'll be impossible."

Ibn Rashed's efforts to have the Americans close the case as quickly as possible clashed with the legal and medical processes, because "rules are rules, and they take priority over people and their wishes!" His indirect efforts with Hajem were foiled by his silly smiles and the workers' provocations. Ibn Rashed thus made his decision privately and carried it out one night, in complete secrecy.

At noon he sent Daham to take Hajem to the medical board, or so he told Daham, and so Daham told the worker in charge of Hajem—for the workers had decided among themselves that one of them should remain with him at all times. Instead of taking Hajem to the medical board he took him to Arab Harran, to Ibn Rashed's tent, where Ibn Rashed had prepared one of his men to travel after dark, to escort Hajem back to his family. And indeed that is what happened. Some money was placed in the saddlebags of Hajem's camel, rather than in his pocket because "he'd throw it away or give it to any bedouin," Ibn Rashed told the man who accompanied Hajem to Ujra, then to Umm Saaf, "because he has an uncle there—turn him over to his uncle and tell him the compensation is on its way!"

When Ibn Rashed was asked about Hajem three days later, he said, "The American doctor took him in, and God willing he'll come back cured." But on the fifth day, Daham grew fearful and anxious and said, "Hajem is with his family. If he doesn't get there today he'll make it tomorrow."

The workers were filled with black hatred when they heard what Daham said, and they vowed never to forget.

46

A FEW DAYS AFTER THE EMIR LEFT, MUHAMMAD al-Seif and Abdullah al-Saad arrived in Harran. They were Harranis who had left a very long time before. Abdullah had always sent his family letters, gifts and money, and although Muhammad had not been in contact for the first three years, after that he began to send letters and money, and the bearer of one of his letters claimed that "Muhammad al-Seif is doing splendidly—he's one of the richest and best-known men in Basra."

Now they were returning, and when they stopped at al-Mattaleh, at the beginning of the Harran-Ujra road, they thought they were lost, and for a moment Abdullah thought he was dreaming. He rubbed his eyes and stared, but he recognized only the two palm trees by the mosque: that was all that had not changed. There was no sign of Harran, which had been in that lowland among the wells. There was a scattering of colored buildings and a group of tents where he remembered houses, and the hills to the east and west were covered with things that had not been there before.

They were silent, looking around, for perhaps there had been some mistake, but when they were sure they had arrived, sure that the astonishing sight before them was Harran itself, albeit a different Harran, they felt frustration and something like revulsion. Why had the Harran they knew been demolished? Where were their families—what had happened to them? Were they themselves capable of living in this Harran they did not know and had never lived in?

The men had much to say, but the shock and the urge to explore and discover left them silent and confused. After a few words of wonderment and incredulity in al-Mattaleh, they jogged along on their camels with this caravan which they had loved at first sight in Ujra. It was a huge caravan, full of people who would never have come together in any other caravan, and carried a full range of goods. They had chatted with most of the other travelers but had not said that they were from Harran, or that they were now returning after years of absence. When one of the bedouin in the caravan asked them if, like him, they were going to Harran to look for work, Muhammad nodded his head yes.

Now they were riding toward the mosque, feeling terribly let down and worried. How would they find their families? Should they ask the strangers who had only just moved here themselves to guide them to where their families lived? Would the families know them after all these years, and all the changes that had taken place everywhere?

"Muhammad, all we can do is go to the mosque," said Abdullah jokingly. "We'll say our prayers and look for whatever old men haven't died yet, and surely they'll know us, or something about our families."

Muhammad laughed. "Like they say in Egypt—'Tell me if you can, young men/Where my father's house has gone.' "

"Trust in God—we'll find them, don't worry."

"I'm not worried, but . . ." Muhammad shook his head and looked closely at Abdullah, then smiled and went on. "Twenty, thirty years ago, we used to blindfold ourselves and race our donkeys from Tel Zeeb to Harran, and we'd always get there!"

Abdullah laughed. "Donkeys can always find their hitching posts."

Harran had not changed completely. As soon as the caravan arrived the people swarmed around it. Much sooner than they thought, at the first looks they exchanged with the people, the two felt enveloped in an atmosphere of home and friends. The people crowded around them as if they had been away only on a short trip. Time had left its marks on all their faces, but these marks were dissolved by the emotions underneath, and these emotions revealed the inner strength which eliminated time and distance, returning their features to their original loveliness.

The men's meetings with their families and friends were deeply moving and at times difficult, for the Harranis were unruly in their happiness and went out of their way to demonstrate it, but there was an unhidden rebuke in their eyes: why did you leave us for all these years? Or: how can a man forget or abandon his roots so lightly? The new arrivals turned every which way and asked dozens of questions without waiting for complete or detailed answers. They were apprehensive: Where were their mothers, sisters and aunts—where were the women of Harran? Could the people be living contentedly after the changes that left no trace of the original Harran? Where were they living now?

Muhammad al-Seif and Abdullah al-Saad made their chaotic way to new Harran amid the screaming and shouting of the children and the agitation of their camels, which was a result of the shouting and general uproar. Many saw Abdullah al-Saad wipe his tears away when he met his mother. She was a very elderly lady who had gone blind and could barely walk. When she met him she buried her face in his chest and did not move for a long time, and even when she moved back a little and lifted her head she still clutched him. She clutched him tightly at first, as if afraid that he would turn away from her or leave her again; she wept copiously and buried her face in his chest every few moments, smelling him and crying, and the people saw Abdullah smile, but it was a tearful smile. After a while she freed one of her hands to explore his face while holding him fast with the other.

These were hard and violently emotional moments for everyone present, not only for Abdullah and his mother. She was silent as she moved her hand back and forth, as if using this hand to ask questions, to search and to reassure herself. She felt her son's small beard tenderly, with evident delight, and kissed her own hand, then stood on tiptoe to kiss the beard itself, and when she was sufficiently reassured, or intoxicated, she loosed her hands, though she repeatedly stretched out one or both her hands again, as if stroking an infant, to feel this strange creature who had suddenly appeared.

Abdullah was surprised that his mother had lost her sight; no one had told him about her blindness and he had not expected it. When he saw her this way he felt wretched, guilty of a misdeed so great that he could never forgive himself; when his sisters embraced him he felt the terrible weight of time's passage. Even his youngest sister, whom he had left as a girl of ten, was married with two children; she was carrying one and holding the other by the hand. How had all these years passed—why was it so heartbreaking?

Abdullah was surprised by what he saw, but Muhammad,

who could not be surprised by a sightless mother, since his own had left this world when he was a boy, was surprised by everything else. Even after days had passed, in which they came to know all the young of the town and asked for all the older ones, toured the new houses of Harran on the western hill, visited the market and the wells, and walked along the beach, they still felt no repose in the Harran they saw. It was not only unease they felt—it was fear.

Instinctively, the townsfolk of Harran surrounded the two new arrivals in love and fear to fight any thought they might have had of leaving again. The people felt what women feel before men—that the two men could turn away and say whatever they liked, make any excuse to go traveling again. They sensed it in the men's eyes and the solemnity that had possessed them shortly after arriving, though the two had said nothing.

The townsfolk all felt responsible for Muhammad al-Seif, though not as the result of any plan or explicit decision, but the old blind lady took charge of her son Abdullah on her own and joined in with the rest of them besieging Muhammad al-Seif to prevent him from leaving. They all felt abandoned, in need of some kind of protection, protection that could only come from within their number—not from the emir or anyone else. It was this feeling which made them act and talk as they did with the men and which informed the desires that overcame them every so often. The days passed, and within a month Abdullah told his mother that he would send his brother Ibrahim to Basra to bring his family; he would send a letter with Ibrahim to his partner there in which he advised him that he would be a long time in returning. The old lady nodded and tears flowed from her eyes, but she said nothing. A few days later Ibrahim was ready to go. The night he left, Muhammad al-Seif said, "I have my money, and any place else is as good as Harran. If I don't leave this year, I'll leave next year."

47

IN THE BARRACKS RESENTMENT MOVED LIKE A BIRD FROM one man to another. It circulated constantly, for any reason or even for no reason. Daham, who used to be so strong, with his powerful voice and self-confident gait, who thought nothing of cursing—he considered it one of his natural talents—became meticulously wary after Hajem's absence and Ibn Rashed's departure. Daham spent little time in the camp, on the pretext that he had work to do or business to attend to in Arab Harran or the American compound. The workers had not seen Naim since Mizban's death. After taking part in Mizban's funeral as the official representative of the company (as he kept pointing out), he disappeared completely. Some of the workers said that they had seen him from a distance, and others said that he had gone on a long journey and might never come back. As to the personnel office, as that phantom was called, no one knew if it was still operating; the workers received several orders from the foremen and the emir's men, but these were later canceled.

New groups of workers arrived about this time. They had been recruited by Dabbasi, not Ibn Rashed, and Saleh Dabbasi showed an unusual interest in receiving these workers and assigning them to the recently completed barracks. They were advanced a half month's wages "in case they needed to buy supplies from Harran, or for tea in the cafés." In addition, the clothing and other things handed out to the new recruits were better than those given to the original workers. Saleh inquired every day to make sure of that.

The new men, who came from all different places, brought with them the fresh air of the world outside Harran. They told stories which were medleys of dreams, wishes and lies—how new recruitment offices had been opened in Ujra and al-Samaayineh and on the Sultan's Road, and how Ibn Rashed's men attached to the offices or roving in the interior to look for workers boasted of the privileges in store for men who were ready to join the company: excellent food, wonderful pay, short hours with no end of free time and free housing in homes surrounded by water and gardens.

Their eyes explored every corner, looking with the desire to know and discover. Some of the lies would survive a little while, but the new barracks, though better and cooler than the older ones, wrecked the newcomers' expectations and gave notice of the harsh and difficult life before them.

The personnel office, so long a phantom, now resurfaced to inform the men that interviews to determine their classification would be held within the next few days. One of the emir's men told the workers so and told them to get ready! Get ready? What did that mean—what would they do? What did the "classification" of the workers mean, and what would it lead to?

Such an announcement might ordinarily have had no great effect or inspired no dread, but three days later the workers were told that they would be split up into groups: the first group would go for interviews and the rest of the groups would report to work as usual. Daham read out the names of the first group on the spot, asking the others to go off to work, and the selected workers were led off to the American compound.

A long time, several months, had passed since they were last there, and some of them had never been in the compound before.

American Harran looked like a new place to all of them. Even the buildings they had worked on, in whose shade they had rested, looked completely different. The Americans had added many new touches such as trees—where had they come from?— and the soil had been dug up and replaced with a strange substance. The trees were tall. There were large and small clumps of different vegetation here and there, and even the barrels had been painted white, filled with plants and placed all around. The streets, whose packed dirt had been coated with black liquid within the first days of work, were different as well: there were new buildings beside the ones they had put up, and there were rows of small houses not far from Central Administration.

The sight of all these new and strange things in American Harran bred both awe and wariness, especially when the workers saw the Americans going from building to building staring at them curiously, as if to ask: what are they doing here—who brought them?

Silence like the shadow of a heavy tent hung over the group of some twenty men. There was no sound but their footsteps— the friction of sandal leather and their breathing. There was nothing they could say to each other out loud. Even the questions they'd asked each other as they left their camp for the American compound now increased their unease and suspicion with every step they took.

One of the Americans told them, with a wave of his hand, to halt. They stopped thirty or forty steps short of the Central Administration office, at a roof supported by poles, but they could not all fit underneath, so some of them stood in the sun. They could look around in all directions: to the east was the large swimming pool and two rows of houses, and on the other side was the restaurant where the emir had dined, part of another pool and a row of small houses. Directly in front of them, beside the administration building, was a large structure about as wide as the restaurant but elongated, with small rooms along one side.

They watched silently. None of them dared ask a question—if they had, none of them could have answered it. At first they avoided looking at each other's faces so as not to see how pale and afraid they all were, but after taking in the whole scene in all directions, and waiting a good while in this place, they began to exchange looks of uncertainty and terror. Their eyes never stopped talking, and enigmatic muttering had displaced the silence.

Suddenly, as they waited, Naim came at them, as specters rush out of tombs. He headed toward them from the Central Administration building, not looking at them once while walking from the building to the place where they stood. He was looking at the ground, and though the strength of his features showed when he came near and they saw him, it was the strength of hatred or contempt. He wore loose clothing, unusual for him—his clothes were usually tighter and less varied. As he surveyed them with one brief, sweeping glance to determine where the group began and ended, Daham spoke up decisively. "They'll enter in groups of five, alphabetically." Daham drew the list of names from his pocket, read out the first five names and added, "Follow me."

A sudden cold breeze in the long, dim corridor chilled the five workers and gave them gooseflesh. It was like a blast of winter wind or late-night air. They turned every which way to see where the wind was coming from but saw nothing. The rooms on either side of the corridor were locked and quiet; they could hear only their footfalls as they walked nervously behind Naim. They walked a long way, and when they reached the end of the corridor Naim halted abruptly, so they stopped. He looked at them with one side of his face, then opened the door in front of him and went in. They did not know whether to go in or to wait, so they looked around at each other and then at the open door a few steps away. Naim stuck his head out of the door like a magician and said, "Come in."

They walked in to find themselves in the presence of a very dark-skinned man sitting behind a desk. There was a group of chairs to the side of the room. The man gave them a cool, neutral glance. He spoke with Naim for a few moments, then they both stood up. They opened the side door and went in, closing it behind them. Voices were heard from inside. The workers stood in the middle of the cool room—no, it was cold, very cold. They turned around and looked at the walls and chairs, then at each other. They were absolutely quiet, their throats were dry, and their hearts were beating violently.

The same door reopened and the two men came out. "Come with me," said Naim to one of the men, and "Sit down here" to the rest of them, indicating the chairs to their right in front of the door. They tried to sit down, but two of the men bumped into each other when they both headed for the same chair. Once they were seated their gazes were drawn to the brown man, who reseated himself behind the desk, and the door through which Naim and Ibrahim al-Faleh had disappeared.

The very dark-skinned man—darker than anyone they had ever seen, and so exquisitely clean that he seemed bathed in oil— leaned back in his chair and gave them a long look, more kindly than he had before, and when he saw them looking at him he smiled. His teeth were very white, or perhaps they only seemed so because he was so dark. The men looked away quickly and kept quiet. They involuntarily moved their hands and feet and one of them shifted in his chair, and when their gaze met his again he smiled more broadly than before. He tapped his left index finger twice on his chest, smiling. "Musulman . . . Musulman. Ali Iqbal."

They smiled nervously but said nothing. They did not understand a word of what he had said. Was it supposed to be Arabic? They looked at each other curiously. What did the man mean—what did he want from them? Had he asked them a question? Was he expecting some kind of answer? He looked at them and nodded, then slapped his chest with the palm of his hand and spoke again. "*Alhemdu Alah, rabb al-alameyn. Al-rahman, al-raheem.*"

So he considered this gibberish Arabic. This time his smile was a grin, but again they looked at each other and said nothing. The man raised his two index fingers in an even line and pointed them to his chest as a sign.

"Musulman."

They were nervous and afraid. They understood and did not understand at the same time. They said nothing.

When Ibrahim al-Faleh went in he found the room very large and cold. It was at least three times larger than the first room, but just as cold. In the front of the room was an empty round table, and three Americans. He recognized them immediately: two of them were always visiting Arab Harran and knew Arabic, and the third was the one with the huge red beard. They were sitting in a semicircle in the approximate center of the room, and there were several empty chairs. He could think of nothing to say to them, though he wanted to greet them, to say something, but he was too nervous, so he jerked his hand and said nothing. They looked at him from head to foot as he approached them. One of the two who spoke Arabic smiled at him and asked him to be seated, pointing to a chair. He sat down, and Naim sat nearer them, leaving the chair nearest him empty.

The Americans glanced at each other and spoke a few words he did not understand; then Naim turned to Ibrahim.

"We are going to ask some questions, and we'd like you to give accurate answers." When he saw the fear in Ibrahim's eyes, Naim said kindly, "They're easy questions, just routine ones. Anyone could answer them."

The Americans spoke English and Naim translated, but before asking him any questions one of the Arabic-speaking men moved over to the round table and sat behind it, ready to write. After a short silence the questioning began.

"Your name—full name, father's and grandfather's?"

"Ibrahim al-Faleh al-Ibrahim."

"The name before your grandfather's?"

"Ibrahim al-Faleh al-Ibrahim al-Muhammad."

"Great-great-grandfather?"

"Ibrahim al-Faleh al-Ibrahim al-Muhammad al-Ibrahim."

"Which tribe?"

"The Atoum."

"Which branch?"

"The Harb."

"Mother's name?"

Ibrahim al-Faleh gave Naim an astonished, shocked look, then looked at the three Americans, and when he saw them awaiting his reply he asked, "What do you want with my mother?"

Naim shot him a serious, almost rebuking glance, then turned to the Americans and translated what Ibrahim had said. The three Americans roared with laughter, and one of them who knew Arabic spoke. "The information we need is quite simple— and necessary." He paused for a moment and smiled, then stood up, went over to Ibrahim until he was opposite him and patted him on the shoulder.

"Do you have a mother?"

Ibrahim nodded yes.

"Does she have a name?"

Again he nodded yes.

"What is the name?"

Ibrahim sighed like a wounded wolf and shook his head despairingly. He looked at the American who stood over him, then at Naim, and said patiently, "My mother's name is Muzna."

"Is she living or dead?"

"Dead," said Ibrahim, smiling.

"And your father?"

"My father is alive."

"Did he marry several wives?"

"What's wrong with you—can't you talk about anything but my father and mother?"

Again the three Americans laughed, and Naim joined in after he translated what Ibrahim had said. The American who had been standing by him went to have a word with the other two, then said something to Naim that made the other two smile, and Naim nodded vigorously to show that he understood or agreed.

"Like I told you at the beginning: the information we need is simple and necessary, and it is confidential too. No one will know about it, so you can answer freely, without fear." He paused a moment and added in a different tone, "All this information is necessary for us to raise your salary—for your promotion. It can help us send you to America for training."

Ibrahim curled his lip to show he did not care. The questioning resumed.

"Did your father marry anyone besides your mother?"

"Yes, two others."

"What was your mother's position in relation to the others?"

"What was my mother's position?"

"Was she the first wife? The last?"

"The first."

"The wives after her—during her lifetime or after she passed away?"

"One before, and the last one three or four years ago."

"You mean after her decease?"

"Yes!"

"How many brothers do you have?"

"Three, and I make four."

"Are they older than you or younger?"

"I'm the oldest; they're all younger."

"How many sisters?"

"God help me—leave me alone!"

"We told you," said Naim firmly. "This information will remain confidential and no one will see it. It is important for the company to know."

Ibrahim al-Faleh mumbled. Indistinct sounds came from his throat.

"Number of sisters?"

"Five."

"Are you married?"

"No."

"Are your brothers and sisters married?"

"Three of my sisters are married."

"Did they marry relatives or men outside the family?"

"Relatives."

"Now we're through with the family questions." One of the Americans smiled. "Naturally there are plenty of other questions that have to be asked, but no more of those." He paused and looked for Ibrahim's reaction, but seeing him silent and visibly distressed, he turned to speak to the man with the red beard, then resumed asking questions.

"You are a Muslim, correct?"

Ibrahim nodded yes but said nothing.

"Do you pray?"

"Sometimes."

"Why sometimes? Why don't you pray all the time?"

"What do you care!"

"We want you to answer accurately. Why don't you pray all the time?"

"Listen, prayer is God's—not His servant's."

"What do you mean?"

"If I'm with people who are praying, I pray."

They smiled, and some of them exchanged glances.

"Besides prayer, which religious duties do you observe?" asked the man with the red beard.

"I fast."

"Do you fast because your family tells you to, or for other reasons?"

"Because the Lord God said: 'Fast.' "

"Do you fast any time other than in Ramadan?"

"No."

"Have you made the pilgrimage to Mecca?"

"No."

"Don't you want to?"

"God willing, I'll go."

"Any other religious observances?"

Ibrahim exploded. "Tell your friends," he said to Naim, "this is just useless talk, and they had better stop it."

The man with the red beard shook his head in surprise when Naim translated what Ibrahim al-Faleh had said, and he exchanged a few words with the two others, one of whom took over the questioning.

"How many members does your tribe have?"

"As many as there are grains of sand. More. I don't mean to brag."

"Do you like the sheikh?"

"If he's a real sheikh, loves the people and fights beside them, and is one of them, then I'm with him."

"Does your tribe have quarrels with other tribes?"

"That's our business. It is no business of yours. At present, no." He laughed and shook his head as he said no, but they pretended not to notice.

"Do you like the emir?"

"Yes!"

"Have you spoken to him? Have you visited him?"

"No."

"Do you like the job you have, or would you like to do something else?"

"I wouldn't go to the sea. I'd go home to my family before I'd work at sea, but all the other jobs are the same. I've carried rocks here and there, and done digging all around. It's all the same."

"How many of the workers are your friends?"

"They are all my brothers."

"What about friends?"

"Trust in God, my friends—all people have good in them."

"Would you like to go to America for training?"

"No."

"Why not?"

He laughed loudly and did not know why he said, "The jackal is a lion in his own country."

They laughed when Naim translated this saying, after asking Ibrahim al-Faleh what his word for *jackal* meant. When the laughter died down the Americans looked at each other as if deciding to end the questioning there, especially after one of them looked at his watch and then at the ceiling as if calculating how long the interview had lasted. They conversed among themselves, and then one of them spoke to Naim, who nodded several times in agreement.

"As we told you, the questions we asked you, and your answers, will remain confidential and no one else will know about them, so we must ask you not to mention anything to the other workers if they ask you."

Naim escorted Ibrahim to the other room, told him to go directly back to the camp without joining the other workers and asked one of the four workers waiting outside to come with him.

48

B Y THE TIME THE WORKERS RETURNED TO CAMP that afternoon, fifteen of them had been interviewed; the others were to be interviewed at an unspecified later date. Although some of them were quiet at first, not speaking, asking or answering questions, a feeling of anger and unrest pervaded the camp. Their inner turmoil made the men behave moodily and raise their voices for no reason; some of them went straight to bed, though they did not usually go to bed this early.

When the other workers—those who had not been called in for interviews—returned early that evening the mood in the camp changed: the questions and discussions began. The questioners were motivated by mere curiosity, not fear or misgiving, but once they had begun their ingenuous inquiries they were

shocked by what they heard from those who had been interviewed.

"The bastards want to know everything," said Ibrahim al-
Nasir. "Even why my father got divorced and remarried. They
wanted to know if I was unclean, because I didn't pray all the
time. They asked if I had a lot of wet dreams, and they laughed.
The bastards want to know who has planted every seed and laid
every egg in history."

He spat angrily.

Fawaz bin Miteb al-Hathal could not keep his patience. Though
he tried to keep quiet, he spoke up sharply and loudly enough
for everyone to hear when one of the workers asked him to write
letters for him—he wanted a letter of resignation and one to
inform his family that he would come home soon.

"Did they tell you what they told me? 'You're one of the best
workers we have. You have a future here. We've got to send
you to America for training—you can learn English and go to
college and someday you'll be a manager.' " He paused to take
a deep breath, then went on. "If you had been Miteb al-Hathal's
son they would have asked you, 'We'd like you to tell us why
your father quarreled with Ibn Rashed, and where he is now.' "

They had asked Suweyleh to sing, and when he curtly refused
the red-bearded one told him that they only wanted to write
down the words of some of the songs because they loved what
they'd heard him sing at Dabbasi's wedding. He hesitated and
refused again, but finally had to give in because Naim kept
nagging him: "These fellows just like our singing and only want
to hear the words so that they can understand them."

The men's piecemeal narrations produced consternation; their
attempts to convince the others that it was all true—what they
were asked, and what the Americans wanted—did not wholly
succeed. Some of the others felt that they were wrong to have

told everything: perhaps they should have kept the sessions secret, as Naim had constantly warned them to.

It was the workers' custom to go to Arab Harran every once in a while to buy supplies and sit in the coffeehouse that Abu As'ad al-Helwani had opened near the beach, which he called the Friends Coffeehouse—but tonight they could not get out of the camp fast enough.

They needed to walk, and it was a good distance from the camp to Arab Harran. Such a long walk might help them to forget, and if it were not long enough, at least their errands in the market, socializing with the people and a good session in the coffeehouse would soothe them. But they could not just sit quietly in the camp and look at each other, nor did any of them feel like talking. The silence was harder to bear than the fights that broke out between them now and then. If they did speak, they would be watched and spied upon by informers, and the Americans would summon them again to hear Naim's wheedling tones: "I've told you a thousand times: rules are rules. I could talk to rocks or walls and the rocks or walls would finally understand, but with you it goes in one ear and out the other. We've overlooked it time and time again but not this time!" And the questions would begin again, and the questions would lead to other things they could happily do without.

They noticed several new shops in the market in Arab Harran; now there were only one or two empty lots between the shops, and even those were cluttered with the heaps of stones and sand that Ibn Rashed had put there in preparation for construction. They also noticed that a great many workers and foreigners had arrived and were sitting all over the place: by the tents, near the mosque and in the shops. When they reached the Friends Coffeehouse, Abu As'ad al-Helwani beamed at them and at the few empty seats in the coffeehouse and could not stop repeating the same words—"Welcome, men! Welcome, welcome, welcome!"—

as he rushed back and forth to make room for so many unexpected guests.

In Arab Harran they ran into Ibn Naffeh and Abdu Muhammad, who told them that some of the men from Harran who had been away were now back in town.

Ibn Naffeh felt sure that an evil wind had blown the workers into Arab Harran in such large numbers. Anyone who worked with and lived beside the Americans had to be crawling with ill spirits. It was his custom to be sure and hear every new thing that was said, but tonight he was afraid; after offering his hand two or three times to shake the hands of the men who were coming in droves, he pretended to be busy with his prayer beads and refused to meet their eyes as they passed into the coffeehouse. But he listened carefully. From what he was able to glean, he understood that the Americans had summoned the workers to their compound and asked them about all kinds of things. He shifted excitedly and opened his eyes and ears, and with his never-changing supplication—"I seek refuge in God, I seek refuge in God from Satan the accursed"—intermixed with sporadic mutters of "Yes, yes . . . what did they say then, my boy? What can they possibly want? Did you talk? Did you tell them anything? The bastards, every one of them is a devil," his voice rose and fell between the questions and answers, incredulous to the point of real pain. The workers spoke loudly on purpose; they wanted Ibn Naffeh to hear what had happened. When Ibrahim al-Nasir told how they had asked him if he had wet dreams, Ibn Naffeh stood up and began to rant and rave. "Cut their cocks off, people of Harran, and throw them to the dogs! The Americans have come between our men and their wives; they've made fools of us and tomorrow they'll use their witchcraft to turn men into women and women into men! They'll conjure us into monkeys! God damn them and the day they came here! God help us—I seek refuge in God from Satan the accursed!"

He stood in a transport of rage and hatred and glared at the faces around him, then spat several times as loudly as he could and left.

"The haj has gone to the mosque to say his evening prayers," observed Abu As'ad al-Helwani placidly, to calm the atmosphere.

Abdu Muhammad was sitting in a far corner with his back to the room to prevent anyone from sitting or speaking with him; he did not want to talk about his new pictures. The workers were used to him now and kept the distance he desired and imposed on them, especially now that they knew he was in love, but tonight they were immersed in this new problem that had jolted their lives with a disruption they did not know how to counter, so none of them went near Abdu Muhammad. Some of them greeted him loudly from across the coffeehouse, to let him know that they had seen him but that they did not intend to disturb him, and he responded to this gracious gesture by turning around to acknowledge each greeting and even stood up when he responded as a mark of respect and affection.

At one point some of the workers noticed that Abdu turned as if afraid or reluctant, in order to follow the mood in the room, to see that the others were immersed in their own problems and discussions. He heard everything Ibn Naffeh had said. Some of them saw Abdu extract a photograph from his pocket and look at it for long moments as he smiled, murmured and shook his head slowly, then return it to his pocket and sneak a glance in this direction and that to make sure that no one had seen him. This he did several times; had the workers been in any other place they might have made comments or asked questions or called each other's attention to what Abdu Muhammad was doing, but those who saw him only shook their heads and said nothing. When Ibn Naffeh threw his fit of anger, Abdu Muhammad turned his chair directly around to face the others and began to listen to the proceedings from his corner. When Ibn Naffeh used the vulgar words that made all the workers shout with laughter, Abdu placed his hand on his genitals as if to make sure that they were still there, and shortly after Ibn Naffeh stormed out and quiet had returned to the Friends Coffeehouse, he stood and walked through the maze of small iron tables toward the door. Some of the men spoke to him, but he only muttered in reply, and though they invited him to sit with them, since they missed his company and had come a long way on foot from their camp to see him, he only gave his usual answer. "Dawn waits for no man. Tomorrow you'll all be hungry. 'Abdu, where's the bread!' "

49

T HE ECHOES OF THE MEN'S CURSES AND FEARS were not long in reaching the personnel office, and reverberating from the personnel office to headquarters, where the reaction was silence and a halt to the interviews.

Administration gave no sign of anger or even dissatisfaction; indeed the conduct of the Americans, especially the ones who spoke Arabic, became milder and more cunning. They continued to visit Arab Harran but accepted invitations much less frequently than before, and even in the rare instances when they visited homes or individuals, they limited their conversations to the weather and the meanings of certain words and expressions.

On one occasion, they visited Abdullah al-Saad when Ibn Naffeh happened to be present. He stared at them a long time and shook his head, and asked them if they wanted to separate

men from their wives, or brothers from their brothers. Then he
asked them where they kept the jinn, and if they wanted to fetch
a number of demons equivalent to the number of Harran's residents and the surrounding tribes. When he put the questions to
them, suddenly and aggressively, the Americans looked at one
another and laughed, and began to quote some verses from the
Koran. One of them said that "accusing Christians and Jews of
unbelief was a sin against God." Ibn Naffeh's jaw dropped when
he heard the Koranic verses. He could not believe it at first, and
when they quoted some other passages he got up furiously and
screamed: "Satan has a thousand faces and a thousand tongues!"

Although Abdullah al-Saad was deeply embarrassed by Ibn
Naffeh's conduct he stifled his anger, but on hearing these words
he lost his temper, and when his brother Rashed tried to calm
Ibn Naffeh and make him sit down again, and Ibn Naffeh shouted
and tried to get free and shouted more curses, Abdullah spoke
up loudly to his brother so that everyone could hear: "Rashed,
leave the door open, wide enough for a camel, so that any guest
of ours can come in, and so whoever doesn't like our company
can go where he chooses—God's earth is wide!"

Ibn Naffeh came back when he heard this and stood in the
door of the room where Ibn Saad and his guests were sitting.

"Yes, by God, the earth is wide," he snapped angrily. "God
have mercy on those who sleep on the hard ground, like your
father, who used to pray God to build a wall of fire between
himself and all infidel sons of bitches."

He paused for a moment and looked the frightened Americans
in the face, then smiled mockingly and went on. "My boy,
foreign lands are corrupt, and foreign people bring corruption,
and money corrupts worst of all."

Abdullah al-Saad's lips tightened in disgust but he said nothing. There was silence. In the doorway Ibn Naffeh waited to
react to any remark, and to curse, but he saw that he was unable

to provoke them any further and so turned away, facing them in profile.

"Tomorrow they'll bite your hands, but it will be too late to be sorry."

The Americans visited the workers' camp too. The first time they did so on the pretext of examining the water pump, and again in order to determine a site for the new barracks, and both times they stayed longer than was necessary to examine the pump or select a site, and both times they waved at and spoke with the workers.

The third time, four of them came, including Naim and one other who spoke Arabic. It was on a Friday, the workers' day off, in the morning. They said that they wanted to build a mosque and a clubhouse for the workers and had to name a supervisory committee: would the workers prefer to elect the committee or to leave the selection to the personnel office? The workers were asked if they had any other proposals to make. The workers were extremely cautious and said as little as possible, and when they were asked directly they told Naim that they preferred to elect the committee themselves.

Despite the friendliness of the Americans' words and behavior, they gazed intently into the workers' eyes and closely watched their movements and reactions to every proposal or idea they put forward. They wanted to keep talking for a long while; they wanted the workers to respond frankly and fearlessly, but with these impassive faces and brief words it was difficult or impossible to keep a conversation going for long.

At one point the Arabic-speaking American, who had been on the team of interviewers, said that he wished to make it clear to everyone that the company had come to serve the workers and for their sake, and that it would be better able to serve their interests if it could obtain more helpful information: What kind of food did they want? What kind of work did they like best?

When, for example, the company asked the workers if they prayed, it was only in order to know whether or not it was necessary to build a new mosque, or if the mosque in Harran sufficed.

The American discussed these matters in a manner intensely serious and yet comical at the same time, for his accent was all but incomprehensible, and twice he had to ask Naim for words he did not know. When he finished, he was delighted to see the workers smiling and exchanging glances. He knew that the reason for this was his way of speaking, but he had been trying to establish some intimacy and mutual confidence.

After an hour of discussion and questions, during which the workers smiled and winked at one another, the Americans said that, having heard the workers' views and requests, they would convey all they had heard to headquarters. Within a short time steps would be taken to begin construction on the mosque and clubhouse.

This was not the only action the Americans took: they sent presents to Arab Harran and the camp. They also informed the workers, by way of the personnel office, that the interviews would not be resumed; in their stead, green questionnaires would be circulated, asking the name, age and hometown of each worker. As to the section dealing with family matters—marital status, number of children and so on—Naim had made it clear before the questionnaires were sent around that the purpose of this question was to allot pay raises to married workers and those who had children; the amount of the raise would correspond to the number of children. Naim was taken by surprise when Abdullah al-Zamel asked whether the raises would take into account only the number of children, or the number of wives as well.

"Administration hasn't considered that," he answered somewhat perplexedly. "We'll check it with the legal department."

50

AFTER FOUR MONTHS OF UNRELENTING LABOR, the dredging of the shoreline and expansion of the port in front of the American compound were complete, and a number of roads were opened. One linked the compound directly to the port and another beside it led west along the beach to Arab Harran. A third road, a short distance from the harbor, connected the second road with the workers' camp.

With the expansion of the port and construction of the roads, Harran changed once again: large and small ships came in every day, carrying people, goods and new fears as well as strange objects in gigantic crates. Harran trembled with the arrival of every ship and filled with anxiety as it watched everything and every move through the eyes of its children and old men. The children occupied themselves with counting the new people that disembarked from the ships, while the old men watched and meditated, overcome with worry; they turned back to go to the market of Abu As'ad al-Helwani's coffeehouse, where they discussed the latest news with an air of fright and bitterness until it was time for the sundown prayer. Then they left the coffeehouse for the old mosque of Harran, where before and after prayers they spent long periods immersed in silent meditation. After that they rose up again, strong in body but with heavy hearts, to trudge back toward the new city of Harran on the western hills.

There was no limit to the diversity of the new arrivals in Harran or to their strange conduct. Some of them went straight to the American compound and were not seen again until much later. Another group was furnished by the Americans with a field of tents near the beach. It happened that the tents were erected before they arrived, so as soon as they came off the ships they reported to the tents, though within a fairly short time some of them were housed in new barracks and others were moved to the American compound itself. No one knew where some of the others went; they did not enter the American compound and no tents were put up for them; indeed there was no one to welcome them off their ship. They waited a long time for their ship to drop anchor and took their time disembarking, and looked thoroughly bewildered and lost as they stood on the beach amid the piles of their luggage and belongings. It was clear from the way they looked around them that they thought there had somehow been a mistake in choosing their destination. They wandered around looking for other places, carrying their suitcases and parcels with them, behaving noisily and acting very confused.

In no time they were everywhere: in the market, in Abu As'ad's coffeehouse, in the mosque and outside the camp.

Most of the people who arrived on ships like this one were

poor and terrified and never refused any work they were offered; no sooner did Daham or Dabbasi or anyone else from Harran invite them to work in the camp, at stonecutting or in house construction, than they readily accepted. With unhesitating zeal, in their desire to please and be allowed to stay, they agreed to any salary and any type of work.

Harran itself hummed, changed and grew bigger every day.

The emirate building rose broad and tall on the northern hill, and two or three hundred yards to the east the emir's residence grew higher. Anyone standing on the beach or anywhere else in Harran could plainly see the two buildings stretching taller with every passing day.

Abdullah al-Saad did not wait or procrastinate as Ibn Rashed had done in deciding to build a house on the western hill. He recruited a number of Harranis to help him build the house, and they were eager to be of assistance, as if driven by an unseen force to challenge the emirate and emir's residence on one hand and to prove to the Americans that they were just as capable of building houses on the other. To aid them they enlisted the services of Abu Abdu al-Teli, from Ujra. He came with a number of assistants, and after a few days spent touring Harran and testing the soil and rock, they went near the American compound to "inspect" the houses there; they had been refused entry to the compound in spite of all their requests. After all the tests and the "inspection"—accomplished with a great deal of whispering and clear apprehension—Abu Abdu al-Teli and his men went to work with supreme confidence, and before the coming of winter that year the last stone arches over the windows were in place, but work never stopped.

Even Ibn Rashed, who was traveling, did not stay away long. He returned to Harran one week before the emir. As usual, he had a number of new men with him. Although no one knew what they would do, Daham made no secret of Ibn Rashed's intention to put up a modern building in the market district. He said that it would be the most magnificent building in all Harran and for miles around. It would have three floors: the ground story would be a huge bazaar with several spacious shops, the largest of which would be Ibn Rashed's office. The two upper floors would provide Ibn Rashed's living quarters, with each of his wives having her own floor. He refused to talk about this directly, but when he was asked about it one day as he sat in Abu As'ad al-Helwani's coffeehouse, he smiled and avoided the gaze of those seated around him. "All property is God's, my friends." When they looked at him and smiled he laughed. "Harran is packed with people now, and it doesn't make sense to live in the desert anymore—certainly not for a man with wives."

Not only that; he spoke again, more to himself than to anyone present, his brows knitted: "As you see . . . this market isn't big enough anymore. Harran needs more than one market."

They understood that Ibn Rashed would bring his family to Harran after putting up this new building, and that he would do so very soon.

Within a few days of his arrival, most of the people saw him strolling through the market, near the mosque, with some of the men he had brought. He looked excited and preoccupied at the same time. Another day he was seen, in the early morning, with his robe tucked up in his broad belt, with a long rope or what resembled a rope. He and another man were measuring the plot of land and writing something on a piece of paper—no one knew exactly what, but everyone was sure that Ibn Rashed would begin construction before long.

At about the same time it was rumored that Saleh al-Dabbasi would marry Muhammad al-Seif's sister; the two men's close friendship, the long hours they spent together, the close ties that bound the Seif and Dabbasi families, and .what the women, especially Dabbasi's wife said, made another marriage, aimed at strengthening and renewing these ties, seem inevitable. But everything had to wait until the elder Dabbasi came back from his trip.

As to Hajem, who had left so mysteriously—or, more precisely, been made to leave, with no one the wiser—he too reappeared, accompanied by an old man, two days before the emir returned.

Hajem's return had the impact of a bolt of lightning, especially for Ibn Rashed. Everyone had assumed that the problem was gone, to be forgotten with the passage of time, so Hajem's strange reappearance gave Harran one of its most painful and difficult nights.

Hajem was extremely thin, as if he had not eaten or slept for days, and apparently in a complete stupor. He could not even hear the voices around him and seemed unable to perceive the faces and eyes that looked at him. When the old man wanted to address him, to tell him something, he grasped his forearm and gave him a shake. Hajem flinched violently, as if returning from a distant reverie or waking from a deep sleep, and looked at the man with sorrowful eyes, like those of a wounded animal, and his eyelids fluttered several times as he nervously jerked his head. Even when the man was sure that he was paying attention, he asked loudly, "Hajem! Are you listening, Hajem?" If Hajem nodded yes, he went on. "Tell me, my boy, do you want to eat? Drink? Aren't you hungry? Thirsty! Aren't you thirsty?" Hajem made a motion with his hand to indicate that he did not know.

As soon as Ibn Rashed heard that Hajem was back, in the company of that cross old man, he was filled with fear and bewilderment, and for a while he vanished completely. No one knew where he had gone or why; as soon as the news spread that the caravan had arrived and was near the mosque, someone brought word to Ibn Rashed, who was sitting in Abu As'ad's coffeehouse, that Hajem had come back with a cross old man who was cursing and threatening and asking about Ibn Rashed. Those who had seen Ibn Rashed go into the coffeehouse, those who had seen him in the coffeehouse at sundown, did not know when or how he left. They looked for him in the tents, in the market and in the workers' camp but had no luck.

With every minute that passed, as they searched in every likely place for Ibn Rashed, never finding him, the old man accompanying Hajem grew angrier, cursing and threatening vigorously.

"Where would Ibn Rashed go? By God, by God, if he ran to the remotest corner of the earth I'd find him. If he flew up into the sky I'd grab him and haul him down, and even if he tried to creep back into his mother's ——— I'd fetch him out." He paused a moment and groaned, and looked around him at the people's faces. "Does he think that human beings are cut from trees? Doesn't he have family? No, Ibn Rashed, a human being is not a dog, a person is a person, and if you send Hajem off with a bedouin and say that's that—no, that's not that. Hajem and his brother Mizban—where is Mizban? Did you bury him and say that's that?

"No, it's not over yet, Ibn Rashed, I'm onto you, and time is long."

The men looked at Hajem. So changed was he that they hardly recognized him. They held out their arms to shake his hand and saw him look at them without seeing them. They shook the limp hand that hung at his side and said, "How are you? Are you fine, Hajem?" but his stare did not change and he did not utter a word, not even his lips moved. The men felt a crushing sadness and could not bear to look in his face, especially his eyes. They grew even sadder when they remembered how this had been the "small fish," and Abdullah al-Zamel, who came running when he heard that Hajem had come back, buried his face in the boy's chest and did not move for several long moments. When he lifted his head to look at the men around them, some of them said that his eyes were red with weeping, and others swore that they heard him sobbing when he buried his face in Hajem's chest.

Harran, wretched with grief, could do nothing to soothe the old man's anger. The Harranis invited him to their homes to rest and have some supper, for Ibn Rashed might not be found until the following day, and a solution for the problem could be reached then, but the man gruffly refused their invitations. After he waited a long time and grew tired searching for Ibn Rashed all over town, the old man went back to Abu As'ad's coffeehouse and shook Hajem awake.

"Get up, boy. We'll show Ibn Rashed."

When they got up to leave, Hajem smiled for the first time. The old man looked at him and then at everyone in the coffeehouse.

"I'm onto him—time is long."

51

THE TOWNSPEOPLE OF HARRAN WERE USED TO
Ibn Rashed's sudden departures and reap-
pearances, but no one had thought him ca-
pable of vanishing this quickly. After searching for him in all
the likely places without finding him, some of them said that
he had left town. Others said that he had left even before the
caravan arrived, because some of the men he had brought to
Harran stayed only three or four days and then departed, and
he must have gone with them. Still others said that he had not
left at all, that he was still somewhere in Harran—but no one
knew where.

Two of those who had said their evening prayers in the mosque
of Harran, and who had seen and heard what Hajem's companion
had said, reported that, as they were crossing the market on their
way to New Harran, they saw Daham and Naim walking toward

the emir's encampment. They could not be sure whether there was a third man with Daham and Naim because the night was very dark and only Daham returned their greeting; Naim and what might have been the other kept walking briskly so as to meet no one.

Harran's sleep was sad and uneasy that night. Hajem and the man with him went to sleep in the mosque, and no one knew what happened after that. The men who usually sat up until late in Abu As'ad's coffeehouse saw and heard nothing as they played cards or immersed themselves in learning the new games Abu As'ad had brought from Damascus to encourage people to come in and sit for long stretches without getting bored.

An hour or so after supper three men sent by the emir's deputy went to the mosque, apparently because they knew or guessed that the two men asking for Ibn Rashed were there. Without asking anyone they went straight to Hajem and the man with him. One of the emir's men knew Hajem. The men took them away calmly, and Hajem's companion actually seemed delighted; his eyes twinkled when they asked him if it was he who sought Ibn Rashed. When he smiled and nodded yes, they asked him and Hajem to come along with them, and in no time they found themselves before the deputy emir, who addressed them severely, almost angrily. "Who are you and what brings you to Harran?"

The man answered politely but firmly that he had come to Harran to get what was due him; to find out how his nephew had been killed and who had killed him; and to find out how his other nephew had lost his senses. He indicated Hajem, who was standing at his side.

"Why are you making such a fuss about Ibn Rashed?"

"Ibn Rashed is my enemy!"

"Do you know Ibn Rashed?"

"I haven't seen him, but I know all about him."

"Who told you he did it and left?"

"Everyone knows it."

"Everyone knows it? What about the government?"

"I want the government to help me get my rights."

"So why haven't you gone to the government to ask them to get involved?" The deputy emir paused a moment to glare at him, then shook his head and went on. "If you were thinking you could get your due by showing your muscle or pushing people around, you'd better know right now that those days are gone. Now the government is above everybody. The government isn't afraid of anyone; it and it alone secures people's rights, but you bedouin only learn from a beating."

Without waiting for a reply he addressed his men, who were standing by the flap of the tent. "Take them away."

Earlier, as the man had struggled up the hill to the tent gripping Hajem's arm, he had expected to get his rights at any moment; surely the emir had seized Ibn Rashed and perhaps even tied him up pending their arrival. The emir would hear the whole story of how Hajem had been sent to him with the bedouin. The old man would take the money from his pocket and place it in front of the emir and say, "Here is the money." The emir would fly into a rage and punish Ibn Rashed to show how problems should be solved.

Now, as the men led him out of the tent to he knew not where, and having heard what the deputy emir had to say, he could not believe his ears; he could not believe what had happened. Had there been some mistake he had not understood? Didn't the emir know what had happened; had he heard nothing? The whole story, which had taken place right here, in Harran, which everybody had heard about, not just in Harran but in far distant places like Ujra, al-Rawdha, Umm Saaf and Wadi al-Uyoun, was still the subject of gossip . . . the emir did not know this story that people knew in all these faraway places? Wasn't the sight of Hajem himself sufficient evidence of Ibn Rashed's disgusting treachery?

How had Ibn Rashed been able to get to the emir so quickly? Where was he now? Why didn't he show himself and speak in front of the emir if he did not consider himself responsible or guilty?

The emir's men did not know where they were supposed to take the two men, for Harran had no prisons—had never had a prison. There was no need for such severity toward the two men, they felt, especially since they knew how Mizban had died and could see Hajem for themselves: the remnants of a man, with a simpleton's gaze, oblivious to everything around him. If there had been a prison in Harran, was it possible to consign such a man to it?

The employees of the emirate looked at each other and then at the two men in the half darkness of the tent, lit by a dim hanging lamp. They were completely bewildered and downcast, and when they looked at Hajem's face their bewilderment turned to fear. "A madman is capable of anything; he might burn or kill. He might piss on other people while they are sleeping." This is what some of the men were thinking; this is how they looked at such unfortunates, with fearful and pitying impulses . . . but for now, what were they to do with this imbecile?

A shout from the deputy emir interrupted their confused and bitter thoughts, and one of the men ran to answer the call. When he returned a minute or two later his tone suggested rancor akin to obscenity. "God has deserted men's hearts—they've become vipers."

When the others asked him what he was talking about, he turned his back to Hajem and the man so that they would not hear and said that the deputy emir had ordered that the two men be tied to their hobbled camels. The emir's men were shocked; they protested, and the man with Hajem supposed, in a final deluded moment, when he heard the deputy emir's call to one of the men, that the deputy emir had come to his senses and wished to rectify his error, or retract his words or apologize. When he heard what the deputy emir had told the man he laughed derisively—feeling, at that moment, an urge to weep or scream. He had to do something to keep from falling down dead. When he looked at Hajem and the boy returned his gaze with those wretched cheerful eyes, and smiled, he grasped his upper arm tightly and spoke up loudly enough for everyone—including the deputy emir—to hear: "If a man doesn't take his rights using his own muscles, he'll die and get nothing."

52

THAT NIGHT THEY ALL SLEPT NEAR THE CAMEL stand. A low, uneven stone wall, about waist high, separated them from the camels. The ropes they had been ordered to use were looped carelessly and angrily; none of the emir's men had made any serious effort to carry out their impossible orders. After looking at each other and then at the two men's faces, they decided to sleep and told the two, "We'll sleep here" and pointed to a spacious corner filled with sacks of straw; they said not a word more.

Harran seemed harsh and oppressive that night, though the coolness that filled the night helped the old man to forget; even so, deep unbroken sleep eluded him. When he looked over at the five sleeping men, Hajem among them, it seemed to him in the light of dawn that he knew them, that he had seen them before. When one of them rolled over, his face directly opposite him, he thought for a split second that this was Mizban! Mizban's face had looked just like that when he had last seen him, three years ago. The camels constantly made chewing noises with their lips; he could see their shoulders and heads as they shifted in their sleep. They were sadder than any camels he had even seen, straining their tongues and throats as if cursing, and looking around them resentfully. The man was burning with anger, no, not only anger; it was mingled with something as black as pitch and oozy thick as old blood that had not dried yet. He sat on his bed in the first light of dawn and asked himself, "Is the world now so depraved that a murderer's victim is at fault, that a man is imprisoned for seeking his rights? Can a man take all this and remain silent?" He looked around. He saw a number of tents and two huge, crude buildings. "Ibn Rashed won't get away from me even if he learns how to fly, even if everyone in the world is on his side." He shook his head and looked at the sleeping men around him, and they seemed more familiar than before. Hajem, asleep on his back, his face to the sky and his arms stretched out, his lower lip slack as if in a smile, looked like a small child. He was like the other children, only larger. "If their mother knew, she would kill herself."

If there had been some mistake the night before, because of his anger, or because his words had been understood as direct threats against Ibn Rashed—if they thought he had come to take revenge and kill him instead of to seek his rights as was customary—if there had been some mistake the night before, then the deputy emir should act differently today. So the old man reasoned, but when morning came and the sun rose to the movement and noise of the area, especially in the two buildings, and when they were told to go into the small tent and stay there, he was beset by doubts all over again. They were more than doubts, for had the deputy emir wished to discover the truth, he would have asked the people what had really happened so as to solve the matter as quickly as possible, but the deputy emir's leaving him thus imprisoned, tied up, not knowing why or for how long, made rage drift, like a vapor, to his head. Hajem, who slept late, not waking until the sun crept above the wall to shine on his face, stayed silently in the tent; his gaze was fixed on the lamp. He did not notice when a piece of bread and a glass of tea were placed in front of him, but he showed greater fear than ever before when the old man grabbed his arm and shook him. He ate only a small fragment of the bread and drank the tea cold.

Three men came in the afternoon, as the emir's men moved around here and there and Hajem and the old man sat in the tent. One of the three walked quickly, nervously, and the other two tried to catch up. The first man glanced at the two seated men out of the corner of his eye, then adjusted his black cloak and walked away. The other two men exchanged a few words as they looked. The old man looked up, recognizing none of them, but when he turned to Hajem and saw him smiling broadly, as he had not smiled for days, his heart missed a beat and fear seized him. He watched the workmen washing their hands and faces in the barrels of water nearby, and he let this and the other movement around him absorb his attention.

Shortly before sundown, when he was asked to appear before the deputy emir, he felt uneasy, and when he went in and saw the three men seated he knew that the man seated next to the emir was Ibn Rashed. At first Ibn Rashed did not look at him; the other two watched him attentively and a little fearfully. The deputy emir asked him and Hajem to sit down, as he had done the night before, though he now seemed more prepared to listen.

There was a long silence.

"Do you know your enemy?" asked the deputy emir.

The old man looked at the faces around him and took a deep breath.

"My enemy knows himself," he said contemptuously.

"You say that Ibn Rashed is your enemy. Take a good look. Do you recognize Ibn Rashed among these men?"

"If the Almighty does not deceive me, that's him!"

He pointed to the man beside the deputy emir.

Ibn Rashed sat up with a mocking and self-confident smile, and spoke in a loud but stammering voice. "This Ibn Rashed you're talking about, who you've spared no disgrace in all you've said about him, who you've never laid eyes on—he's the one who wants to secure your rights for you, even from the lion's mouth, but you don't care about that."

At that moment the old man knew he was in the presence of his enemy, and he spoke in a menacing tone. "Listen, Ibn Rashed, if you are Ibn Rashed, truth is truth and it is a boon from God, not from you or anyone else. Men are not money, and you don't bury men's blood at night. You're an Arab, and you know how men secure their rights."

"Are you threatening me? Did Ibn Hathal and the others send you after me?"

"Listen to me and understand: truth is truth, and rights are rights. That's all."

"I have nothing to do with your rights."

Angrily, Ibn Rashed began to tell the story again, before the deputy emir, who nodded to show he understood. Suddenly Ibn Rashed turned to the man and spoke sharply. "These are witnesses, they wrote the petitions, they wore themselves out trying to get you some compensation, and the money you received was sent by Ibn Rashed. It was from Ibn Rashed's own purse."

The man extracted an old wad of cloth from within his shirt and threw it in the middle of the floor.

"Then the money is yours, Ibn Rashed, or someone else's, and here it is, and now your witnesses are my witnesses."

He pointed at Hajem, who sat looking at Ibn Rashed and smiling.

Ibn Rashed looked at Hajem, perhaps for the first time. He might have seen him before, but he seemed alarmed to see him now. He shifted several times and addressed the deputy emir. "The Americans said, 'We have no medicine for this man. Go see someone else.' You know, Your Excellency, that the Arabs' medicine is better than American medicine. It can cure burns, and injuries, and illnesses."

"And Mizban, Ibn Rashed?" This from the old man.

"He died. It was God's will."

"You took him to the sea and drowned him and you say it was God's will?"

"Don't you understand? Life and death are from God."

"If you hadn't taken him away to the sea he wouldn't have died."

"I didn't take anyone away anywhere."

"So I took him away?"

"The company, the Americans, they're the ones who took him away and they are responsible. They say that they will pay compensation."

The old man grew angry and shook his finger threateningly. "Listen, Ibn Rashed, a man's blood doesn't flow into the dirt. I don't know anyone but you, you who ran all over the place hiring people and herding them around, and now you say you're not responsible?"

A confused and fearful Daham began to tell how he and Ibn Rashed—he pointed into the distance—did everything in their power to obtain compensation, how they went to the personnel office and met with Naim personally on several occasions. The petition they presented to the personnel office, which the personnel office submitted to headquarters, had been composed with Ibn Rashed's cooperation, and the company had promised to study the matter, "though up until now the personnel office hasn't conveyed any response."

Daham's speech was halting, confused and cold, and added nothing to what Ibn Rashed had already said. The old man listened and looked at Daham and the glowering black man, then spoke to the deputy emir. "You see what has happened to our children, Your Excellency. One is dead and buried, and this is the other."

He pointed to Hajem, whose gaze wandered aimlessly as he smiled. The old man shook his arm.

"Hajem!" he shouted. "Do you hear me, Hajem?"

Hajem turned to him his wretched, sad and imbecilic face.

"Hah, my boy—how are you?" shouted the old man.

Hajem stared at him but said nothing. The old man addressed Ibn Rashed. "Was he in this condition when you took him away from Ujra?" He smiled derisively. "And his brother Mizban—does he have a grave or did the fish eat him?"

Ibn Rashed answered sharply. "The company owes you your due. There is their door."

"I know only one door—this one."

He pointed to Ibn Rashed, who seemed angry. Ibn Rashed spoke up animatedly but with fear in his voice. "Do you hear this, Your Excellency?"

The deputy emir seemed deep in troubled thought. He turned to the old man. "You'll get your due." He added decisively, "Everyone will get his due. You'll be our guests for three or four days, and then we'll see."

And so Hajem and the old man remained the "guests" of the deputy emir for another day. Ibn Rashed stayed around for a short while, then left with the two men who had come with him.

53

T HE EMIR RETURNED SUDDENLY FROM THE HUNT; no one had expected to see him again so soon. More surprised—not to say shocked—than anyone was Ibn Rashed himself, for after Naim's visit to the deputy emir with Daham, Hajem and his uncle were "restrained" or "detained . . . in order to prevent any disturbance resulting from their accusations and threats, or unrest on the part of the workers in the company," which Ibn Rashed convinced the Americans would be inevitable when he talked to them that night, which he spent in their compound; and Naim told them the same thing. The question of cash compensation for Mizban's death was still very complicated, because the company's legal department judged that "the company is neither responsible nor liable, since the transfer of the workers to the company's responsibility was not effected until after the decease." The compen*ation due Hajem would, it was promised, be paid "within the coming few days, on condition that law and order prevail." This was why Hajem and his uncle were kept under detention: so that the disturbances might die down and the threats against Ibn Rashed cease. Payment would be made via the emirate, and the case would be considered closed.

This is how it was planned, and how it was carried out. Mizban's death months before had caused a great deal of silent unrest among the workers, the recent interviews had aroused much fear and suspicion in everyone, and nothing had been done to ease these ill feelings, which had spread to Harran itself—thus, Naim explained to the Americans on several occasions, the situation could bear no further strain or disruption.

Now, Hajem's reappearance in Harran was a painfully obvious indication of the treatment of these human creatures and the way the Americans viewed them. In addition to this living, breathing example were his uncle's threats and the contagious anger of the workers—"things are bound to lead to an outcome the company would prefer to avoid."

As the emir neared Harran he was captivated by the two buildings even before he arrived. He saw them from afar—at first he could not make them out clearly and asked if they belonged to the company, though the company's buildings were clearly visible from that distance. When he was told that they were the emirate and the emir's residence he could not hide his joy.

"Never mind if we didn't get all the birds we wanted," he told Dabbasi jokingly as they rode together toward Harran. "Just look at our consolation prize!"

He pointed delightedly at the two buildings and seemed determined to get home as fast as he could. They arrived in the midafternoon, as the workmen were about to go home, and headed straight for the site to inspect the progress that had been made. The deputy emir, who rushed out to meet the emir, and who was clearly excited, assured the prince in broken, breathless words, as he trotted by his side, that he had overseen all the work personally, and that His Excellency's instructions had been followed to the letter. He pointed to the large window openings on the southern wall and thumped the thick walls with his palm to show how solid they were. The emir asked if the work had gone on steadily for the whole period of his absence and how many workmen were on the job; he asked about the materials they used and many other related things. Dabbasi was making the tour with the emir, and his astonishment showed plainly; he praised the construction and the quality of the building materials and said he was "truly awed"—if all the work was of this standard, he said, then the building might well stand for hundreds of years: "Furthermore, this is what the buildings in Egypt look like—some of them were built in the days of the patriarch Joseph, peace be upon him, and are still standing!"

The emir was happy as a child and praised the workers effusively, telling them that were it not for their dedication and loyalty the construction would never have come so far or been so impressively solid. The workers, who were pleased by the emir's praise, made a few brief remarks about the window arches and their breadth as well as the fact that "the cement had to be poured several times before it settled right, but now it will never crack." All this was explained to the emir, who again praised their efforts. He asked how much longer it would take to complete the building and whether the noise and dust were as bad now as they had been in the beginning, and when his deputy assured him that he was thinking of the preliminary stages, and that the heavy equipment that roared and stirred up the dust was no longer in use, the emir addressed the workers, standing a few feet away, in his loudest voice. "Those things that dug the foundation were enough to split your head open and blind you!" He paused to laugh. "Praise the Lord . . . we've seen the last of them."

Dabbasi, who insisted on accompanying the emir until the end of the tour, said, when the emir invited him to have supper, entertain himself and spend the night before going back to his family, "I think it better, Your Excellency, that you visit with some of your other friends." He smiled before going on. "There are so many besides me, Your Excellency, waiting to see you!"

"The way you talk, Abu Saleh!" The emir laughed. "Every word you utter has a thousand meanings."

The two laughed together, and after they drank some coffee Dabbasi went back to his family, and the emir asked his deputy what had gone on in his absence, what caravans and people had come to town. He listened to a few responses without really taking them in, then got up to go and see his family in another tent.

"So it goes with people's problems," he said. He took a few slow steps and laughed. "There is no end to people's problems, Abu Rashwan."

His deputy laughed. "In Harran, Your Excellency, there is no end to people's problems, or to the people—even death doesn't rid us of them!"

"Trust in God," said the emir.

54

I BN RASHED WAS AMONG THE FIRST TO VISIT THE EMIR the morning after his arrival. He came earlier than usual. The emir was inspecting the buildings, happy and relaxed, slapping his palms against the walls to test them as his deputy had done the day before. When he saw Ibn Rashed coming at this hour, he did not know what to think: Was he coming to greet and supervise the workers? Did he do this every day, or had he heard of the emir's arrival and come only this once to show how loyal and ambitious he was? If he had come to pay his respects, his timing was wrong. The emir spoke while Ibn Rashed was within a few hurried steps of arriving. "Why so early? Something is amiss, Ibn Rashed."

"It's almost noon, Your Excellency!" said Ibn Rashed, attempting a smile as he hurried along nervously.

"Are you telling me?" replied the emir.

Ibn Rashed did not know what the emir was getting at, whether he was praising or rebuking him. After greeting the emir warmly and asking whether the hunting trip had been enjoyable and the prey plentiful, Ibn Rashed joined the emir in inspecting the two buildings and made many observations regarding the strength of the structures and the care with which they were built. He assured the emir that everything would be complete within a month, and he said that only the interiors needed some finishing touches. With a little encouragement, Ibn Rashed said, no doubt the Americans would do for His Excellency what they had done when building their own homes: no sooner had their doors, windows and many other ready-made furnishings been hauled out of their crates and wrappings than they were installed. The emir was greatly interested in having some of these things and wondered aloud if the Americans would give them without being asked; he hinted that he was ashamed to ask for them himself.

Ibn Rashed immediately perceived the emir's weak point.

"I shouldn't allow you to ask for them, Abu Misfer," he said. He smiled and added, in a different tone, "With your approval, Your Excellency, just leave it to me."

He paused for a moment and spoke through his nostrils. "I'll keep after them night and day. I'll tell them, 'The emir's house has to be just like the Americans have.' "

Craftily and brilliantly, Ibn Rashed promised the emir to act on his behalf in talks with the Americans to fit out the emirate and emir's residence exactly like their own houses. The emir took happily to the idea, though his eyes and other features seemed to express some reservations; in an attempt to overcome his doubts and give Ibn Rashed a chance, he looked directly into his eyes and said, "Trust in God, Ibn Rashed, and don't let up on them. Keep after them, only don't let anyone know that it was I who asked."

Ibn Rashed nodded wordlessly, with a confident little smile.

A few moments passed. He struck his chest with an open palm and said, "You will get just what you want, and no less, Your Excellency."

He resumed his tour with the emir, and when he saw two or three of the workers arriving he shouted at them sternly and somewhat sarcastically: "God—God! It's nearly noon, my friends!"

When the workers saw the emir they were struck with fear and unease and said nothing. Ibn Rashed went on in a paternal tone: "Get going, men! Let's move it along—you've all got work to do!"

To spur them on he shed his black cloak and threw it on a heap of rocks, then tucked up his robe into his broad belt.

"Let's get going, all together now!"

In an atmosphere of noisy excitement and exaggerated energy they began to fill the water barrel, shift the bags of cement and prepare the sand. Ibn Rashed's participation, his energy and the orders he gave confused the workers more than they helped the pace of the work, and the emir, watching from a distance with a smile—whether a smile of pleasure or of pity it was impossible to tell—spoke to him. "Get your cloak, Ibn Rashed, and let's get some coffee."

Ibn Rashed quickly washed his hands and snatched up his cloak as if he had been waiting for these words; he ran behind the emir, who had begun to stroll away. When he caught up he spoke to the emir as if talking to himself. "If you don't stand right over them, Your Excellency, they just fall asleep."

Ibn Rashed was deeply worried and upset, for in the same measure that he needed the emir's approval and confidence, he was afraid that this confidence would be demolished by any investigation of the case of Hajem and his brother Mizban not carried out with careful planning and in the right atmosphere. He still remembered what the emir had said long ago when the case was first investigated; he had been harsh and almost hostile, telling him, "Look after your own, Ibn Rashed, and give us a rest from these complaints." If he told the emir that Hajem and a kinsman were now in a tent only twenty or thirty steps away, that they were imprisoned because the kinsman had been making threats, that he had thrown away the money he had sent; if Ibn Rashed said anything like this the emir would surely fly into a rage and turn the world upside down on his head, whereas if he told him that he had agreed to detain them with the approval of the Americans and the deputy emir, the emir would surely feel insulted; he might ask sarcastically, "Who's the emir—you or me? And since when do the Americans have anything to do with it?" Worst of all—what would the emir say if he saw Hajem this miserable and destitute? And what would the deputy emir say in his own defense?

His head was a whirl of thoughts and imaginings. He felt besieged and threatened; the smiles he now saw on the emir's face were only a deceptive veil, especially since "that bastard Dabbasi must have raked me over the coals but good on their hunting trip!" There was no doubt that Dabbasi had stirred up the emir against him; if he were to see Hajem and his companion, a single word from the latter and a crazed stare from the former would settle things once and for all.

"You seem preoccupied, Ibn Rashed," said the emir, looking directly into his eyes. He paused a moment and then laughed loudly. "Trust in God—you can't change the past, Ibn Rashed."

Ibn Rashed sat up abruptly and pretended to smile when he saw the emir looking at him that way.

"You said it, not I, Your Excellency."

"And you know as well as I do that worry burns the heart—it kills."

"That's the truth indeed!"

"Your heart is troubled, Ibn Rashed."

"People have troubled it, Your Excellency."

"People—or money?"

"Money does not disease the heart, my dear friend."

"Money is the disease and the cure."

Ibn Rashed sighed deeply, as if preparing what he was about to say, and spoke in a humble voice when he saw the emir smiling. "Your Excellency, please hear what I have to say. Judge me afterward, and I will accept whatever judgment you make."

These words took the emir by surprise. When Ibn Rashed began to tell the story of Hajem with a fearful and nervous excitement, the emir sat up, drew back slightly and began to nod his head methodically as if recalling what he had said before, how he had wanted the problem solved quickly and with good-will on all sides. But when Ibn Rashed came to how Hajem had returned with one of his relatives, their threats and subsequent imprisonment, how the problem was worsening every day in the workers' camp and among the Americans, and how Ibn Rashed did not know what to do, what with the Americans refusing to pay compensation—at this point in Ibn Rashed's narrative the emir made an angry gesture with his hand. "I told you, Ibn Rashed: the problem is money."

He shook his head a few times and spoke in a contemptuous tone. "Between you and the Americans the people's rights have been lost, Ibn Rashed."

Once again Ibn Rashed tried to explain how he had done his utmost to obtain compensation for Mizban and how the Americans still refused. Compensation would be paid out to Hajem, but not all the necessary steps had been completed yet. How he had sent a sum of money from his own pocket to placate them and as evidence of his own good intentions, and how he was still doing his best to clear up the matter as quickly as possible, in spite of the Americans, who had stipulated that nothing would be paid out until things had quieted down and Hajem's friend had stopped making threats.

As he talked Ibn Rashed gestured with his hands and waited for the emir's reaction. He watched closely, because his reaction was all-important to him, for if the emir heard him out, his heart might soften and all manner of doors would be open to him, meaning that he could remain powerful, whereas if the emir opposed him and refused to listen, there would be no end to his troubles.

"If you give me your consent now, Abu Misfer," he said slyly, "I will go from your presence straight to the Americans and not leave them alone until they resolve both questions: the question of the doors and windows and the question of Jazi's sons."

The emir spoke up wearily. "Pull your thorns with your own hands, Ibn Rashed. We'll see tomorrow."

55

ALL EFFORTS TO RESOLVE THE PROBLEM FAILED. The company stubbornly refused to pay any compensation, or even to make a nominal payment, because "the law is the law, and rules are rules." Their excuse was always that responsibility for the workers' welfare had not been transferred to the company until after Mizban's death, "and before that date the company did not recognize or assume any rights or liabilities; the agreement reached with Ibn Rashed obliged him to provide day workers, and he was solely responsible for them." The emir's attempts to "divide the heap in half—half from the company and half from Ibn Rashed—" failed as well: Hamilton and Naim visited the emir and emphasized to him that "basically it's not a question of the amount of money under discussion, it's a matter of principle, of legality, and on that basis the company refuses to discuss details." Hamilton added that the company would pay compensation for any subsequent accidents, whether loss of life, total or partial disability, loss or injury of limb or organ, eye, leg or ear, or even less serious injuries; the compensations would be generous, just as if the Arabs were regular people!

Ibn Rashed was desperate to place the burden of compensation on the company, "because my money, Your Excellency, has all gone into people's bellies, into buying steel and stone." When the emir decided that Ibn Rashed should pay the whole amount himself, since the company had refused, he shrieked as if he had been burned. "I barely have enough money to pay the workers' wages, Your Excellency! Try to intercede with the company, and if they agree to give me a loan for one year . . . I'll pay."

The emir lost his patience.

"I will not intercede. You know the company better than I do—go and borrow money from them, or from the Devil." The emir turned away to where his deputy sat and told him sharply, almost menacingly, "I've listened to enough of this!"

Ibn Rashed made a blatant attempt to influence the emir, exploiting the presence of the deputy.

"The Americans have agreed to everything, Your Excellency. They said your doors and windows will be just like the ones in the company houses, even better." He paused to take a deep, anxious breath. "Right now they don't have three or four big doors ready to install, but tomorrow, Your Excellency, they'll take the measurements and make them to size, and they'll be ready in a few days' time."

The emir's features softened, but he did not look directly at Ibn Rashed, as if he had not heard or had no comment on what had been said. Ibn Rashed had said something very similar after his first visit to the Americans, though nothing as decisive and final as this. At the time the Americans shook their heads and looked at each other and said, Ibn Rashed recalled, that they would have to look into the availability of the requested doors and windows; now, in light of the impasse he had reached, he tried to pressure the emir, to make him change his mind or at the very least to soften his stand.

The deputy emir made an attempt to propose a settlement that would secure the money they needed from a source outside the company, and at the same time preserve peaceful and friendly relations with the Americans.

"Forget the company. Talk to Dabbasi or al-Seif, or Ibn Saad. One of them might give you the loan."

"Let's change the subject," said the emir disdainfully. He turned to give Ibn Rashed a fleeting glance and then addressed his deputy: "Don't worry about this one, money is no problem for him. He knows how to raise money."

Ibn Rashed almost wept to express his inability to find the money. He said that he had spent all that he possessed, a mistake that he could never forgive himself for making, because "land is worthless, and there was no other madman like himself in Harran who would squander his money on land and in people's bellies." He said that if things went on like this much longer, he would have to leave town, because he could no longer face the empty mouths that asked him for money day and night.

The emir seemed to be weakening. "To listen to you, Ibn Rashed, one would think you needed charity."

"What do people have but appearances—nothing but talk."

"As Abu Rashwan said: talk to Dabbasi. Go see al-Seif."

"You know them as well as I do, Your Excellency."

That is what Ibn Rashed said. He paused a moment and then went on sarcastically. "Ibn Seif wouldn't give me the time of day, and Dabbasi lives for the day I sell my cloak and go begging!"

Dabbasi was indeed waiting for an opportunity to deal the death-blow to Ibn Rashed—or at least a blow hard enough to weaken and humble him—so as soon as he heard the tale of Hajem and his reappearance, on his first day back in Harran, he got to work.

He visited the emir at noon the next day. The majlis was crowded with guests of the emir, most of whom who had come to pay their respects. The emir was in good spirits, even cheerful, especially when they asked him how the hunting trip had gone, but he referred the questioners to Dabbasi with a meaningful smile and a gesture of his hand for Dabbasi to respond. When the crowd thinned out a little Dabbasi approached the emir and whispered a few words in his ear. The emir turned this way and that and answered him loudly. "I know—I know, Abu Saleh."

When the majlis was completely empty, with only the emir and his deputy remaining, the emir turned expectantly to Dabbasi.

"Hah, Abu Saleh. What are the people saying?" He looked at his deputy out of the corner of his eye. "Our return was a mercy for the people, not just for the birds, Abu Saleh."

"For the birds, yes, by God, Your Excellency," said the deputy emir in an effort to defend himself. "As for the people, I don't know—they're busy with their daily worries and concerns, and were it not for that troublemaker, they couldn't be any better off."

"Speak, Abu Saleh," said the emir grimly.

"There's so much to say, Your Excellency, but the story I heard yesterday, when I arrived, and which I heard again today in the market, is the story of the bedouin who went simple-minded—Ibn Rashed's man."

None of the three men needed any further details on the subject, for no sooner had Ibn Rashed left the emir for the American compound to see about the building of the emirate and emir's residence, and the deputy emir arrived, than they summoned Hajem and his uncle. When the two had finished listening to him, the emir spoke. "You'll get your due. Hold your tongue." The emir peered for a long time into the man's face and then into Hajem's, looking sad and pained, and added, in a calm but firm voice, "Do you hear me? Do you understand what I said?"

When the man nodded to show that he had heard and understood, and seemed reassured by the emir's face and words, the emir spoke again. "If you wish to remain as our guest you are most welcome, and if you wish to go down to the market, that is the market road."

The old man muttered a few rapid and jumbled words which were taken to mean that he wished to go, so the emir called out for one of his men. "Show him the way to market. And give him something."

When Dabbasi made his way to the emir's tent, he did not see Hajem and his uncle, but many people reported seeing them in the market, near the mosque and in Abu As'ad's coffeehouse, and although the old man did not answer any of the questions put to him, his eyes were blazing, and his grim silence said more than any words; Hajem, walking by his side, looking curiously and surprisedly into people's faces, smiling every so often in his peculiar way, aroused their pity and anger at the same time as he emitted sounds like the neighing of an injured horse.

Dabbasi was deeply affected when he heard this, realizing at the same time that he had his opportunity to strike.

"If he had listened to you, Abu Misfer, none of all this would have happened."

"Money infatuates, and ambition blinds, Abu Saleh."

Dabbasi and the deputy emir shook their heads and said nothing.

In the following few days Ibn Naffeh took over. As soon as he saw the two men by the mosque, the afternoon of the day after the emir arrived, he began to shout wrathfully. This he did spontaneously, without provocation, and after he greeted the old man warmly everyone heard him shouting. "This man"— he pointed so that his index finger almost touched Hajem's face, as Hajem grinned at the people's faces—"this man has no problem. Death is every man's right and no one fears it, death is closer to man than his jugular vein, and his problem is not death. No. Death is an institution. A demon has possessed this man. The Americans came and the demons came with them. Anyone who drinks their water or eats of their provisions will have a demon enter him, if not today then tomorrow, and if it doesn't show right away, it will show in its own time."

Ibn Naffeh looked into the men's faces to see what effect his words had had upon them, and when he saw them standing silent with bowed heads he spoke again in a louder voice. "Ibn Rashed has gone roaming east and west and gathered people from the four corners of the earth and handed them over to the Americans. He's handed the sheep over to the wolf, and for every beast, for every head of them, he gets his money from the Americans and they ask him, 'Have you got any more of these?' and he runs off and gathers more and tells them, 'Here you are!' And he and the Americans are like hellfire, never quenched, never satisfied."

He sighed deeply and grasped Hajem's shoulder, which he gave a strong shake. "My boy, illness and treatment come from within."

He turned to the people around him and pointed to Hajem. "Today it's him, and tomorrow it will be all Harran. As our ancient friend put it: 'I see the demons entering through your nails to clothe themselves in your bodies and take up residence in your brains.' "

The uncle's head nodded unceasingly, and rage was evident in his eyes and other features. When he was asked if he had seen

Ibn Rashed, and how the emir had received him, and before that the deputy emir, he only gazed in his questioners' faces for a long time and shook his head silently. When the questions were repeated, with no response or explanation, Ibn Naffeh shouted again. "The Americans are the problem—they're to blame!"

When the question about Ibn Rashed rang out—no one knew whether it was directed at Ibn Naffeh or Hajem's uncle—Ibn Naffeh made obscene gestures and answered contemptuously. "Who is Ibn Rashed? Ibn Rashed is a bag of shit."

He went on, laughing. "Ninety needles don't make an awl, and Ibn Rashed is even smaller than a needle, but the Americans are an awl. Tomorrow or the next day they'll make us swallow a needle and pull awls out of here." He pointed to his buttocks.

Ibn Naffeh's words made them laugh and were repeated everywhere, inspiring wonder and fear. People whispered and commented and sneaked glances at him. A bitter severity was drawn on the old man's face, as if he did not see or hear what was happening around him; when he looked up at all it was to stare at Hajem and shake his head.

Dabbasi missed nothing. He listened and knew everything that was happening, especially the proposal of the emir and his deputy that Ibn Rashed take a loan from him. He was not in a hurry. He made a simple, almost naive remark, which by the time it had been passed from mouth to mouth had become like a fiery skewer. He commented on what he had heard Ibn Naffeh say near the mosque—that Ibn Rashed was nothing but a needle—in Abu As'ad's coffeehouse that same night.

"God Almighty, my friends! A man's nature never changes." He was silent for a while, then spoke to the group of Harranis around him. "Fear whoever does not fear God."

He shook his head and spoke to one of the men seated near him, loudly, so that everyone might hear, "Make sure these fellows get something to eat, and let them sleep upstairs."

They understood that he meant Hajem and his uncle.

Three days later the emir's deputy sent Daham to ask Dabbasi to loan Ibn Rashed the sum of money they had agreed upon as compensation for Hajem and his brother.

"I have the money. This afternoon, at the emir's," said Dabbasi. He added, smiling, "Tell Ibn Rashed to be there. The world is only life and death."

Although Dabbasi was ready to lend the money, Ibn Rashed stalled—perhaps the Americans would come through after all—but in the end he seemed ready to go along. What no one realized until after that afternoon was that Hajem and his uncle had left Harran the previous night. They told no one they were leaving, and no one saw them go. All that evening's efforts to locate them in the mosque, the coffeehouse, the market, even in the workers' camp, ended in failure.

"Ibn Rashed has put us in a plight—God help us," said the emir when he heard that they had left.

He looked dejectedly at his deputy as if to rebuke him. When Ibn Rashed arrived to pass on the news he had just heard about the departure of Hajem and his uncle, the emir replied, "Money exalts and humbles, and makes men masters or slaves."

A heavy silence fell, and most of them knew that there was a great deal more yet to come.

56

WITH THE END OF SPRING AND THE TEMPERATE, refreshing days and nights sometimes blessed with coolness, the pitiless, oppressive summer came in. The people, accustomed in former years to the slow advent of summer, heralding its own arrival with rising heat and humidity, were surprised by this summer's sudden, early assault. It began with searing winds and tumultuous sandstorms. Harran was nearly obliterated by these tempests that raged in from the desert, under the heaps of sand and dirt which the winds swept in from miles around by day and night. Even the nights falling at the end of every spring, so mild and soothing in their coolness, enabling the people to forget the heat of the day, were harsh and heavy this year, more like midsummer nights. The older men said that they had not seen such a spring in long years, and others said that there had never been a drought like this one; it would raise prices, especially for wheat and barley, and make people's lives miserable—and the animals? They didn't have a chance of survivng into the hottest part of the summer. Only Ibn Naffeh ignored what the people said; he maintained that the heat that filled the air came not from the sun but from the earth, and from within certain spirits, "since the new demons live under our feet, and waste no time in conjuring themselves into the bodies of men and beasts; before long they'll take over everything, for within every creature dwells a small black demon, which grows ever bigger unless man makes some effort to kill it."

The people of Harran generally expected the arrival of a caravan or two at this time of year—caravans bringing news, letters, money, cloth, sugar and flour—which changed the tenor of life in Harran, bringing cheer and liveliness, or fear or disquiet because of news or the lack of it. This year was different from all previous years, however, in that no one was awaiting any specific caravan, for they were so plentiful now that barely a week went by without one. In addition, news and goods came now not solely from the direction of Ujra but from many sides, especially from the sea. These caravans, too, brought fear and disquiet as well as many new residents nearly every day, and no one knew how they would live or what they would do.

In past years the absence or delay of caravans was a source of great worry, especially among the elderly, but the caravans that came now, with their news, rumors and travelers, made them all feel that Harran was no one's property, no one's city. So chaotic and crowded had it become that everyone asked and everyone answered, but no one heard or understood. The men who spent most of their time in the market, going several times each day to Abu As'ad al-Helwani's coffeehouse, carefully monitoring the rise of the new buildings, watching the newcomers with a wary fascination—these men watched, listened and asked questions, but they did not know how to explain what was happening around them, nor did they know how their own lives were changing, so they sank into silence and anxiety. When they went back to their homes and tried to explain to their wives some of what they had seen and heard, they ended up talking only to themselves, for the women, having their own problems and cares, neither looked nor listened to them. If they did chance to look or listen they understood nothing of what the men said, and their faces showed signs of genuine surprise at these problems that occupied their menfolk, and at the fear the men displayed for no apparent reason. When the men's hidden anger burst forth, or they emitted short, sharp shouts, warning that everything might come to an end any moment now, with the earth opening up and everyone dying, the women knew that life around them was taking a turn for the worse and that their men had much on their minds, though they did not realize it. Within a few moments, in a highly secretive and sly manner known only to mothers and other experienced women, the children were put to flight, and every woman acted as gently and sympathetically as she could at a moment's notice. So expert were they that the harshest and coarsest of the men softened and were all sweetness and apologies. Their anger was replaced by a placid sorrow more like despair, as if they were confronting an unchanging and unyielding force.

These were the days that followed the disappearance of Hajem and his uncle, that mysterious and sudden disappearance. Some of those who attributed the depression they felt to that occurrence no sooner said so in front of a large number of people than they forgot the reason, though the depression did not leave them; it grew stronger every day. Even the severity of the emir, who had come to treat Ibn Rashed harshly and speak to him rudely, and who became extremely upset when any reference was made to what had happened, was transformed into a bitter sarcasm, and his anger and resentment were replaced by defiance.

Ibn Rashed himself, who could hardly believe anything that had happened, as if it had been a dream, was a changed man. At first he was shocked, then his shock turned to bafflement and silence, then both turned to fear. He became a desperately uneasy and fearful man, afraid of everything and everybody. He started and stared, frightened by every sound, and looked into people's faces with an almost accusatory curiosity. This transformation took place within a very short time but quite slowly, and for a while it went unnoticed by many, but the panic that showed in his conduct and actions, and in his troubled relations with others, and the irresolution that marked his every move, drew the attention of most of them and made them wonder.

When Ibn Naffeh heard the men in Abu As'ad's coffeehouse discussing Ibn Rashed's daze and silence in awed tones, he said, "The demons have started to eat him up." He shook his head and laughed.

"We'll see, if we live that long."

57

D AHAM AND DABBASI WERE MOST AWARE OF IBN
Rashed's new condition: Daham through his
direct daily contact with him and Dabbasi
through conjecture and reasoning in addition to a number of
unrelated remarks, rumors and information that came to him
from various sources, having to do with the man's words or
behavior. Each of the two men, not knowing what the other
knew, decided independently to finish Ibn Rashed off and make
him pay dearly.

After long and difficult bargaining and haggling to force Ibn
Rashed to pay compensation, he consented in spite of himself,
and since he did not possess the required amount, Dabbasi agreed
to lend it to him. After Hajem and his uncle made their sudden
departure, Ibn Rashed reckoned that there was no need for the
loan at the present time, but Dabbasi spoke to the emir. "The

money is safe in my pocket, Your Excellency"—he paused a moment to look at Ibn Rashed—"but if you ask for it tomorrow it might not be there."

He changed his tone completely as he redirected his speech to the emir. "Perhaps, Your Excellency, the old bedouin has gone to find an ally, a gang, to help him get a few more coins out of us."

He resumed his former tone, addressing Ibn Rashed. "If he comes back tomorrow, don't come to me—'Come on, Dabbasi, hand over the money, Abu Saleh.' "

Reasoning this way, they decided that the money should be held in trust by the emir until such time as the bedouin came or the problem was resolved. Since the money was to be held in trust, and Ibn Rashed was unable to raise the sum in the foreseeable future, this was required of Dabbasi, so he spoke to the emir to conclude the business. "Abu Muhammad, God bless him, has put all his money into people's bellies." He took a sudden deep breath and said in a different tone, "And that's like putting your money down the well—it's gone for good!"

Barely a week later Dabbasi said, in the coffeehouse, that he had made the loan to Ibn Rashed and now wanted to make a deal with him: he would let him keep the money, and he would take over the piece of land west of the mosque, "since that land is worthless anyway, and no one would ever think of buying it." When a garbled version of this proposal reached Ibn Rashed, he only shook his head and said nothing, but then a messenger from Dabbasi came to ask him "if he really needed that land west of the mosque, because Abu Saleh would like to build a house and the western hills are too far away for him, and he'll pay whatever price you ask." When the messenger came and talked like that, Ibn Rashed knew that the land west of the mosque would be taken from him one way or another, but he could not say yes or no.

"I will go along with whatever Abu Saleh wants," he told the messenger. He sighed and looked him in the face. "If we meet we can settle it."

Dabbasi considered this response satisfactory and auspicious enough for the time being, so he did not insist or even mention the subject again. On the strength of Ibn Rashed's evident unease and fear, however, rumors began to circulate in the market and Abu As'ad's coffeehouse to the effect that a number of travelers had spotted Hajem and his uncle in Ujra. This time they were not alone: they were with Miteb al-Hathal himself and a group of armed bedouin. Some said they'd heard that Miteb al-Hathal would arrive in Harran any day now; according to other reports, some of the new residents recently arrived in Harran were actually close relatives of Hajem's and had come to seek revenge.

Did Ibn Rashed hear any of this? Did anyone tell him what was being said? No one could confirm or deny the story, but Abdu Muhammad, who had heard some of the story making the rounds, and who still kept to his own corner of the coffeehouse, roared with laughter when he heard these kind of suppositions.

"My friends, why don't you ask *me* about Ibn Rashed?"

He paused a moment and shook his head as if recalling or visualizing the many stories he knew and added, "Ibn Rashed is worse than the devil himself. He knows who planted every seed and who laid every egg."

The people heard this and looked at each other in amazement—how could he know everything? Who had told him? When they could find no satisfactory explanation they were surer than ever that whatever they heard surely had to reach Ibn Rashed's ears, perhaps even before they knew. They had heard that Ibn Rashed had not left his house for days, that he had not left town, nor had he visited the emir or the American compound, although he was in Harran . . . knowing that, they realized that something new had happened: what was being said about the presence of Hajem and his uncle in Ujra with Miteb al-Hathal, and how they would come to Harran with the next caravan, was all true. This was why Ibn Rashed had gone into hiding, as he had done before.

When Ibn Rashed appeared in the market—and he was no longer seen without two or three of his men at his side—he seemed greatly distraught and much changed: he moved quickly, and his eyes were extremely alert and fearful; he was constantly turning nervously to look behind him for no apparent reason. Sudden noises, even the voice of one man calling to another or the sound of a falling object, terrified him. Once in the coffee-house, where he turned up after a long absence, he jumped violently when a bedouin dropped a vessel for roasting coffee beans and looked around in terror. When he calmed down, he collapsed in his chair limp as a sack, cold sweat running down his brow.

When the people saw Ibn Rashed in this state they were positive that something new was growing and developing in front of their very eyes, and that it would surely get worse.

Daham watched like a hawk, and listened, and made his plans. No sooner had two or three weeks passed, with Ibn Rashed's problem becoming plainer every day, especially to Daham, than Daham began to represent Ibn Rashed in all dealings with the Americans, even in following up the work on the emirate and emir's residence, particularly since Naim had made clear his displeasure with Ibn Rashed's insistence that the company should pay the compensation and with his threat to stop procuring workers.

In order to emphasize his new role, and since he had to meet with the emir every now and then, Daham decided to dispense with his overalls and cap for good; he now wore Arab clothes at all times. He had inspired surprise and some derision when in the beginning he had been the first to put aside Arab clothes, as an example to the rest, but his return to his old clothes, plus his hurried purchase of a black cloak, caused quite as much surprise and wonder. He explained his decision to Ibn Rashed. "Your life, Abu Muhammad, is as dear to me as my father's or brother's. But the American clothes are tight enough to show a pimple underneath, and I can't hide this."

He wagged a pistol in the palm of his open hand, as if testing it or playing with it.

Ibn Rashed's surprise at the sight of the pistol was evident, and he did not understand the connection between it and the talk about the American clothes. He looked perplexedly at Daham, and for a moment he felt an obscure fear. Daham smiled to allay his suspicions.

"You should keep one with you day and night, Abu Muhammad."

Ibn Rashed shook his head and did not reply, but he sighed deeply, for he had heard what people were saying.

"These clothes," Daham went on confidently, indicating his Arab clothes, "can hide ten of these." He tucked the pistol expertly into his belt and whispered, "With a cloak over it all, Satan himself wouldn't know what you were carrying."

Ibn Rashed understood, and to show his courage, and respond to what was being said in the coffeehouse and the market, he smiled and spoke through his nostrils. "God has not yet created the hand that can touch Ibn Rashed, my man."

"Tie up the jackal with a lion's rope," said Daham to end the discussion, "and you won't have to worry about a thing."

Thus Daham came to be seen everywhere and at all times wearing his Arab clothes, and people stopped talking about him in the workers' camp and American Harran. They got used to him like this and could not imagine him any other way.

More than Daham's clothing changed: his behavior changed,

as did his manner of dealing with people, and even the way he walked. Now he walked quickly, just as Ibn Rashed had walked when he was busy or did not want to get into a conversation with anyone. He removed his cloak when his work required him to do so, in order to show the power he now enjoyed. Anyone seeing Daham tuck the end of his robe into his belt might well have thought, at first glance, that this was Ibn Rashed himself.

How did he change so profoundly, so quickly?

He went to see the emir for the first time to suggest putting iron bars over the windows on the ground floor of the emirate building. The deputy emir and Dabbasi were there as well.

"Hah!" the emir said. "Are you trying to bury us alive, my boy?"

He laughed when Daham looked uncomfortable, unable to say a word.

"Tell your friends to be generous with their iron—but not to us." He added, in a different tone, "Tell Ibn Rashed he's been absent too long. We want to see him."

"What's this, my friends?" wondered the emir aloud after Daham had left. "What's happened to his pants?"

The men laughed and nodded, the emir laughed and made a gesture of disgust with his hand.

"God Almighty, now he talks about iron and wood, about what should be done and what not."

"He's Ibn Rashed's deputy, Your Excellency," said Dabbasi slyly. "Like it or not, Ibn Rashed can't lift a stone without his advice—and his approval."

The emir curled his lip and motioned with his hand.

"He's a dolt," said Dabbasi, "but he has a good heart."

The conversation turned to Ibn Rashed. Dabbasi had spoken in a meaningful way in the coffeehouse, in front of the others, about the report that Hajem and his uncle were in Ujra with armed men and how it prevented Ibn Rashed from venturing outside, but at the emir's he said that Ibn Rashed's problem was only an idle notion, not fear; perhaps the illness had brought it on.

Ibn Rashed's specter never left the workers' camp. The stories that circulated, the news that spread through Arab Harran, in the market and the coffeehouse, all quickly reached the camp. As the news made its short journey from one place to another, new details and distortions were added. A number of the workers said that ever since Hajem and his uncle had come to town, Ibn Rashed had lost control over his bladder and constantly pissed on his clothes, and that was why he could not leave his house. The ones who related this story swore that they could not sit near him in the coffeehouse because he smelled like a corpse. He emitted a damp reek of urine and perfumes that gave severe headaches to all the people seated near him, one of whom loudly asked Abu As'ad if he had any incense or perfumes.

Others maintained that he sometimes disguised himself in beggars' rags, and two workers said that they had seen him with his face daubed completely black! Still others claimed to have seen him late one night, putting a cap on over his headcloth in an effort to disguise himself.

While there was a great deal of imaginative distortion in these narratives, the one certainty was that fear had entered Ibn Rashed's heart. Ibn Naffeh said that "fear will not leave the man until Mizban leaves his grave." As for the talk about treatment with irons and bloodletting, "it might help Hajem, but not Ibn Rashed," as Ibn Naffeh said.

When the workers talked about the armed bedouin who were to avenge Hajem and Mizban—for they were all sure that they would come today or the next day—they lowered their voices and agreed that they would prepare a place for Ibn Hathal and his bedouin to stay; they would be hidden in places that no one would discover, and Ibn Rashed would never find out.

In the past the workers had had varying opinions about Daham, though all at the very least differentiated between him and Ibn Rashed, but when he became a new Ibn Rashed, and showed up in the workers' camp wearing his Arab clothes, Abdullah al-Zamel slapped his hands together. "God, God! Munir leaves and Munawar comes in his place!"

He shouted with laughter and turned to the men around him before Daham arrived.

"Be careful, my friends—like Ibn Ghitar's donkeys: the loose one is worse than the one who's hitched up!"

When Daham began to make some requests of the workers and to give them orders, as he had done many times before, Abdullah al-Zamel whispered into the ear of the man nearest him, and they both laughed loudly. Daham looked cross, but he turned the other way and said sternly, so that Ibn Zamel could hear, "A rational man, a good man, is not misled and does not change."

He paused a moment and looked at them.

"You all should know that today is unlike yesterday, and tomorrow will be different from today. We shall see."

After a long and wide-ranging discussion about work, the barracks and the new workers, Daham left the camp. The workers asked Abdullah al-Zamel why he had laughed and what he had said.

"Like our sheikh said, 'Today is unlike yesterday, and today is not like tomorrow. We shall see.' " He shook his head several times and said angrily, "The fool thinks we don't know him. Like a blind man who shits on the roof and thinks nobody sees!"

The workers kept questioning Ibn Zamel, and the man who had been laughing with him replied. "He asked me, 'This sheikh we see, is it our Daham, the friend that we know?' And I told him, 'Who eats their figs does their bidding—this is Ibn Rashed the Second.' "

At about the same time, during one of Ibn Rashed's rare visits to the coffeehouse, he looked sallow, wild eyed and confused in his movements. His appearance provoked conflicting emotions, ranging from sympathy to incomprehension. Several of those present tried to start a conversation with him, but he answered them only with sad smiles and brief, fragmented replies.

Ibn Rashed's visit to the coffeehouse and lengthy stay there may not in itself have excited much concerned discussion, but what happened during his visit caused the greatest commotion and was long remembered by the people.

"The bedouin. Fetch the bedouin," shouted Abu As'ad to the boy who helped him out in the coffeehouse.

Ibn Rashed jumped like a madman when he heard this shout; everyone with him jumped to their feet at the same time and looked in the direction in which the boy ran. Ibn Rashed motioned with his hand and gave a few brief orders. The boy reentered the coffeehouse with a bedouin, who exchanged a few words with Abu As'ad, then sat on the floor and opened a small bag. He extracted a coin and handed it to Abu As'ad, and when he did so Ibn Rashed saw him, as did everyone in the coffeehouse, and all of them, but especially Ibn Rashed, felt a weakness akin to shame. Visibly upset, Ibn Rashed rose and left the coffeehouse, but his eyes did not leave that bedouin for a single moment.

As soon as word of this incident reached the workers' camp, and the ears of Abdullah al-Zamel, Abdullah had them repeat Abu As'ad's words and how he'd said them. He nodded several times and smiled, but no one understood why.

58

THIS LINGERING SUMMER WAS THOUGHT BY MANY to be the worst in living memory. The days grew long and the nights very short, as the harsh blaze of the sun grew ever stronger, and many of the people felt assured that this summer would annihilate men and beasts alike and leave nothing and no one alive. Ibn Naffeh never stopped telling the people, joyfully, almost gloatingly, how demons would soon fly around their feet like mice, and how the Hell that boiled beneath the earth would soon burst out and burn everything to cinders. The people, who were tormented by the heat and humidity as well as by Ibn Naffeh's predictions, lost their appetite for food and fell prey to apathy, distractedness and forgetfulness, remembering nothing but the hour they were living now, seeing nothing but what was taking place before their eyes.

Harran, which had been undergoing constant change since the

hour of the Americans' arrival, knew how to keep people busy and make them run like dogs, why and to where no one knew, for they were immersed in cares that they had never known existed; nonetheless Harran never ceased to surprise itself and others, its residents and those who had come in recent months and days.

In the market, where the newly arrived caravan travelers gathered in throngs with those deposited by the ships, no day passed without dozens of major and minor incidents—from arguments to the endless haggling over deals to buy and sell among the wooden shops and mud houses—when they were built, why and by whom, no one knew. In the mosque, whence men withdrew to take their Lord's counsel, there was no end of prayers and complaints. Between the prayers and complaints the men exchanged news and gossip, shrugged their shoulders and shook their heads, awaiting the days to come.

The workers' camp, which had known some quiet and contentment in winter and the first days of spring, became an unbearable hell in summer. The Americans seemed tough and bigoted at the best of times, as did the emir's men and those of the personnel office, but as June wore on their visits dwindled, then ceased, with the result that the grip of the emir and the personnel office relaxed, and no one knew whether this letup was permanent, if their domination had ended for good. Most of the Americans left on long vacations in July and August and behaved with exaggerated happiness and anger in the few days before their departures; they acted like children.

The barracks, notable the previous summer for admitting burning sunlight all day long, were now so suffocating that no one could stand to be inside for more than a few minutes, just long enough to fetch whatever was needed. They were mere storehouses for clothes, shoes, tools and quantities of food; and when the odors of all these things intermingled with the intense heat and humidity, no one could go inside at all. Some workers insisted on pushing the sacks and stray objects out of the long aisles to clear a place for napping, to escape the burning sun, in the narrow spaces beneath the tent or beside it, and threw themselves on the cement floor inside the barracks, but they soon came out again with haggard faces, drenched with sweat, deeply upset and afraid, for many of them had seen or felt snakes or been stung by the little yellow scorpions that trooped out from under the beds. Those who survived the stings were bitten by insects of types unfamiliar to them, for they had swelling and itching all over their bodies. The big black rats made the barracks their home during all hours of the day, and at night they scattered everywhere, between the tents, near the barrels and in the toilets. They made quick, agile leaps forward, and having reached a safe distance paused and turned around to look at the men they terrified, and some of the workers said that the rats looked at them and laughed; some of them said that the rats laughed just like children.

The Americans guessed—or perhaps knew—that while it was easy to dominate and tame the workers in cold or mild weather, they turned into savage beasts in summertime, growing more brutal as the temperature rose. A man had to stay by them to some degree, but stay away to a greater degree. They were exactly like sharks, which are impossible to soothe, tame or control when they scent blood.

The barracks buildings had been exposed to the blows and insults of the men the previous summer—to the surprise and hilarity of the Americans—but this summer neither the Americans nor the emir's men raised any objection, nor did the Administration object when the workers spread their blankets and possessions on the ground outside the barracks in the early spring; in May, when the heat intensified and the workers asked for tents, it was promised, without long discussions, that they would be supplied. It did actually happen this way, albeit with some delays, and some of the workers went out of their way to find excuses for arguments and fights.

That summer more Americans took vacations than stayed behind in Harran: they left in waves. As soon as the hottest part of summer began the workers got the impression that the Americans who'd stayed behind were unlike those who had left, unlike even the way they had themselves been in the past. The graciousness displayed by those leaving, especially in the last days, the happiness in their faces as they made their preparations and the strong handshakes they offered the Arabs, made those remaining seem even ruder and more hostile. Some of the workers were reassigned, some suspended, and some departments were shut down. Everything seemed confused and temporary—just as it had been in the early days.

The workers moved warily, but every one of their movements, no matter how minor or careful, met with rebukes and shouts from the new bosses, whose angry remonstrances grew louder by the hour. They sometimes ran, they were so angry, and shouted in all directions, and a man did not have to be very bright to figure out what kinds of things they were shouting. The workers, who looked around in genuine bafflement to see what they might do to please their bosses, began to answer their curses with even viler ones, with angry and defiant looks. But nothing was ever settled except according to the wishes of these boorish Americans.

As the hours of the day wore on, relations strained, deteriorated and broke down. When it came time for the workers to head home in the afternoon, everything was at an end. The foremen, so alert in the morning, moving even more briskly than necessary, sagged by the end of the day, even wearier than the men they supervised. Their voices were hoarse and strangulated, and their eyes frustrated, and they got angry over the slightest action or question directed at them. The American bosses, who in the morning hours strutted busily around like roosters, were soon overtaken by exhaustion and futility as their movements slowed and their enthusiasm waned. Their tongues, which never stopped shouting and swearing, almost lolled out of their mouths by the end of the day, like those of thirsty dogs, or else they never showed, as if stuck to the roofs of their mouths. They answered the workers' and foremen's questions with their eyes, or limp motions of their hands, living only for the end of the workday.

The shift ended, and all the men drifted home to the two sectors like streams coursing down a slope, one broad and one small, the Americans to their camp and the Arabs to theirs, the Americans to their swimming pool, where their racket could be heard in the nearby barracks behind the barbed wire. When silence fell, the workers guessed that the Americans had gone into their air-conditioned rooms whose thick curtains shut everything out: sunlight, dust, flies and Arabs.

The workers repaired to their camp for their second shift of hardship: preparing meals, washing clothes, cleaning out the tents, fetching water. Some went to the market to buy bread, canned goods and what was left of the meat, for the best was quickly sold in the early morning.

Every undertaking, every step, brought endless difficulties and disagreements. Although some of them had consented early on to do these chores, usually at the beginning of the week, there were always new discussions and arguments. After growing weary and bored by the arguments, which had been refought dozens of times, they went away in silence, no one talking to anyone else, full of discontent and unfriendliness.

This happened countless times, and this is how it went most days. Night came, infusing their bodies with a kind of narcotic laziness. Exhaustion sucked away all their energy, but with their first cigarettes after supper they felt the first hint of relaxation, and their mood changed; even their voices regained the friendly tone of people who had something in common. They began to tell jokes and exchange bits of news, reflecting on the day just passed. Anyone talking about the bosses or foremen was careful to look around to see that no friend of these was present; then the discussion started in earnest, full of profanities and inside jokes.

The workers did not know Hamilton's name; to them he was Abu Lahab. The use of this name spread to Arab Harran, and some said that Hamilton himself had found out about it. James, director of the harbor project, was renamed Abu Jineeb; the chief of the American compound was named Crooked Camel, because he often stood at the compound gate looking at the footprints on the ground and at the feet of everyone leaving and entering, as if looking for some kind of clue.

Not only the Americans had nicknames—the deputy emir's name was the Barrel; the workers passed on secretly and carefully the name they had chosen because of his fatness and because, during the construction of the emirate, he was always after them to fill the barrel before they left the site. Saleh al-Dabbasi they called Saleh the Donkey, perhaps because of his high-pitched voice or his limp manner of speaking.

In the early evening their conversation was comical and ambiguous, but as night came on with the moonrise and the twinkling of the stars, it turned to other places and times past. Every man has a past, and those who so poetically depicted these distant places and lost times were rare indeed, but they were the backbone of the camp and its most important residents; the workers gathered around them, and they initiated the nightly councils. With every new story or biting comment, or remembrance that stirred their hearts and minds, most of them felt more strongly than ever that they were nowhere, wearing themselves out for nothing, and they were filled with sadness and regret; they felt alone and forgotten. When things reached this point their voices rose in song and they were lost in dreams and memories of faraway places; grief bred grief, and the song that started out graceful and timid gradually became a sad, plaintive lament to life and existence and everything else. Very few of them had mastered this kind of singing, which was a rare treat; the singer burned with emotion and almost passed out until the climactic moment when his voice drowned out the others, to fill the darkness, saying things that the singer himself had not foreseen, for the pain that penetrated his heart like a knife left no choice, not permitting him any voluntary or conscious will.

This was how Harran's nights passed, but Harran, which changed every day, and was new each day, never knew any two of its nights to resemble each other; there was always something new.

59

THERE WAS NO PATIENCE OR PERMANENCE IN HAR-
ran, not in people nor in things; even nature,
including the water and air, shifted and
changed. The people, so preoccupied by Hajem for so long,
saddened, expectant and curious about what would happen after
his sudden departure, forgot the man in the onrush of events,
and even when they remembered him in their nightly councils
other memories carried them away and prevailed over that recollection or blinded their minds and hearts with other matters.

Before Hajem, Abdu Muhammad had diverted the people,
but he was now secluded in his bakery. No one thought of him
or talked about him anymore except as a recollection deeply
rooted in the past.

Even Ibn Rashed had kept the people preoccupied for a while
with his news and behavior, and been very much on their minds

with his comings and goings, and now they saw him leaping like a cat from one place to another, measuring the ground, contemplating the buildings, rummaging through planks and twisted steel, gathering up things that no one in his right mind would dream of gathering . . . Ibn Rashed himself, after all that had happened, and all the talk and apprehension he had caused, was all but forgotten, or at least was not on their minds in quite the same way he had been before. The isolation he had imposed upon himself, and the melancholy that compelled him to go for days without seeing anyone or being seen, this isolation removed him completely. When they thought of him it was usually because he had been seen in Abu As'ad's coffeehouse one afternoon, or walking along the beach with two or three of his men. He was much changed: his rapid stride had given way to a slow, heavy gait; his strong, plump body was now stooped and almost thin, and had it not been for the darting, suspicious glances he still cast around, the people nearest to him would not have known him.

The ships brought more men every day. Tons of cargo came in and were quickly transported, most of them, to the American compound. Buildings were built here and there and grew higher by the day. Crowded shops jammed up against one another, people rushed around, shouting and calling, and their memories were frantic. Unease and unrest mounted: no one knew what the next day held in store for them.

Arab Harran, which retreated as far as possible in an attempt to distance itself and flee its fate, could not resist for long: the mud structures heaped up against one another, which blocked the roads or made them wind and zigzag, could no longer hold all the people, and the people were no longer content to remain as they were. New buildings went up everywhere, scattered like boils on an arm or patches on an old broad garment. The market, which began with three shops, was the strangest place of all.

New shops went up every day, every type and size of shop, some strong and immovable and others made of hurriedly assembled wooden crating. Daham was now a contractor for the hurriedly assembled type of shop: he brought the huge wooden crates from the American compound, and whoever wanted one of them had only to bring in their merchandise and open for business in "the delivered, ready-built shop . . . with profits to be evenly split" between Daham and the new merchant. Everyone liked the crate shops, which suited their needs admirably, and they appeared everywhere: in the central market, by the mosque and outside the workers' camp. Several were installed in the western hills of Arab Harran itself.

Beside these shops were built houses of the same type, though as a rule they were more spacious, and they were renovated to make them more beautiful or better fitted to the new owners' needs. These houses sprang up everywhere, on the seafront, between the shops, on the hilltops, in other words on every plot of vacant land wide enough for such a house, and no one had any serious objection.

As these shops and houses were erected, another type of building flourished as well. These were houses built of well-hewn and tightly spaced stones of a gray, almost black color. The first and biggest of these houses was Abdullah al-Saad's, and Dabbasi followed him, building his house on the open land west of the mosque which Ibn Rashed had agreed to give up, with the emir's approval. Others, al-Salaami and al-Marzouq among them, were quick to build stone houses, though theirs were smaller and humbler.

The emirate and emir's residence were completed in late summer and early autumn, but the emir did not move out of his tents, which had been brought from their old place and set up anew in the middle of the large open space which he had enclosed by a fence to define the courtyard of the emirate and residence.

The reason the emir gave for his delay in moving was "the stink of the new paint—it blinds you and gives you a headache," in addition to the fact that "it is much better for a man to sleep in the open air than to shut himself up in one of those tombs," as he told anyone who visited him or asked him about it.

Just as Abdullah al-Saad and Muhammad al-Seif had come to settle in Harran, two other men made a much-heralded arrival in Harran in this period. The first came from Basra with Ibrahim al-Saad; Abdullah al-Saad had not expected him to come, because Mohieddin al-Naqib—the Shahbunder of Merchants, as he was known in Basra, for his formidable and wide-ranging commercial interests—had business to look after in India, Manchester and everywhere in between. Mohieddin al-Naqib had come out of curiosity; then he decided to stay permanently. The second was Hassan Rezaie. He arrived to a warm, boisterous welcome, on a ship smaller than those of the Americans yet also unlike the poor, miserable ships that brought so many dozens of wandering travelers. Hassan Rezaie arrived with pomp and splendor, and although not a soul in Harran knew him, he visited the prince the moment he disembarked. They discussed any number of things, and by way of introduction and explaining his coming, Hassan Rezaie said that he was exploring and that "he had no objection to offering whatever kind of assistance Harran needed, today or any day." He brought the emir a telescope, which the emir was at first hesitant to accept, but he was thoroughly delighted when he put the telescope to his eye and looked in this and that direction, and pointed and laughed with pleasure and surprise.

Hassan Rezaie stayed in Harran just three days on this visit, "because his affairs and appointments allowed him no more than that, despite the good time he'd had and his wish to stay longer, and his pride in having met the emir." The emir offered him the opportunity to stay on as his guest in the emirate building, but Hassan Rezaie refused very politely, saying that he would spend all of the time "at the court of the emir and in his company, but the bed he was used to, due to his illness, compelled him to go back to the ship." In the process of explaining this and trying to win the emir's consent, he said that while he would be on board the ship, he and the emir could each use his telescope to carry on a long and delightful dialogue, as sailors on shipboard did. He bet that the emir would enjoy this kind of conversation and learn it easily.

The people did a lot of talking about this man, whose origins they knew nothing about. They did not know how he had become so friendly with the emir so easily or how he was able to discuss so many things with him, or how they would continue to communicate, after parting, over such a long distance!

Ibn Naffeh shouted angrily when he heard what the people were saying about the telescope—that it permitted a man standing on the beach to see a kernel of wheat in the farthest area of the western hills and to see the night stars as if they were lamps hanging above his head. "The Judgment Day is drawing near—man no longer fears the reckoning, or his Lord!"

When the people asked him what made him think this way, he shook his head sadly, in utter despondency.

"From the first day the Americans came they brought demons, sins and catastrophes, and no one knows what will happen in these next days." He was silent for a moment, then quavered, "Lord God, our sovereign, the mighty and compassionate, keep me in the faith of my father and forefathers, the faith of our prophet Muhammad. Do not make of me a sinning infidel like the sinners of my tribe. Hear me, O Lord, and answer my prayer."

"Leave this old man now," said a man in the midst of the prayer and supplication. "The ship has arrived."

"What ship?"

"Like the one you remember."

Abdu Muhammad went mad when he heard that another ship of women had come in. He wanted to get rid of the loaves he was working on, to get out of his bakery, out of his skin, out of Harran altogether. He seemed never to have had so much baking; he had never seen so many loaves in one place at once; and not only the bread, the fire was thwarting him; it did not cooperate: Why was the dough not cooking? Why didn't it cook so that he could take it out? Would the ship wait for him? Why did he have to stay behind and burn in this hell while the others, there, sat lazily on the beach, dangling their feet in the water and watching the beautiful shuttling of the little boats back and forth, bearing bevies of ladies. Their eyes followed the delicious, perilous little voyage until its last moment in the water; like seabirds they lit on the beach with their clamorous voices, like nightingales, and showed their white, white, tender white bodies, so near, so desirable, pushing forward like gazelles at a pond, surrounded by hands and watchful eyes . . . God, was it possible that all this was happening, and him so far, far, far away? So what if the people had to wait for the bread they needed so that Abdu could go and watch like the others? Even if they didn't eat for one day, would that be the end of the world?

Everyone was against Abdu Muhammad. That was a known fact, and he knew it better than anyone else. He fed them all, every day, he was proud of giving them the best and tastiest loaves possible, but no one, yes no one, so much as looked at him or felt any affection toward him, or knew anything of the fire that burned in his heart, especially now that he knew the ship had arrived. Why didn't they come now, this minute, to take their bread? Where had they all gone—why had they left him alone like this?

When Abdu took the loaves from the oven, he found them completely burned. He looked at the three or four that were left and said to himself, "I burned up before they did," and could not go on.

He went to the beach, to stand in the same spot he had the year before.

He moved closer. He moved as close as possible, and his face touched the barbed wire, but at this distance he could see nothing but a far-off white ship. He could not even determine the color of its fluttering flag. He argued with Juma; he said that the Americans had sent for him, had asked him to come, but Juma did not listen or reply, as if he had never eaten Abdu's bread! He wandered far from the gate and looked around in all directions to see if he could jump the fence, to get nearer, but all his attempts failed. He saw some boys nearby and asked them if they had seen anyone ask about him, but they laughed and made indistinct replies. He felt bitter regret as he watched them swim out, crossing the American barrier and shouting to one another, because he did not know how to swim.

He remembered what he had heard in recent days about the telescope, the gift the emir had received. They said that since the emir had acquired the telescope, he had spent most of his time lying on his stomach, with the telescope set up, watching everything. If Abdu had this telescope even for a minute, he would be able to watch her. One glance was enough for him to live on her for another year. When he saw her, she would doubtless be searching for him, watching every new arrival and scrutinizing every face.

That day, at about sundown or a little after, a widely believed rumor spread, to the effect that Abdu Muhammad had drowned in the sea. While it was true that some of the people had seen him near the shoreline, no one had seen him after that. The bakery had been closed all day. All the knocking and calling out was in vain. Even his friends, who knew when to knock on his door and what to say, who knew how to rouse him from his hideaway even during his worst bouts of isolation, even they failed and were seized by the fear that Abdu was not there in the bakery. Perhaps he really was dead. Some of them thought of breaking the door down, but they decided to leave things until the next day: "Morning is a blessing, and this is nothing new—the man is feeling melancholy and doesn't want to see anyone."

This same day Abdullah al-Abyad's bakery did business as it had never done before, and with the loaves he placed in the people's hands he filled their ears with the details of Abdu's drowning.

But nothing in Harran was constant, and late that night, one hour before dawn, the men coming out of Abu As'ad's coffee-house saw Abdu on the beach, not far from the coffeehouse. He was crooning sad songs, and sometimes sobbed and cried loudly.

Abdu was thinner and more haggard than usual for the next few days, and his hands shook badly. He was hardly able to put the loaves in the oven and take them out again, and he spoke to no one and did not look anyone in the face.

But within a few days the rumors reported that Abdu, who did not know how to swim and had never gone into the water before, went in that day and beat the water with his arms and legs until it carried him to the distant anchored ship; and he boarded with the help of a rope his woman friend lowered to him, and there he spent long, busy hours. He swam to the beach on his back, holding a woman's picture clear of the water with one hand. It was seen by a number of the men coming out of Abu As'ad's that night. The picture was dry and glossy, for the water had never touched it, and he kissed it as he wept.

60

RUMORS ABOUNDED, IN MIDSUMMER, THAT Daham's visit to Ujra was intimately related to the problem of Hajem. It was said that the funds left in trust with the emir had been withdrawn, because Ibn Rashed had decided to look everywhere for Hajem and his uncle in order to pay them the compensation; he had increased the sum the emir had decided upon, in case it should prove insufficient or unsatisfactory. What enhanced the rumors' strength or credibility was that Ibn Rashed, contrary to his custom in recent days, began to appear among the people, and that although he had never been particularly pious or devout, not going to the mosque unless compelled to, he was seen in the mosque several times; what is more, several people swore that he was deeply engrossed in prayer, supplication and trembling. His eyes were half closed as he murmured his very lengthy prayers, which was a slightly alien thing to do in Harran: neither the bedouin nor the people of the surrounding regions prayed so, and indeed they were a little suspicious and apprehensive toward people who prayed that fervently.

What further added to the strength and credibility of the rumors was the fact that Ibn Rashed was slowly regaining his health: he often sat in the coffeehouse for long periods and went for walks on the beach. True, he paid little attention to the many business matters that had preoccupied him before, but most of the people reasoned that his present moodiness did not allow such concentration; before long, he would be back doing business as usual. Although as had become his wont, he was very quiet and reluctant to do much talking with others, except for brief greetings and fleeting questions, he often sat and talked with the two or three of his men who never left his side.

When Dabbasi was first told that Ibn Rashed had spent an hour or more in the coffeehouse and seemed animated, he feigned sadness. "The wakefulness of death, my friends." A moment later he added, as if talking to himself, "He imagines that if he learns to live with his fear, he'll feel safe."

He sat back for a short while.

"He's in deep touble, Ibn Rashed, and who with? Ibn Hathal and the bedouin. Any one of those would take his revenge forty years from now and say, 'Why was I in such a hurry?' "

To make sure of Ibn Rashed's new situation, Dabbasi sent his son Saleh to visit him and to extend an invitation to his wedding party, for Saleh was to marry Muhammad al-Seif's sister, but Saleh came away with a very confused impression. Sometimes he said that Ibn Rashed had not changed a bit, and other times he said that he detected something eerie, incomprehensible, in his eyes, but what was for sure was that "the man does not want to talk!" Saleh urged his father to go visit Ibn Rashed and see for himself, and they agreed to meet in the coffeehouse.

"He chose the coffeehouse," said Dabbasi to clear himself. "I told him, 'I want to visit you, Abu Muhammad.' He said, 'In the coffeehouse, we'll meet this afternoon,' and we met, and that was that."

The moment they met Ibn Rashed suggested to the men who were with him, rather rudely, that they go away. He stood up as soon as Dabbasi moved near him and said happily, "Just as you see, Abu Saleh, as strong as a horse. Stronger."

"What good is a horse without a mare or two?" replied Dabbasi and laughed.

"We're looking, Abu Saleh," said Ibn Rashed. He paused a moment to turn and whisper, "Once all this is over."

Without Dabbasi asking, Ibn Rashed proceeded to tell him about the band of armed men, led by Miteb al-Hathal himself, who wanted to kill him. He said that they lay in wait for him day and night, but that he was ready for anything; they would have no opportunity. Excitedly he pulled a pistol from his cloak.

"Before they even draw their weapons, I'll get them with this, one by one."

He spoke very sharply and excitedly. Dabbasi was surprised, but he smiled and pretended to be calm.

"Trust in God, Abu Muhammad. The matter is much simpler than you think—it doesn't call for gunpowder and bloodshed."

"Whether it calls for them or not, I know how things stand, and before they kill me I'll kill ten of them."

"I heard they were satisfied," said Dabbasi craftily. "They took the money and shut up."

"They were ready and willing, but the people, the people, Abu Saleh—especially the one that never forgets and never wearies, Miteb al-Hathal." He paused to sigh and then went on. "Every one of my friends still talks to me, they all say, 'Ibn Rashed,' but they know."

He paused again, wiped the sweat that ran down his forehead

and added in a different tone, "That money was a good sum, but so is this, and anyone who wasn't happy with that will like this."

He shook the pistol confidently and looked around him.

At this moment a boy burst into the coffeehouse, screaming: "The bedouin! The bedouin!"

Shots rang out. Shouting and the acrid smell of gunpowder filled the coffeehouse. When the shouting and the echo of the gunshots died away, Ibn Rashed collapsed in his chair. He had fainted.

Ibn Rashed had thought that persons were about to enter the coffeehouse and kill him, so he moved before they did—that is what he said after he came to. He was in such a state of panic and fear that everyone took pity on him.

It might have been written off as a coincidence and forgotten like so many other things, but the cries that began to follow Ibn Rashed, that he heard in his house, as he said, at all hours of the day and night, sometimes the cries of boys and at other times those of men, forced him to seek refuge in his house for days and nights on end. He could forgive the children, but what about those rough voices in the middle of the night? He started from his sleep, terrified, or flew out of his bed like a slaughtered chicken. The voices goaded him to come out if he had any courage. If he kept quiet or hid the cries grew louder, but if he ran out no one was there. When he asked other people they looked surprised and denied hearing or seeing anyone.

Some of the people said, to explain the shouts of the boys, that the coincidence had turned Ibn Rashed's head; no sooner did they learn of what had happened in the coffeehouse than they saw a connection; as for the shouting men, Ibn Rashed was the only one who heard them.

When Daham returned from Ujra with a group of workers and heard what had happened in his absence, and saw the frenzy that had possessed Ibn Rashed, he spoke out in front of everybody. "This is Abu Saleh's doing. Abu Saleh is the father and mother of it all!"

Dabbasi heard what Daham said but pretended he did not hear. Preparations for the wedding were moving ahead, and he was handling most of them himself. He invited the guests and saw that the sheep to be slaughtered were being well fed and had them taken to the beach twice to be washed, so that they would be immaculately white. The lamps with the most powerful lights were brought especially from Ujra and tested the same day they arrived and again on the following night: Arab Harran glittered radiantly in the night on the western hills, and many of the workers who were watching from the camp thought that this was the night of the wedding, though others told them no, that the wedding was Friday night; what they were seeing now was only a rehearsal.

Harran, which remembered the father's wedding the year before, expected the son's to be even grander, "because Saleh is the oldest son, and Dabbasi is richer and more important now than he was a year ago, and he has to prove it." The emir, who was invited, and reinvited time after time by Dabbasi himself, never actually promised to attend because he was secretly hoping to watch the wedding through his telescope; this was very important to him, since he would see it brilliantly lit from such a vast distance. He was busy looking at matchsticks or pictures which his men held up at various distances, again and again. The emir took different bearings, and at one point rolled onto the floor and stabilized the telescope on a pillow. He knelt, propping the hand holding the telescope on the other hand, trying to attain "target identification," as he called sharp focus. Dabbasi insisted, however, and made it clear how important the emir's presence was to him.

"Come this afternoon," said the emir without turning around. "Have some coffee and leave us."

He gave orders for his men to stand the matchsticks using tongs, to put them in a neat line; then he looked at them, first with his naked eye and then using the telescope. He shook his head in wonderment.

"Anyway, we'll see you, Your Excellency," said Dabbasi as he left. "When you come, we'll know how to look after you."

Dabbasi continued to send messengers to give out invitations, and when he sent one to Ibn Rashed, Daham said, after a long silence, Ibn Rashed replied, "I don't think we'll be coming." He paused and added, in a slow, low voice, "Beware of your enemy once, but of your friend beware a thousand times." Not only that; as he got up, saying that he had much to do, he added, "Happy days are short." When Daham told Dabbasi about this answer he laughed angrily and repeated a phrase then much in use among the people: " 'Ride the donkey and ignore his farting!' If I don't ride this mule and make all Harran hear his farts, I'm not Abu Saleh!"

On Thursday morning Dabbasi asked the emir yet again, this time in the form of an urgent request to honor him with his presence. The emir, however, was raptly watching a newly arrived ship, and he did not even hear Dabbasi arrive, much less what he had said. Dabbasi slowly grew annoyed, since he had a great deal to accomplish that day, and he turned to the deputy emir, who gave him a wry look and shook his head.

"I'm depending on you, Abu Rashwan."

The deputy nodded, which Dabbasi took to mean that he would do his best.

Saleh in the meantime made a final visit to the workers' camp and made a loud and openly boastful announcement: "You are all our guests tonight—tell everyone to come. And no excuses!"

The emir was busy into the afternoon watching the ship and counting the men who disembarked, though he could not be sure of the exact number, because five or six of the men who had come off went up and boarded again, and one man might have gone on and off two or three times; the emir was not sure, since the people were crowded together, and dressed and looked alike; and one of the emir's men jostled the telescope when he served tea. His patient, deliberate surveillance made the emir very pensive, and he thought of many times long past and wished he had had the telescope with him then. He told his deputy what an important invention this was and said that someday the mind of man would invent a device using many telescopes, making it possible to see people in faraway places, in Egypt and Syria and even farther away. He brooded over his imaginings and dreams until he was told supper was ready.

After a short rest during which he slept fitfully because of the intense heat and humidity, the emir looked at the western hills as the sun sank in the west and saw throngs of people and something out of the ordinary. He guessed that this was Saleh al-Dabbasi's wedding, and when he took up the telescope, he asked his deputy, who had just come in wearing fresh clothes that smelled of incense, if this was the wedding day, and when the deputy laughed loudly before answering he raised the telescope to his eye and looked at him to see why he was laughing.

"The man is a wreck, Abu Misfer," said the deputy with measured sarcasm. "He says no one's getting married unless Abu Misfer comes."

The emir nodded as if remembering that he had seen Dabbasi that morning.

"Duty is duty," he said to himself.

Before arriving at the large main square of Arab Harran, the emir said to his deputy, "I'll stay until sundown and then come back." He added a moment later, in a different tone of voice, "You, Abu Rashwan, you stay longer, because Abu Saleh will get mad otherwise."

In spite of all his efforts, the senior Dabbasi's wedding was a much grander and more important affair than his son's, and were anyone to wonder why this was so he would not be able to give a clear-cut answer, or the same answer that others might have given. More sheep were slaughtered this time—three times as many, to be exact, and several times as many people attended. The many lights that were strung up all over the place turned the night into day; at Dabbasi's wedding only one large lamp had been hung in the middle, and it had hurt people's eyes more than it had improved the visibility. And so it went with the singing, dancing and other entertainments—this time they were far more lavish, but the people felt that Dabbasi's wedding had been different. Some of the workers pointed out that the Americans had not come this time, but they were told that had the Americans come they would have turned the wedding into an orgy of interviews and picture taking. Still others said that Suweyleh's presence would have made all the difference, but he had departed a few weeks before; no doubt he had himself got married and, being happy, decided to delay his return to Harran or cancel it altogether. Hearing this, most of the guests nodded but had no comment.

The wedding might have ended with the ribaldry of Saleh al-Dabbasi's friends and enemies alike, with everyone then going home, but the elder Dabbasi insisted that everyone stay as long as possible, so that the wedding would be a memorable event. He also wanted to underline the power and prestige he now enjoyed, so when it was suggested to him that the celebration conclude with a torchlight procession throughout Arab Harran, he quickly gave his consent, and no one but a few old men objected to the idea.

"Tonight doesn't belong to you," said Ibn Naffeh in a tone of mild reproof. "There are other people, too, my friends."

No one listened to him, so he spoke up again, this time to himself. "You hear a goblet ring and begin to dance and sing. And all the devils come out."

The wedding might have ended with a tour of the market, a vigil outside the mosque, a visit to Abu As'ad's coffeehouse and a final procession back to the western hills, during which Saleh al-Dabbasi would have been thoroughly egged on to discharge his duty successfuly that night, and that would have been that. But a demon was at work, or perhaps it was only a coincidence, for no sooner had the procession wound its way toward Ibn Rashed's house than a shot rang out. No one knew who had opened fire, but within minutes all Harran was ablaze: there was shooting everywhere. At first there was a general feeling of fear and wariness, but it gave way to joy, anger and excitement. People stood around for a long time, and in the pauses between the gunshots and the sound of bullets striking there were sharp voices chanting, "The bedouin! The bedouin! The bedouin!"

Although there was not a sound from Ibn Rashed's house, and no ray of light, everyone was sure that Ibn Rashed and his men were inside, that they were listening to every word and watching the procession, and that they were doubtless ready to respond to and resist any aggression, but because nothing like this had ever happened before or even occurred to anyone, and since it was really only a matter of boys shouting, perhaps with the help or at the instigation of some of the men, the procession went on and moved away a little. During a lull, a strong voice was heard behind the procession, as if it came from above, a coarse but clear and drawn out voice: "The Donkey! Look at the Donkey! Saleh the Donkey! Saleh the Donkey!"

Some of the men looked at each other and at Saleh al-Dabbasi with questioning faces: Whose voice was it? Daham's? Ibn Rashed's? Someone else's? Saleh's face turned yellow, then black, then blue in the flickering torchlight and shadows. The dead silence was broken again, as the men exchanged glances by the drawn out voice, like that of a wounded dog: the Donkey . . . Saleh the Donkey.

"Don't pay any attention to the crazy fool," shouted a voice, no one knew whose, from the midst of the crowd.

"Let's get going—the bridegroom is impatient," said a second man.

"If the bedouin comes tomorrow he'll cut his balls off," said the first man in the same powerful voice.

The procession started moving again, but slowly and heavily this time, and bitterly. Even though the elder Dabbasi had heard what happened, as well as the shots fired in the market, he tried to inject some gaiety into the proceedings. He danced and asked some of the old men to dance; he fired into the air and several others opened fire as well. Some of the men sang and some women came nearer to see the dancing men and could be heard laughing. In spite of all this, and the fact that the festive mood had returned to the party, when Dabbasi insisted that everyone should stay all night, some of the men proposed to go home, and they smiled and winked suggestively. Dabbasi answered them the same way he had at his own wedding. "Stay, my friends, stay and be merry, for tomorrow we'll die."

He said it laughingly, and winked at his son, whom he wanted to agree with him.

Late that night, before the men left, Saleh al-Dabbasi was wedded to his bride, and the next day the women told each other

a certain item of disappointing news, fearfully and in total secrecy, so the news did not travel far. Dabbasi's wife appeared
rough and angry when she came close to saying it outright.
"Those men wore him out. From the hills to the market, and
the market to the hills—it would exhaust a camel!"

No one alluded to it again.

One month after Saleh's wedding, Abdelaziz al-Rashed died.
It was a sudden death, particularly because no one had seen him
since the night in the coffeehouse, and everyone was sad. They
felt somehow responsible for his death. Even Dabbasi groaned
and lamented loudly when he heard. "Oh, no! Oh, God, no!
There is no god but God! There is no god but God, and He
alone is eternal, He alone is everlasting."

Harran mourned Ibn Rashed in sorrow and silence, and almost
everyone in the town attended the funeral.

61

IBN RASHED'S DEATH IN THE LATE SUMMER, AND THE
way it happened, aroused a great deal of bitterness
and soul searching. In spite of the hatred many people felt toward him because of his coarseness and greed, and
despite the envy he inspired in the hearts of the men who talked
about him, they all felt that he had been unduly wronged, and
that this injustice had destroyed him.

Only a few days after his death, some of the workers could
be heard to say, "God rest his soul—he was better than a lot of
others. What's past is past." Others said, "The dead deserve only
forgiveness. Poor Ibn Rashed thought he'd live forever, and his
ambition killed him."

"My friends, now Ibn Rashed is gone. He's dead and buried,"
Abdullah al-Zamel loudly told a group of workers three days

after Ibn Rashed's decease. "You have to be fair, and say what's in your heart. You have to tell the truth."

He paused to look in their faces before going on.

"Do you know who killed Ibn Rashed?"

Their eyes pressed him, and he nodded his head.

"The Americans. They killed Ibn Rashed."

The workers stared at him. "The Americans killed Ibn Rashed? How? Why?" It was unbelievable, or at least unclear and illogical.

"Yes, the Americans. They're the ones who killed him."

He smiled at their incredulous faces.

"More than three years of him running around like a dog, back and forth, here and there, whatever the Americans wanted. 'Yes, sir, whatever you say, sir!' It didn't do any good. When Mizban died, God rest his soul, they said, 'Ibn Rashed!' Who drowned Mizban? It wasn't Ibn Rashed! He had nothing to do with it. The Americans took Mizban and drowned him, and 'Ibn Rashed, you must pay, Ibn Rashed, do something!' They talk about laws? Aren't there laws for people who drown? Don't they have rights? 'We have nothing to do with Mizban, we don't owe him a straw, we never saw him and we don't know him.' Ibn Rashed, God rest his soul, was blinded by ambition, it drove him mad. And you know the rest."

The workers looked at each other and at Abdullah al-Zamel. Now they understood his words, but they did not know exactly what they meant.

"The Americans have no friends—like wolves and sheep," said one man, whom they called Locust because of his small size.

"No," laughed another man, "they're not like wolves and sheep, they're like locusts."

"No, like wolves and sheep. Locusts eat only until they're satisfied, but your wolf, he kills and mutilates," said the short man forcefully.

"The Americans are wolves—Ibn Rashed was a locust," joked Ibn Zamel. He guffawed and added, "And you know the story. For the sake of a locust birds get themselves trapped."

"What about you, Ibn Zamel?" asked one of the workers sharply. "You killed Ibn Rashed. You kept at him until you buried him."

"Me?" His tone changed. "Shame on you."

"No. You, yes, you killed him."

Abdullah al-Zamel laughed loudly, but it was a dry and forced laugh, and the workers' challenging and almost accusatory stare did not leave his face.

"Listen, my good man . . ." He looked at all their faces, then at the man. "You know, and so does everyone in this camp, that Ibn Rashed and I were like grease and fire. He hated me, I hated him, but facts are facts.

"Maybe I didn't do right by Ibn Rashed," he went on, in a different tone, "I'm not saying I did, but, God rest his soul, he wronged himself more than people wronged him. No one loved him, and he did plenty of disgraceful things. He let the Americans make fools of us. He was never satisfied. That was Ibn Rashed."

"And you say 'God rest his soul'?"

"I said it and still say it."

"By God, you're confusing us, Ibn Zamel!"

"Do you want the truth? Ibn Rashed was a dog, a son of a bitch: greedy, selfish and tricky; but he was a Muslim and an Arab. He knew right from wrong, and that was what ruined him, that was what killed him." Abdullah al-Zamel paused, took a deep breath and went on in a clear and even sharp voice. "The Americans are godless. They are infidels. They know nothing but 'Work, work, work. Arabs are lazy, Arabs are liars, Arabs don't understand.' Ibn Rashed never stopped for a minute. It was always 'Yes sir, yes sir, whatever you say,' and they treated him like a dog; they let him struggle and go mad and die. And not one of those sons of bitches, not even Sh'eira, Nusayis, who came to his funeral, so much as said 'God rest his soul.' "

He paused. He took a deep, sobbing breath.

"We know what honor is. We know the sacredness of death, we know—"

He was unable to continue; the right word would not come.

"Death reforms all men," said one of the workers, who had been standing silently at a distance as if not paying attention. When he realized that everyone heard what he said during Ibn Zamel's pause, he stopped, then stepped forward and added, "When Ibn Rashed died, when he became dust, suddenly God had made no better man?"

Everyone looked at him in surprise, and he went on. "By God, you have no consciences, O sons of Arabs. Every day you have a new face and every hour a new opinion."

He left the tent. And as Muflih al-Arja left, the workers' opinion changed once again.

"It's as clear as day," Ibn Zamel almost shouted at the end of the discussion, which had turned into chaos. "The Americans killed him, and tomorrow you'll know, and not only about him!"

Several such debates went on in the camp, and although many of the workers did not consider the question to be as tangled as Ibn Zamel and Ibn Naffeh insisted it was, at least they agreed that "had the Americans been more reasonable, or had more honor or self-respect, they wouldn't have abandoned the man after all he had done for them"—that was their responsibility. As to the rest of what Ibn Zamel and Ibn Naffeh said, it was all idle talk and exaggeration.

Such discussions also went on in the coffeehouse and market. Even the women of Arab Harran, who hated and resented Ibn Rashed because it was he who had brought all the catastrophes upon them, had the houses demolished and forced the people to

move, began to feel sorry; some even felt anxious when they
remembered how they had prayed so fervently for revenge against
that "tyrant."

Now that Ibn Rashed was gone forever, in a way completely
unlike his short, mysterious disappearances, every person in Harran felt in some way responsible for his death, or at least responsible for leaving him to die like that without doing anything
to help him, not even fetching a drop of water for him in his
last hours, or giving a kind or encouraging look to help him die
more restfully or more at peace with himself or with less guilt.
This feeling haunted the people from the moment they heard of
his death—which at first, exchanging wondering looks, they
refused to believe—but when they were convinced, they moved
as one man, possessed by feelings of regret and depression, to
take part in his burial. His ghost hovered over their heads. They
did not know whether it was a kindly or malicious ghost, and
they did not know why things happened this way.

Dabbasi, who was baffled by this turn of events and seemed
deeply shocked and sorrowful, felt crushed by the passing of
days and wished he had been more generous and tolerant; even
more, he wished that their conflict had not reached such a pitch
of hatred and distrust. He remembered things he had said to the
emir and others and felt responsible for the man's end. When
his son Saleh came to him a few days after Ibn Rashed's decease
and said that "the gate of fortune is open; the obstacle is gone,"
referring to the now permanent removal of Ibn Rashed, Dabbasi
replied with painfully clear bitterness that "fortune is from God,
my boy, and death is from God. Don't gloat over your enemy's
death." But Saleh al-Dabbasi did not pay much attention to what
his father said and went away full of energetic plans for orga-
nizing his business now that Ibn Rashed was gone.

The elder Dabbasi's emotions were mixed for a long time. He
could not join any of the others when they talked about Ibn

Rashed; indeed he actively avoided anyone who talked about him, and when he heard anyone allude to "the deceased," as Ibn Rashed had been called from the moment his death was made known, he said, "Remember your good deeds against your deaths, people of Harran, so that you will not be consumed by regret."

So it remained in Dabbasi's heart, even until death came to him many years later. Ibn Naffeh, on the other hand, needed no convincing: he was absolutely positive that Ibn Rashed had died the moment he placed his hand in those of the Americans, that God had given him a brief respite and not neglected him, but since he paid no heed he died an infidel.

Ibn Rashed's presence lingered for years afterward, until those great and momentous events transpired in Harran and its surrounding area. He was long remembered, and his memory took on features new and vastly different from what it had had in the past, going far beyond the events that had truly taken place.

62

NOT ONLY THE SUMMER, BUT THE AUTUMN AS WELL, was harsh that year. With the last days of September, days far hotter than many that had passed that summer, the Americans began to flood in again. Those who had been away on vacation returned, or most of them did, and new ones arrived as well. Most of them were new. For the first time life in the American compound was hard, as hard as it had been in the early days. Tents were erected all over, several ships were anchored for days in front of the compound, and a large number of the Americans ate and slept aboard the ships. The emir was very active and energetic in this new phase, and he was amazed to see a strange device on the deck of one of the ships, which was unloaded and sat on the dock for barely a minute before it swept into the compound fast as a bullet. The emir saw it with his own eyes, and deftly raised his telescope for a better look, and shouted and pointed with his finger, but he cried out when he saw Hamilton, the deputy chief of the compound, mount the thing and ride it. The emir's face showed signs of rapture and confusion together. True, he had seen the large machines that moved forward and backward and turned this way and that, and Naim and other Americans had told him about smaller machines of the same type intended only for people who steered and rode them at high speeds, and although he had heard this and shown the greatest interest and awe, he had been unable to imagine exactly what such machines would look like. Now he saw one with his telescope, watching its darting movements with bated breath, a little frightened, and when it took the central road, as if headed for the northern hills, he was so filled with surprise and fear that the telescope shook in his hands; he was much less able to follow this than the landing of passengers from the ship or any other stationary target.

This strange, swift machine engrossed the emir and made him reflect uneasily, especially since these things, coming suddenly and all at once, provoked quite as much fear as wonder and curiosity.

When he saw the Americans' commotion on the deck of the ship and focused them clearly in the telescope, he saw that they were naked or nearly naked for most of the time. The emir's shock reached the very limits of intense confusion and fear when he spotted a number of women with them, all as naked or nearly naked as the men. At first he could not believe his eyes, and thought that this was an illusion, or that perhaps his vision was distorted from using the telescope for too long—this had happened to him before—but after he rubbed his eyes several times and closed them to relax for a few moments, and looked at the ship again, and the people on the deck, he screamed. Some of his men were nearby, and his words, slowly enunciated, were clear to all of them. "Oh! You sons of bitches, you Americans . . . naked, all of them are stark naked, my God, as You created me."

The men looked at the ship, in the direction the emir was looking, but they could make out nothing at this distance. They saw the ship but not the people on it; if one were to scrutinize the view for a long while, at certain hours of the day, he might distinguish some kind of movement at this distance, phantoms, but whether male or female could not be told. Now, as the emir said in complete confidence and lust that they were women, naked women, and that he could see them clearly, the men's lewd thoughts erupted and flew over this long distance to reach the ship and touch the women's bodies clothed like a ball of fire. Their hearts and eyes were shocked, and they felt an uncontrollable panic.

What the emir was saying could not be believed, a man could not imagine such a thing: real naked women, wandering among men on the deck of the ship? How could the men stand to have them walking around and coming near without burning up, without exploding like gunpowder, without sticking themselves like tent pegs into every crevice of those warm, beautiful bodies?

Every man's imagination went wild. They wanted to go closer to see, to see and feel, or at least to look through the telescope, even for a moment. Even a fleeting glimpse of the women at this distance would be enough to cool their burning hearts, but the emir grasped the telescope as a mother grasps a suckling infant. None of them would ever have guessed that the emir knew the kind of language he was using now; certain poses of the bodies enchanted him and destroyed him, so he handed the telescope to his deputy to look at the scene or at the women who made him feel as if he were about to explode and dissolve in space. He shouted like a wounded man and struck his head with his right hand, not strong blows and not light ones, as if mourning or lamenting.

"You missed it, Abu Rashwan, good heavens, Abu Rashwan, come and look. Allah, Allah . . . she's as shapely as a filly, she gleams and glistens, she shines, Abu Rashwan. I'm on fire; my patience is gone. Come here, I swear to God, come and look. She's sprawled out now, her leg is out, she's turning over, Abu Rashwan, she's as radiant as lightning. She's killed me, Abu Rashwan, come and look . . ."

When the deputy emir took the telescope and aimed it at the ship, he could not see anything clearly, not even the ship.

"I can't see anything, Abu Misfer!' he said softly.

"On the left. Start from the west of the ship and keep moving until you reach the middle and you'll see her sprawled out like a mare. Do you see her? Are you sure?"

When the deputy emir shook his head no, he shouted sharply. "Give it to me, give it to me, Abu Rashwan."

The emir snatched the telescope from his deputy and turned to speak to one of his men, but no one was there.

"I told them to leave us, Your Excellency," said his deputy a little fearfully.

The emir turned around again to look for a stirrup or some cushions.

"If the people find out, if the Americans find out, we'll be disgraced, Abu Misfer," said his deputy in the same tone.

With a precise movement he often used, with his tongue and left hand, the emir grabbed like a chameleon and made a half circle with his hand to show that he was not afraid and did not care. Then, like an old woman used to sitting all day, he stumbled to his feet, and after pulling a stirrup out of the tent and carrying it two or three steps he threw it at the entrance to the tent and knelt like a camel. He steadied the stirrup on the ground and mounted the telescope on top of it, and adjusted them several times.

"Come here. Come here, Abu Rashwan," he shouted.

He grasped the telescope even more tightly and his voice changed, becoming thick and a little crazed. "She's not by herself now, now there are two of them—a mare and a foal, each lovelier than the other, shining like the sun. They walk like cats. If the first doesn't kill me the other one won't leave a breath of life in me. Come on, Abu Rashwan, have a good look."

Anyone who saw the emir and his deputy taking turns falling prone on the ground and shouting, rubbing their hands and exchanging comments and information would have thought that they had lost their senses. Sparks flew from their eyes, which glowed visibly red from lust and contact with the telescope; their lips were limp and trembled nervously, and the occasional involuntary shouts from one of them spurred on the other, who pleaded, anxiously and pathetically, to let him have his turn quickly so he would not miss this glorious moment.

At one point, after several frightened and tentative efforts, one of the emir's men cleared his throat, before coming forward, to announce his presence, but the two men were alarmed: some stranger might be spying on them from behind. As soon as they sat up, however, and the deputy emir put away the stirrup, one of the emir's men stepped forward to tell them that lunch was ready.

During the lunch break and their customary time of rest, neither of the men could calm down or even close his eyes for a moment. They were silent and their thoughts were far away.

Although the emir went to sit on a hilltop after washing himself, as was his custom at sundown each day, and stayed there until after evening prayers, telling stories and chatting with his visitors, today was completely different. He sat there until late, strolling over the slope and watching the ships carefully with his telescope, and in an attempt to hide what he was doing he also surveyed the western hills of Arab Harran and the American compound, but he looked longest on the ships. He saw many bare-chested men but no women. In the early part of the evening they talked mostly about the steel crate delivered to the chief of the compound, and how that crate which was the yellow-green color of a chameleon in early spring moved around quickly with no one pushing or pulling it. Two or three of the Americans had entered the crate with the chief of the compound and disappeared completely. This subject had greatly aroused the men's interest, exciting wonder and curiosity, and might have moved the emir to discuss and explain the nature of that machine to the others, how it traveled long distances without getting tired, but his confused mental state prevented him from addressing this matter. He did not recall what he had been told previously, when the first machines arrived to begin construction on the emirate building, because he had listened inattentively and forgotten most of it, but he felt compelled to speak, to say something. He shook his head; there were a great many things on his mind.

"The crate is like a lot of other things, you have to have a good look at it, examine it closely, before you talk about what it might be."

"You should ride it, Abu Misfer!" said the deputy emir, who grasped what the emir was saying.

"You said it, Abu Rashwan, yes—ride it and try it out!"

When the emir and his men went to dinner, the deputy approached him, laughing. "I'm afraid, Abu Misfer, we're getting like that Sumatran."

The emir laughed. "It's already happened."

That night the emir did not fall asleep until late. He felt deeply troubled, but when he tried to figure out why, he could not, not even in the days that followed. The women explained this as being the result of exhaustion and the heat, and worries, especially after the arrival of the ships.

The emir remembered that on the first night, and on subsequent nights, he had seen himself on the deck of the great white ship, in a dream, turning the women over one by one as a man turns over sheep to check their sex; as soon as he lay his hand on any buttock or thigh and held it a moment, he heard profuse muffled laughter, but when he drew his hand away quickly from the buttock or let the thigh drop, he felt a trembling mass in his soul and all his limbs shook. This happened times without number; he was mad with confusion, running back and forth to find the fattest and most beautiful woman, but when he reclined on one of them, she laughed continuously, as a cat purrs, and he woke to find himself covered with sweat and other things, feeling exhausted and feverish. His breath was short, and his pounding heartbeats filled his chest and head.

The events of the first day were repeated again and again: there was a rumor to the effect that the emir and his deputy had fallen prey to a mysterious illness, that they spent all their time alone, unable to speak to or receive anyone, but as soon as the white ship left Harran, taking some travelers with it, leaving others settled in the compound, and after certain other things happened in Harran, the health of the emir and his deputy was restored, though unlike his deputy, the emir seemed sunk in utter distraction.

63

WHEN IBN NAFFEH HEARD THAT THE EMIR WAS
suffering from a mysterious illness, he found
that he did not have the right medicines, so
he went to the gate of the mosque as the men were filing out
after sundown prayers.

"Get ready, Mufaddi," he said. "His Excellency needs the
irons." His tone changed as he added, almost to himself, "If
cautery doesn't do him any good, he'll die—the underground
demons have got to him."

Ibn Naffeh dared to say out loud what no one else, even those
who wondered among themselves in hushed tones, almost whispers, about what was ailing the emir, dared say; they had no
satisfactory answers. Some said, with a hint of resignation, that
the emir's harsh treatment of Ibn Rashed and Ibn Rashed's tragic
death had brought on the illness.

Dabbasi, who heard that the emir was not receiving visitors and did not wish to visit others, found in this a way out for himself, for he was in a bad mental state, being very depressed, and did not want the emir to see him this way. But within a few days the deputy emir came and told him to prepare for another hunting trip, as he had done last year, because nothing else could cure the emir. Although it was still early in the year for such a trip, Dabbasi liked the idea. He believed that a hunting trip could cure both of them: in the depths of the desert, where a man found himself surrounded by endless silence and nature still in its primeval stages, there was no sense of events taking place; the making of a new man was an arduous task that demanded calm and silence.

When Dabbasi asked about the emir's illness and whether or not he might see him, the deputy shook his head sadly. "The disease is spreading, Abu Saleh." After a moment of silence he added, "Today he said, 'I don't want to see anyone, and if he comes tomorrow or the next day, you see him.'"

Dabbasi did not press him and asked no more questions. He went away to prepare for the hunting trip, but with no sense of urgency.

That day, as suddenly as the ship had left, the emir was seized by a kind of agitation that turned into anger. He lost his temper at the slightest word or action, and it took nothing for any man to become, in his view, an enemy. He felt deceived; the departure of the ship and its passengers was a plot against him. The Americans seemed to have heard what he was doing; no doubt someone had told them and he was doing nothing but watching the ship, especially its female passengers; the informer must have been one of his own men, he reasoned, and that was why he made the sudden and unexpected decision to leave for a while.

The emir began to have doubts about everyone around him, and every one of his men was a suspect. He looked at their faces, and especially at their eyes, with a curious and doubting gaze, and if any of them seemed uneasy or afraid, he asked him, between his teeth, "You . . . hah?" If the man tried to speak or ask a question the emir flew into a rage and began to shout. "Get out of my sight, get out! I don't want to see your face—I'll settle with you later."

The man hurried away not knowing what he had done or why the emir had spoken to him in this way. So it went, day after day, as the emir banished all of those who did nothing but spy on him and report all of his deeds to others, and it was this behavior that led to the rumors of his depression and illness.

It was considered something of a joke at first, but with the passage of time the deputy emir began to perceive that the matter was now so serious that something untoward might well happen, so he sent the men away from the emir and kept his condition quiet. When the ship put out to sea and the watching game ended, he hoped that everything was back to normal, but what he had seen of the emir's agitation and anger, and the suspicions and shouted curses that marked his relations with almost all others, made the deputy emir wary and on edge, so he contacted Dabbasi to have him arrange the hunting trip and summoned Naim to have him ask the Americans to invite the emir for a demonstration of the steel crate. He tried several different tactics to protect the men from the emir, and when he saw him cursing, threatening and being cruel to Johar, who was the closest to him, he waited for Johar to stumble out of the room before addressing the emir. "Would you listen to a few words from me, Abu Misfer?"

The emir looked at him and said nothing, so he went on. "Please listen, Your Excellency." He paused a moment and smiled. "Truth is truth, Your Excellency, and a man has to speak the truth."

The emir's gaze did not waver, but his face showed signs of displeasure.

"Our men are our men, Abu Misfer. You can take one of them and cut his head off and he won't say a word." He forced himself to go on. "But they're people like us—you see them, but they see you, too . . . Your Excellency."

The deputy emir seized the telescope, shook it several times and said sharply, "This is the trouble right here!"

For the first time the emir listened attentively, as if surprised by what he heard. He nodded and opened his eyes wide.

The deputy emir continued. "As I hear it, Abu Misfer, the women we saw on the ship were all whores—they're loose and dissolute, and the red and white you see on their faces is nothing but dye and cosmetics. They are nothing but trouble."

The emir felt his strength ebbing. He did not like the way his deputy was speaking to him, but he felt weak enough for any man to crush him. Something inside him rebelled, but he was nervous and unable to say what he was thinking, as if his thoughts dissolved before they crystallized and settled.

"What you say is true, Abu Rashwan," he said in a final attempt to break the siege he felt enclosing him. "But I still want them."

This was the beginning of his recovery.

Two or three days later Hamilton and Naim came to visit the emir, and during this visit they discussed the many huge projects the company would undertake between Wadi al-Uyoun and Harran. Every effort would be made to find the large numbers of new workers that the work required; the company would construct other new buildings and installations in Harran itself as well.

At the end of the visit they invited the emir to come to American Harran and inspect the new projects and installations. They made reference to the company director's private automobile, saying they would all be delighted if the emir came to acquaint himself with all these things firsthand.

The emir was silent during the visit, only listening and nodding, though every so often he surprised his visitors by suddenly staring at Hamilton, then just as suddenly shifting his gaze to Naim. He longed to find out what they knew about him, especially what they had heard recently. Although his behavior somewhat frightened Naim, who showed alarm more than once, his thoughts drifted off to other subjects, perhaps to Hajem and Mizban, or perhaps to Ibn Rashed. He accepted their invitation to visit the compound but did not set a date.

"I told Abu Rashwan, when the ships were coming in front of us, here—" said the emir, pointing and nodding his head, " 'See to these people, ask them if there's anything we can do for them . . .' "

He paused a moment and looked straight at Hamilton and added very seriously, "If any more ships come, I have to see them for myself!"

His convalescent period might have lasted much longer, or taken a different direction, had not Hassan Rezaie arrived about this time. He explained to the emir why he had come back. "Anyone who drinks of Harran's water is bound to return."

His voice was so low that he might have been talking to himself, but when he saw that everyone was listening to him he went on. "Since the day I left Harran I've been constantly on the move, every day in a different town, but Harran was always here—here." He struck his chest with his fist, then tapped his forefinger and middle finger on his temple. He smiled and looked at the emir.

"So you stopped everywhere?" asked the emir, who wanted him to keep talking.

"The world is endless, Your Highness," said Rezaie quickly, "and no matter how far a man travels or how many places he visits, there are still places he must go, that must be visited. Even if everything in this world had an end and a limit, man's yearning to know and discover would still be endless and limitless."

He paused and shook his head, remembering all the places and things he had seen in his travels, and when he noticed the emir listening closely to all that he said, he went on in a different tone. "Your Highness, we should go somewhere together, travel in this world and get to know it."

The emir's laughter rang out, and he turned to his deputy.

"What do you say, Abu Rashwan?"

"Traveling by sea isn't very pleasant at first," said Hassan Rezaie, "but once you get used to it, there's nothing to compare to it."

"I prefer dry ground," replied the emir. He looked at his deputy and said ambiguously, "This seashore, here, in front of us, is killing us. What do you say we see what's beyond it?"

"The high seas are very different from these shoals, Your Excellency," said Hassan Rezaie enthusiastically. "The open sea is a different world!"

"The shallows are better." The emir laughed. "The shallows are safe and near home."

While they were speaking, three of Hassan Rezaie's seamen came into the tent, three of the employees who worked for him on board ship. Sweat ran down their burned red faces, which were the color of old copper. Two of them were carrying a medium-sized sack, containing something very heavy and valuable to judge from the way they carried it and placed it on the ground. The third carried a square black object that look like coal.

In silence, amid rapt attention, Hassan Rezaie got up confidently, took a short knife from his pocket and opened the sack. He asked one of his men to pull out what was inside. He did so very carefully, and Rezaie looked at the emir as he placed the gleaming box with one cloth side—it looked like wool—in front of him, but he remained silent. The emir had never seen anything like it before, and could not guess its purpose. When the ropes, or what looked like ropes, growing from the rear side of the box were connected to the black cube beside it, and Hassan Rezaie announced that everything was in place, he rubbed his hands, smiled broadly and sat beside the box, and looked at the emir and the others before proceeding to the next step. They were utterly silent and seemed a little afraid and curious. Rezaie cleared his throat. "This is a gift I have brought you from far away, Your Highness, and it will bring the whole world to you and bring you to the farthest point of the world, as you sit there."

The emir's eyes opened wide and he nodded continuously to show that he understood and grasped perfectly everything Rezaie was saying. He did not say a word but waited to see what would happen next.

"This machine, Your Excellency, is very sensitive and precise," said Rezaie in a different tone. "No one but yourself may touch it."

The emir looked even more surprised and somewhat afraid, and his men looked at each other.

"Now, we begin," said Rezaie, smiling confidently and rubbing his hands.

He moved his hand to one side of the box and waited a moment, his eyes trained on its middle, his face very close, as if whispering to it. A green light went on in the machine's middle, and the emir looked at the others, and though he tried to be calm his looks were looks of fear and alarm. Rezaie turned some of the knobs on the box, and suddenly sharp voices burst from no one knew where. Everyone present started violently, and a number of the men retreated a few steps, and one man hid behind some others. The emir shifted in his seated position and looked at the others as if to ask them to be strong and prepared for anything. Rezaie moved the knobs more energetically than before. The green light grew brighter, then almost faded away, with a piercing squeak. He touched a knob again, and there was a burst of music. The sound of the music was clear, as if it came from within the tent. The men looked at each other, mildly shocked, and the emir crept toward the box, smiling. Rezaie adjusted the sound and turned it up until it filled the tent.

With pleasure mixed with terror the men listened to the music in silence. After a few minutes, with a quick and crafty movement no one saw, Hassan Rezaie stopped the music. A long, profound silence fell, so palpable that a man could have stroked it with his hands.

Rezaie spoke. "That was music, Your Highness, that was just one station, and there are so many others!"

With the same hidden deftness Hassan Rezaie moved his hand, and there was a distant sound. It rose and fell, and the green light on the box glowed and faded, and when the light glowed, the men heard a voice clearly.

"—And when a king of the land of Serendip dies, he is tied to the rear of a low cart, on his back, with the hair of his head brushing the soil of the earth, as a woman with a broom sweeps the dirt onto his head, crying, 'O people, yesterday this was your king. He owned you and held you in his power, and now he is as you see. He has left the world, and King of Death has taken his soul. Do not be fooled by life, ye who come after,' and so on for three days. He is then bedecked in sandalwood, camphor and saffron, and cremated. His ashes are scattered in the wind."*

This is what the men heard. They looked at each other, unable to believe what they had heard. The voice intermingled with other voices and the green light went out, and then they heard nothing.

They look uncomprehendingly at one another: How could this box speak and make music? Who was playing the instruments? Where did he sit? How could he eat and sleep, and how did that tiny space hold him? The speaker sounded like Ibn Naffeh or an eloquent imam! Was he playing the music, too, or was that someone else?

"One . . . two . . . and now three," said Hassan Rezaie delightedly.

Once more he moved his hand on the box, and it began to sing.

> O ship about to depart!
> I have among your happy riders a dear friend
> My eyes were bathed in tears when we said farewell
> My heart wept as I heard the news
> The sun has sunk beneath the horizon
> My soul sighed, I drew my last breath
> When my love embraced me and we said farewell
> My fate fled with him when the sails unfurled . . .

When the song ended, a voice said, "This is the Near East Broadcasting Service." The emir moved closer to Hassan Rezaie and spoke like a child who cannot hide his pleasure and delight. "Now let me do it! Just show me how."

---

*Ibn Sairafy, a geographer of the fourth century A.H. From Dr. Shakir Khasbak's *Radiant Writings of Arab Geography*, p. 88. This passage is from *The Book of India and China*.

"Let it rest. It has to rest!"

"Just once! Then it can rest."

The emir crept nearer, as a child who knows what fire is creeps nearer to it. Patiently, carefully, he placed his hand where Hassan Rezaie indicated and did as he was told. When the box emitted loud music he started and drew his hand away, and when the music rose to fill the tent he retreated slightly and looked into the men's silent faces. They watched his every movement warily, as if he were conveying to them that he knew more than they did, as if he knew what they didn't. After a few minutes of nodding happily, as if he had conjured up this music from an unknown place, as no one else could do, and after a short silence, Hassan Rezaie spoke uneasily. "Your Highness, it has to rest."

Quietly, expertly, he moved his hands on the box, first on one side, then on the other, then disconnected the ropes from the black stone and put them back. When he was done he rubbed his hands and looked at their faces, especially the emir's, asking them wordlessly what they thought of what they'd seen and heard. Their faces were impassive and uncomprehending, but the emir's head was nodding as if jogged by a strong wind.

"The world around us is a strange one, full of secrets," said the emir. "Almighty God 'teacheth man that which he knew not.' The important thing is for him to keep his intentions holy and open his heart so that Almighty God may inspire and teach him."

The emir's words seemed obscure and meaningless. He addressed his deputy. "The spyglass shows you a hair from a long distance. The yellow steel crate runs like a gazelle and doesn't get tired. This box talks, sings and prays!"

After a moment he spoke in an awed tone. " 'Glory be to God, who teacheth man that which he knew not.' "

64

NEWS OF THE EMIR'S WONDERFUL NEW GADGET spread faster than any item of news ever had. Even the "steel crate," as they called it, though some others called it "the jinn's steed" and talked about it for days although very few of them had actually seen it, and even then from a great distance—even the jinn's steed in American Harran didn't excite nearly as much curiosity, wonder and fear as the new machine did. No one could describe it or say anything specific about it. When the emir sent some of his men to the coffeehouse and the market to invite some of the people to visit him, without giving any reason for the visit or saying what would happen afterward, everyone began to talk about "the new wonder," and three or four of the men said that they had heard a voice, during the day, which seemed to fall from the sky or spring from the earth. One of them said that one day he had heard a voice calling him, but when he turned around there was no one there. Some of them talked to the emir's men, to understand from them anything about the device, but no matter how the emir's men tried to describe it or give them some kind of idea of what it was, they failed. Those who asked about it in the coffeehouse and market did not really know what to ask, and the answers they got only deepened the mystery. The answers were very brief and cryptic: "Something people had never heard of before." "Seeing it is nothing to hearing it." One of the emir's men, named Shihab, whose duty it was to extend the emir's invitation to Ibn Naffeh, Seif and Dabbasi, had to hurry away to extricate himself from the crowd.

"Tomorrow, people of Harran, when you see it," he told them, "you'll go crazy!"

Everyone had been invited by about two hours before sundown, but some of those who had not been invited could not stifle their curiosity or wait to hear what the others would report, so they determined to go and stand nearby; when they got a chance they would find some pretext to push their way in to see the wonderful device and then tell the rest of the Harranis what they had seen before anyone else could.

The emir was profoundly agitated that whole afternoon. He did not sleep and did not leave his tent, and his eyes never left his new gadget. He stood and paced around it to look at it contemplatively close up and from all sides, and he probed it with his fingers to explore its solidity. For hour after hour he devised ways of taking over the operation of the thing for himself, without any help from Hassan Rezaie, and planning the right moment in which to ask him to teach him all the moves—how to begin and where, the second and third steps, until he knew all the operations—so he asked Rezaie to come with the rest of his guests for the demonstration of the wonderful thing. All the townsfolk of Harran would be amazed; they would feel that this was the first day of their lives, or at least the most important. They would shout like children, joyful, afraid and awestruck—how could they not, when he, the emir, was still full of wonder and astonishment at this device that no one had ever seen or heard of?

At one point the emir gave orders for his majlis to be prepared earlier than usual. He was a little afraid that it would not be possible to move the device outdoors.

"I forgot to ask you," he said to Hassan Rezaie nervously. "Today, our majlis in the desert, here, right nearby. Can we take the thing out with us?"

Rezaie assured him that it would be easily accomplished, that he could move it there or anywhere else he pleased, only it had to be done very carefully: the thing must not be shaken or set down too hard, and nothing must be placed on top of it. The emir was delighted to hear this and imagined many places and things.

"Now I want you to teach me to use it," he said in a friendly, confidential tone. "Tell me everything."

"It is your right, Your Highness, to know everything, to try out everything," said Hassan, grinning broadly. "For today I'm here to offer any help you need, and tomorrow I may not be."

The emir could not have been more pleased. The man was giving him all his secrets, strengthening his position among others, setting him above them all. He spoke again in the same tone of friendly confidentiality. "God bless you—may He make many more like you."

Hassan Rezaie began to explain to the emir the nature and importance of the machine. He spoke long and copiously. He said that other countries attached great significance to the radio and spent a great deal of money on it. Like a mirror, it reflected the power and standing of a country. It was found in the houses of the rich, who used it to discover what was happening in the world, to learn all the news and events. When the news was over the entertainment began: music, singing, useful lectures, stories, poems and much else besides.

The emir could not understand or follow a great deal of what Hassan Rezaie told him, but he remembered the word *radio,* which kept recurring. He was burning for the man to finish talking so that they could both get the machine working, so that when the men arrived he would not need any assistance or instructions.

"Actions are better than words," he told Rezaie jokingly. "Now let's say, 'In the name of God' and begin."

Without waiting any further he crept close to the radio and sat by it, waiting for Rezaie. He caressed it with a loving hand, as a man pets the face of a loved child, and tapped it gently with his forefinger, as if this was a sign to begin.

Hassan Rezaie began with the same speed and light dexterity. Perhaps he began too quickly for the emir, or perhaps the emir could not grasp everything, for he spoke up almost immediately. "Easy, easy! Take your time!"

"Just as you say, my lord!" Rezaie smiled. He had mastered this form of address to a degree that was unusual in Harran, but it pleased the emir and made him feel important. This way of speaking had caught his attention from Rezaie's first visit, and he realized that he liked it. When he heard him say "my lord" this time, he thought to himself: "People in other places are far more polite than we are; they know everything, especially how to address a man as befits his station."

"Once again, slowly," said Hassan Rezaie.

"Yes, yes, once again, slowly!" replied the emir. "Take your time!"

Before long the sound of the radio filled the huge tent and the surrounding desert; it could even be heard in the tent reserved for the women. Rezaie lowered the volume.

"Now, Your Highness," he said confidently, "you can do it all yourself!"

The emir went to work, but he was anxious and afraid of making a mistake. To make it as easy as possible for the emir, Rezaie said, "The best way, Your Highness, is to count." He paused a moment and nodded as if he had hit upon the ideal way to teach the process, and showed him how.

"One, two, three, and this is four."

He put his hand on the battery, the first step, then on the switch, which was step two, pointed to the dial, which was three, and step four was the volume control. He did it somewhat rapidly, which moved the emir to comment, "Counting is a good way, but it's not how the bedouin pray!"

Rezaie laughed though he did not understand what the emir meant, and when its meaning—"fast or incomplete"—was explained to him, he laughed harder. He spoke as if teaching a child. "One . . . this is one. Good?"

When the emir nodded to show that he understood, he pointed to the switch. "After one is two. This is two."

The emir nodded vigorously, and Hassan asked, "Shall we go on?"

"Trust in God," said the emir regally.

"This is three, Your Highness, and it's the hardest step."

The emir nodded to show that he understood and could handle the difficulty.

"And this is four. It's easy. If you want it loud, so that all Harran can hear it, turn it to the right, and if you want none but yourself to hear it, turn it to the left."

After several tries, during which Hassan Rezaie gave him additional instructions, especially as regarded the battery and the tuning dial, the emir looked pleased.

"This is the last time," he said, "and then we'll let it rest, so that the rest of them can be amazed when they come and hear it." He laughed loudly. "By God, I'll let it roar to the stars until morning!"

The majlis was prepared earlier than usual. The emir's men moved the radio under his supervision, and he gave them sharp orders before and as they moved it. When he was sure that everything was ready, and in order to impart a sense of thrill and importance to the operation, he draped his cloak over the radio to cover it completely.

The emir tried to act and speak naturally, even simply, with his men, and though it felt strange, because he was not used to doing so, he adopted a friendly, fatherly tone, but his inner tension drove him to unusual activity, rapid pacing and a mood that bordered on fright. This was a new experience for him, and although he felt confident and self-assured, there were lingering doubts: "What if the thing just dies, or I make a mistake turning it on or running it? What if I make a mistake counting or confuse the switches, as Hassan Rezaie called them?" He would feel shame if he failed, and if Hassan Rezaie then came to move him aside and take his place and did not fail, but did it easily, Rezaie would look at him out of the corner of his eye, and the others would watch and smile. If that happened, wouldn't he seem, at least to himself, wanting or stupid? His anxiety mounted and he grew more tense. He now wanted to have one last try: "We should try it out once in its new location." But what would Hassan Rezaie say?

Shortly before sundown the men arrived. First came Dabbasi, who was expected to come early, before any others, because he had not seen the emir in several days, and because he felt a vague sense of guilt. Perhaps this was because of Ibn Rashed's death, or perhaps because it had been so long since he'd visited the emir, or perhaps because of his general feeling of futility. In any case he did feel guilty and had not been overly excited by what all the people were saying in Abu As'ad's coffeehouse about the emir's new gadget. He had said more than once, in the coffee-house, "If you were to travel and see the whole world, people of Harran, you would never believe it was the world you were seeing." He said nothing more, and no one knew what he meant.

Abdullah al-Saad and Muhammad al-Seif arrived together, and al-Zawawi and Ibn Naffeh arrived together, conversing volubly as they hiked up the north hill—about the corruption that was spreading in the world, and the evil that was now so common, the terrible ruin that afflicted the world, and the approaching day of judgment. They talked about what the emir was doing, what was happening in Harran under his very nose, and his contemptible silence in the face of all the trouble. They could not explain his silence or his indulgence toward the Americans; it was more than they could understand, and they could not overlook or tolerate it. And the emir's surprising new gadget—Ibn Naffeh spoke loudly enough for everyone to hear. "We've already seen enough and more, Abu Mohsen. He's like that black man who saw his mother's cunt and went crazy—he wants to drive everyone else crazy, but he won't succeed."

When the sun sank behind the western hills, leaving nothing behind but steadily darkening orange rays, all those the emir had invited were at last present, including three workers, one of whom was Ibn Zamel. Daham al-Muzil was the last to arrive; he had been rushing and stumbled into the tent covered with sweat. The emir looked aound to see that all those whom he had invited were present, noticing two or three uninvited Har-ranis—what did they want?—then rose to speak.

"It is much pleasanter outdoors, my friends."

The men all stood. There was a certain rustling clamor as they stood, but no sound of spoken words. The emir walked a step or two ahead of the rest and seemed confident, but he still had some doubts. He signaled with his hand for Hassan Rezaie to remain close to him, to come nearer, and the man replied with a courtly but spontaneous gesture. Ibn Naffeh's eyes never left Hassan Rezaie for a moment; he had ignored all others to concentrate on him from the moment he arrived. Hassan Rezaie smiled whenever his eyes met Ibn Naffeh's, but Ibn Naffeh did not return the courtesy and never averted his eyes. When he saw the way the emir treated Rezaie he said to himself: "No one knows whether God or Satan brought this man here, but like they say, if a disease comes from the stomach, where does the cure come from? This bastard, this devil, has got into the emir's armpit, and must be the curse of his ancestors and ours."

As soon as the men were seated, all gazing with intense curiosity at the marvel that sat to the emir's left, under his cloak, the emir spoke in a slightly trembling voice. "The world has changed, my friends; it is no longer as it was. It is smaller. It came to the prophet Adam; he did not have to go to it."

None of the men understood what the emir was saying; in fact his speech made them feel even stranger. He went on more confidently. "A man doesn't believe until he's seen with his own eyes, until he has tried something for himself." He turned to Hassan Rezaie and smiled, as though they shared a secret, and said, "When they have seen with their own eyes, they will believe."

He pounced like a cat to pull the cloak aside.

"Do you all see this?" he asked theatrically, pointing.

The men nodded to show that they saw the device.

"It roams the whole world in the twinkling of an eye, and tells you everything."

The men sat silently. The emir rubbed his hands, exactly as Hassan Rezaie had done when he'd worked the radio.

"What you see talks, then it weeps, then it prays!"

He paused to look at the radio, then at the men, and nodded.

"And now we place our trust in God, and begin."

In a barely audible voice the emir began: "One." He touched the battery, waited a moment, and added, "Two." He sat before the radio, his back to the others, and when the green light appeared he leaned over to work the tuning dial, and when he found a station—he was sure, because he heard a few words, and saw the green light flash brightly—he turned to the men.

"Listen—listen," he said in a husky voice. He turned up the volume.

"They were told that Ibn al-Khattab wept when the treasures of Chosroes were revealed to him," they heard, "and he said, 'This was never shown to any nation without bringing them to despair.' "

The sound faded away as soon as this was heard, and it was followed by a loud, continuous buzz. The men looked at each other and at the device that the emir was impatiently working at; they stared and their jaws were slack. The buzzing died away.

"I do not fear poverty for you, rather I fear that you will submit to the world as did they who came before you, that it will make you dissent and fight one another as it did them. The Prophet, peace and blessings be upon him, said, 'Be in this world as a stranger or a traveler passing through.' "

The emir watched every face to see their reactions, and when he saw them looking at one another in silence, and then glancing perplexedly at the radio, he rubbed his hands and laughed.

"That's one." He turned the volume all the way down and said, "You have seen with your own eyes and heard with your own ears. Now listen again."

He leaned over again until he was almost reclining and spun the tuning dial with his ear glued to the radio. He heard a sound, then turned up the volume and laughed.

"This is two."

The sound of music surged out to fill the air. He looked at

them, nodded and laughed, and turned the sound even higher so that it roared more loudly than before. The men trembled and held their breath, and their hearts pounded. They did not dare look into one another's faces but stole looks here and there from the corners of their eyes. Each was terrified that men would spring out of the box to kill them all. The emir was plainly delighted, and he exchanged long looks with Hassan Rezaie, and they winked at each other when they saw the powerful effect the radio was having; the emir now wished that he had invited all the townspeople of Harran instead of these few—"If all of them had come, we would really be seeing a marvel"—but he gave up this thought, "because secrets are for adults, only for those who understand." After the music there were a few garbled words, and lightly, as Hassan Rezaie had done, the emir switched off the sound.

"That was two, but there're a lot more."

He reclined as he had done before, turning the knob and watching the green light, and when it emitted an even sound he sat up again.

"Now, three."

"It is related that there was a certain seabird, said to be a tern, who dwelt on the seashore with his wife, and when it was time to hatch their young the female told him, 'Let us seek out an inaccessible place in which to hatch, for I fear that the Lord of the Sea will make the water rise to take our chicks.' He told her, 'Hatch them where you are, for we have water and flowers nearby us.' She said, 'O heedless one, think again, for I fear that the Lord of the Sea will take our chicks.' He told her, 'Hatch them where you are, for he will not do that.' She said, 'How sure you are, do you not remember his threats against you? Do you not know yourself and your power?' But he refused to obey her, and when she insisted and he did not listen, she said to him, 'He who will not heed counsel will suffer the same fate as the tortoise who heeded not the two ducks.' And the male said, 'How did that come about?'

"The female said, 'It is related that there was a pond with pasture, in which there dwelt two ducks, and in the pond was a tortoise. Now the tortoise and the ducks loved one another. It befell that the water in the pond diminished, and the ducks came to the tortoise to bid her farewell. They said, "Peace upon you, for we are leaving this place because of the want of water." She replied, "There is a want of water, and I know, for like a ship I can live only in the water, but since you two can live anywhere, take me with you." They told her, "Yes," and she asked, "How can you carry me?" They said, "We will each grasp one end of a stick; bite it in the middle, and we will fly you through the air. Hold fast with your mouth, and beware! If you hear the people talk, say nothing." So they took her and flew into the sky, and when the people saw, they said, "Wonderful indeed, a tortoise flying between two ducks!" and when she heard that she said, "May God blind you, O people!" And when she opened her mouth to speak, she fell to the ground and died.'

"The male said, 'I hear your fable, but fear not the Lord of the Sea.' When the water rose, they fled with their young, and the female said, 'I knew this would befall.' Said the male, 'I will take my revenge,' and he betook himself to the council of birds, and told them, 'You are my brothers and my trusted friends— help me.' They said, 'What do you want us to do?' He said, 'Let us go to the rest of the birds and tell them what we have suffered from the Lord of the Sea. We shall say, "You are birds as we are—help us." ' The council of birds told him, 'The griffin is our mistress and our queen, let us go and seek her counsel. She will appear to us and we will recount to her what you suffered from the Lord of the Sea, and we will petition her to avenge us upon him with her power and authority.' They then went with the tern and sought her aid, and she appeared to hear their tale, and they asked her to fly with them to combat the Lord of the Sea, and she consented. When the Lord of the Sea learned that the griffin was seeking him with the other birds, he was afraid to fight, a powerless king; so the tern's young made peace with him and the griffin flew away!"*

The emir was delighted and anxious at the same time. The men were perfectly silent as they listened, their tongues tied, awestruck. He found their rigid, silent aspect almost comic, but when the story went on and on and the stories intermingled, and he missed some of the words as he turned and watched them, he became afraid that the device was tired. No sooner had the men heard the last words of the tale, and their faces relaxed, than the emir pounced like a cat on the radio, and some of them heard him say, "Four, three, two, one!"

When the radio was switched off, he returned wearily to his place and sat. He took a deep breath and looked at the sky, and he spoke when he perceived the heavy silence that hung over the group. "As you have seen, my friends, 'God teacheth man that which he knew not.' "

Each of the men had a great deal he might have said. Those who had traveled and seen the world wanted to do nothing but talk; true, Dabbasi had seen a radio before: he had seen one in Egypt at the house of Ibn al-Barih, but it did not strike him as particularly incredible, "because everything in Egypt is incredible." That was how he usually summed up his impressions of Egypt, with no attempt to supply details. Abdullah al-Saad leaned over to Muhammad al-Seif and whispered, "Our friend Ibn al-Naqib in Basra has one, and I've seen it!" The others, who had never been anywhere farther than Ujra, were deeply confused and afraid, and most of them wished that the emir would cover

*Kalila and Dimna.

the radio up again and put it away, because "anything can happen in this world." Most of them were not ready to hear any explanation or comment, because the strange device could talk, sing, tell stories and perhaps do many other things as well, in spite of its tiny size. The people inside it might be strange enchanted creatures, probably badly deformed as well. The only one to dare ask a question was Ibn Naffeh, though he was apprehensive and a little afraid.

"Who made this calamity?" he asked Hassan Rezaie.

Rezaie was a little irritated at the hostile stares Ibn Naffeh had directed at him the whole evening, and he answered him brusquely. "Man invented it."

"Tell me—tell me: the Germans or the Americans?"

"This radio was made in Holland."

"Holland?"

"Yes. It was manufactured in Holland."

"Do they know Arabic there? Do they pray and fast and say 'There is no god but God'?"

Dabbasi spoke up, feeling that Ibn Naffeh was becoming more hostile toward Rezaie.

"If Abu Misfer agrees, let's ask our friend to buy one for us and bring it to us on one of his visits to Harran, and if he likes we'll pay for it right now!"

Ibn Naffeh was horrified.

"And put it in our houses, Dabbasi?"

"Trust in God, man, be patient!" Dabbasi smiled.

"And put it in our houses, to attract wolves to our sheep?"

"By God, Ibn Naffeh," said the emir, "you don't like anything not from the Nejd. You don't like anything at all—you say that everything is sacrilegious." He softened his tone and addressed the whole gathering. "My friends, you all heard with your own ears what it said about the Prophet, peace and blessings be upon him, and what it said about Ibn al-Khattab, and others."

Ibn Naffeh got up angrily.

"My friends, be wary of the green of new manure." He paused a moment and added sarcastically, "It has one eye, like Satan, a green eye, and that is what the Prophet repudiated and called the green of new manure."

He added, in a threatening tone, "Tomorrow it will drag you to Hell."

65

THE MEN WHO SAT IN ABU AS'AD'S COFFEEHOUSE
that night, watching and waiting, said they
had heard unusual noises coming from the
north hill; the noises, they said, could be heard, though indistinctly, when night fell and the sea waves calmed. Abdu Muhammad, who spent more time than usual in the coffeehouse
that evening, said that he heard the melodies of songs he knew,
and that the melodies flowed to him directly from the north hill.
Othman al-Asqi, who was deaf in one ear, decided to go to the
emir's gathering uninvited, because he could not stifle the curiosity that gripped him when he heard everyone talking about
the wonderful device, though some of the men wittily suggested
that he had gone only to get a free meal.

Al-Asqi was the first to arrive at the coffeehouse after the visit
to the emir and the demonstration of the new marvel. For a long

time he was silent, shaking his head and hands in wonderment. When they asked him to describe the radio, he waved his hand to indicate that he could not, because what he had seen could not be explained or described. When he tried, after a great deal of patient insistence from the others, and much hesitation on his part, he said that the emir possessed something truly marvelous: a box, but not like any box. Like a tea chest, smaller or perhaps a little bigger—he was not exactly sure—but when you hit it on the head it shouted and began to talk. It had only one eye, a green eye, the color of spring grass; and if you hit it again, gently, it made pipe and drum music. If you hit it yet again, on the side, it went mute and died.

Abu As'ad asked him loudly, and with hand gestures, if the box had round black knobs, like the round loaves that Abdu Muhammad baked, only smaller, and if it had a large funnel like a fat funnel or larger, and if a tall, thin protuberance had to be adjusted before it spoke. After Abu As'ad explained, with the help of several of those present shouting into al-Asqi's ear, Othman said it was nothing like that, that he had not seen the things that Abu As'ad described since he had sat as far as possible from the thing. Abu As'ad asked him if it had small switches and a glass pane in the middle with a moving needle, and al-Asqi said it did have something like that. Abu As'ad leaned forward in his chair.

"Why didn't you say so before, old man!" he said patiently, then shook his head, laughing, and shouted, "That's a radio, my friends!" He turned to Othman. "A radio! Right?"

Othman curled his lip and shrugged to show that he did not know.

"Al-Asqi was watching and listening with his stomach," said one man, who longed to know what a radio was. He was seated at a distance and had been closely following the discussion and gestures.

"If Harran had electricity we would all have had radios long ago," said Abu As'ad, who felt that he knew a great deal more than the others.

He went on to explain to all of them everything he knew about radios, and how they were found everywhere in Beirut, Aleppo and Damascus, and many other places he had lived in or visited. He said that the homes of the rich and eminent were never without a radio, and pointed out that the Nadim Coffeehouse in Beirut's Sahet al-Bourj had both a radio and a gramophone. Then he explained to the men what a gramophone was, how records which resembled thin loaves of bread emitted songs, never tiring of spinning around night and day. People came in throngs from far-distant places to the Nadim Coffeehouse only to hear the songs, and the coffeehouse manager, Wajih Halabi, played songs at the listeners' requests. Abu As'ad kept repeating the word *listeners*. He repeated that as soon as Harran got electricity, the first radio would be installed in the Friends Coffeehouse. He shook his finger in mock warning, however.

"Listen! When we get it, no one may touch it but me!" He paused, then laughed. "And another thing: I can't have you all saying, every minute, 'Abu As'ad, turn this on' and 'Abu As'ad, shut that off.'"

That night, they all said later, Harran did not sleep. The emir's soiree lasted longer than anyone expected or wanted. The sound of the radio, like the song of a distant camel driver in the early evening, grew progressively louder and stronger and everyone heard it. When Hassan Rezaie said with exaggerated politeness that he would like to go home, but that he would be at the emir's disposal at any hour of the morning His Highness desired, the emir announced that the evening was concluded. When they all left, the emir accompanied them for a good distance—longer than he usually did for his guests—and bid them good night, and they all said that the sound of the radio followed them as if the thing were walking behind them, even after they got to the bottom of the hill and reached the market. The sound was clearly audible, and they all laughed when al-Zawawi fell into a ditch in the road.

"That thing opened our ears, Abu Mohsen, but it blinded our eyes!"

The emir lingered after his guests left and turned up the volume of the radio several times, nodding happily in time to the music. He moved it from one place to another, first into his tent and then to the area behind it where he slept; there he was heard talking loudly about the wonderful gadget. He turned the radio up even louder, and the delighted and frightened voices of the women joined in—everyone in the coffeehouse heard. The sound of the radio rose and fell. Abu As'ad was gathering up the chairs in the coffeehouse and talking to his last two customers.

"God willing, within a month we'll have a radio, and we'll hear the songs reaching the sky!"

Ibn Naffeh, who left early and went straight home to Arab Harran, refused to say anything about the radio, and the sound of his praying was heard until late that night, and because of that, or the distance, no one in Arab Hassan could hear the radio. When the others and those who lived in the western hills left the emir's, they all talked about the radio but none of them could describe or explain it.

Before dawn the next day, the emir was seen asking Massoud and another man to move the radio. He went with them all the way and lifted the tent flap himself so that they could move it in easily. Some of the more malicious townspeople said that the emir spent several sleepless days by the radio with his loaded rifle, ready for any surprise that might come from the thing. Ibn Seif said that on one of his visits to the emir he saw two men lifting the radio high into the air while the emir examined the bottom of it with his telescope. When he saw nothing, he moved closer and struck it with the palm of his hand as if knocking on a door. Hearing no sound from within, he crept around it in a circle to look at it from all angles with the telescope, rapping it with his knuckles and palms.

In the mosque, market and workers' camp there was talk of nothing but the new wonder, and everyone longed to see or hear it. The emir, who was completely preoccupied by the radio and let none of his men touch it or go near it in his absence, had entered a new phase of his life. It began by coincidence, when he heard some songs which affected him deeply, and which he and many others remembered for a long time to come.

66

T HE EMIR VISITED THE AMERICAN COMPOUND WITH
his deputy and Hassan Rezaie and inspected
the automobile carefully. He asked whether
Americans, like Arabs, gave names to the things they rode—
Arabs named their horses, for example. He was delighted when
Henderson told him that the automobile did indeed have a name,
Ford, and turned to his deputy to say, "I told you!" He asked
many other detailed questions: How long did Ford live? Did it
use gunpowder? Would it respond to different riders? Did it need
training, or was it naturally tame? After the emir asked these
and many other questions, nodding gravely as he heard the answers, Henderson proposed that they all ride the automobile.
The emir seemed inclined to refuse and asked Hassan and his
deputy in a certain tone if they wished to try it out or not, but

in the face of Henderson's willingness and Rezaie's deference he had no choice but to accept.

It was a festive ride, marked by surprises, shouts and explanations. When the automobile suddenly took off at great speed, the color drained from the frightened emir's face and he shouted "God help us!" Afraid of falling, he reached out to grab Henderson's leg beside him, to steady himself. When Henderson roared with laughter the emir withdrew his hand, ashamed, and gripped the side of his seat instead.

"My friends, we should have said our prayers first!" said the emir to his deputy and Hassan Rezaie, without turning around.

When Henderson took a sharp turn the emir was overcome with fright and grabbed the wheel, and there would have been an accident had Henderson not acted quickly and pushed the emir's hand away. Another accident was narrowly avoided when Henderson stopped abruptly to keep from hitting a dog; the comments and screams that issued from the automobile were long remembered. Whenever Henderson reminisced about the first automobile in the compound, he recalled the emir's face: "He was absolutely terrified, and jabbering indistinctly, like he was praying to God or begging. He almost caused a couple of accidents, while we were moving and standing still. At one point he almost jumped out! He grabbed the door handle while the car was moving, and if it hadn't been for my quick thinking they'd be saying that the Americans killed the emir."

When the automobile sped past a group of workers, who shouted and waved to the emir and his companions, the emir did not budge but kept his grip on the side of his seat. He was amazed to see Henderson put his arm outside the window to give the men a carefree wave.

"The thing leaps like a locust," said the emir afterward, when they were going up the hill. "You have no way of knowing when it's going to fly."

"Our donkeys are better and safer, Your Excellency," said his deputy.

"It was faster, but dangerous."

"The inventions of man are endless," said Hassan Rezaie after a short silence. "There are thousands of inventions and new things every day, but the origin of all inventions is gunpowder."

The emir nodded in agreement, but his thoughts were so confused that he could not say anything clearly. He was surprised to hear himself say, "If they used gunpowder to push it, it would be better and stronger."

They could not continue the discussion, and the emir could find no clearer way to express the thoughts that suddenly filled his head, while Hassan Rezaie perceived that the distance that separated him from these people was so great that he could not really be serious with them, or discuss any topic in earnest.

As soon as the emir reached home he looked first at the radio and then at his men, to see if any of them had gone near the radio or played with it while he was away, and when he decided that they had not, since they seemed guiltless and calm, he spoke to them to create a cheerful atmosphere. "Why should a man race all around from place to place? It's much better to let the world come to him!" He headed straight for the radio.

"Now it's easy for you!" said Hassan Rezaie even before the emir got it working.

No sooner had the sound of music burst from the radio to fill the tent than the emir began to sing.

"Our days are over and our fate has overtaken us/ The journeys we've made are more than enough." A moment later he added in a sad voice, "When I hid my sorrow, my passion awakened/ The sleep of my eyes was replaced by wakefulness/ I cry out, for my passion excites my thoughts/O passion, flee but do not leave me/ My soul languishes between heartache and peril."

Hassan Rezaie clapped rhythmically, surprised that the emir could memorize and recite poetry; he had never known or guessed at such a thing.

"You have to relax," said the emir in an effort to justify his exuberance. "When your heart gets weary you die!"

Coffee was served in a relaxed and very cheerful atmosphere. Hassan Rezaie lowered the volume of the radio, and when the emir did not object, he addressed him. "Your Highness, I must ask your permission to travel."

"Fear God, man, we've hardly seen you," protested the emir.

"My business affairs require me to leave, Your Highness." He paused and then added, "Whenever Your Highness commands me to return, I will do so."

The emir looked at his deputy but directed his speech to Rezaie. "No."

"Just as you say, Your Highness," said Hassan with feigned regret.

There was silence, then the emir spoke in a more decisive tone. "We need you here these days."

"I am at your service, Your Highness."

The music had died away. The emir leaned over slightly and asked Hassan and his deputy to move nearer.

"I asked the Americans to send us over the translator this afternoon," he whispered in their ears. "We want to see what their needs are and how we can help them."

"I don't think I should be present when you discuss private matters, Your Highness!" said Rezaie with false modesty.

"I have told them that you are one of us, that there is much you can do for them."

So Hassan Rezaie stayed for days that turned into weeks, until he signed a three-year contract with the company, which required him to recruit manpower for the construction of the Wadi al-Uyoun–Harran pipeline, to take over the import of supplies, to subcontract the paving of the Ujra–Harran highway and to procure all necessary supplies except for asphalt and machinery, which the Americans would provide.

After the contract was signed, one evening when all the emir's guests had departed, Hassan Rezaie spoke, apparently to himself, but so that the emir could hear. "I really should listen to the London broadcast." He drew a watch on a gold chain from his pocket and added, "Still forty-five minutes until the news."

He stirred as if preparing to leave for his boat, where he might listen to the news bulletin.

"This radio brings in London?" asked the emir.

"Most certainly, Your Highness!"

"So let's all listen to it."

"I don't want to be a burden on you, Your Highness." He smiled. "You need your rest."

"I'll rest later." The emir laughed. "It's still early!"

"I want you to listen to the news from London every night, Your Highness," said Rezaie in a completely different tone. He lowered his voice to add, "Nothing in the world happens without that station knowing it first, and knowing the most about it!"

He paused for a moment as if recalling some event.

"I first heard of Harran, Your Highness, on the London news bulletin. British Broadcasting was the first to know all the news of Harran: the petroleum port, the refineries, supply depots for the whole region, for all the ships, and all the rest.

"I said to myself: 'You have to visit that place, to get to know it. A man could be of some use, he might help out.' "

"All that is going to happen in our Harran?" asked the emir. He could not hide his astonishment.

"Yes indeed, Your Highness, all that and more."

"These damned Americans never told me! They never told anyone!"

··

"They're bastards. They don't give away their secrets."

"Even that little coward who came to us that day, the translator I saw, never told me a thing!" The emir shook his head in disbelief. "So when are all these calamities going to happen?"

"It's already begun, Your Highness. Once the pipeline from Wadi al-Uyoun to Harran is completed, it will all be finished."

The emir laughed. "There are hard times ahead!"

Hassan Rezaie laughed along with him, and when they both stopped laughing Hassan turned to him earnestly.

"I have a request, Your Highness."

"Granted!"

"Next time, in a month or two, if we live till then, I will need your help, Your Highness, in choosing a piece of land. I want to build a house, and the closer it is to you the happier I'll be."

"Bless you—choose any land and it's yours."

"I'll take the land you choose for me."

"Bless you."

For a moment they said nothing.

"A short time back I had never heard of Harran and never thought of it," said Hassan in a profoundly humble tone. "And now, as you see, Your Highness . . . praise the Lord."

They turned to the radio, and Hassan Rezaie managed to locate the London station.

"Right here, at night, London will come in loud and clear," he said confidently. "But in the daytime it's somewhere else."

And they listened intently to the news bulletin.

67

A YEAR AND A FEW MONTHS BEFORE THE PAVING of the Ujra-Harran road was completed, two large trucks appeared in Harran. The driver of the first—its "boss"—was an Armenian, Akoub, and the other one was Raji, "Abu Aqlein." These were not their real names, but most people knew them only by these titles. Even in the official papers later drawn up for Raji, he wrote beside his name: "Raji Suleiman al-Nunu, known as Abu Aqlein."

There was no consistent schedule for the trucks' departures or arrivals; these depended on Akoub's and Raji's estimations of how business was in Harran, or on their moods. In Ujra, on the other hand, they were completely subservient to whatever Abboud al-Salek wanted.

A single truck coming from Ujra carried between twenty and twenty-five men with their own and others' cargoes. The trip between the two towns, which were no more than 145 miles apart, usually took about thirty hours, because the truck always got a flat tire or broke down on the road, and in either case it had to be emptied of cargo and men, all of whom had to help unload, push the truck and load it up again. This generally took several hours and often happened two or three times on each trip. In addition to that the truck had to stop and cool down once or twice—to be exact, at the 75-mile station, which had long been a stopping place between the two towns. All the caravans stopped there because there was a well, but there was also a station at 110 miles, set up during the road-paving project. The stations were composed of small coffeehouses, which served tea, coffee and sometimes food, and since the two drivers often changed shifts, no one was surprised when the journey lasted two days. Even if a truck experienced no delays on the road, it was certain to lose time at one of those stations. The passengers also faced unpredictable waiting periods before the trip began. When Abboud al-Salek opened his "Desert Travel Office" in Ujra, it was the sole agency for arranging travel and transport between the two towns: anyone wishing to travel or seeking to ship goods to or from Harran had only to see Abboud al-Salek at the Desert Travel Office's small storefront in Ujra, which took charge of all business and services.

Abboud lounged in the doorway of the Desert Travel Office like an old fox waiting for prey to happen along. When he caught sight of a bedouin, or men seeking work, his practiced instincts told him that they wanted to go to Harran, and he instructed his young assistant to shout, "Harran! One passenger needed for Harran, one more rider for Harran!" Abboud himself slipped like a fish into his shop to sit behind his old desk, on which a set of scales stood, to hunch over his huge ledger and look thoroughly absorbed in writing or reviewing his accounts. The bedouin or stranger fell directly into Abboud's trap: he re-

sponded immediately to the boy's shouts, though naively pretending that he had no desire to travel, and went into the shop,
where he could not help gawking. In any case Abboud never
showed interest or any sign of hurrying his work. Even when
the traveler gave in at once by coming out and saying that he
wanted to travel to Harran, that he was ready and impatient to
leave, Abboud waited a good while before raising his head,
looking tired and exasperated. Seeing the eager bedouin anxious
to settle his business, he said regretfully, "What a shame—if
only you had come an hour ago, my friend. The truck left an
hour ago." After long negotiations, which were very laborious
on both their parts, Abboud stipulated that the bedouin pay the
fare immediately to reserve a seat, since "there's a truck leaving
for Harran tomorrow, God willing." The bedouin was extremely wary and hesitant to pay, claiming that he had left his
money with his friends, but Abboud only waved him away
scornfully, telling him to get out and leave him to his work.
Then the bedouin agreed to pay half the fare, and to pay the rest
when he boarded the truck. Firmly but not impolitely Abboud
refused the offer, and after a long silence, during which Abboud
absorbed himself in his huge ledger, the bedouin found himself
forced to pay. The bedouin asked only that his seat be booked
until he came back with the money. Abboud got up from his
chair to gaze outdoors.

"Payment first, then booking." He walked past the bedouin
seated on the floor and said, "Pay now and take your ticket, and
you're as good as on your way."

The bedouin went out, leaving Abboud seated on a crate with
his back against the storefront.

"If you're late, my boy, you'll have to wait for the next one,"
Abboud called after him. "That's in a week, or two weeks, God
only knows."

When the bedouin returned an hour later, Abboud held out

his hand wordlessly, rubbing his fingers briskly to indicate that he wanted the money right away, no delays this time, and when the bedouin tried to insist on paying only half the fare now and the other half the next day, Abboud grew angry, or pretended to be angry, and stood up to shout at him. "You're not going anywhere with us, do you hear me? You're not getting near any of our trucks."

These words had no effect on the bedouin; he seemed not to hear, though he was still confused and uncertain. Eventually he reached into his shirt and drew out a carefully tied purse and sat on the floor.

"Tomorrow we go?" he asked before untying it.

Abboud nodded and motioned for him to pay quickly, but the bedouin was still deliberate, unhurried and afraid. Here Abboud left him, for "better bend than break," as he often said to describe his shrewdness. He went to his desk, opened a drawer and took out a round iron piece that looked like a smooth old coin, though it was larger and thinner, and a slip of paper half the size of his palm. He scribbled his complex, sloping signature on the paper and waited while the bedouin drew out his money, counted it two or three times and handed it over. Abboud's trained eyes had counted it even before the bedouin was finished. He pushed the metal piece and the paper toward the bedouin.

"Return the iron piece to the office before you leave, and give the paper to the driver."

The bedouin picked up the paper and the metal piece and stared at them a long time but could make nothing of them.

"If you lose them you don't travel and you have no claim on us, you hear me?"

The bedouin nodded, undid the purse he had just finished tying and placed the metal and paper inside. He carefully bound it up again.

"When do we go?"

"Tomorrow or the next day, if we live that long." When he saw the fear in the bedouin's eyes he added, "Tomorrow, after the afternoon prayer, drop by here. God is great."

"After afternoon prayers? Tomorrow?"

"Come at noon."

"And when do we leave?"

"We still need a few more passengers. If we get them we'll set off today."

When he saw fear flare up in the eyes of the bedouin, who felt cheated, having paid his money without knowing when he might travel, he spoke to banish his worries.

"If you have any friends who want to go to Harran, bring them to see me. Come by in the morning and we'll see," he added to end their conversation.

When the bedouin showed even more fear and uncertainty, Abboud ordered him some tea and asked him where he came from, what tribe he belonged to and why he wanted to go to Harran. Without waiting for all the answers he went on to explain how Harran had become a great city full of projects. He concluded by saying, "When you get there tomorrow, God willing, you'll be a big success and I don't think you'll ever leave."

This is what most of the Desert Travel Office's customers were like. Abboud collected them, one by one, stalling them day by day, sometimes for as long as a week or ten days, making the excuse that "the Armenian has gotten depressed and refused to work, and if I force him to go he might kill all the passengers." When he reckoned that he had gathered enough passengers and cargo, and one of the trucks had come in from Harran and had a chance to rest for a day or two, preparations for the journey began. It was an extraordinary day in Ujra, no less important than the arrival of a hajj caravan. There was chaos and confusion throughout the market: last-minute sales, gossip about the passengers, loading of merchandise and much else. When the travelers were banded together, each of them trying to get in front of the rest and secure a place better than the others', subjected to Abboud's shouts and swearing as well as his threats to cancel the trip, Akoub strolled silently around the truck to inspect all its parts, often losing his temper at Abboud and the passengers, and when they had all done as he commanded, putting the heavy luggage in certain places to balance the whole load and to simplify unloading in the event of a punctured tire, he gave his last clipped orders and lent a hand in the final loading. If his orders were not obeyed, or if Abboud took too long to collect the metal pieces from the passengers, leaving them to do as they pleased, then Akoub behaved differently and addressed Abboud angrily. "Take your time, take your time, my dear friend, but now I may have to unload everything!"

Akoub would turn away and walk toward the coffeehouse until Abboud ran behind to appease him; then the truck was ready to go. But if he made it to the coffeehouse and heard of the total chaos ensuing at the truck, that Abboud was at the end of his wits and everything was topsy-turvy, then his mood turned sour and no one could appease him; his anger might last for a day or two. All the cargo had to be unloaded and then put on again according to his own instructions while Abboud fled to his shop, furious. Sometimes Akoub refused to let a passenger on board, claiming that he had lost his metal piece, or demanding more money for baggage that he deemed excessive. Heated and complicated discussions took turns that no one could have predicted.

When everything was settled and the old Ford was ready to take to the road, with all the cargo trussed to the roof—it did not seem possible that it had been organized and massed up there—Akoub had a final look around the truck, and when he was satisfied that everything was right, he started it up. If he and Abboud were on good terms, Abboud rode on the running board as far as the crossroads, all the time shouting advice and warnings as well as his farewells. At the crossroads Abboud left the truck to its long, arduous journey toward Harran.

When the trucks arrived in Harran with their cargo of men and goods, and Akoub alit by the mosque beside the livestock market, the men who crowded out of the truck could not be distinguished one from the other. They were completely covered with dust; and even their eyelids, when they opened and closed, looked as though they had been coated with flour or sand. The unloading of all the cargo was accompanied by a great deal of shouting, as well as warnings and questions, and Akoub, who supervised it in silence, still had duties to perform: packages to the emirate building, to Daham and the many others, which they had ordered on the previous trip or which others had sent them from Ujra, letters and sums of money all had to be delivered to their owners.

This stout, middle-aged man was silent most of the time, except when the curse of song afflicted him and he chanted from his nostrils, whether from joy or grief no one could tell; the only word that others understood from his song, because he constantly repeated it, was "Peace, peace."

No one knew exactly why he had come here or where he had come from. Once he said he was from Aleppo, but another time he said he was originally from a far more distant place. Once, in a happy and rather defiant mood, he told them that he was from the most beautiful place on earth and would go back there someday.

Akoub became part of Harran. When he was not actually in Harran he was on his way there and was expected at any time. Just as caravans had come in the past bringing provisions, cloth and letters, "Noah's Ark"—as the emir called Akoub's truck— arrived two or three times each month bringing everything imaginable. People awaited it with longing. In addition to the provisions, cloth and letters it carried were the new things Akoub never failed to bring, and these were what caught the emir's attention and made Akoub his friend; when the radio battery wore out, for example, and Hassan Rezaie could not supply a new one because he was abroad, and the sound of the radio was too weak to hear except late at night—and even then only as a garbled rattle—Akoub saved the day. He recharged the battery and promised to do so again whenever necessary. He said, to everyone's astonishment, that even a dead battery could be brought back to life. The emir in particular was incredulous and did not believe him at first, but when he heard the powerful voice burst out of the radio, he praised the Armenian as "a very devil." The small gas stove Akoub used to prepare his food was at first considered a wondrous thing, but when he offered to bring three or four of them to Harran and sell them cheaply, everyone wanted to buy one. Being honest, he said that he could not promise to bring more than three on his next trip and that he would bring more from Aleppo in two or three months' time. Another time Akoub brought lamps that operated on dry-cell batteries. They were small enough to be carried by hand and were very useful for people who stayed up late or walked home at night, for the streets of Harran were now full of deep holes, and there were piles of rocks and sand everywhere. When Akoub brought a small machine for grinding meat for Abu Kamel to use, everyone watched raptly as Akoub installed it at the edge of a table and then as Abu Kamel stuffed a big piece of meat in one end and pulled the small pieces out the other.

The thermos Akoub drank from was an intricate mystery to most of the people, since they could not explain the heat it emitted, and he himself never discussed it because if the emir heard about it he would surely try to get one or take Akoub's. Akoub could not do without it, so he hid it from everyone. He kept it in a place no one could ever find, which led to rumors that he drank "devil's piss"—alcohol.

He brought dozens of other wonderful things: polished bone combs, mirrors, small syringes, sandals made from automobile tires, needles and strong thread. No sooner did the people first see these things than there were clamorous demands for them. Every Harrani wanted at least one thing, though Akoub only rarely thought of doing business in them. He used dry-cell battery lamps to inspect the truck's engine or when he slid underneath the vehicle to examine certain mechanisms, and when they saw him do so they turned the lamp on and off for fun and they all came to want one. Although Akoub nodded his assent to most of their requests, he was unable to fill all the orders. When he agreed to try, he drew a pencil from behind his ear and scribbled on a piece of cardboard he kept in the door of the truck. They watched closely to see that he was recording their orders but were bewildered by the barbed, mysterious script he used— it went in the wrong direction and they did not consider it writing; it was more like comical drawing. When they asked him about it he replied testily, "You ask more questions than Turkish soldiers!" When they kept quiet and Akoub calmed down, he told them in his barely comprehensible accent, "My dear, you want something or you want something else?" When the maker of the request nodded or said what he wanted, Akoub laughed and added, "Let Akoub do it his way!"

So it went time after time, and Akoub's importance to Harran increased daily as he constantly made new friends. The men he transported to Harran said, in spite of all his delays and his terrible swearing, and the exhaustion of the trip, especially when they had to clamber out and lift the truck while a flat was fixed, that they forgot all the hardship; all they remembered, and could never forget, was that it was Akoub who had brought them to Harran. They had become residents, with the feeling of power and distinction that set them off from mere visitors. Those who had not come to Harran with Akoub had at least benefited by some service—he had delivered a letter to them, sold off their goods or done them some favor. Ibn Naffeh, for example, despised "that infidel," but when the stove he had surreptitiously purchased broke down and he angrily went to confront Akoub over the evil merchandise he supplied, Akoub was quick to repair the little stove and install a new part. He gave it a good shake and returned it to the old man in working order. When Ibn Naffeh tried to pay him for his trouble, Akoub repeatedly refused to accept anything.

Akoub worked the Line, as the Ujra-Harran road came to be known. Raji Abu Aqlein was tall, skinny, and bald—what hair he had formed a crescent around the back of his head. He was quick to anger and full of curses, and very different from Akoub in yet other ways, but he had a good heart and was quick to forget, especially offenses or insults. Whenever he arrived in Harran he headed straight for the coffeehouse, leaving his assistants to unload the truck, since "a game of backgammon with Abu As'ad is enough to make a man forget that he's in this shit hole called Harran." If he found Abu As'ad busy or not wanting to play, he sat in the coffeehouse, called for a hookah and supervised its preparation himself, which led to a stream of invective, and within an hour he had picked a fight with everyone in the place, forcing them to listen to his unreasonably harsh opinions about everything. So he sat, refusing to be quiet or calm down until Abu As'ad agreed to play with him. A murmuring crowd gathered as soon as the noisy match was under way, with all the usual shouting and slamming down of playing pieces, and the dice being thrown so hard that they flew off the board, and the war of nerves that Raji regarded as indispensable to a tense and exciting game.

Raji was one of a kind; there would never be another Raji. He gave the dice an interminable shake and looked at the faces of the spectators, lifting his head as if searching for someone. When he located the person who, he felt, had the luck, he shouted, "Here's to you!" When the dice showed what he wanted, he turned to the one he had been looking at to crow, "My luck and yours together could break rocks! Come sit near me!" If this individual accepted the offer to sit beside Raji and follow the game like his partner, the winnings were always Raji's and the losses the fault of this poor soul. Raji glanced at him between throws and sometimes spoke as well. When he was winning he said, "What hands you have, Raji—this isn't luck. It's all in the throw, and Master Raji knows how to throw," but when he began to lose he shouted, "It's your turn, try your luck," and then he would be quiet until he muttered between his teeth: "Don't look at me, brother, look at the board." Not everyone could make out what he said, but they guessed. Since Abu As'ad had only two concerns, namely winning the game and seeing to it that the customers never lost money, he did everything he could to control the board and keep the wagers at a reasonable level.

"Listen!" he once shouted at Raji in mock anger. "These people have nothing to do with us—this is between me and you and this thing!"

He pointed to himself, to Raji and then to the backgammon board. Raji, unconvinced, shook his head and raised his voice. "Listen, Abu As'ad, don't put me in the middle like this." He pointed at all the spectators. "They're all your friends, they're all with Abu As'ad. Poor Raji is a dog and a son of a dog—let him lose a hundred times over!"

In their heated discussions, Abu As'ad swore that he was playing a clean game and that no one was interfering in it; Raji's complaints about the customers' so-called partiality were only an attempt to cover up his poor showing, to end the game before he was beaten. After this discussion Raji agreed to keep playing, but on the condition that no one watch every game and every throw of the dice. Abu As'ad blamed Raji for attracting the spectators with his shouting and contentiousness, so the only practical way to get rid of their audience was, he said, to refrain from making any noise themselves, to play quietly, and soon after they would find that no one was paying any attention to them. Raji consented and they went back to playing, but as soon as Raji's position improved or deteriorated the problem began all over again. He could not enjoy victory alone and could not savor his moves without an audience there to appreciate them. Whenever he lost it was either a mistake or the dice were "dead—dog's bones!" He said that an evil eye followed his every move and perverted every throw of the dice.

Raji lost countless times, but he always forgot them quickly, remembering only the times he had won. He always remembered the final score, who had been there to watch, the weather, time of day and what they'd done after the game.

Raji was just as important to Harran as Akoub was, but in a different way. Raji was capricious and generous and loved to interfere in everyone's business, to offer help or advice. Unasked, he transported poor travelers to Harran for free, which led to arguments when Abboud found out—arguments that were always settled when Raji agreed to forfeit from his pay an amount equal to Abboud's lost commission on the ticket. Abboud always went along with this concession hurriedly, since he had no desire to see Raji lose his temper—there was no telling what might happen then. "Raji Abu Aqlein is crazy—he'll punch you, or hit you with anything he can get his hands on—a tire iron, the big wrench, anything at all—he'd blind you!" Everyone who knew Raji was very careful not to anger or provoke him.

Akoub and Raji were rarely in the same place for more than a very short time; sometimes they met on the road, but as a rule one of them was in Harran and the other in Ujra, or one headed in one direction on the Line and the other in the other. If they happened to meet at the Mile 75 or Mile 110 stations, or anywhere else, they had little to say to one another after exchanging the usual questions about the road conditions and how the business was faring. When they parted, Raji always commented, "He's a midget—he's one foot tall. The steering wheel is higher than he is. Those poor passengers—they could be killed at any time because he's so short he can't see the road. Short and practically blind! If his eyesight gets any worse he won't be able to see two feet in front of his face. Those poor passengers!"

So Raji would begin, and if his listener showed interest or seemed to be listening with his eyes, he went on: "Granted, height and sight are from God—everyone knows it. Almighty God made one man tall and another man short, but Akoub's problem is that he doesn't know how to drive. His driving is just chaotic, and he thinks he's God's gift to driving and the lord of mechanics. That's the problem."

When his companion looked at him askance, which Raji took to express doubt or disagreement, he lost his temper.

"Don't roll your eyes at me," he shouted. "Go and ask him how many flat tires he got the trip before this last one. Ask everyone at Mile 110 how many times their tractor had to pull him out of the sand. If there were more drivers around you'd realize how bad he is, but among the blind, the one-eyed man is king!"

When he saw that his words had little effect, he tried another tactic.

"Let's forget the son of a bitch. He's the world's biggest miser.

He eats alone, he drinks alone, he never says a word. He does nothing but work, and even his work is a cheat. All day long he's either carrying some tool around or lying underneath the truck taking things apart. It's a lot of nonsense. He's just trying to fool people, but he's as obvious as a baboon's ass!"

Akoub only smiled and said nothing when he eventually heard about what Raji said. He was extremely self-confident and sure of his abilities. He was quick to admit his inability to do certain things, but he always tried and often succeeded. There was an abandoned pump at Mile 110, which an American engineer had been unable to repair—he said it needed spare parts, without which it could not budge an inch—but Akoub kept at it and fixed it. So, too, with the water pump on the road, which he repaired after everyone else had completely given up; so, too, with the tractor.

But if Raji went too far in talking about Akoub, especially about his avarice, Akoub got profoundly angry, though he hid his anger. He only said, "Never mind—we'll see tomorrow." He was not in a hurry. The people who watched this battle, seeing in it no justification or reasonable motive, were sympathetic to Akoub and regarded Raji as cruel and slightly crazed.

So it was for a long time. The paving of the road progressed with each passing month, and the passengers who had come to Harran on one of the two trucks settled there permanently after finding work. Akoub still brought novelties along with the letters and his services. At times Raji remembered Akoub and started in on him. Akoub heard but said nothing.

This obscure battle might have ended violently in time had Akoub been struck by one of his fits of temper, which were rarely seen but which flared up now and then—he might have killed people and laid waste to the land; his temper might just as easily have subsided on its own; it might have ended either way, but it did not.

One time Raji had been absent from Ujra for a particularly long time, longer than he had ever been absent before, and there was enough work available to require a truck journey every day, unlike the moribund demand in Harran. Although their agreement with Abboud provided that the trucks should complete one trip and return again as soon as possible, on this journey, Akoub, just setting out for Ujra, met Raji, who was bound for Harran, at the Mile 110 station; and after Akoub loaded up and returned again, he found Raji still stranded at Mile 110. His truck had broken down.

It would have been possible for Akoub to stop and offer his assistance before continuing, or to gloat at the sight of Raji reduced to a black blot from the oil and grease that covered him after several fruitless days of trying to repair the truck, but as soon as he took in the situation Akoub plunged in like a bull, with a determination that knew no passivity or hesitation. Raji hovered around him like a bee, showing Akoub all he had tried to do and offering explanations. Akoub heard and did not hear, looked at Raji and through him, and after narrowing his eyes to two black slits he asked him for tool number six, and then tool number five. After struggling for a good while, he asked for another tool, and another. He assembled, took apart, wiped the machinery and then asked Raji to start the engine. For an hour or more they both tried to start the engine.

"That's it," said Akoub confidently. "It's fixed. Start it up. I'll drive behind you."

After sitting at Mile 110 for days, the truck roared to life, strong as a horse, and despite his weariness Raji was the most anxious to continue the journey. A few hours later, the two trucks arrived in Harran together.

This incident deeply wounded Raji but did little to change his attitude toward Akoub. He never missed an opportunity to provoke him, though Akoub always listened in silence. He never referred to what had happened at Mile 110; all he said was that "if you see a friend in need and don't help him, you're no better than a scorpion—and scorpions die when they sting themselves."

Although Raji still treated Akoub with never-ending provocations and curses, something new had happened: he got angry at anyone who swore at Akoub or spoke a single word against him. Only Raji had the right to do that. If any man made the slightest remark about Akoub, even if he were only repeating something he had heard Raji say, he became an enemy. "Who are you, scabface?" Raji would ask. "Raji can say what he wants. He knows what he's doing and so does Akoub. But you, who are you to talk?" If anyone were audacious enough to say that Akoub was a miser or drank devil's piss, Raji shouted, "Go on! Now we're going to hear from one of the companions of the Prophet! Ahmad bin Hanbal is about to deliver a pronouncement! Speak, O infallible one!" Then he turned to the speaker to say, "Who are you! You lousy, flea-bitten idiot, you're nothing but a louse yourself. If you don't leave decent people alone I'll pave this road with your bones."

This was the new Raji. No one knew how to deal with him anymore. Should they believe him when he cursed Akoub? Agree with him? Disagree? It took nothing to "provoke this madman and fill him with God's fire." If anyone nodded agreement with what he said, he shouted derisively, "Oh yes, by God, the flea has become a horse!" He had been known to slap anyone who looked skeptical as he cursed Akoub. "So now you open your mouth, and your balls hang down! You're like a cat, happy that his masters are blind!" But if anyone openly contradicted the curses he heaped on Akoub, he shouted, "Shut up! I'm an adult! Children should be seen and not heard."

Raji and Akoub came and went in the people's memories as had other subjects and other cares in past days, depending on whether they were there, on whether Raji's curses were heard, on what kind of incidents happened. One rainy day, they saw Raji drive into Harran, towed by strong ropes behind Akoub's truck. No one would ever have been able to imagine such a thing. They were used to Raji bragging about his vehicle, which he said was "worth ten of Akoub's broken-down heaps." He had adorned it with ornaments and lights, and it always seemed bigger and shinier than Akoub's. No one ever guessed it would be dragged behind Akoub's like a dead thing.

Ibn Naffeh laughed when he saw one truck towing the other. "The rock you despise trips you up." He shook his head, still laughing. "The same way you see a donkey pulling camels, even though the camels are bigger, now we see cats pulling rubbish!"

The townspeople of Harran talked about this incident for a long time and almost got into fights with Raji only because they had watched and laughed. When the two trucks parked by the mosque to unload their goods and passengers, and only a few men were present, Akoub looked at Raji uncertainly.

"Listen, Raji, it's your truck. What do you say we go back to Ujra together and come to terms with Sami or—" He paused a moment to look down and smile. "Or shake hands like friends, and God—"

"No, my friend," said Raji quickly. "You're enough; forget Sami and all the rest."

Akoub laughed heartily and raised his hand so Raji could see. "I am here. Akoub is ready. That's all."

"That's all?"

"No. No *gula,* no *galmedee.* Agreed?"

"Don't worry—agreed." Raji embraced him.

Those who watched the two men working together said that they came close to having a fight. Akoub shook his fist, they said, and almost walked away, but at the last minute he backed off and returned to work. At one point he looked distinctly annoyed, dropped his arms at his sides and seemed ready to quit.

Raji addressed him in a loud voice before three or four other men. "Give your bread to the baker for baking, even if he steals half of it." He patted Akoub on the back somewhat mockingly and said, "Brother Akoub, this job is too big for you."

He turned to the other men.

"You give a gentleman a chance and he thinks he's an expert." He laughed. "It was an accident, my man."

Akoub heard and did not hear; he did not understand most of what Raji was saying, so he kept working. A few hours passed, and Raji saw that it was all in vain, so he decided to go to the coffeehouse.

"Mr. Akoub!" he said sarcastically and bitterly. "Put all that away, and come with me—I'll break your head in a game of backgammon."

"God go with you, dear man. Go. Never mind," said Akoub.

Akoub stayed on the job while Raji gathered information between games of backgammon. He had something to say about every bit of news and every game, and his listeners alternately laughed or were sad. As soon as Raji had won the first game he turned to face all the spectators.

"Listen, go tell Akoub that the first head is broken. Tell him I'm ready for his head now."

Manawar al-Khodeiri went away but came back to tell Raji that Akoub had pulled out all the insides of the truck and taken them apart.

"By God, I'll pull out *his* insides. By God I'll strangle him with a dog's insides."

Raji folded up the board vigorously and shouted when he had won his last game.

" 'Should we wish to destroy a village we will use ease and luxury so that its people stray, that it may be said we have destroyed it truly; how many villages before thee have we destroyed!' And truly Akoub is the worst corrupter in Harran, and after him or even before him is the miscreant Abu As'ad al-Helwani!"

A second and then a third round of backgammon began by the last light of day, then by the light of a lantern, while by the light of the electric lamp that Akoub had rigged up near the machine, his attempts to repair the truck continued. Akoub finished his task just as evening prayers were coming to an end. He started the engine and drove over to Abu As'ad al-Helwani's coffeehouse. Raji's heart pounded when he heard the roar of his truck approaching, and nervously, ruining his throw of the dice, even though he was ahead, he started up to hear the sound, and when he saw the truck rumbling forward he knew it was his because of the small colored lights twinkling at the sides. He surged up involuntarily with the strength of a horse, and those who saw the two men meet in the light of the headlights said that tears streamed down Raji's face as he leaned over to embrace Akoub and bury his face in his chest. Akoub then sat in the coffeehouse and drank two glasses of tea as he watched the new game between Raji and Abu As'ad, but he said nothing. He only spoke to answer a few questions, mostly about his health and well-being. He replied very briefly but with a smile, and before the game was over he said that he was very tired and wanted to sleep.

Once again, shortly after this incident, Harran sank back into its own worries and people began to wonder what new events would be caused by the paving of the Ujra-Harran road, what new joys and sorrows, since every day brought new gossip and expectations. Most of the news and expectations had begun to come from a different direction in recent years—instead of coming in from Ujra, from the caravan routes, they came from the sea, from cities and lands none of the Harranis had ever heard of before.

Now that the road was nearing completion, the two trucks

competed for the record of the fastest trip between Ujra and Harran. It was no longer a matter of thirty hours or two days: a truck set off from Ujra in the morning, and before the end of the afternoon it had been unloaded in Harran. It was also at about this time that the trucks started carrying more goods than people. Even Abboud, who derived great pleasure from handing out the metal pieces to the passengers, and from the admiration his complicated signature always aroused, for they all said it was unique in the world, now stopped handing out the coins. One day the boy who worked for him brought him ten of the coins which had been thrown away near Sami's shop—Sami was the only mechanic in Ujra. When Abboud compared them with his own metal pieces and rubbed them with sacking, he found that they were almost exact copies—mixed in with real ones, they could fool anyone. That was why he decided to stop circulating his own. He kept using his signature, albeit with a few modifications, and after the Desert Travel Office expanded—Abboud annexed the land behind and beside it for a warehouse with a wide gate, where the truck could enter and be loaded up with ease—he decided to take an important step forward, as befitted the new era, by ordering special ledgers, receipt books and signets from Damascus. He put them to immediate use in spite of the error in the town's name: the calligrapher had written "Ghunjra" instead of "Ujra." Abboud had to correct every single receipt. He did this at his leisure, to pass the time. His receipts and signets became a new hobby—he loved to fill out each passenger's name and the amount of payment, but he cackled as he crossed out the spaces for indicating the departure time and seat number, saying to himself, "Why don't they leave spaces for the passenger's mother's maiden name and the arrival time in Harran!"

Each receipt had to be signed and stamped with the round signet. Abboud breathed hard on the face of the seal two or three times to make sure that it was damp enough to leave a clear impression. Although the trucks carried fewer and fewer passengers, so that it was virtually impossible to miscount them, just as it was impossible for any of them to evade paying the fare, Abboud always made a point of recounting the receipts at the last minute.

"Present your tickets, brothers!" he said firmly after all the passengers had climbed aboard the truck.

If any of them searched for the small slip of paper or forgot where he had put it, Abboud shouted at them: "Don't hold us up! Present your tickets!"

68

THINGS WENT SMOOTHLY FOR ABBOUD, AKOUB, Raji and their trucks in the first month after the completion of the road. Abboud, who had decided to go to Harran and open a full branch office there, postponed his journey time after time, because a hajj caravan was due to return soon, and he felt sure he would be able to persuade one or two of the caravan drivers to settle in Ujra and work for him on the Ujra–Harran route. Two trucks were no longer enough, and Akoub's truck was constantly breaking down despite his efforts to repair it.

Akoub and Raji made peace at about this time; in fact, they became fast friends. They spent a great deal of time whispering together in the Mile 75 coffeehouse, exchanging news and confiding in each other. Raji dealt with any passenger who insisted on resuming the journey quickly, whether it was one of Akoub's passengers or one of his own. He shook his finger and shouted at them. "God damn these times we live in! Pimps! Sons of sixty dogs!"

When the passenger's jaw dropped in amazement, because he did not know whether Raji was referring to him or to someone else, or what precisely was meant, Raji shouted even more threateningly and brandished his fist. "It used to take a week or two weeks to get from Ujra to Harran—and that was *if* you got there!" Then he spoke in an entirely different tone. "Have some tea on me, or pick your toes, just let people drink their tea in peace."

If the passenger persisted in protesting against this language or about the delay, Raji lost his temper.

"Every word, every bit of your sermonizing will delay you one hour. Keep it up, by God, and you'll be spending the night here!"

Since most of them knew Raji or had heard about him, or other passengers told them what he was like, most of these incidents ended with the jokes or stories that al-Ghanem, the owner of the Mile 75 coffeehouse, loved to tell.

Akoub became better known to them at Kilo 110. He sang often and ate and drank with the others, though he never drank the bitter coffee that al-Ghanem was so proud of, often saying that it was the best in the region. Al-Ghanem used to tell him, in a tone of sincere apology, when he refused to drink it, "You have no faults but your voice. And you talk about bitter!"

"God, in His wisdom did not give him a sweet voice, that's all," said Raji as Akoub nodded.

They learned that Akoub came from Aleppo, though he was born in the mountains behind it, near the most beautiful lake God had ever created—that was what he said. In the terrible first part of the century, marked by great upheaval as a result of the massacres of the Armenians, Akoub, who had lost his father,

mother and most other members of his family, was taken in by
his grandmother. She brought him to Aleppo and they settled
there. The truck represented his life's savings, and since he was
getting on in years—though he never told his age—he said that
in two or three years he would go back to Aleppo to marry,
and he and his wife would go to live by that lake. He wanted
his children to be born there. And so what if he was getting
old—he wouldn't have to worry about combing his hair!

Akoub's plan, if he was able to keep working for another year,
was to sell "the old heap" and add the money to what he had
saved, to buy a newer automobile. A year or so after that, or
two years at the most, he would bid Harran and the Line *Kula
Gula* and head home, first to Aleppo and then to Armenia.

Thus he thought and dreamed and planned, and when he saw
his thoughts clearly outlined in his head his features relaxed and
his face shone, and sometimes he laughed delightedly. When his
whole face laughed and his silver teeth gleamed in his mouth,
no one could guess his age, he looked so boyish and strong, and
yet at the same time whatever remained of his youth seemed to
fade away.

"You are Arabs," he would tell Raji as the darkness began to
fall, to excuse himself from going on to give away more of his
secrets. "You have a thousand and one nights. I'm Armenian—
I have only three hundred and sixty-five days, and I have a lot
of work to do!"

He rose with the strength of a horse. He walked with his feet
apart. Perhaps his legs were bowed, or perhaps his powerful but
generous body made his thighs rub, so that he walked like a
duck. Watching him made Raji laugh hard, as if someone were
tickling him, and when Akoub had gone some distance, with
his distinctive walk still noticeable, Raji called out to him. "Akoub,
Akoub!"

When he turned around, Raji began to sing: "My love, my sweetheart, she walks as a gazelle!"

Akoub shook his fist menacingly but tried unsuccessfully to walk differently, and as he leaped lightly up on the running board of the truck he could hear Raji singing: "My love, she leaps as a partridge he leaps!"

Raji generally sat for another hour while al-Ghanem brewed another pot of coffee—"If Raji didn't taste it there would be no point," as Raji said to explain his delay there, and al-Ghanem quoted this saying back at him to make him stay yet another hour, "because if Akoub goes, and you go, there'll be nothing for me to do until one of you comes back again."

It had been a little over two months since the completion of the Ujra-Harran road. The hajj caravan had come through, the company trucks plied the Line beside those of Akoub and Raji, and Abboud held long and difficult but apparently indecisive negotiations; his promises got him nowhere, so he decided to go to Harran and see about opening an office there. Because he was afraid of riding with Raji, for a variety of reasons, he tried to make his journey appear sudden, a spontaneous venture. The physician accompanying the hajj caravan had decided to stay behind in Ujra, leaving the medical care of the returning pilgrims and escorts in the hands of his assistant; after making thorough inquiries about local job opportunities, he decided to go on to Harran. As soon as he paid his fare and took his ticket from Abboud, the two men fell into a deep conversation, and when the doctor asked for a forward seat, beside the driver, Abboud decided to go to Harran as well. The doctor agreed to postpone his trip for one day, because he was told that "the Armenian fears God and drives well, unlike that madman who races along

and screams so that you wonder if you'll ever get there alive."
And so Abboud traveled to Harran in the company of Dr. Subhi
al-Mahmilji.

The two trucks met at Mile 75, or rather Raji's truck was
parked there when Akoub's rolled in. Raji was astonished to see
Abboud there, and pointed at him as he turned to al-Ghanem.

"That's that thief Abboud those bedouin were telling you
about."

Abboud tried to smile, so as not to show his annoyance, and
to face all of the eyes that looked at him with one stare.

"Watch out, Abboud," Raji continued, "there's no iron or
paper in Harran. They take a man's word there."

"I'll take care of that tomorrow!" Abboud laughed heartily as
a means of defense.

"Everyone who passes through here to Harran speaks well of
you," said al-Ghanem to Abboud, to lighten the atmosphere.
To remove any lingering doubts Abboud might have had, he
added, "Everyone says, 'If it weren't for Abboud's trucks, we'd
never get to Harran.' "

After this the people mingled and their conversations mingled
in the air. With his fair, pink-hued complexion, neat clothing
and eyeglasses, Dr. Subhi al-Mahmilji seemed otherworldly.
The Harran road, which had seen growing numbers of people
every day for years, had never seen anyone like him; even the
two teachers who had passed through three weeks before were
not nearly as elegant, clean or healthy. The American and other
engineers who had stayed at the coffeehouse seemed like mere
laborers by comparison; some had even eaten with their hands.
Raji leaned over toward Akoub to ask about this elegant gentleman. "This effendi. Do you think he'll make it to Harran or
melt on the road?"

Akoub laughed but did not reply.

"That son of a bitch Abboud is like a saw. He gets it coming and going—takes his money and then rides beside him!" He turned to Abboud and asked innocently, "So, Abu Najm, you're off to Harran? Who do we answer to there?"

"It's just for a few days and then I'll be back," said Abboud. He paused. "Don't worry. I've got a fellow there and he knows what he's doing."

Raji could not contain his laughter. He waved his hand in the air and asked, "What about the signets and signatures?"

"You have a big mouth, by God, you bastard," said Abboud irritably.

"Everything about me is big!" exclaimed Raji, getting up from his chair and pointing to several parts of his anatomy.

Harran shocked Abboud. This town that he had last visited four years ago was completely different from what he remembered, or rather it bore no resemblance whatsoever to it. Had it not been for the people he saw in the street, the coffeehouse, everywhere he went, people he had dispatched to Harran himself, he would not have believed he was in Harran.

Four days after his arrival he reached an agreement with Shihab al-Dreihi for the opening of a travel office in Harran as a branch of his Ujra operation. He showed him the receipt books and signets, and explained the commissions he would collect on every passenger and shipment he carried. They agreed on the details, such as ordering new ticket books and seals from Damascus for both offices. Shihab al-Dreihi would have a special stamp with his name on it, for since he did not know how to read or write he could not sign his name either. Abboud explained to Shihab several times that a signature had nothing to do with reading or writing: every man had to have a unique way of signing his name, so that no one could copy it. When they had gone over all the details and all the wonderful opportunities that lay in store for the new office, they headed over to Abu As'ad al-Helwani's coffeehouse.

As they sat sipping coffee several men came in to talk about the cargo being unloaded from the ship that had come in the day before, which included, among other things, eight huge new trucks, bigger than any that had ever been seen in Harran. When the eight trucks were set on the dock several drivers with other men climbed into them to start the engines; they would begin moving out at any moment.

Shihab looked at Abboud curiously, almost accusingly.

"You've come at the right time, Abu Najm. So much for the Salek-Dreihi office."

That afternoon, before sundown, the eight trucks, five of them International and the rest Mack-Pickering, cruised from the sea to Harran as far as the mosque, then set off toward the Ujra road and were gone for an hour. Finally they parked in a row on Rashedi Street near Rezaie's offices, almost blocking the street.

That evening, in the coffeehouse, the market, the mosque, in Arab Harran and the workers' camp, everyone talked of how a new era had begun, and of how no one could predict what joys and sorrows it would bring. Would it bring benefits to Harran and its people, or more of the same suffering that they had known since the coming of Satan's ship more than four years ago?

Everyone was greatly bewildered. None of them knew what to think about the new development.

"Poor Akoub," said Ibn Zamel in the camp.

The workers looked at him with questioning eyes. Why was Akoub, of all people, so unfortunate?

"These new trucks are going to devour everyone's business, and first to be devoured are Akoub and his truck."

Akoub watched the procession of trucks with the rest of them. He had just come in from Ujra. There were signs of worry, fear and happiness in his features, and no one who looked at his face could tell whether he was smiling, or dark and melancholy. He walked toward the trucks when they parked by the mosque and circled closely around them.

"Man is better than machines," they heard him say. "Akoub is stronger than International and Mack, but Akoub is poor."

Akoub and Raji stayed on the Line. The new trucks flew down the road like lightning, fast and huge. Akoub strained visibly to keep control of his truck in the windy wake of these trucks when they passed him. Sometimes these trucks seemed to be playing with them, running so close as almost to force them off the asphalted road, or speeding up from behind so fast that Akoub was afraid of a collision. He would make a sharp turn to avoid crashing, and when the new truck was almost close enough to touch, its driver swerved at the last minute to follow the road at the same speed, grinning at his power to frighten the old man. Because all of those trucks were of almost identical size and color, it was not easy to find out who was behind these "games."

The games continued. One day, at Mile 75, Raji caught sight of two of the drivers. He leaped out of his truck and hit the ground running. He wanted to start a fight, to beat them to death. He had often told al-Ghanem that he wanted to do this, and it would have been easy except that al-Ghanem was there and watching him. When he saw Raji running he ran after him and grabbed him, and with the help of two or three other men was able to restrain him. The two drivers looked terrified.

"By God, you fucking sons of whores, before I die I'll take a bath in your blood!" he shouted at them.

He tried to break loose, but they held him tight. He was frothing at the mouth. "You sons of bitches, you cowards, if you think that because your trucks are new, you'll turn our trucks over and kill us, you're wrong. Before I die, me or Akoub, we'll have your blood running from Ujra to Harran."

They all tried to calm Raji down. They said that those drivers were not the ones, that they had done nothing. Perhaps the others had done something or tried to.

"The biggest son of a whore is Rezaie," shouted Raji. "If we don't wreck his trucks, we'll let him see the blood of one of those dogs."

The two drivers slipped out of the coffeehouse and were told to continue their journey to prevent trouble. When they had driven away Raji sat and fumed.

"Listen, me and Akoub, this road, before they tarred it, broke our asses. We rode it a thousand times. We were on this road for years. Our trucks are old, yes, but just because a man's truck is old doesn't mean he has to die on the road like a dog. Rezaie bought new trucks. We all saw them. We didn't say a word. Maybe he stole them, or maybe God blessed him with them, that's between him and the Lord, but Rezaie went looking for the last drivers God made and told them, 'Get rid of Raji and Akoub. Kill them, crash into them on the road, and they'll die God's death or end up slaves.' "

He rested a moment, sighed and smiled. "Never mind. I was wrong. I have nothing to do with children. I'll go for the big one."

The games stopped. That same day, the story was told in Harran by the two drivers and by a host of others, and as was usual in Harran everyone in the city was discussing it by the end of the day. Akoub, who had just left Ujra, no sooner noticed one of Rezaie's trucks from afar than he stiffened, then slowed down and moved as far as possible to the right. He was expecting this truck to play with him as he was used to all of them doing, but he was surprised to see that even at this distance the other truck—in daylight, no less—flashed its directional lights, slowed down and kept to the right. Akoub was frightened and slowed almost to a stop, and when the other truck approached he slowed down even more. When the truck pulled abreast it seemed to Akoub that the other driver smiled at him. Then the driver waved. Akoub laughed.

"So Raji's done it," he said to the men sitting next to him.

That was the end of that means of warfare, but there were others.

Rezaie's trucks began to transport goods and passengers to and from Harran at no charge, or for a nominal fee. The truck in Ujra which carried cement, lumber and some provisions also took anyone who cared to go along; all that was needed was the driver's consent. Many people in Harran rode Rezaie's trucks, not because they were real travelers but because they had nothing else to do, and since the trucks left empty it was possible to spend a pleasant day or part of a day in Ujra before returning to Harran with the last truck.

Akoub and Raji sat in the coffeehouse at Mile 75. Raji was bringing two bedouin and three sacks of flour from Ujra, and Akoub was returning alone with an empty truck, since his assistant had decided to stay in Harran to find other work. Akoub sighed in remembrance. "You say walks as a gazelle. Like a rooster. Listen."

Akoub almost stopped. There was a long silence as his mind wandered far away, but after a while he continued. "Thirty years ago, forty years ago, in Aleppo, I got ill. My grandmother said, 'Akoub is going to die.' I had a dog. The dog got ill. The dog didn't eat or sleep, and he slept at my feet. One week, two weeks later I got medicine, I got better, but the foot didn't heal. You say as a gazelle? Look."

Akoub lifted his trouser leg. His lower leg was pitifully thin, and the calf was bowed.

"Hah! You see?" He laughed, as if at someone else's story, and then went on. "The dog got like Akoub. His leg got crooked."

He roared with laughter, then patted Raji's leg. "No, not crooked. The eye gets crooked, bent round like a wheel, like a tire."

Akoub fell silent again. It seemed that he did not know why he had said all he'd said, and when he remembered that he had to drive to Ujra alone, his head filled with thoughts.

"A truck is like a dog," he said quickly. "It can get sick and die."

He could find nothing more to say, and after sitting for a little more than an hour, they parted.

When Raji was on his way back from Harran the next day, he came upon Akoub before reaching the Mile 75 coffeehouse, trying his best to repair his broken-down truck. He was having no success. He could not fix it. When Raji towed him to the coffeehouse, a distance of less than four miles, Akoub seemed sadder than he had ever been. They sat at a table, and Akoub spoke up before either of them could start a conversation or ask the other if he was hungry or wanted a glass of coffee or tea.

"A truck is like a dog. I got ill and it got ill!"

Both of them were ill. It was a mysterious disease and at times seemed incurable. Akoub, who knew how it had started and would develop, when and why it struck, had recently begun to experience symptoms which he had never had before, and which he could not explain. Even the doctor he'd driven to Harran, who had rented three shops side by side and opened a clinic for treating the sick, which even had beds for him and for patients requiring urgent surgery or overnight treatment, even Subhi al-Mahmilji could not diagnose his disease or explain the pains he complained of. The pain started at the base of his skull and spread all over his body, causing weakness, loss of appetite and high fevers, especially at night.

Akoub took aspirin, and sometimes various herbs which he picked and prepared himself, but neither the herbs nor the aspirin did much good.

He treated his truck the same way. When he felt it weaken, seemingly unable to continue the journey, he spent long hours inspecting every part of it, at times searching out the malady and trying to figure out why until the day became night, but most of the time he failed. After resting for a day or two, but preoccupied with the hidden malady day and night, and not finding any likely cause, he told himself: "Even if the truck was fine, Akoub is still sick. If the truck was shit but Akoub was fine, that's no use. Even if the truck was fine and Akoub was fine, there's no business. The market is shit."

Even Abboud, who had strutted around like a rooster and taken such pride in his signature and metal pieces, in his receipts and signets, felt weak and depressed because of Rezaie and the competition, which was no less dire than he'd expected. He often joined his young assistant in crying, "Harran, one rider for Harran." They would then leave the store and cross the sidewalk, sometimes going as far as the mosque or the beginning of the Sultan's Road looking for a single passenger for Harran. Abboud got angry at the stupid, penniless bedouin who did not respond to his shouts or his efforts to fill a truck for Harran.

"Let them ride with Ibn Rezaie, but tomorrow when he takes their last penny, they'll come looking for Ibn Salek with a lantern and find nothing but ruins."

With time, Abboud al-Salek's office in Ujra became a shop like the others. He sold rice and flour and bought salt and dates. He waited for the hajj caravans; he waited, as he put it, for a blind coincidence—some unlooked-for opportunity—to strike.

It was in this period that Mohieddin al-Naqib imported two buses, much in the same way that Rezaie had brought in his trucks. The yellow buses were Harran's latest prodigy—the peo-

ple spent long hours pondering these strange creatures that had
suddenly appeared on the Ujra road. Everyone stood for a long
time and looked inside them, while some of the children crawled
screaming underneath to see the "belly," as they called it, and
others tried to scale the rear ladder to reach the roof, but the
driver and some of Naqib's men saw them and shouted for them
to stop. Later, the steps and ladders were wreathed with barbed
wire to keep anyone from using them, so the boys were content
to draw shapes and pictures on the buses' sides. This they did
with the greatest pleasure and total absorption, and the shapes
they drew did seem very strange and beautiful, especially when
the dust on the bus sides was very thick.

Harran was excited, as it had been so many times before. At
first the people did not know the purpose of these two strange
vehicles, but then a huge banner with large red lettering appeared
over the building Mohieddin al-Naqib used as his office: NAQIB-
SEIF DESERT TRAVEL AGENCY. There were shouts of "Ujra! Ujra!"
and then a broadly smiling Muhammad al-Seif came along to
address them in his powerful voice. "All the people of Harran
desiring to travel to Ujra, or from Ujra to Harran, step right
up. Your journey is on us—none of you will pay a single piaster!"

The people stared at each other and at Ibn Seif, and their eyes
were full of questions: from Harran to Ujra, and Ujra to Harran,
free? Nothing to pay?

The buses came and went busily for three days, transporting
their "travelers" inside, with the luggage tied to the roof. Everyone rode the bus or at least tried; some of them made the journey
two or three times while many others went down, some of them
very early, and waited, but when they saw the seething crush
of people and the intense competition between the prospective
travelers, they gave up.

The buses rested on the fourth day, and the drivers gave them
a good cleaning as rumors circulated that from now on rides on

these fast, powerful, comfortable buses would be very expensive indeed, more expensive than Akoub's and Raji's trucks, perhaps even twice or three times as much; but the people were surprised to learn that the fare would be the same: "the same as the heaps." Abdullah al-Seif tried to clarify the matter to a number of men in his office on the second floor of the Naqib-Seif Desert Travel Agency.

"We want the buses to cover expenses and the drivers' salaries—God curse seekers after profit!"

So began the bus service between Ujra and Harran. One bus left Harran in the morning and arrived in Ujra shortly before noon, and left Ujra for Harran in midafternoon, with the other keeping the same schedule in the opposite direction. Both buses broke the journey at Mile 75 to give the passengers a rest.

Raji and Akoub sat at the Mile 75 coffeehouse watching the passengers stream off the bus, jostling to be first in line to get something to drink.

"You and me, Akoub, are like little fish—if we keep our distance we'll survive. But how will the big fish survive?"

Akoub curled his lip and said nothing.

"You'll see. Naqib has shafted Rezaie from his ass to his eyeballs. You'll hear the screams any time now."

Akoub laughed. "We're the ones who got the shaft, effendi."

"Right! We got shafted, but now along comes Naqib with ten shafts."

"Ten? For whom?"

"Rezaie, of course! Rezaie is eating shit."

"Effendi, Rezaie eats meat, he doesn't eat shit." Akoub paused a moment before adding sarcastically, "You and me, effendi, *we* are eating shit."

"Wrong!"

"Wrong, not wrong. You'll see."

"My friend, in him God truly has something to answer for."

Instead of getting up quickly, as he usually did, Akoub sat for a while longer. Al-Ghanem prepared some coffee and brought it to him, but he refused to taste it.

"I've told you a hundred times"—al-Ghanem laughed—"in this place, this stinking desert, you have no choice. Bitter is all you get." He offered him the cup again. "Drink. Listen to your brother. Drink."

"You drink. Leave me alone," snapped Akoub.

Naqib stole Rezaie's passengers just as Rezaie had stolen the passenger and cargo business from Raji and Akoub. Rezaie still moved most of the cargo; his trucks linked Harran with far-off places. All eight of them transported cement, lumber and many other goods directly from Beirut. He bought more trucks, some of which towed large trailers behind them. Ibn Naffeh had a good laugh when he saw Akoub's truck pulling Raji's into Harran, but he gaped in surprise when he saw the long trucks towing the trailers. He shook his head in angry mockery.

"We'll live to see them tow Harran itself behind them. They'll tie it on with a rope like hitching a donkey and say, 'Giddy-up, boy, let's go.' "

Things went from bad to worse for Raji and Akoub. Most people felt sorry for them and said that they deserved better than this, but no one could stand up to the two powerful new giants. While many people still depended on Akoub if they needed anything brought from Ujra, and some still preferred to travel there in his old open truck, these were comparatively few in number and diminished every day; besides, they traveled rarely, perhaps not even once a year, and many of the things they wanted could now be found in Harran.

A month or two short of a year after the paving of the road,

Raji came upon Akoub in the Mile 75 coffeehouse, which had become something of a place of refuge for both of them.

"Boss, it's all over. There's no work for us."

Akoub nodded in agreement but said nothing.

"Hah . . . what do you think, boss? Do we stay here like this?"

Akoub shrugged his shoulders and hands in resignation.

"Listen," said Raji. "A few days ago Rezaie sent one of his people to see me."

Akoub opened one eye to show his interest, and nodded for him to go on.

"To make a long story short, he said, 'Sell your truck to us and we'll hire you as a driver.' "

"Did you accept?"

"I asked them for a few days to think about it." He paused a moment, looking confused, then added, "I asked them 'What about Akoub?' They said, 'If Akoub wants to sell his truck we'll buy it.' So I asked them, 'Would you hire him as a driver?' and they said—"

Raji stopped. He could not go on. His face showed his grief, and when Akoub smiled to make it easier for him, he swore. "The sons of bitches." He sighed deeply and said, as if to himself, "We have to make a shaft to use on them, Akoub."

There was a long silence as they thought.

"The sons of whores," said Raji between his teeth. "They said, 'Forget it, Akoub's too old.' " His features twitched and his voice changed. "Akoub is stronger than their God. He'll bury them all."

He reverted to his calm, conspiring tone. "If we don't give them the shaft, my name isn't Raji!" He moved close to Akoub and whispered, "This is my idea. We'll agree to sell our trucks, yes, we'll sell them, but as soon as we have the money in our hands we'll drive out of here."

"I'm not selling," said Akoub fiercely.

"Look, I wouldn't work for Rezaie if they cut my head off," explained Raji. "I might work in the company, or for Naqib, but him? No."

Akoub gestured toward his truck. "That's mine and I'm keeping it. You, God keep you, my dear."

Raji had left Harran only hours before on his way to Ujra, but he felt the need to stay with Akoub, to talk with him, to sit for a while until they agreed on something, so he decided to go back to Harran.

"I'm going back to Harran with you," he said to keep the conversation going.

"Harran?"

"Yes, Harran." He laughed. "As long as there's no business in Harran or Ujra, what's the difference?"

So they went back to Harran.

No one in the world would have dreamed that these men had been enemies, that such a thing would ever have been possible. No one could have guessed that these apparently strong and happy men hid in their hearts so much misery, disappointment and confusion. As soon as they arrived in Harran, after unloading the ten head of sheep, three bedouin and their cargoes of flour and barley, they set out together. They strolled in the central market, which was now known as the Rashedi Market, although Hassan Rezaie had bought most of the land it stood on; the people had named it. They stood in front of Rezaie's offices, under an immense signboard that read HASSAN REZAIE & HIS BROTHER ABBAS/ GENERAL TRADE AND TRANSPORT. There were three new automobiles parked in front of the building, one of them black and larger than the other two. After standing there awhile they headed to the eastern market; here was Abu Kamel the butcher, and Abdu Muhammad a short distance away, and, at the end of the market street, facing the sea, Abu As'ad al-Helwani's coffee-house.

They strolled and talked like two youths in the prime of life. One of them would stop the other at times; what he had to say was so subtle and important that he had to look his interlocutor in the eye, or make sure that the gestures that accompanied his words were clearly understood. They laughed and stood talking with many of the friends they ran into, and responded kindly to their warm invitations never to leave Harran and to visit more often.

This was on their way to the coffeehouse. When they got there it was crowded to bursting, and they were obliged to stand for a while with Abu As'ad. He readied them a place at some distance, on the beach, and Raji himself helped to prepare the hookahs. Abu As'ad told Raji that as long as he was free for a few minutes he would play him a game of backgammon to get even.

"Some other time," said Raji.

When Abu As'ad insisted on playing, this very night, Raji said, "I've taken an oath not to play tonight."

Had Raji, or any of the others who sat with the two, recalled the night's conversations he would have been unable to remember anything remarkable, anything worth repeating. If any of them cared to think back on how the evening had started and ended, he would have been unable to recall anything that was out of the ordinary or that stuck in the memory. Even so, it was a great night and a highly unusual one. Akoub told Abdullah al-Zamel, who had spent more nights with him and Raji than anyone else, and tried to convince them to go with him to the camp to spend the night, that he would drop by the camp the next day, since some of the things the workers had ordered were still in the truck and he could not go and get them at this late hour.

People said they had never seen Raji as calm and smiling as he was that night. Abu Kamel said that the meat for the pastries they ate that night had been put aside; he had been planning to take it home to grill and eat himself, but "everything in this world is luck and chance," so they all ate it. Abdu Muhammad, who never touched flour or dough at that hour of the night, readily agreed to Abu As'ad's proposal that he bake the pastries. Ibn Naffeh, who passed by quickly, avoiding the door of the coffeehouse, bumped into Akoub and Raji, who were sitting facing the sea; he would have kept on to the mosque had it not been for his sudden desire to chat with Akoub.

Many others besides them dropped in, and many other small incidents took place, but no one remembered them because what happened afterward made them forget, or at least made them unable to remember.

After Akoub and Raji went back to the trucks, which were parked near the mosque, and each of them prepared his bed in the back of his truck, Raji went over to Akoub's truck.

"That son of a bitch Rezaie, if he buys my truck, he'll use it for a urinal."

Akoub laughed heartily in the still night. It was a belly laugh, a roar. He grasped the side of his truck to climb in and turned to Raji, who was surprised by the guffaw. "Effendi, pissing does as much to relieve a man as sleeping does."

"By God, Akoub, I won't rest until I've pissed on Rezaie." Raji's words came from between his teeth, sharply.

"Effendi, enough talk about pissing," said Akoub. "Let's get some sleep."

"I won't be able to sleep until I've pissed on Rezaie."

"Very good, effendi. Go ahead. Good night."

And so they slept.

Raji said, the next day, that after this conversation with Akoub, silence fell; there was no sound save for the barking of the dogs who circled the camp and the market. He did not know how long he slept, but he woke with the sound of mooing in his ears, such as one hears when an animal is slaughtered. He looked around his truck for a bull but found none, then heard an even louder bellow. It was a heavy, trembling, insistent voice, and it came from Akoub's truck, from the back. At first Raji thought that Rezaie's men had come and had begun to kill Akoub. He grabbed the club that he always kept beside him and leaped from the truck.

"God damn you, Rezaie, you sons of bitches!"

When he came upon Akoub but found no one else, Akoub was still moaning and covered with sweat, and his face was dripping. Raji screamed and called to him, and shook him, but Akoub was writhing, though his eyes were closed, as if he were in another world.

Raji said, the following afternoon, "I was terrified. I didn't know what to do. I opened the water bottle and poured it over his face and chest. I slapped his cheek. I pulled up his head and shouted, 'Akoub, Akoub,' but he didn't respond or say anything, and he was writhing like a butchered animal. He was in pain, and moaning, only with his mouth shut. I wanted someone to help me, to be by my side, but I shouted and no one came. I left Akoub and ran to the doctor. The effendi woke up an hour later, and he was very angry and irritable. He told me, 'You and he come tomorrow morning.' I told him, 'The man can't wait that long, he's dying.' He said not to worry. He had almost gone in and shut the door, but I told him, 'Doctor, please come quickly,' and I brought out the club. He was terrified! He went as yellow as a lemon. He asked me, 'Who is it anyway?' I told him, 'It's your friend Akoub.' He said, 'Who is Akoub?' I said, 'The same Akoub who brought you from Ujra, the driver.' Anyway, he came along all right. He was afraid and took his assistant with him. When we got to the truck he was even more afraid—he didn't think anyone slept there. He said, 'God bless you, please leave me alone. I have children.' He was almost crying. I told him, 'Don't be afraid, just see this sick man.' He said, 'Where is he?' When he heard Akoub moaning in the bed, he gasped. He looked inside the truck and then went in with the little lamp in his hand. He saw Akoub and gave him a shot with a needle, but by the time the morning prayers came he was gone. No . . . just as the call to morning prayer was sounded, he died exactly then. The doctor told me, 'God rest his soul.' "

That late spring day was a dreadful and sad day in Harran. There had never been anything like it, and long years would pass before a comparable sorrow broke the town's heart. Silence filled the houses of Arab Harran, and at night the women wept. For the first time in three years no one came to Abu As'ad's coffeehouse; it was open but all the chairs were empty. Abdu Muhammad did not attend the funeral, thus touching off a lively rumor that he had left Harran, but he failed to take part because he could not bear to, indeed he refused to believe that Akoub could die. Abdullah al-Zamel and dozens, or rather hundreds of workers marched out of the camp, fearlessly and without permission. They simply informed the personnel office that one of their colleagues had passed away, and they had to attend his funeral. The personnel office neither consented nor refused, but referred the matter to Administration. Beyond this measure of solidarity, Ibn Zamel, Ibn Hathal and every one of the other workers did what they could to express their love and respect for Akoub.

Even so, Akoub's death generated a great deal of uneasiness in Harran. It was not like any other death: shortly after word of his death circulated they began to wonder how and where to bury him, and who would take charge of the arrangements. The imam of the mosque, Ibrahim al-Hmeidi, refused even to discuss it, since "the deceased was a Christian and an infidel," and would not even touch him, but Ibn Naffeh's plan, and the testimonies of some other citizens, solved the difficulties one by one, resulting in a funeral that was attended by all, with the sole exception of Abdu, who was not seen or heard from all that day.

"Wash the body," Ibn Naffeh told Abdullah al-Zamel, "and afterwards, we'll see."

This was Ibn Naffeh's own initiative. When Abdullah had carried out his task he told Ibn Naffeh everything was fine, as anyone could tell by looking at the index finger of the deceased's injured right hand, fixed in a gesture of doctrinal witness. Raji swore before the assembled populace that Akoub's soul had been released to its eternal reward at the instant that the morning prayer call was sounded, and the crowd murmured: "I testify that there is no god but God, and Muhammad is His servant and His prophet!"

Ibn Naffeh seemed ready to pray over Akoub and eulogize him, but there was one last thing that bothered him: had the man drunk devil's piss or not? He turned to Raji with uneasy sorrow. "It is true that a man's reckoning is God's and no one else's, but tell me: did your brother drink infamy? Did he drink devil's piss?"

Raji swore by all he held sacred that Akoub had never touched liquor and never drank it.

"What was the drink he put in his bottle?" Ibn Naffeh asked him in a whisper.

In spite of his mourning, Raji raced to the truck and snatched the thermos from under the seat, and ran back shouting. "It's coffee, sweet coffee. It's all he ever drank."

Ibn Naffeh asked Abdullah al-Zamel and Manawar al-Khodeiri to taste the coffee, and when they had done it and confirmed that it was coffee, real coffee, like everybody drank, only sweet,

Ibn Naffeh spoke up so that he could be heard by all. "May God curse the Devil! Everyone used to say that he filled that bottle with devil's piss!"

The funeral procession set out from Abu As'ad's coffeehouse. It was a sorrowful procession. There was no sound from the silent marching men but the words "God give him peace; there is no god but God."

At the grave, Ibn Naffeh prayed over the body, but when the time came for the eulogy, no one knew Akoub's full name or his mother's name. Ibn Naffeh looked at the faces around him and spoke without asking anyone and without hesitating. "O Yaacoub son of Fatima, when you come to the abode of the righteous and your Creator questions you, say 'God is my Lord and my faith is Islam, Mecca is the focus of my prayers and the Muslims are my brethren.' Witness that there is no god but God, and that Muhammad is His servant and His prophet."

In silence Akoub was lowered into the grave, which was filled with soil and topped with a rock as a headstone.

Harran slept that night and the following nights with a sorrow it had never known before.

A few days later, Fawaz bin Miteb al-Hathal engraved a prayer on the stone with a large nail, with the words HERE LIE THE REMAINS OF YAACOUB AL-HARRANI.

69

THE CONSTRUCTION OF THE PIPELINE FROM WADI
al-Uyoun to Harran consumed a great deal of
toil and time; instead of taking twenty-two
months, as planned, the work lasted twenty-seven months. The
Americans were in the same nervous, quarrelsome frenzy that
had possessed them during the dredging of the harbor, with one
difference: this time they were in the desert, in the midst of Hell
itself. They were used to going back to their compound every
day, to its swimming pools and air-conditioned rooms, but here,
now, they were like animals surrounded by raging fire. They
ran around, shouting and fighting among themselves and with
others, seized with fear and a sense of impatience. When the
workday was over they returned to their tents but could do
nothing; sleep was impossible. They had vacations every month;
after a month of work, or twenty-five days to be precise, they

went back to Harran for a whole month while another shift reported for duty, but instead of relaxing or changing them, the month of rest made them less willing to return to their onerous tasks, which they could not do efficiently and confronted with an almost murderous ill will.

The year the road construction began was marked by the loveliest weather in years. Work began in early winter, and despite the cold nights the intensely beautiful weather spurred the workers on during the day, especially after the long months and harsh years they'd spent in and around Harran. The plentiful rains rushed through the desert trails and filled the brooks, green vegetation bloomed and birds and animals appeared. Life was easier and less oppressive, and the workers spent long hours gathering flowers and herbs or chasing rabbits, even sometimes gazelles. The early winter evenings were great fun, for in addition to the games the workers invented to stay warm after the sun began to drop past the horizon, gusts of nostalgia filled their chests and made them sing.

The workers knew how to adjust to the ocean of desert around them, and knew even better how to infuriate the Americans and make them lose their tempers. Besides the games they invented spontaneously, they expertly wove strong slingshots from wool with which to hunt kangaroo rats and lizards and hit targets with stones. The clean, polished stones hissed and whistled as they few through the air, and the Americans scattered in all directions to flee these "missiles," which they heard but could not see, and cursed and shouted, asking the workers to stop.

Besides these there were a number of workers whose sole pastime was collecting wood. After leaving it to dry in the sun for days, they built fires and made tea and coffee, and no sooner did the fire catch, filling the camp and surrounding area with smoke, than a new problem arose, as if the dust thrown up by the earthmovers, the winds that gusted up to blow the dust close by and the storms afar off were not enough. The smoke caused no end of bother to the Americans. Despite the heavy goggles they wore, and the thin cloth they pulled over their noses and mouths to screen out the dust, as soon as the flames rose and the smoke meandered in the air and spread quickly, the Americans flew into a rage. Some of them tore off their masks and goggles and threw them on the ground, like children or madmen, while others were seized by fits of coughing and ran toward the fire or their tents, to do something or merely flee.

When these annoyances had run their course, or if, in the eyes of the workers, they had not gone far enough, there was always someone particularly gifted or brilliant at devising practical jokes to play on the Americans. One such was the short, thin, soft-spoken Majalli al-Sirhan. He knew how to throw people into panic every day, with no one aware that he was responsible.

No one could count the times Majalli al-Sirhan let loose rats and lizards in the Americans' tents. He hunted these creatures with tireless zeal, and when he had found a good number he tied them by their legs or tails and pulled them along, and if the time was not right to release them he kept them nearby, and when evening came he dragged them to an American tent and released them. The terrified lizards and kangaroo rats, which had been tied up for long hours, ran for cover as soon as they were let go. They darted into the tents or leaped into the trenches where the workers labored, zigzagged between people's feet, and when the workers heard the Americans' piercing screams, scuffles and cries for help, they looked around for Majalli. He was usually among them or nearby, and they looked at him closely to try to discover if, once again, he was behind the incident. There he was, silent, his features radiating innocence—sometimes he even offered to help the Americans.

Sometimes Majalli gathered snakes to let loose in the tents. He did this twice at least, during successive winters, the first

time when the camp was being built around Station H2, halfway
along the new highway. He explained, at the time, that the area
was full of snake pits, and that the nearby wadi was the snakes'
breeding ground. He spread this story around, and soon the
Americans did not dare go near the wadi. They spent long hours
of the night searching out snakes, and the supplies they urgently
ordered to help combat these dreadful creatures, which speedily
arrived, helped their campaign but did nothing to allay the fear
that filled their hearts.

The second time was during Mr. Hamilton's visit, after much
progress had been made on the pipeline. This time Majalli did
two things the workers were to talk about for a long time to
come. One of the engineers asked Majalli to hand him his toolbox, and Majalli brought it to him while Mr. Hamilton was
inspecting the installation of some equipment. When the worker
opened the box, he screamed and ran away, because a lizard as
big as a cat was reclining on top of the tools, glaring at the
American with his gray eyes and drawing deep, crazed breaths.
Mr. Hamilton, whose face turned yellow and horror-struck,
could not budge forward or retreat. The engineer who had fled
in fright stumbled and fell. He was in a lamentable state: sweat
poured off him, his lips trembled, and the color of his face
changed from blue to yellow to waxy white. Majalli, who had
been standing silent and still amid the fear and horror, stepped
forward, snatched the lizard by the neck and pulled him from
the box, his arm stiff as a stick, heaved the lizard above his head
and struck him against the ground. The lizard got dizzy and ran
off, then changed direction. The Americans, who had been
standing, stunned with fright, now ran away, colliding with
each other to escape the perilous beast. They had no idea what
it was or where it had come from.

More to explain the lizard than to explain his fright, the engineer said that it was his mistake; he had left the toolbox open,

and because it was deep and cool it attracted creatures that wanted someplace to go.

That day Mr. Hamilton ordered that all toolboxes be kept closed; everyone would be held responsible to see that they were. The engineer put locks on the three boxes that were in his keeping.

On the third day of Mr. Hamilton's visit the workers killed a large snake that was as black as night; they put it in an open place, near the tent where the Americans slept, and spread a rumor that this was only one of three snakes that had been together, but that they had been unable to catch the other two. For two nights terror engulfed the entire camp, and Mr. Hamilton left the second day—whether his sudden departure had anything to do with the snakes, no one knew.

Such was life in the three stations that grew up in the course of building the pipeline. The Americans gave these stations names deriving from the name of Harran, since that city was the outlet, with a different number for each—they were H1, H2 and H3— but the workers used the old names for these places or gave them names of their own. The first, Muteira, was about two days' journey from Wadi al-Uyoun. They named the other two stations Askar, "Soldiers," and Quss'a, "Eats." Askar was named for Percy, the chief engineer at H2, who insisted on a head count of workers twice each day, once when they reported for work and again just before they left, always making them stand in a long line; that was why they called it Askar. Quss'a got its name from the Indian cook, who, when asked if the food was cooked or not yet, always answered, "Eats are all finished" or "Eats are not finished."

The three stations started out as names only, with the exception of Muteira, which had a well and some tents, but new wells were dug one after another, tents and equipment piled up, more men arrived, and a new life began, one which the workers got used to and came to love, though the Americans grew unhappier, more uncomfortable and more overcome by difficulties. They ran into endless frustrations in their efforts to heat the tents in winter and cool them in summer, because the generators they set up by the tents, which roared day and night, created more problems than they solved. The machines, which could not start up or shut off properly because of the wind and dust, were soon stopped altogether.

The workers' tents were cooled by the open air every day, and the workers, who endured wordlessly as they huddled in a circle of warmth around the fire and coffeepots during the winter nights, or raised their tent flaps when the summer came after fixing the entrances to face the breezes, often sat and watched the Americans fussing with the generators, which they repaired time and time again. When their bare, burned bodies began to run with sweat, like punctured waterskins, the workers felt a mixture of wonder, joy and pity, because they enjoyed a distinction the Americans lacked.

Had the hardships consisted of nothing but the harsh weather and the problems associated with work, they might have been tolerated or overcome, but one strange night in the fourth month, a night full of rain and thunder which seemed bent on annihilating the desert's thousands of years of silence, a ghost burst on the scene to destroy their tranquillity and fill the Americans' nights and their lives with an almost maddening fear.

It happened unexpectedly. That night, a little before dawn, there was a great commotion at H2. At first it was muffled and confused, but as it grew louder gunshots were heard, the roars of camels and whinnying horses. In the insufficient space of time it took a man to open his eyes, to remember where he was and distinguish the sound of men's voices from the thunder that filled the night sky and the chugging of the machines that had rung in his ears for weeks, in those few moments fire broke out in several of the tents.

No one knew how they could catch fire on such a wet night, and so quickly. As the workers came out to see what the noise was about, the tongues of flame began to consume three tents, among them Mr. Percy's tent and the one that served as an office.

The terrified Americans, who screamed and ran around in every direction, not knowing what to do or where to go, finally clustered around Mr. Percy, who appeared so feeble that a number of workers thought he had been struck by a bullet, and what with fighting the fire and lending assistance to Mr. Percy, the Americans were unable to be of any help. Three of them tried to use fire extinguishers, but they were too late. The workers had already begun heaping sand on the flames, and, having no other options, the Americans threw down their equipment and began to snatch at the sand themselves.

With the first light of dawn they all surveyed the scene, and the questions began: Who did this? Why had he done it? All the cryptic whispers and queries had but one answer: Miteb al-Hathal. He was the only person conceivably willing or able to do such a thing. No worker said it outright or pronounced his name out loud, but his specter filled the whole desert. On the third day a group of men, accompanied by two Americans, arrived from the Central Province to conduct an investigation and fired hostile questions at the workers about who might be behind the incident and which of them were related to Miteb al-Hathal or how well they knew him, and whether they had seen or heard anything about him recently. After the investigation they were all sure that Miteb al-Hathal, who had been gone for long years, no one knew where, was back, and that he would make the desert a hell for the Americans. They were delighted, but their delight was tempered with a certain wariness and anticipation. What they could not explain was that Fawaz bin Miteb al-Hathal and Suweyleh were brought to H2. Some of them said that if Miteb al-Hathal knew that his son was in the camp he would not attack it again; others said that Fawaz was a hostage, and that the Americans would take their revenge on him if anything happened, but Majalli al-Sirhan said that nothing and no one could stand in the way of Miteb al-Hathal.

A guard unit of six men was dispatched from Ujra and was joined by reinforcements wthin a few days, and before long there were as many soldiers as there were Americans in the camp. The workers secretly gave them the same titles and nicknames they had bestowed upon the Americans. Despite the fact that Miteb al-Hathal had vanished once again, it was said that several patrols had set out in pursuit of him—according to one rumor, one such patrol actually met up with him and his gang and killed a number of them, including Miteb al-Hathal himself. The workers heard these stories, circulated by Ghattas, the translator at H2, uneasily at first, but when they saw the head of the guard detachment, Nimr al-Suheil, passing out extra ammunition to his soldiers and barking orders, saying that "Miteb al-Hathal can come on such a black night as this, as dark as the grave with the soil heaped over it, and take you all by surprise!" they were all sure that Ghattas's stories were mere inventions. Miteb al-Hathal, who had taken refuge in the dark and the desert, would be back.

Once again Miteb al-Hathal filled the camp with anxiety, combined with the silent but growing antagonism between the workers and the Americans. The intense surveillance, especially during break periods, and orders to report any strangers or passing travelers to the guard detachment, at first silently ignored by the workers, later provoked curses and arguments. Many of the workers let it be known that they wanted to leave and quit the company, and others insisted on preparing their own meals, which compelled the Americans to ease up on the measures they had imposed and use other means: in addition to bringing in a large number of foreign workers, they began to transfer the Arab workers frequently. The number of observers increased. Ghattas, who'd been far warier and harsher after that night and had clashed with the workers several times during the interrogations, soon left all contact with the workers to Nimr al-Suheil—"He's the only one who can deal with them." Nimr, who was a very rough man and had seemed stern in the first months, now changed completely, and it was said that this was on the orders of the emirate of the Central Province, because force would only create a thousand more Miteb al-Hathals.

The workers slowly returned to their normal routine, and all began to forget Miteb al-Hathal, or pretended to forget him, though rumors resurfaced time and again, circulated by shepherds and passing travelers, which assured them that something was going to happen soon, and that it would be Miteb al-Hathal's doing. Nimr al-Suheil created an atmosphere of provocation and terror by staging frequent search raids, acting on instinct or muddled information, late at night when the workers were in their beds or when they were away from the tents, and while no one ever mentioned weapons or said that they were the object of the searches, they all understood this to be the case, especially after the confiscation of their large knives and other objects that were considered potentially lethal.

The atmosphere of watchfulness and expectation lasted for several tense and uneasy days. The workers' every action was invested with a new meaning; every whisper and every movement was cautiously and fearfully watched. When one of the shepherds tied a tin can to a dog's tail and sent the animal running into the camp, the incident provided the Arabs with hours and hours of sarcastic and pitying smiles, but even the Americans could find no excuse or explanation for the blow the shepherd received from Nimr al-Suheil.

Another time, the guard detachment arrested a man passing by the encampment after dark, and when they found that his name was Miteb, the soldiers and the Americans were delighted, if visibly nervous. The guard unit's movements were cautious and expectant, full of grave anticipation, and so it remained until the following afternoon. That first night, Nimr al-Suheil summoned four workers who were natives of Wadi al-Uyoun and asked them if the detainee was Miteb al-Hathal, but he did not believe them when they said he was not; he regarded their denial as an act of collusion, an attempt to cover up for Miteb, and suddenly he grew very rough and angry with them, shaking his fist in their faces. The next day he summoned Suweyleh to identify the man in the presence of an American; he wanted others to see Suweyleh's reaction if he tried to deny knowing him. When he subsequently had Fawaz brought the man seemed bewildered, not understanding what was happening around him or what was expected of him. Not until the afternoon did things clear up, when two men Nimr knew came from Muteira in search of their father, who had left home four days earlier. They did not know why he'd left or what had become of him—he had lost his grip on reality after the death of his wife.

Miteb al-Hathal remained a phantom, appearing and disappearing for the whole period of the pipeline construction. The Americans resorted to an endless variety of schemes, threats and inducements to get the project finished. They were very wary and worried, never more than when the pipeline was on the verge of completion, at which time they became different people: the slightest word angered them, and any action, especially by Nimr al-Suheil, threw them into fits. One morning, when the third phase was completed with the last weld in Muteira, they were almost insanely happy, more than they had ever been, and began rapturous preparations for a party.

There had been celebrations before, first when the work was

initiated and again when the pipeline reached the station at Quss'a, but this time the Americans were much louder and more excited, as if they wanted to do something completely different.

The exhausted workers, who finished the last of their work in the morning, were much more tired than hungry, so some of the food offered them went uneaten. They needed an hour of rest to relax their mental state and get ready for the party that night.

Shortly after noontime, small waves of workers began heading over to the big encampment set up near the station. Many of them felt something brewing—something would happen that night.

The men felt, in that desolate place, a mixture of triumph and fright: after twenty-seven months of continuous work, of co-existence in the desert with every inch of progress, of daily fights, the work was finished at last. Each of them felt personally responsible for this achievement: had it not been for their efforts, under constant surveillance and in the face of threats, it would never have happened.

Majalli al-Sirhan, who'd been completely absent the night before—many of the workers assumed that he had left for good— was the subject of rumors in the morning when they discovered he was still nowhere to be found. Even Nimr al-Suheil was worried and posted his men all around, and forbade the bedouin to come near. At first Nimr even barred the shepherds who arrived in the morning to get water, but later he rescinded this order on condition they tell all they knew about Miteb al-Hathal and any strange occurrences they had noticed in the recent past. They had nothing to say, and when his warnings and threats got nothing out of them, he let them fetch the water and go. When Majalli al-Sirhan showed up in torn clothes at sundown with a small jackal he'd caught and minor wounds on his body, they were more sympathetic than surprised. They told him to take pity and set the wretched animal free, and to wash his hands and accompany them to Muteira.

"My friends"—he laughed mockingly—"the Americans have sinned, too."

The men were silent; they did not know what he was getting at. He looked at the jackal.

"This son of a bitch almost killed me!" He changed his tone. "I said to myself, 'As long as the Satan's pipe project is ended, the Americans' lives should end now.' I want them to die from fright, but as you see, after all the trouble I went to this beast nearly killed me before I could kill the Americans!"

Ghazi al-Sultan, the odd old man who had filled the men's heads with his weird stories and been the cause of countless problems in the weeks past, asking the Americans to pay him and set him free, as he put it (the Americans said they would give him nothing unless he stayed on the job until the end, at which time he would collect all his pay and be left alone), even Ghazi al-Sultan, Abu Ayesha, seemed unhurried toward the end, as if he no longer wanted to leave the job. The men congratulated him and said that he was a free man at last.

"By God, you sons of bitches, you bedouin," he told them roughly, "you have no souls!"

They were shocked.

"I thought you'd have some respect for an old man," he went on crossly, "and I said to myself, 'These brothers won't desert Abu Ayesha.' Was I wrong!"

In this atmosphere of confused and contradictory emotions, the men began to whisper to each other, at about sundown, that they were late, but that they should delay longer yet. When Ghazi al-Sultan and two or three others told the rest to get moving—it had the tone of an order—they began to move, group by group. Majalli finally consented to let the jackal free, though not before spitting in its face twice and cursing it out roundly for wounding him, but he took along to the party a box of three lizards. He sang as he carried the box containing the wretched, hissing, struggling creatures:

> "O blue-eyed Americans, wherever you go
> Wherever you try to flee,
> The sun is above and the scorpions below.
> The lizards mangle your balls
> And the foxes feast on your asses,
> O blue-eyed Americans, wherever you go
> Where will you flee, O eyes of blue?"

In this fresh atmosphere of turbulent gaiety the men began marching to Muteira, about two miles away. Any conversation would have changed their mood, but as they marched on and the tent and men came into view, with the smoke twisting up into the sunset sky like a light misty cyclone, they felt that their mission was accomplished, and that they were now more relaxed and emptier than ever.

When Mr. Middleton finished his speech marking the completion of the oil pipeline, and Ghattas declaimed his incompetent translation of it, of which the workers understood very little, everyone clapped, some for a long time, until it was clear that they were expressing only sarcasm. Then Ghazi al-Sultan struggled to his feet like a senile camel. He shuffled toward Middleton with everyone's eyes upon him. Middleton recognized the old troublemaker, and usually ignored him, because when he decided to work even the young men envied his strength, so everyone was expecting a surprise. Middleton looked around, aware that something was going to happen. When Ghazi came near him he reached inside his cloak and drew out a handful of coins, then grasped Middleton's hand, placed the money on his palm and closed the hand.

"As long as those who have the money don't give, the poor should give, so this is from me—it's yours, free and clear!"

Middleton was completely taken by surprise. He did not understand why Ghazi al-Sultan was putting the money in his hand or what it was supposed to mean, and for a few moments he was so astounded that he could not catch his breath. He looked embarrassed when the workers roared with laughter, but when Ghattas translated what Ghazi had said, he burst into peals of loud laughter and patted Ghazi's shoulders and began talking, though Ghattas did not translate all of what he said. He announced a pay raise for the workers, effective from that day, and said that all the money the workers had earned would be distributed during the three-day vacation.

Amid the general mood of happy approval, Majalli al-Sirhan stood and carried his box to Middleton. The workers caught their breath, all positive that there was no way the Americans would like this surprise, but Middleton, who thought that this surprise would be like the previous one, was for a moment assailed by doubts that the workers were presenting him with a gift on the occasion of the pipeline's completion; he tried to guess what was happening, but couldn't.

There was total silence as Majalli placed the box in Middleton's hands and retreated a few steps. It seemed as if this skinny bedouin, who had never smiled in his life, was up to something. Majalli moved farther back.

"Is this a present for the project or for me personally?" asked Middleton with feigned innocence as he placed the box on the ground.

His words were translated, and Ghazi, who still stood nearby, spoke up. "Like the money tribute the workers gave the Americans—only this is tribute from the whole town!"

Middleton did not understand a word of what Ghazi was saying, so he asked Majalli again whether the gift was for him or for all those who had worked on the pipeline, and when Majalli told him, by pointing, that it was meant for him personally, he opened the box cautiously. With unexpected energy, one of the lizards leaped out. Middleton looked frightened and stepped back, but when the workers roared with laughter he laughed too, pretending that he had not been taken by surprise and that such joking was tolerable, not to say perfectly acceptable, on this day, and to show his leniency he went closer to the box, which one of the Americans had carefully closed up, and put both his hands on it. He picked it up skillfully and shook it, and when the lizards flew into a commotion inside, he shouted, in a strong but cheerful voice, for Majalli to take his present back.

The workers were called to dinner in this atmosphere of disorder and merriment, and the Americans were so friendly that the Arabs wondered if these were the same people they knew—what had happened to them?

When Middleton and his two guests left, the party was officially over, and Ghattas rose to his feet.

"Attention—attention please!"

They all looked at him, and when there was silence he spoke. "You are all instucted to report to Administration in the morning, and to be ready to leave by noon!"

The workers looked at one another but said nothing.

70

THERE WAS NO END TO THE PROBLEMS DR. SUBHI
al-Mahmilji faced during his first three months
in Harran, and more than once he thought of
leaving for good, to go back from whence he had come, but
every time he reached this point he put off the final decision
until the next day, because his philosophy in life was "Never
make a decision in anger or excitement." So with the passing
of his "condition"—as he called the source of his anger or irritation—he began to calm down and think "with a cool head,"
because "Life is nothing but difficulties, and the proof is that a
child leaves the womb crying and shouting." The doctor laughed
and added, "The difficulties mount with every passing day, from
the moment of birth until the moment of death, made bearable
only by divine grace, and only death puts an end to all the

trouble, and the proof is that the dead feel no pain; they stop crying and complaining, leaving that to those around them—the living."

It was this cool head, then, that guided the doctor's steps and made him think differently from other men, and since he was this way he had no real friends—"Friends are a burden to a man. A wise man depends only upon himself and does not need others." He had no friends even in his hometown. He had many acquaintances, "but friends are like ghouls and griffins." He did not like small talk and hated people knowing his personal business. His wife, who had at first had a very different personality from his, changed with time. She used to discuss him with her women friends, and often talked about what the doctor liked and disliked, what time he went to bed and what time he got up in the morning, but when he learned of this he scolded her angrily. That was in the early years of their marriage, and it taught her to keep quiet, so after that she was content to listen to the stories of the others. When she gave birth to her third son, she stopped attending their receptions altogether and spent all her time raising her boys and looking after the house. This she did with no fuss or formality, but with his piercing intelligence her husband realized it before she ever said a word, and told her later on, "People's talk brings only blindness and deafness!"

The doctor had spent several years in Aleppo before coming to Harran, and before that he'd lived in Tripoli, but details about his family were sketchy and largely contradictory. When he was asked about it he gave vague answers. He said that his grandfather had served as treasurer to the Turkish governor of Anatolia and had often accompanied the governor on the hajj to Mecca in his royal camel-borne litter, the *mahmil,* but had spent the rest of his life nearby in Medina. His father was the private secretary of the governor of the vilayet of Greater Beirut. The doctor said this quickly and indistinctly and added, smiling, to forestall any questions or discussion, "That was long ago . . ."

As to why Dr. Mahmilji had left the hajj caravan to come to Harran, he ascribed his motives to humanitarian concerns and his desire to help the people of this isolated region. When Emir Khaled asked him about it, after the two men had become friends, he laughed. "Stagnant water putrifies, Your Excellency, and man is an ambitious animal. You know that riders tire out a good horse, but when it's time to race she wins."

The emir, who wanted the best possible relations with the physician, as well as the frankest, agreed and nodded. "A man has nothing to say about where he'll be born or where he'll die."

The doctor sometimes alluded, secretly or ambiguously, to the truth about the motives that had drawn him to Harran. There were two: first, his grandfather the treasurer had bequeathed to him title deeds for land in Arabia, on the Sultan's Road, which he wanted to research and make inquiries about—it might come to something, he said. The second motive was his passion for new places, which he'd acquired in his many travels and from the stories he'd read when he was a student in Berlin about the travelers and explorers who had reached the New World, how they had become rich in a short time and left their influence wherever they went.

He only seldom made reference to these motives; indeed, he usually pretended, even to himself, that the inheritance his grandmother had told him about was irretrievably lost: after all, his father had come here before him and spent three years uselessly running from place to place, returning with a sheaf of torn, shabby documents, full of bitterness and disappointment. He'd left the matter to his son, who took the documents eagerly and tried tirelessly to mend and restore them, because he still dreamed that something might come of them. He always told himself,

"Anything is possible in this country, if a man applies himself and stays patient."

The doctor's arrival was one of the most momentous events in Harran in that period. He wore clean, neat clothes into the coffeehouse just hours after his arrival and asked detailed questions of those seated around him there—about the population of Harran, whether or not any doctor had come there before him, the going rents for shops and houses, and the medical services, if any, that the company offered the workers and citizens. Then he asked about the emir—what kind of a man he was, how old he was and what his interests were. These questions called attention to the doctor, and the people wondered about him and watched him carefully. When he had all the information he wanted, he debated with himself whether to go and visit the emir directly or to ask for an appointment. He decided that the best thing was to go and see him as soon as possible, without anyone else's good offices, so that evening he headed for the emirate building with his black medical bag. The emir had heard of the doctor's arrival and was expecting him to visit, but he was not expecting him to come so soon, or at night.

" 'I seek refuge in God from the accursed Satan,' " the emir whispered. Then he turned to those around him and asked, "What will we do for our health, since these devils make their money from sickness and death?"

Then, with exaggerated hospitality, as if the two men had long been friends, the doctor came forward and greeted the emir with warmth and courtesy, and said that he was delighted to be in Harran, and that with the emir's gracious permission he would offer his services to whomever in Harran needed them.

"God willing," he concluded, "I will do my utmost to ease the pain of those suffering from illness, and to offer modern cures."

The emir listened in silence and watched this broad-shouldered white man, wondering to himself what kind of a man he was, and whether or not Harran needed any doctor other than Mufaddi al-Jeddan. He peered at him. "And how do we know that you can cure people?"

The physician smiled confidently and looked into the faces that stared at him.

"The lives and health of the pilgrims to God's holy mosque in Mecca were my own responsibility, Your Excellency." He smiled before continuing. "Anyone can tell lies or make wild claims—except where the practice of medicine is concerned."

He deftly opened up his medical bag as the emir watched.

"With these medicines and instruments, I can cure any sick man. A degree to practice medicine isn't awarded until you take the oath."

He said these last words with a little embarrassment. The emir gazed at the opened bag and felt the urge to examine the contents. Sensing this, the doctor pushed the bag forward so that some of the medicines and instruments showed.

"Do you know how to cure all diseases?" asked the emir.

"With God's help, Your Excellency."

"Where did you work before coming to Harran?"

"I was the doctor for the hajj caravan, Your Excellency, and when I heard that Harran needed a doctor I put my faith in God and came."

The emir nodded and said he had no objection to his staying on to practice medicine in Harran, and the conversation and questions turned to other areas.

This kind of welcome and interrogation was enough for the doctor to close his bag and think of leaving Harran at once, but his weariness after the journey from Ujra, and his intention to rethink his decision the following day, made him stay where he was.

What followed, later that night and in the days that came after, left him even more confused and eager to leave. He had difficulty finding a house, food and a place to get his clothes laundered, and since the people of Harran were unused to having a doctor among them, no one ventured to visit him at first. Most of them predicted an early departure for this man who had come at the wrong time to a place that needed no doctor other than Mufaddi al-Jeddan, but subsequent events made many of them change their minds. The emir's son caught a fever that no one could cure, so Mahmilji took over his treatment and did splendidly. The emir himself watched the doctor's every move attentively, as if trying to learn or understand every detail. The doctor followed all the emir's movements and reactions out of the corner of his eye and showed as much brilliance as he could, exaggerating every move and explaining the condition with as much precision as possible. The emir stared at the medical instruments, so Mahmilji showed him the stethoscope, thermometer and blood pressure gauge. The emir held the stethoscope gingerly, then put it to his ears with the doctor's help, and looked amazed when he heard the strong, regular heartbeats. He could not find the indicator on the thermometer, although Mahmilji did his best to point it out. He regarded the blood pressure kit as too complicated and potentially dangerous, and did not understand what it was for.

When the boy's temperature went down and he was back to normal on the third day, the doctor began to enjoy a great deal of respect and inarticulate awe. This incident was the beginning of a close relationship and the point at which Dr. Subhi al-Mahmilji's star began to rise.

The doctor's brilliance was proven and everyone was already talking about him when Johar, one of the emir's bodyguards, was seriously injured in an accident. He had a wound in his leg and a high temperature, and Mufaddi al-Jeddan, who oversaw his treatment before the doctor arrived, nearly killed him—so

Dr. Mahmilji repeatedly claimed—by insisting that the leg be amputated. The doctor arrived in time to show his artistry. The emir watched carefully as he anesthetized Johar, opened and cleaned the wound, then stitched it up again, all this in the tent beside the emir's own. Had it not been for the doctor's intervention, things would have gone very differently. Within a week of treatment, Johar was able to leave his bed, though he had to lean on a cane when he walked. With time he became proud of the cane and put it to other uses!

These two incidents sealed the doctor's reputation, and established his social standing, since they occurred early in his stay, in spite of the many rumors and reports that Mufaddi al-Jeddan circulated. Dr. Subhi al-Mahmilji was a person of note in Harran. When he rented three adjacent shops from Dabbasi and ordered extensive remodeling to create a surgery and night wards, everyone knew that he had come to stay, and would long remain. Mufaddi al-Jeddan chose a spot near the clinic where he sat for long periods, muttering provocations and curses. He thought nothing of snatching the medicines from the hands of patients on their way to visit the doctor and throwing them away. He said that they were full of small demons which caused irritation to the chest, because they were manufactured by people who did not fear Satan and had not blessed them in the name of God. The doctor, whose doorman and assistant told him everything that Mufaddi was doing, pretended not to know what was going on outside the clinic; he was waiting for his chance to answer "that quack," as he called Mufaddi, for once and for all. Until that opportunity presented itself, he concentrated on building a special relationship with the emir, the officials and the rich citizens of Harran.

The doctor felt alone and defenseless, especially since it was his nature to keep others at a distance; he could not, as yet, send for his wife and children, since Harran was still, in spite of its many residents and more plentiful markets, an unfinished town, or at least one unable to accommodate too many people or cater to their needs. The recently opened elementary school was confined to the first four grades; there were only five boys in the fourth grade, and they were the children of the school's principal and three teachers. There were also two al-Rashed children. Mahmilji's children were too young to go away to school in Beirut and live with their grandmother there while his wife joined him in Harran. He had also not found suitable housing yet—had not, actually, looked around seriously, for he had not yet made a final decision about staying.

The other thing that made him feel so lonesome was the fact that his assistant, Muhammad Eid, who had worked with him for the past seven years and accompanied him on the hajj caravans, had promised to show up within a month, or two months at the outside. Now three whole months had passed, and he had not arrived or sent word. Muhammad Eid was not any ordinary assistant, whom the doctor could easily replace or manage to do without, for in addition to carrying out the usual duties of a doctor's assistant, he was highly intelligent and a quick learner, and he often executed important tasks that the doctor himself neglected or forgot about. Besides, there was the congenial intimacy bred of their long years of work together, and Muhammad's willingness to do chores completely unconnected with his formal duties—he cooked meals, cleaned the clinic and wards, and did other things as well.

Only Muhammad Eid could do all this, and the doctor could not train anyone else and expect him to be like Muhammad— if for no other reason, his age and this place in which he found himself made it less possible.

The doctor's head was full of these reasons, and he reviewed them every day during the long wait for Muhammad Eid's arrival, but in fact there were other, far more important reasons that made him truly miserable and gave him the compelling feeling that he was alone and friendless amid all these strangers. Muhammad Eid was the only person who could make and keep friendships between the doctor and other people. Such relations meant a great deal to the doctor. Muhammad Eid knew how to talk about him and represent him to others. He talked about a living legend, a man possessed of supernatural powers, who wrested the sick from the grasp of Azrael, the Angel of Death, and told him to get lost! This was when others doctors had given up and admitted their total inability to prevail, and "only Dr. Subhi told Death, 'I'm stronger than you,' and saved the man's life!" Muhammad Eid spoke not only of the many times the doctor surpassed all others, but of the instances in which he outdid himself, because "he's passionate about his profession—he was born for it and nothing else." He had an extraordinary ability to tell the simplest stories in a magical and deeply affecting way, and even after he had told them dozens of times they always seemed new, as if they had happened only yesterday. He knew when to tell the stories and to whom. Sometimes even the doctor was struck when people asked him about the stories; as a rule he could not recall all the details his assistant described!

Another factor that strengthened the relationship between the two men was that Muhammad Eid was a good judge of people and knew how to deal with them—"The doctor is very busy," he would say when relatives or friends dropped by. "The doctor is in the middle of an operation," when the police came to question an accident victim. "The doctor is out," when poor people came in. True, he sometimes made mistakes in certain instances or toward certain people, but these were small mistakes that he could always explain later; the people concerned eventually forgot about them, and he himself forgot them the same day.

The doctor, who was fond of his assistant, spoke highly of

his services and praised his diligence, often warned him, "I didn't see or hear anything . . . you understand?" Muhammad Eid would smile and nod and step back after delivering his report, and add, "Don't worry, Doctor, leave it to me. I'm in charge."

There were other reasons the doctor never mentioned. He'd say, "Give him the good needle," and Muhammad Eid would take charge of the first or final touches with most of the patients. After registering the patient in large but indistinct letters, his condition and early symptons, always in the illegible scribble doctors use, he wrote "stomach pains," "rash" or "irregular pains in the extremities." After this he began to prepare the patient mentally, telling him that his ailment was minor, or that he had come in time, or that God Almighty had shown him mercy by sending him to Dr. Subhi. After a long pause, to let his words sink in, he smiled confidently. "After the doctor examines you and prescribes medication the needle will be ready, and it will take effect in five minutes—God willing, it will do the trick."

There were very few patients whose posteriors were not pierced by Muhammad Eid's needle, and even fewer were those who failed to ask if the doctor would prescribe them a needle, and if it would be of the same type and potency as the one Muhammad Eid would administer. Dr. Subhi gave very short answers, leaving the patient confused until being turned over to the assistant. After asking, or rather ordering, the patient to hurry up and get ready, because "the needle is waiting," Muhammad Eid took the prescription and read it appraisingly, nodding to show that he recognized the condition and considered this the appropriate treatment. In that tiny cubicle, which had once been, perhaps, a hideout or lavatory for a single person and was now the smallest room in the world, barely big enough for one man to stand up in, the patient prepared himself behind a drawn curtain as Muhammad Eid asked, "Are you ready?" On hearing the reply he deftly lifted the curtain to reveal the lower half of the patient's body. He finished his task quickly, always repeating, "This is what you needed," or "The good needle!" It was worth the cost of the whole visit, which was all-inclusive and not broken down by services, so that no one was told, "The cost of the needle is this much and administering so much more." No patient was allowed to request that anyone other than Muhammad Eid administer the needle, though this never happened. When the doctor raised his examination fees, the cost of "the good needle" went up as well. Dr. Subhi had embarked on his medical career charging less than other doctors, especially the well-known ones who were established in Tripoli and Aleppo before him, who often scoffed at his competence and integrity when his name came up. They cited the supplementary fees he got from here and there, referring to "the good needle," as it was widely known, and his practice of selling the medicines he had obtained as samples.

So the reasons for the doctor's loneliness and isolation were real enough, and when Muhammad Eid finally arrived early in the fourth month, the doctor's appearance and behavior changed drastically—he was a new man. The silence he so often used as a barrier, and his brusque conversation, gave way to a new smoothness . . . Muhammed Eid's. The assistant obeyed the doctor in everything and asked no questions. The food Dr. Subhi complained of so bitterly, fearing even to touch it sometimes, "because no one here knows how to cook, or wants to help me," was no more, now that meals were prepared by his assistant. The doctor's worries faded away and his strength returned; much could be said about his cleanliness, new clothes and the way he watched and bargained with the market craftsmen. A number of things came together within the first few days of Muhammad Eid's arrival, and the clinic, which was now finished and organized, looked just like the clinic Dr. Subhi had had in Tripoli twenty years earlier. He was a little unhappy with his residence, which was in the shop next door to the clinic, after hearing of some of the remarks people made about it, but he had a side door built and painted light blue, over which he placed a sign made by one of the schoolteachers who had been sent out to Harran. It read, in magnificent calligraphy, DR. SUBHI AL-MAH-MILJI—RESIDENCE. Another sign painstakingly designed in Ujra for the front entrance of the clinic, in the main street, read, DR. SUBHI AL-MAHMILJI, PHYSICIAN AND SURGEON. SPECIALIST IN IN-TERNAL AND VENEREAL DISEASES, UNIVERSITIES OF BERLIN AND VIENNA.

The "venereal diseases" specialty, which was one of his many special fields, and which he always referred to only fleetingly, was important and impressive. He knew its importance, since it provided him with intimate though complex ties with many people.

He had not been in Harran long before establishing a close relationship with the emir—so close that many people were convinced that they had met before. They were led to think so by the way Dr. Subhi had gone to see the emir on his first night, and by their long private meetings. In the beginning, and in all cases when others were present, the emir was very fond of discussing diseases and their causes, symptoms and remedies. He paid rapt attention to Dr. Subhi's explanations, although most of the others present rarely understood anything. They got so confused that they could not understand how even the doctor could retain all this information. The doctor was always listening and nodding. The emir usually expressed his desire to use the stethoscope on one of his men so he could hear his heartbeats. The instrument never failed to amaze him, and he would have given anything to own one. Whenever the two met, the con-

versation inevitably turned to that sensitive but exciting topic
"the sexual question." The doctor gave out information only
sparingly, but his responses to their questions aroused even more
powerful curiosity, leaving each of his listeners deep in thought
and determined to make an appointment with him.

With the passage of time and the consolidation of the friendship between the doctor and the emir, the questions became more
direct and far less naive.

Dabbasi, who had eagerly rented the three shops to the doctor,
consented quickly to his proposals for remodeling them to suit
his needs for a clinic, ward and doctor's residence. He was proud
that Mahmilji had chosen these shops, since he coveted his friendship, and he agreed to make any subsequent modifications. This
led to indirect and inconclusive discussions about the possibility
of adding a second story and even a third, to provide for an even
larger hospital and more fitting residence for the doctor and his
family.

Dabbasi gave more time than was his custom to the supervision of the remodeling. He spent a great deal of time with the
doctor, and although he had decided, after much thought, to
work the conversation around to the subject of the medicines
and restoratives that he now felt in need of for the first time, he
could never summon the courage. He felt embarrassed and uncomfortable. When he got close to the topic he always found
obstacles to bringing it up and had to leave it until another time.

As the doctor's friendship with the emir and Dabbasi grew
stronger, so did his relations with the "Shahbunder of Merchants" Mohieddin al-Naqib, Hassan Rezaie and others. Even
Ibn Naffeh, who had been very wary and watchful at first,
listening to what Mufaddi al-Jeddan and others had to say, often
saw the doctor in the mosque and was impressed by his piety.
He also knew that he had been the headman of the hajj caravan,

and so came to tolerate and even approve of him. After Muhammad Eid came to Harran and told his repertoire of hajj
stories, of how the doctor had saved dozens of pilgrims from
certain death and spent long days and nights caring for the sick,
and had answered many of Ibn Naffeh's questions, the old man
made up his mind. He told many people that Ibn Jeddan was
wrong and did not know what was best for the Muslims because
he was slandering an upright man. He went further than that,
saying that if Harran could cope with its large population of
merchants, which grew every day, then it would surely not be
harmed by having two doctors—the sick, after all, could seek
treatment from whomever they chose, from Ibn Jeddan or the
new doctor; there was no difference. Ibn Naffeh quoted several
instances from the life of the Prophet which extolled cleanliness
and the care of the sick.

Mufaddi al-Jeddan would have been the last person to suspect
that Ibn Naffeh would give his support to the new doctor. When
he found out, he rolled up his right sleeve and shook his fist in
the faces of a group of men. "Ibn Naffeh must be dreaming!
Does he think that man can save a life that God has decided to
end?" He shook his fist and laughed. "Tell him to put that idea
out of his head. He must be blind."

Ibn Naffeh flew into a rage when he was told what Mufaddi
al-Jeddan said; he frothed at the mouth. "Tell him, 'Ibn Naffeh
does it every day and every night, and if he doubts it, let him
bring me his mother, and he can wait by the door to look and
listen for himself.'"

The feud between the two men deepened and grew more
complex, but the doctor did not intervene directly. He heard all
of what was said—his guard, Hadib, told him everything that
went on, and Muhammad Eid supplied many of the details.

"If Ibn Naffeh wanted," Dr. Subhi told the emir confidently

one evening, "I could turn him into a youth of twenty so that he could make up for everything he missed."

The doctor's fleeting remark, which he intended as a joke, rang for a long time in the ears of his listeners, and those who had never thought to broach this subject with him, because they felt no need to, felt that they might someday require these new and amazing powers. Those whose potency had already diminished, who urgently needed some kind of help, felt as though they had finally found what they had prayed for; they hung on the doctor's every word, and their eyes never left him. Without having wished it, unknowingly, Dr. Subhi al-Mahmilji became the ideal and the hope of many.

Dr. Subhi knew that Harran needed a doctor, but he had not given sufficient attention to the medicine or pharmacy problem. He had kept most of the medicines from the hajj caravan and asked his assistant to bring certain other drugs with him when he came, but Eid had found only enough to last a month, and the supply would surely be depleted the following month, so the doctor began to think, among other things, of making friends with the Pakistani doctor who worked for the company. He spoke to Muhammad Eid one night as they prepared prescriptions. "To get the medicines we need, we have to establish direct contact with the source, and right now the source is the company, at least until our friend Sidqi al-Mufti or someone like him comes along."

Dr. Subhi used all of his brilliance and cunning to cultivate Dr. Muhammad Jinnah and exchange visits with him. At first they were only courtesy calls, which were a little awkward because Dr. Jinnah could speak only English and a few words of Arabic, and Dr. Subhi's English was "a reading knowledge, not give-and-take English," as he said, so at their first meeting they had to use other methods—writing, gestures, the dictionary and a few common Arabic words—to communicate. It was easier on subsequent occasions because the Pakistani doctor learned more Arabic words and Dr. Subhi more English, though his pronunciation was so strange that Dr. Jinnah could hardly understand him. As time went by his heavy accent became the object of good-natured amusement, and the two men's relations developed almost into friendship as they came to understand one another in their special way.

71

ARRAN APPEARED—TO ITSELF, IF NOT TO OUT-
siders—to be a dangerous city during the in-
auguration of the oil pipeline. For a week or
ten days before the ceremony there was a constant stream of
arriving policemen, government employees, guards and servants, in addition to huge quantities of foodstuffs and sheep.
The emir received an uninterrupted series of sometimes contradictory instructions.

The people did not know quite what to think. They felt a little
uneasy. There was unusual bustle at the emirate building and in
the daily messages between the emirate and the American compound, and the emir summoned many of the town notables for
long colloquies whose topics were the subject of much gossip
in Harran. Three senior Americans paid an unexpected visit to
the emirate, and the next day the emir went to the American

compound for a tour of the shoreline area and the three tents the Americans had set up within their compound, in a spacious garden near the swimming pool. It was said that these were for guests, because the sultan's deputy—the crown prince—would stay at the emir's residence or in the emirate building.

The unceasing movement, memorable for its chaos, confusion, the emir's sporadic fits of anger, and those of the deputy emir and even their subordinates, went on for days, as did the questions of the people who never paused in the activity for a single moment, which almost no one seemed able to answer, whether they dealt with the number of guests due in Harran or how long they would stay, or the last-minute instructions to shopkeepers, especially in the three main streets which the procession would pass down. These shopkeepers were instructed to decorate their premises with colored flags, banners and other ornaments to demonstrate their joy, but they did not know exactly how to go about the decorating since they had never done anything like it before. They watched Muhammad Eid putting up wooden planks in front of Dr. Subhi al-Mahmilji's clinic with the help of the carpenter who had remodeled it; within a few hours there was a great arch that almost completely covered the clinic, and several carpets that the doctor had recently purchased from a merchant ship were draped over it. All of his carpets, with the exception of three which he'd laid out in his clinic and bedroom, were spread over the arch and surmounted with colored paper that he usually kept in his large medicine cabinet. The noted calligrapher from Ujra, Raouf al-Saqqa, who had recently relocated in Harran, decorated one long banner with slogans the doctor himself had spent most of the night thinking up and writing down, refining and polishing until he found the right ones. Dr. Subhi could not have been more delighted with the final result, and it was strung across the street, right in front of the marketplace, under his direct supervision. Several times he asked that the ropes be pulled tighter so that the banner would hang higher, and when it was done he went to the end of the street to look, then walked back with his eyes never leaving the arch and the banner. He was delighted.

"Great men and great achievements deserve this and more!" he shouted.

The doctor's initiative showed the way to many others, and even the emir himself wasted no time in going to Harran to visit the doctor in his clinic the very afternoon the arch was erected. Although he explained that his visit was spontaneous, Muhammad Eid remarked confidently that "the emir's visit to the doctor pertains to much bigger and more momentous questions." He paused and looked at the faces of those who had asked him about it. "You know how close they are—they're not just friends, they're brothers."

No one in Harran really understood what the visit was about, but they all talked about it.

Everyone in the city was agitated and impatient, but the emirate was in even greater turmoil; no one had ever imagined that such important people would visit Harran, let alone in such numbers, and now that they were coming everyone wondered how they would be impressed by what they saw and heard. Although the townspeople were awed almost to the point of terror, their feelings of pride, which bordered on haughtiness, prevailed and grew stronger, and many of those who had not been instructed to do any decoration went ahead and displayed what ornamentation they could find, even if it was only some flags or colored rags.

The only person who refused, to the point of utter scorn, was Ibn Naffeh. When he walked into Rashedi Street and saw Dr. Subhi's triumphal arch, he was so deeply shocked that he began to screech. "Oh . . . you son of a bitch! You Albanian! We thought you were an honest man, and you turned out to be one

of them!" He paused and went on in a tone of withering sarcasm.
"Like they say! The greyhound is brother to the cur!"

Ibn Naffeh would not stop shouting and cursing in spite of
Muhammad Eid's efforts to calm him down and explain things.
The group of men standing underneath the arch in front of the
clinic, looking alternately at Ibn Naffeh and the decorations,
which they thought magnificent, did not take his shouting seriously at all; they said that he did not mean a word of it—such
behavior on the old man's part had been taken for granted since
the coming of the Americans, and he could not abandon it now.
One of the men spoke up with the intention of creating new
discord. "My friends, the whole problem is that the doctor won't
give Ibn Naffeh the needle he craves!"

The men winked and roared with laughter, and the laughter
had scarcely died away when Muhammad Eid addressed them
jokingly. "If that's the only problem, listen, maybe I can talk
the Haji into it!"

"And who are you to say that—you Albanian?" asked Ibn
Naffeh angrily. He was enraged. Muhammad Eid, surprised,
only shrugged and said nothing.

"Listen . . . listen," said one man from a distance, to escape
Ibn Naffeh's wrath and possibly a blow.

When everyone looked toward the voice, the man turned as
if to leave.

"When you get old, your ——— gets shorter and your tongue
gets longer. That's what old age is all about!"

Ibn Naffeh could not believe that anyone would talk to him
that way, or say what the man had said. For a few moments he
was stunned, and when all the men laughed and their eyes scalded
him to see his reaction, he turned his back on them and strode
toward the nearby shank of the arch, pulled his clothes aside and
shook his member at them, then squatted down to piss. Silence
fell as the men's faces showed their surprise and shock. He stood

up again and laughed in anger and mockery. "You Albanian, tell your master that Ibn Naffeh is as strong as an ox and wants nothing from him, and I've paid a fitting tribute to his monstrosity here!"

Ibn Naffeh walked away with his head held high, paying no attention to the stares and whispers that followed him. When he was gone, the doctor's voice was heard from his office, shouting for Muhammad Eid to come at once.

Ibn Naffeh was the only person in Harran to show any sign of dissatisfaction, but his actions, though they made the men laugh and frightened Muhammad Eid, were soon forgotten in the preparations and general commotion. Even Johar, who had been promoted to chief of the guard units, responsible for the security of the guests, shook his baton and laughed when he passed by the arch and laughing men and was told what Ibn Naffeh had said.

"Let the old man rave," he said. "He's crazy—his balls are bothering him."

The preparations continued and were speeded up in the final three days. On the fourth day the sultan's deputy, Crown Prince Khazael, arrived.

The motorcade was preceded by a dark green pickup truck carrying eight guards armed with long rifles, swords, bullet-packed bandoliers across their chests and curved daggers of various shapes and sizes. Johar sat in the front seat of the vehicle, beside the driver, with his baton-wielding hand outside the window. There had been eight cars following the pickup when it left Ujra, but only six entered Harran because two of them broke down on the road; had Crown Prince Khazael not been paying attention, the riders of those two cars would have been left stranded on the road between Ujra and Harran. As it was, they piled into the other cars, so that all except Prince Khazael's car were bursting with soldiers of indistinguishable rank. The prince's car was a blood-red Cadillac; the others were gray or beige except for one black car. They were all Fords and Chevrolets.

Prince Khazael's car rode in the middle. Its size and shape, even its color and its fluttering flag, made it look like a slaughtered sacrifice in the middle of a moderate feast, or a white sheep surrounded by a herd of goats.

Beside Prince Khazael, like a wary cat, sat Emir Khaled al-Mishari. People who saw the motorcade enter Harran, and who ran beside the red car, said that Emir Khaled was silent and dripping with sweat and did not wave to the boys who rapped on the car windows. In the other cars, the prince's retinue, including the guards and drivers, were all smiles and showed a great deal of good-natured tolerance as the motorcade wound through the streets of Harran. The procession stopped twice because the men and boys blocked the street while others held sticks aloft and danced, and it paused a third time when Dr. Subhi's arch caught Prince Khazael's eye and he asked the driver to slow down while his secretary read him the message written on the banner. When the motorcade pulled up to the emirate building, the deputy emir, Dr. Subhi al-Mahmilji and other Harran notables were waiting.

The emirate was in a state of chaos. The movement of the men inside, especially the guards and attendants, was too much and disrupted many of the carefully planned arrangements, so that many of those waiting were unable to get near Prince Khazael or greet him. This was the case with Daham, Ibn Jeddan and two schoolteachers, but Mohieddin al-Naqib was shoved forward as he was being presented to the emir, and had he not regained his footing at the last minute he would have fallen on his face. Prince Khazael greeted him warmly and smiled as Emir Khaled whispered in his ear who Naqib was.

Dr. Subhi stood out prominently in the crowd because of his elegant though not extravagant clothing, his eager look, his white complexion and the smile that never left his lips. He rarely looked directly into anyone's eyes, so that he would not feel embarrassed; as soon as his eyes met anyone else's, especially those of Prince Khazael's attendants, he looked away as if in apology or in greeting from afar. Even so, he did not miss a single one of the men. When he went to bed that night and recalled the day's events, he was able to summon up almost every face and detail he had seen. He remembered everything that had been said, reviewed it all carefully and thought it over at his leisure.

Dr. Subhi had a special presentation to the emir. True, he was presented after Hassan Rezaie, Dabbasi and Naqib, but this did not diminish his importance, for the emir had mentioned early on, even before presenting him to Prince Khazael, that it was he who had erected the arch that had caught the prince's attention, at least so the doctor deduced from the prince's effusive handshake. He did not actually hear what the two officials had said to each other.

The doctor's high standing, not to say his total supremacy in the community, became clear after the cups of coffee were drunk. The school principal longed to deliver Harran's official speech of welcome to Prince Khazael, and had done his utmost to induce the deputy emir to choose him, but after long discussions in the emirate, and on the instructions of Emir Khaled himself, it was decided that the principal would read an introduction and answer questions that came up during the visit, but the speech would be delivered by Dr. Subhi. No explanation was made and no reason given. The principal, who submitted disgustedly to the decision, talked longer than a master of ceremonies ever should, which made the doctor visibly restless, not least because the schoolmaster was saying many of the things that he himself wished to say in his welcoming address to Prince Khazael. He did not stay angry for long, though, for before he knew it his own voice rang out in the large tent erected inside the emirate building.

Dr. Subhi was different from other men. He was, among other things, the greatest physician in the Near East and the Middle East, as Muhammad Eid loved to point out. Eid loved these cryptic geographic designations, though he often wondered to himself, and intended to ask the doctor or others, exactly what regions they referred to and which countries they encompassed. He never actually discovered the answers, but he insisted on using these expressions, especially when he was boasting.

No one disputed that description of the doctor, but no one knew or even suspected that he was also an eloquent speaker who had memorized numberless poems and proverbs, stories and anecdotes, which he always recounted in a strong, clear voice. Even the principal, who had introduced Dr. Subhi al-Mahmilji very briefly, as if to belittle his importance, shook his head in astonishment, and many people saw that, when the doctor rose up before the gathering as if he were the only person there. Even Prince Khazael, who was not used to such speeches, preferring stories and poems to what he called, among his close friends, "dervishes' sermons"—even he was bewitched and paid close attention to what the doctor said, especially since his pronunciation was never more beautiful than when proclaiming the titles "deputy to the sultan, and crown prince."

The speech was not long enough to be boring or so short as to seem an onerous duty. The doctor had chosen a specific length and included three verses of poetry and one proverb.

"Harran will remember," he said in closing, "for scores of years, for hundreds of years, this singular day of her history, the day she was visited by the son of the greatest sultan of all time, our beloved Prince Khazael, the day his hands graciously opened the pipeline of blessings and prosperity for this people, that love might flow for all people, near and far, and that all of us might enjoy a more comfortable life.

"On behalf of Harran, in the name of its men and women, old and young, in the name of the city and the desert, in the name of Emir Khaled, who has toiled day and night; on behalf of all those present, and in my own name, we offer you, Your Royal Highness, the most solemn assurances of our appreciation, love and loyalty. 'And say, Strive, for God and His messenger will guide your acts.' May the peace and blessings of Almighty God be upon you all."

Afterward, that same afternoon, a feast given in the American compound to celebrate the completion of the pipeline, and followed there by a dinner party in honor of the prince, which was limited to a number of guests, including Dr. Subhi, boasted the same pomp, splendor and grace. Unnoticed by all but a few, a strong and trusting friendship and even affection was built up between Prince Khazael and Dr. Subhi al-Mahmilji by way of small details of conversation, stories, proverbs and poetic verses at lunch in the emirate, in the tent at the compound, and that night at the emir's residence. When the next day came and Prince Khazael was preparing to leave, Dr. Subhi approached the prince's closest adviser, Zaid al-Heraidi, in a state of visible agitation and whispered in his ear. Zaid laughed and spoke loudly enough for the prince to hear. "It's his affair . . . he will accept the gift."

When the prince turned to them questioningly, Dr. Subhi took a small carpet from the hands of Muhammad Eid, who stood behind him, and presented it humbly to the prince, who took it and looked at Zaid al-Heraidi, then at the doctor.

"A humble gift, Your Royal Highness," said the doctor. "Its only value is in your accepting it, and I shall remember this honor for the rest of my life."

The prince laughed delightedly and unrolled the carpet. He asked how old it was and where the doctor had bought it.

"A gift from my grandfather to my father," said the doctor humbly, "and from my father to me, Your Royal Highness, and from me to the greatest of men!"

That evening, when the doctor and his assistant were recalling the events of these two days, so that they would forget nothing, Muhammad Eid suddenly shifted around to face the corner where the doctor had piled the carpets he'd recently purchased, asking the question with his eyes before he finished his sentence: "I think, doctor, that we had bought a carpet just like the one that—"

The doctor answered quickly, averting his eyes to avoid his assistant's gaze. "No, that was another one. There was a certain resemblance, but they were as different as day from night!"

72

MUFADDI AL-JEDDAN WAS NOT ONLY THE "PHY-
sician" for all Harran before the coming of
Dr. Subhi al-Mahmilji; he was also its "odd
job man," as they called him. When no one needed his medicines
or remedies he fetched water to homes; when he got tired of
doing that he did small chores, helping the fishermen or making
short boat trips, earning his bread by helping the seamen with
the rowing. On shore he helped the construction workers and
stonecutters, kept an eye on roaming camels or went to the desert
to gather herbs. When he got tired of all these jobs, as he often
did, he hunted rabbits and mountain goats and came back with
an impressive number of them, which he generously gave away,
often keeping none for himself.

His appearance had changed very little, and imperceptibly, in
the many years since he first came to Harran. His face was like

that of a child, with its bold eyes, loud, innocent laugh and large, gleaming white teeth, and his slim, lanky body seemed carved from smooth stone or wood. He was as solid and permanent as Harran's well or hills. Even the women of Harran, who had known him for as long as he'd been there, said when they saw him now that "it was like his mother weaned him yesterday—the years don't touch him."

Despite the long years he had lived in Harran, becoming one of its sons, or even more than that, he had never married, did not own a house and had only enough possessions to fill a medium-sized saddlebag. Most of these were his medical items—irons, instruments for bloodletting, and the herbs and remedies which he kept in small, tightly sealed bags. He knew each by its feel, without having to open it, and when similarities in the size or shape of a bag mixed him up, one sniff was enough to tell him what it was.

A long time afterward, after Harran underwent the changes and the floods of people moved in, men would sometimes pull money out of their pockets and tell Mufaddi, "If you can tell me how much this is worth, it's yours." Mufaddi would turn the coin or bill over and examine the lines and marks upon it, then return it, saying, "Do you want the truth? By God, I don't know!" The men would laugh a little and then try again with another piece of money, with the same results.

Mufaddi had never worked for money and did not hide his contempt for it, nor did he trade his services for favors. He got extremely angry when anyone offered to pay him, no matter how much or how little.

"I swear to you, people of Harran, the day will come when they try to sell water!" he muttered, shaking his head in distress and looking at the ground. "Fear God. Keep the faith, my friends!"

Because he was like that, the people viewed him more tolerantly than they did others and treated him kindly. He freely entered any house in Harran as if it were his own, and he never hesitated to ask for food or drink. When his clothes or sandals wore out, he thought nothing of demanding new ones. While it was true that he did not do this often, since he always mended his clothes and replaced his sandal straps several times over, sooner or later they would be beyond repair and he would approach some of the more prosperous folk to ask some for sandals and others for clothing. Others frequently spared him the trouble—Khazna often did this for him. She too was a village doctor, treating mainly women and children. In spite of her poor, blurry eyesight, she was always the first to know that Mufaddi's robe was torn or his sandals worn out, and she went about ingeniously getting him new ones in such a way that no one knew about it. Once, one of Harran's rich told Mufaddi that he needed to meet with him about an important matter that very day and then gave him new clothes and sandals. That was how it went, despite Mufaddi's protests.

This was Mufaddi, who had lived so many long years in Harran that people had forgotten that he had moved here, just as so many others had. They had even forgotten why he had come. As to why he had never married or acquired a house, no one knew but himself, although Khazna once said, in a moment of absentmindedness or confusion, that there was a woman waiting for Mufaddi, and that was why he had left his hometown and family, though he would surely return someday.

Khazna said this to Ibn Naffeh's wife and Abdullah al-Saad's mother, and when the two women asked for more details she tried to avoid answering, then changed the subject; she subsequently denied that she had said anything of the kind, but had instead only been guessing or speculating on her own. When Ibn Naffeh asked Mufaddi if there had been a woman involved in his coming to Harran, he paled and appeared deeply disturbed, and denied that any person, man or woman, had caused him to move; then, as was his habit, he changed the subject.

Could that have been the real reason behind the two men's silent feud? Were they really enemies or only estranged friends, or were their stars wrong, as Mufaddi said? Ibn Naffeh said that Mufaddi did not know the Lord because he did not fast and avoided prayers whenever possible. When the fasting month of Ramadan came around, he went to sea or into the desert, and when asked why he was not fasting he said it was because he was traveling. When it was prayer time, he pretended to be busy to escape that duty, or if he had no excuse he prayed only very briefly and was the first to leave the mosque, hurriedly, lest someone stop him.

Harran changed every day, but Mufaddi never changed. The bedouin who came from the desert by way of Ujra always went straight to him if they were ailing. They went to him or sent for him whenever they were sick or in pain. They knew the symptoms from the first, and if they did not know the cure or did not have the necessary remedies, they rushed to Mufaddi before the aches and pains overtook or incapacitated them. Town dwellers came from the same direction but from more distant places, though they did not expect his kind of treatments and hesitated to consult him or put themselves under his care. Some of them made fun of him, but as their pains worsened by the day and then the hour they had no choice but to go to him and do as he told them. These were the two groups of people that were bound to Mufaddi and he to them. While the bedouin did not complain or hesitate to go to him, some of the town dwellers still had their reservations about his prescriptions and were quick to forget all the times he had cured them. They heaped abuse and slander upon him and said he was senile and a quack, but they considered themselves even more foolish than he for believing him and actually taking the bitter potions he prepared.

Those who came from the sea did not know Mufaddi at first and so were indifferent to him; they had brought their own doctors and medicines. Some of the poor who had never seen doctors kept their own remedies in small colored-glass bottles or wrapped in rags. The few times they saw Mufaddi in the market, outside the mosque or in Abdu Muhammad's bakery, as he applied hot irons to the ailing, they turned away and felt afraid of him, and they avoided him. Some claimed to have terrible black nightmares after seeing him at work in the marketplace—nightmares in which they were his victims.

Khazna al-Hassan, Mufaddi's partner in this demanding profession, was a proficient healer, though years after Mufaddi's arrival in Harran it was said that he was more capable than she. She looked after the women and children, healing them as best she could, and serving as a midwife, especially after life changed in Harran. She also kept vigil with sick and dying men and women to pray with them, help them to drink water and recite what short Koranic verses she knew. She had a very low, subdued voice, and Ibn Naffeh often said that this was because she knew nothing of the Koran but the Sura of Praise—she recited in a low and indistinct voice so that no one would hear her mistakes. All the same, everyone forgave her mistakes and was quick to forget them; the mere mention of God's name over the heads of the dying soothed them and helped them enter the hereafter more comfortably, their souls at peace, and perhaps without sin as well.

Khazna often borrowed medicines from Mufaddi, consulted him in certain cases and referred her patients to him when there was nothing she could do to cure them. She often claimed that only her "famous brother"—Mufaddi—could deal with such a case, and he always accepted the challenge. When the patients who came to her were female, whether townswomen or bedouin women, she could not refer them, and so Mufaddi worked indirectly, giving her advice and instructions so that she could treat them. She did all this because of a vow she had made after her son left; he had gone to sea for a few days which stretched into months and then years, and there was no word of him. Khazna al-Hassan vowed that she would treat the sick and do all that was in her power to do for them until her son came back, and this she still did, awaiting his return.

It was easy, or at least possible, for Harran to provide a living for both doctors, Mufaddi al-Jeddan and Subhi al-Mahmilji, because the population grew every day, and most of Mufaddi's customers would not have dreamed of visiting the new doctor or having anything to do with him. Others, those who welcomed Subhi al-Mahmilji as if they had been waiting for him, had grown tired of Mufaddi months before the new doctor even came. Most of those who earlier had never hesitated to give him new clothes or sandals had stopped doing so, because Mufaddi, who knew nothing about money and refused to deal with it, who scorned it, drew no distinction between his own money and that of others. Now that Harran was flush with money for the first time, now that it flowed into everyone's hands, Mufaddi underwent a strange change, and his change grew more noticeable as wealth proliferated. Mufaddi, who had been a nearly silent man for long years, was silent no longer. Khazna al-Hassan felt the change more strongly than anyone else, and she was the first to notice that Mufaddi al-Jeddan was on a dangerous course, and she was positive that this course could have only one outcome: his downfall. The people he was cursing and threatening were more powerful than he was! She could not begin to understand Mufaddi's new madness. She guessed somewhat obscurely that he was at the end of his tether, that whatever inner force he had been stifling was stronger than she had ever imagined, that this was at the bottom of the change that now possessed him.

One day she saw him with his head bandaged from a wound.

"That son of a bitch Daham would strike his own father," she told him. "He killed Ibn Rashed and then said 'He died God's own death,' but there you go making trouble for Daham and anyone else you don't like. Let them be, old man."

He wagged his head. She did not know whether he was agreeing with her or getting ready for the next round.

"You need some time to recuperate. Turn your thoughts to God, you lucky man."

Mufaddi laughed mockingly but said nothing.

This happened after Daham sent one of his men to beat up Mufaddi and bloody him because he had dared to say that Daham was robbing people, Arabs and Americans, the living and the dead. Mufaddi was beaten again after that incident, this time in the market, though no one knew whether Saleh al-Dabbasi or Mohieddin al-Naqib was behind it; he had cursed and slandered both of them. There was a third time, as well. One day the saddlebag in which Mufaddi kept everything he owned was stolen, and two days later he found it thrown on the ground near the mosque, with all the medicines and remedies it contained spoiled and mixed with dirt.

That was not all. Some men had recently arrived from Ujra to work for Daham, and though they did not know Mufaddi yet, they said that he had been responsible for the death of Turki al-Muflih.

When Mufaddi heard what people were saying, his eyes opened wide in fright, shock and amazement at the baseness of the rich, who would spread such a false, trumped-up story. Instead of laying low or staying on his guard, he raged like a bull.

"People of Harran!" he shouted in the street. "Let those present convey this to those who are absent: Ibn Jeddan is the same man he was, he has not deceived or betrayed anybody. He owns nothing in this world and fears no one but Almighty God. People of Harran, money has corrupted many before you. It has corrupted nations and kingdoms. Money enslaves, it subjugates, but it never brings happiness. You can see that with your own eyes! Look at Daham and Ibn Dueij and Ibn Farhan, look at al-Naqib and Ibn Seif and al-Salaami, any one of them would kill his father and mother and brothers, and nothing they have will last. You will see that tomorrow. By God, by God, I'll keep at them until I curse their parents. God is my witness."

The people who heard Mufaddi al-Jeddan did not understand the mania that had taken hold of him and could think of no explanation for his behavior.

This was Mufaddi before the coming of Dr. Subhi al-Mahmilji: embittered, angry and confused. He could not understand how houses were built, land bought and pockets filled so quickly. He felt, for no very clear reason, that most of those making money were doing nothing but stealing, stealing both when they bought and when they sold, and when he saw the doctor, surrounded by those rich thieves, and heard that this man would stay in Harran always, to demand payment for illness and death, he could not believe it. When Dr. Subhi opened his clinic to receive the sick, sending them away with those small colored boxes, charging undreamed-of sums, he knew that a new kind of stealing had been added to all the other kinds. He set up his post near the doctor's clinic, to help prevent this stealing, to do something. The doctor, who wanted to make a strong beginning, wanted to clear all obstacles from his path, to eliminate all those who presented a threat. When Mufaddi al-Jeddan appeared, the doctor did not hesitate to call him a quack and, secretly, to stir people up against him. He slyly derided those who killed people on the pretext of curing them, though he never mentioned Mufaddi by name. He talked a great deal about microbes and inflammation and other things that his listeners could not begin to understand, but as long as he was talking about Mufaddi they agreed with him and added defamations of their own.

Dr. Subhi never took part in the war himself. He only egged on the others, and even that was subtle because one of his basic principles was that "war should be between equals—a war between equal rivals is the only kind that does honor to the antagonists, even the loser. In an unequal war, even the winner loses." He said this to himself and smiled when he saw Mufaddi's face. "If you have a servant, you shouldn't dirty your hands." He saw in his mind's eye the images of those madmen who wanted to get rid of Mufaddi that very day and smiled, and continued his provocation.

The days passed, however, and Dr. Subhi forgot, or made himself forget Mufaddi al-Jeddan, so when he saw him at the reception for Prince Khazael he completely ignored him, although they stood face to face. At first they were beside one another, but then Abdullah al-Seif spoke up. "If you get any closer, Doctor, Mufaddi will bleed you or get his irons out!"

The doctor then glanced at Mufaddi and moved away. After that, when Mufaddi tried unsuccessfully, because of the crowds, to greet the prince, the doctor felt even more important. He felt prouder yet when, two or three months after the dedication of the pipeline, he received a gift from the prince: a green automobile. This was as good as killing Mufaddi al-Jeddan.

For Dr. Subhi, who was on his guard against Mufaddi, even though he did not say so, and continued to provoke him, forgot the old man as he became absorbed in more important matters. A strange building began to rise on the large site that al-Salaami owned on the north side of the road to the American compound. At first people said it belonged to the company, but when they

saw Dr. Subhi there several times, giving orders, they knew
that it was his. They were sure it was his when a signpost
appeared on the compound-emirate road, reading SHIFA HOSPITAL
with an arrow pointing north; there could be no more doubt
that the building belonged to Dr. Subhi al-Mahmilji. At about
this time the doctor left town two or three times, to go no one
knew where, but he returned with a whole group of people after
one trip, and everyone assumed they were his family, because
of the resemblance. Within a few more weeks, the Shifa Pharmacy opened its doors, and not far from it Dr. Wasfi Agha
opened a dentistry clinic. The principal of the school said that
Wasfi was only a dentist's assistant from Aleppo, because he had
known him there; it was out of the question, he said, that this
man would have got a medical degree in his fifties! But in spite
of all that the principal said, "Doctor" Wasfi began seeing patients in the early winter, and one of his first patients was Emir
Khaled, for whom he made a set of gold teeth that caught everyone's eye.

At about this time several of Harran's rich citizens married.
They all married in the same time period, or at least during the
same winter, as if they had planned to do so among themselves,
since it was the custom in Harran to plan these things well in
advance, and there was always a great deal of talk and rumor
about them. This time it was different; as soon as winter came
these notable citizens began to have their weddings. Most of
them were friends of Dr. Subhi, and one of them was Emir
Khaled himself. What was noticeable was that the weddings took
place with very little public show or celebration—that had never
happened before—though everyone talked about it privately,
and concluded that Dr. Subhi had something to do with it.

Also that winter Johar began to wear a military uniform. It
looked bizarre, and at first everyone thought it was some sort
of joke. A diminutive man had shown up two or three months

after Prince Khazael's visit, in a green automobile accompanied
by two soldiers in a pickup truck, and asked with timid courtesy
how to find the emirate building; those who saw him expected
something unusual, but they found out the next day that the
small car was the crown prince's gift to Dr. Subhi. The pickup
contained a load of military uniforms, cords, braid, colored ribbons, medals and a large assortment of other things. The three
men's mission was to set up a military unit; the short man's job
was to administrate and supervise as the other two men delivered
the "requisites" to the emirate in accordance with their official
instructions, then carried them back out to distribute them to
the Emirate Detachment, as they called the emir's men. After
three days of hard and continuous labor, which went on until
long after dark, the Emirate Detachment was formed.

The men drilled presentably enough, but the sight of them in
their full dress uniforms reduced everyone to incredulous laughter. Their movements were hampered by the heavy boots and
the multicolored cloth, braid and medals, so that they looked
like small children who did not know what they were doing—
never more so than when, on the third day, the "assignment
ceremony," as they called it, took place with the emir in at-
tendance.

The ceremony was talked about for a long time afterward.
The soldiers had drilled since morning and wore their colored
and beribboned full dress uniforms. Johar led the detachment in
a gaudy embroidered uniform with several colored sashes across
his chest and rammed in his armpit a baton—whether it had
been entrusted to him from the "requisites" or whether he had
found it somewhere, no one knew. When the climax of the
ceremony came, in total silence, with every eye on the emir as
he stood at the gate of the emirate waiting for the detachment
to present itself, Johar dropped his baton and lost his composure.
He did not know whether to pick it up or to leave it and continue

marching toward the emir. He doubled over suddenly to pick
it up, but as he did so he tripped over his clothes and fell. It was
a tense moment that excited both sympathy and some laughter,
and when he stood up again his clothes were dusty and showed
sweaty patches. He turned around to face the detachment, still
deeply embarrassed, and shouted almost angrily. "Company,
march!"

The soldiers tried to shuffle into neat ranks to proceed to the
emir in orderly fashion, and, somewhat pacified, Johar shouted
like a muezzin. "Company, halt! At ease. Present arms! Forward
march!"

The men did as they were told and then moved forward once
more until they were just two or three steps away from the emir.
Johar shouted more loudly than ever. "Salute!"

They raised their hands in salute to the emir, who promptly
smiled delightedly, showing his gleaming gold teeth. Contrary
to his instructions, Johar stepped forward and shook hands with
the emir. When the emir embraced him and Johar buried his face
in the emir's chest, the baton could be seen behind the emir's
back as if Johar were stabbing him. When Johar straightened up,
a number of those standing near the two men heard the emir
say, "Your staff, Johar, is like Moses's staff!" They all smiled,
including Johar, and as he retreated, still facing the emir, he
replaced the baton under his arm, clasping it tightly there until
he was four or five paces away.

"Company, right face!"

They turned as one man and everyone, even the emir, burst
into applause. That was the first day of the Desert Army.

A year or more later, Mufaddi al-Jeddan said to himself in the
dark cubicle under the stairs, "Glory to God, it is a strange world,
stranger than any man knows. Everything in it changes, and
nothing changes more than man himself." He shook his head as
he remembered, and put his hand to his chest to feel the wound.

When the pain throbbed more than usual, he said, "Nothing changes a man more than money and a uniform . . ." He almost said something more, but shame prevented him.

Mufaddi was remembering Johar and the day he arrived with Emir Khaled, the day he fell ill and Mufaddi healed him with irons, and another time when he cured him by bleeding him. He remembered the time when he treated the wound in his leg and the Albanian came hurrying in, shouting and cursing, and drove out all those present. When Dr. Subhi saw the wound, he shouted, "Where's the quack that touched this? I'll break his hand—he should spend the rest of his life in prison. He's killed the man! Even if he lives, his whole leg may have to be amputated." He remembered this, and then thought back on the first time he saw Johar wearing his military uniform and carrying his baton. In the beginning, Johar had always sat in the coffeehouse and talked to people and socialized in the shops. He used to smile at the boys who gawked at his uniform, and he didn't object when some of the men reached out to touch the heavy medals and colored ribbons. He threw out his chest proudly so that everyone might see the medals and the braid, and passed around his baton so that they might heft it in their hands and see whether it was wooden or metal. That was Johar in the beginning, but he changed. "The goddamned uniform changed him," said Mufaddi al-Jeddan to himself. As time passed Johar began to frown and spoke only rarely, and when he went in the coffeehouse, which he did only occasionally, he entered arrogantly, looking at its patrons with an almost hateful disdain. He sat only with a selected few, mainly the rich and prominent of the town. "The uniform has ruined him, ruined him completely; it's like a saddle on his soul." When he walked through the market he did not look anyone in the face and returned greetings curtly. He shouted and often struck people. What made things much worse was the conversion of one wing of the emirate building into an office for Johar and headquarters of the Desert Army: even the youngest soldiers, who had only put on their uniforms yesterday, began to behave like Johar. The soldiers swaggered through the market carrying sticks, hitting people for the most trifling reasons. Johar himself was now rarely seen. He spent most of his time at Headquarters, as the Desert Army's wing was called; when the Desert Army's own building was completed, beside the emirate, it was called the Command Center. The Command Center was composed of two stories and a storeroom underneath reached by a dark staircase. Mufaddi al-Jeddan had been there twice before, and this was the third time.

Mufaddi al-Jeddan was Harran's first prisoner. True, the emir's deputy had tried to imprison Hajem and his uncle some years before, but at the time there had been no place they could really call a prison. Now, in the storeroom that held piles of supplies, automobile tires, barrels and firewood, they sectioned off a room, all the way at the end, on the right, which was the prison.

Johar was embarrassed the first time they brought Mufaddi in. He sat behind his desk, bareheaded, and only looked at Mufaddi once or twice. He gazed at the floor and told Mufaddi he had orders to detain him, and that he had no choice but to carry out the orders. Mufaddi stared at Johar, trying to meet his eyes, and smiled when he heard these words. Johar stood and addressed him as two soldiers stepped forward to lead him to the cell. "God willing, this matter will be cleared up within a few days."

Mufaddi smiled but said nothing. The matter that Johar hoped would be cleared up within a few days took forty days. The charge was suspicion of theft; the accused, Mufaddi al-Jeddan. After Hassan Rezaie's store was robbed, two of Hassan's employees alleged that they had seen Mufaddi al-Jeddan lurking around the premises for two days running; that had been one day before the robbery.

The second time, Mufaddi was locked up after a quarrel with Saleh al-Dabbasi; they arrested him but not Saleh. They said that Mufaddi was the aggressor, in spite of the wounds and bites on his body, and the cut under his eye that was swollen for weeks. Saleh finally agreed to have Mufaddi released into Ibn Naffeh's care three weeks later. When he was released, Johar scolded him angrily. "You're nothing but a troublemaker, Ibn Jeddan. You have a new problem every day. We've decided to let you go this time, in Abu Othman's custody, but next time we'll see that you rot down there."

Mufaddi could hardly believe that these words were being addressed to him. He opened his mouth to speak, but Johar cut him off, shaking his finger at him. "That's it. Shut up—one more word and you're going back downstairs." He turned to Ibn Naffeh, who was following everything, and told him, "If we didn't trust and respect you, Abu Othman, we would not let this old fool free."

Now, Mufaddi had been imprisoned for the third time, in the last cell on the right, on the charge of being a "vagabond." This was how Dr. Subhi al-Mahmilji had described him in his conversation with the emir when the emir presided over the dedication of a new wing of the Shifa Hospital. It was a casual conversation; the doctor had been reminiscing with the emir about his first days in Harran. "There was no doctor here then except for that quack—I forget his name. He was killing people with his so-called medicines, and ranted and raved when we began to practice modern medicine, but now Harran is free of those vagabonds, and this hospital is the proof." He stressed the word *vagabonds*. Three days later, someone reported that Mufaddi was sitting in Abu As'ad al-Helwani's coffeehouse and saying that the Albanian, meaning the doctor, had made all his money by illicit means, and that the price of such illicit living was eternal damnation. When word of these statements reached the emirate, Johar was ordered to arrest this "vagabond" who did nothing but curse and defame people. Although Johar did not understand what a vagabond was—the word brought no picture to his mind—he carried out the order in under an hour, and in worthy style. He ordered the soldiers who went to arrest Mufaddi al-Jeddan to "teach him a lesson" before bringing him to the Command Center. The soldiers carried out their instructions perfectly, because Mufaddi was brought in more dead than alive. Even a youth in the prime of life could not have withstood the beating, kicking and insults he endured. He was silent the whole time, for he understood even better than those who beat him what orders had been given. One month later, when he was brought up to see Johar with one arm tied behind his back, he was forced to listen to language he never imagined Johar knew or would address to him. After this he was again locked in his cell, without being allowed to speak a word; when he tried to speak, he was struck so hard across the shoulders and back with a bamboo cane that he cried aloud. When he was being led back down the stairs he was pushed, and he fell down and shrieked like a wounded animal, "Ruin comes to all oppressors—take heed, you bastards, ruin will come after you, by God, God damn your fathers and Johar's father and the one who dressed him in the saddle." He continued to scream and curse for a long time after they shut the door on him.

Six months and some days in prison, then he was free. Once again Ibn Naffeh assumed responsibility for him. This time he did not meet Johar; he was met by one of his aides, a young town Arab with a clean-shaven, almost girlish face.

"You have one week in which to report to work in the stone quarry, or leave Harran for good," Mufaddi was told.

The aide uttered this one simple sentence and stopped. He looked at Mufaddi contemptuously, as if goading him to leave the room immediately. Mufaddi, whose eyes hurt so badly that he could hardly see, did not know what to say. He was utterly confused and weary to the point of collapse. Ibn Naffeh, who stood beside him, looked now at the young officer whom he did not know and had never seen, now at Mufaddi, who looked old—ancient. The long months in the tenebrous cell had destroyed him. He did not know what to do.

After a silence that seemed long to all three of them, the young man spoke again. "What do you say—the quarry, or will you leave Harran?"

Mufaddi did not speak, but Ibn Naffeh spoke to end this gloomy game. "Never mind. I'm responsible for him. Trust in God, my boy, and let us hope for the best."

Mufaddi shuffled out. Ibn Naffeh grasped his arm to keep him from falling.

73

MUFADDI AL-JEDDAN DID NOT REPORT TO THE quarry, nor did he ever leave Harran—he never intended to, and everyone knew it. Even Johar, who had told his assistant to give him that choice, the quarry or exile, was certain that Mufaddi would not obey the order. Nevertheless, Abu Othman was summoned to the Command Center on the third day, and the same young officer asked him whether Mufaddi would obey the order or not.

"My friends, you are believers," Ibn Naffeh replied somewhat angrily. "You said one week, and the third day isn't up yet."

"You are responsible for him," said the slender, clean-shaven young man, smiling menacingly. "If the week runs out and the order has not been carried out, you'll both be our guests here."

"Don't act so important, my boy—we are all guests in this world."

"Orders are orders."

"Trust in God, boy—orders are God's alone."

"Fine. Let the week go by, then we'll see."

During that week many things happened that could never have happened in any other week. After one day in bed, Mufaddi rose a new man. He bathed and put on the new clothes that Abu Othman had given him and sat in the small courtyard to receive visitors. Those who had not heard of his release and were unable to visit him the first day did so in the days that followed. It seemed to them in the first three days that Mufaddi was exhausted and emaciated, but the sunlight that troubled his eyes soon spread new strength through his body and eyes. His voice grew firmer, and a new smile, one that threw out a challenge, never left his lips.

After the first three days there were visits of another kind. Ibn Ajil, for example, had sold all his land west of the emirate to pay the doctor's bills he had incurred at Dr. Subhi's clinic and hospital, although his condition only worsened, so his children carried him to Ibn Naffeh's house and set him in front of Mufaddi al-Jeddan. Mufaddi administered his irons and gave Ibn Ajil remedies, and within a few hours he was able to move and almost stood up. Two days later he was able to walk again, holding the wall for support.

Dabbasi had a pain in his right leg, from the hip to his foot, and all the medicines that Dr. Subhi gave him did no good at all; he was so frightened that he had begun to stutter, and his right arm was in pain, so he went to Ibn Naffeh's house. He went on the pretext of visiting Abu Othman and pretended to be surprised when he saw Mufaddi, but within a few hours he was lying in an inner room where Mufaddi bled and massaged him. He kneaded the flesh between his hip and testicles, and in spite of his discomfort and moans, Dabbasi swore, when he left

Ibn Naffeh's house leaning on his cane that evening, that the pain he had come in with had disappeared. Within a few days he was walking like a young man again, though he kept his staff.

Hamdan al-Rai visited Mufaddi every day. He seemed delighted though he could not speak, perhaps from joy, or perhaps he had got out of the habit of speaking, but something seemed to be preventing him from being completely happy. Mufaddi found out that the problem was his dog, which had fallen very ill, and told him to bring the dog. Abu Othman had a horror of dogs, never letting them come near his house or touch anything of his, but he gave his permission for the dog to be brought in for treatment. Mufaddi treated the dog, then opened his jaws and spat into his throat. The dog sneezed, struggled up and tottered a few steps, then trotted away, cured.

The three workers whom Dr. Subhi al-Mahmilji had refused to admit to his hospital—at that time the company did not pay for the workers' medical care at the hospital, since it was still in its training and trial stage—could not afford to pay his fees themselves and so had no one but Mufaddi al-Jeddan to turn to. He treated one of them with irons and gave the other two some of Khazna al-Hassan's medicines. Two of them seemed better, but it was too early to tell whether the condition of the third would improve or remain unchanged.

Everything that happened in Ibn Naffeh's courtyard, no matter how trivial, became public knowledge in no time. Everyone in Harran talked of nothing but what Mufaddi al-Jeddan had done that day. Even the patients in the Shifa Hospital, some of whom had lain there for weeks, with no inch of their backsides safe from Muhammad Eid's needles, would have given anything to escape and turn themselves over to Mufaddi al-Jeddan in spite of the pain they knew well enough to expect from his irons and special massages. An hour of pain was better than the pain they endured here for weeks on end, lying on their backs day and night, moving only when Muhammad Eid came to turn them over.

Mufaddi went about his practice happily and grew prouder with every patient he treated, and with every curse he heaped on Johar and whoever had given him his uniform. Everyone talked about these curses, and they grew more elaborate with every retelling, though no one told Johar or the emir anything very damning. Those whom Johar and the emir questioned said as little as possible and tried not to laugh, but when they were alone or among themselves they smiled or roared with laughter.

Khazna al-Hassan had not left Ibn Naffeh's house since the moment of Mufaddi's arrival. She seemed more senile than ever before and older, twenty years older, and cried so much over her missing son that her eyesight suffered, but she changed for the better when Mufaddi moved in; she seemed stronger, and some people even said that they had seen her laugh. She did everything she could to assist Mufaddi and gave him all of her herbs and remedies. She took charge of some of the patients and spoke roughly to them when they showed fear or doubt. Ibn Naffeh's daughter Amna, who was only ten years old, was her assistant. The girl ran to fetch hot water, cloth and firewood and watched Mufaddi with fascination as he applied his irons to the sick. Her mother, Sabha al-Abdullah, kept her distance and moved like an old cat, unaware of all that went on around her. She had only one concern: how many mouths she had to feed, how many loaves to bake that day. When the little girl asked her for something Mufaddi or Khazna needed, she looked exasperated and pointed to the small room where the supplies were kept.

The northern and western hills kept a close watch on everything that went on in Ibn Naffeh's courtyard. Johar heard the stories going around and shook his head. He was waiting for the end of the warning period he had decreed, "And, by God, if this week passes and Ibn Jeddan is still here, I'll really give them something to talk about!" He smiled and said to himself, "By God, I'll chop his nose off. I'll cut out his tongue. This stick will go up his behind and out his mouth, and God help him after that." The more Johar heard about what Ibn Jeddan was doing, the angrier he got.

Even Dr. Subhi had completely forgotten Mufaddi al-Jeddan, remembering him only in the way one remembers an old tale, but when he heard that he had been released from prison, and that he was treating the sick, Dabbasi among them, he said somewhat despairingly to Dr. Wasfi, who was visiting him in the hospital, "I'm in trouble, and so are you."

Dr. Wasfi looked at him with questioning eyes, for he did not know what Subhi was talking about, and Dr. Subhi went on as if talking to himself. "These people are bedouin, Wasfi—jackasses. If you tell them you have a bull, they'll want to milk it." He went on in his former tone. "Even the rich are jackasses, and Dabbasi is the biggest jackass of all. You know Dabbasi. He has given us nothing but problems, but we've treated him here. Every day he was examined and given a shot, and you know the rest. It was all useless. After all our trouble he took himself and went to see a quack, a bedouin worth a franc who used irons on him, and God only knows what else."

Dr. Wasfi laughed and shook his head in disbelief. "The government—how does the government let this kind of nonsense continue?"

"We've told them a hundred times, we've gone all through it, but they're all jackasses, from the top to the bottom."

Nothing was known of what Dr. Subhi discussed with the emir after this, but when Ibn Naffeh was summoned by the young officer a second time, on the fifth day, it was clearly only to make threats and to demonstrate that there would be no postponement.

"There is no good left in this world," Ibn Naffeh told Mufaddi and Khazna when he returned from the emirate. When they looked at him he bowed his head and said nothing for a long time, then went on. "They think they own our lives. The next thing you know they'll tell a man to divorce his wife."

He spat.

"Tell us more," said Khazna quickly. "Abu Othman, tell us what happened."

"The whole story is this. They want Mufaddi to leave, forever, either to go work in the quarries or just to get out of Harran."

"By God, they don't like it," said Mufaddi, laughing. "What you throw to the sky falls to the ground. They're trash. After prison what's left but death? We've seen their hostelry, Johar and his uncle Khaled al-Mishari, and now we'll see what kind of hostelry our Lord will provide me with."

"Listen, cousin," said Ibn Naffeh testily. "This house is your house, and you know me. I am not afraid of them, and they won't dare touch me, but I'm afraid for your sake."

"God help us," said Khazna. "Those strangers rule us and make their plans, they say what will be and what not. By God, the depths of the earth are better than its face."

"Trust in God, woman, the world is still young," said Mufaddi. He seemed as happy as a child. His whole face laughed and he felt like dancing or going straight to the emirate to curse and scream, to spit in the faces of Johar and ten more of them.

"They said one week," said Ibn Naffeh sadly. "That leaves only tomorrow and the next day."

"Too long for them, Abu Othman."

"And too short for us, cousin."

"Don't worry about it, man."

"Whatever you decide, I'm with you."

"What do you say I leave your house, Abu Othman?"

"Leave my house? Leave your house? God forbid!"

"Go see the emir," said Khazna angrily. "Go talk to the men. There's still time to settle this."

Just then Amna ran into the room behind the little fawn given them a month before. She was very attached to the fawn; she fed him and played with him and was constantly trying to carry him, but as soon as she picked him up he felt cramped and began to kick and wail, and usually broke free.

"Leave him alone now, like a good girl," said her father as he watched her chasing the animal. "Stop it now, my dear. It's not enough he's a prisoner, you have to strangle him too?"

The little girl looked at her father and then at the fawn. She wanted to catch him, to cuddle him, but did not dare. She stood waiting, and when he trotted out into the courtyard she ran after him.

The three were silent, as if they had nothing to say, or as if their minds had wandered far afield among their endless thoughts and memories. Ibn Naffeh and Khazna were sad and pensive, but Mufaddi looked like a child, smiling happily, his eyes shining with menace and pugnacity. After some time they drifted back from their thoughts and memories, or at least Mufaddi did.

"Don't worry, friends," he said mockingly. "They're like everybody else, tomorrow they'll be history."

"Today is what matters, dear man," said Khazna in the same tone. She turned away and said, more to herself than to either man, "Live, old cart horse, until the spring."

Their conversation might have continued or moved on to another subject, or another dejected silence might have fallen, had Naama Dakhlallah not come in. She was sobbing and weeping and leading a small boy by the hand. She said, between sobs, that she had brought the boy to everyone in the region of Ujra and Harran, to the Syrian doctor and his friend the Albanian, who gave him shots and some green and red medicines, but to no avail. She spoke at first without noticing Khazna, but when she saw her she smiled and greeted her by laying a hand on her shoulder.

"Khazna knows the whole story. God bless her, she did all she could."

Khazna explained to Mufaddi that the boy had been afflicted by an evil eye and had not been able to speak since then.

The boy stared at them and seemed about to burst into tears or run away. Mufaddi nodded several times to show that he understood the condition.

"If not today, tomorrow," he said softly.

Nothing happened that day, but the next morning, when a sick worker came and Mufaddi decided to treat him with irons, he asked that the child be present as well. Contrary to his usual custom, he lit a big fire and put all his iron instruments in it. When they were red hot he tested them on hardwood and then in water, all the time watching the boy's reactions out of the corner of his eye. When he was ready to treat the worker he asked him to cry out in pain, and the worker was so confused and frightened that he almost ran out, but he briefly explained why, and the worker obeyed. As soon as the hot iron touched the man's leg, at the ankle, the man cried out. It was a genuine cry of pain and ended in a wail. When Mufaddi was finished with the man he turned to the boy, replaced his irons in the heart of the blazing fire with the tongs and other tools, and shouted, his eyes glittering. "Grab him! Bring him here."

He caught the terrified child, who writhed like a fish in his hands. The boy kicked and pushed, but when he saw that Mufaddi's hold was too tight and felt the heat of the flames on his face, he began to bellow. With that, Mufaddi pushed him onto the bed and moved away.

"There you go. I hope he doesn't have a relapse."

That was on the sixth morning; Ibn Naffeh was at his wit's end. He did not know what to do or how to face Johar if the time ran out and Mufaddi was still in Harran or had not gone to the quarry. This was the cruelest experience he had ever known in his life. He had never imagined that the day would come when people would be forced to abide by rules they did not understand or approve of. What did Johar and these others want? What did it matter to them that Mufaddi was here or anywhere else? Did the emir know what was happening to the people, and if he knew, why was he silent? Ibn Naffeh strode out of the house and said, to keep from choking, "If you never get depressed you never cheer up."

No one knew what Mufaddi did between morning and afternoon that day, where he went or who might have seen him. He left the house shortly after Ibn Naffeh went out and told Amna only that he would be back before nightfall. The little girl said nothing but watched him walk down the hill toward the market and disappear.

Why did Mufaddi go down to the market? Was he intending to go to the coffeehouse or the emirate, or was he leaving Harran? Had he stopped in the market and spoken to anyone?

Mufaddi's every step and every movement, and every minute he spent out of the sight of the little girl after walking down the western hill, were shrouded in mystery. In spite of the mystery, every person in Harran claimed to have seen Mufaddi, albeit from afar, heard his voice or felt him near. That was for certain. The workers in the stone quarry, questioned that night, said that they had seen him; he had been walking ever so slowly up the hill toward them. They had stopped working to wave their arms and shovels, and two or three of them had called out to him.

Three fishermen returning from their long night at sea said that they had seen him in a white rowboat. He was far away, and alone in his boat. When he glided by them he raised the oar, smiled and greeted them, then kept rowing. He turned when they called out to him but kept moving. The workers in the camp, or at least those who were near the beach, and others at Station 4, saw Mufaddi with their own eyes. He passed by them and paused, chatted awhile and then smiled and left quickly. He woke some of them suddenly from a deep sleep, but they were not angry at his visit; they were glad to see him and greeted him and shook his hand, but when he asked them to go back to sleep, saying that they would meet again after they woke up, they told him that they could not go back to sleep.

In the market, the main street and the small, narrow avenues, many Harranis said that they had seen Mufaddi pass by and stop in a number of shops. He had smiled and talked, and joked with some of the boys. Everyone sitting in the coffeehouse that morning said with absolute certainty that they had seen Mufaddi when he walked past. He stopped for a few minutes to talk to Abu As'ad. They said that Daham came by in those few minutes, and that Mufaddi joked with him.

The women at home, even those in the distant houses in the western hills, said that they had seen Mufaddi al-Jeddan hurrying by, and though he did not stop to talk with any of them he did smile and wave.

The Command Center was, at this same time, in a state of tireless and tormented alert. Johar could not stop shouting and cursing all morning, and his assistant and the others were the same way. Two soldiers told friends of theirs that they had seen Mufaddi walking, that he had smiled at them when they met near the water tanks, even though one of them had beaten him up the last time he was in prison.

Ibn Naffeh could not bear to stay in the house, and so he went out, but since he could not stroll in the market or sit in the coffeehouse, and it was still too early to go to the mosque, he decided to go back home, and in doing so passed by the water tanks. Whether out of weariness or because he heard something, he paused there, and when he looked over to the north side he saw Mufaddi, lying on his face and moaning softly, his fingers dug into the soil. There was a trickle of blood on the ground, running from his hip. At first Ibn Naffeh could not believe his eyes; he thought he was dreaming, or his eyes were deceiving him. When he moved closer he recognized Mufaddi's back, hands and clothing. He turned him over on his back. He was smiling.

Mufaddi tried to make himself light as he was being carried, and he moved his feet. When he reached the house, carried by Ibn Naffeh and three others, he looked around as if trying to remember the place, then closed his eyes. Two of the men went to fetch Dr. Subhi.

There was nothing Khazna could do. She wept copiously and her hands trembled. The little girl cradled her fawn off by the low room, crying without realizing it. Ibn Naffeh went up to the roof three or four times to watch the road and see if the doctor was on his way yet. He was nervous and lightheaded, and repeated vile curses. Sabha al-Abdullah had been baking in a corner when they brought Mufaddi, and she left it when she saw them, so the dough burned in the oven.

The two men who had gone for the doctor returned and said, "The doctor is in the middle of an operation." One of them added, "Muhammad Needle said to bring him to the hospital." When Abu Othman heard that, tears began to run down his face, and Khazna said, "Let the man sleep." One of the men said, "We should get him to the hospital before it's too late." The little girl wiped her tears on the fawn's back. When Sabha al-Abdullah could not stand it any longer and began to scream, the fawn started with fright and escaped, going over to Mufaddi to smell him. Ibn Naffeh leaned over Mufaddi, his tears falling fast. "If we don't take him to the hospital now, he'll die," said one of the men. "Let him sleep," said Khazna.

At noon, great numbers of people in the market and the workers' camp, in addition to one of the fishermen, said they felt a trembling come over them. Two of the workers in the quarry said that they shivered so badly that they dropped their pickaxes, and in his coffeehouse Abu As'ad al-Helwani dropped a tray filled with tea glasses, and all the glasses broke; both events happened at the stroke of noon. Naama Dakhlallah wept with joy when her boy told her he was hungry and wanted something to eat, but it was a sorrowful joy. Hamdan's dog, which had been sleeping, woke suddenly at noon and began to howl. "Shut up—shut up!" said Hamdan, and when the dog kept howling he threw a rock at him and hit his left foreleg.

The men decided to carry Mufaddi to the hospital, and Ibn Naffeh stepped out of the way, but when they touched him and found him cold to the touch, they hesitated. Khazna screamed through her tears for the men to leave him alone, the sleep would do him good. When Salman al-Zamel and two others arrived, having heard the shouting in the market, and saw Mufaddi, Salman leaned over and put his ear to Mufaddi's chest, then grasped his hand. He let the cold hand fall, and shuddered, and did not say a word.

Ibn Naffeh came forward to have a closer look at Mufaddi, and when he saw his staring eyes he gently closed them. He did not move until Salman al-Zamel helped him up and said, indistinctly because his voice was choked with tears, "God bless you and reward you, Abu Othman."

Mufaddi al-Jeddan was buried that afternoon, and all Harran turned out to bid him farewell. Even the emirate was represented by one of the emir's men. The funeral procession started out from Ibn Naffeh's house and wound its way to the graveyard by way of the mosque. Several of the mourners reported that as the procession crossed Rashedi Street near Dr. Subhi al-Mahmilji's clinic, there was a momentary disturbance, as if the corpse had stirred, and some of the men carrying the bier said that they felt a sudden strong tremor, so strong that the bier nearly fell from their hands. They also said that Ibn Naffeh separated himself from the others at the clinic and went to piss in front of it. Others denied that Ibn Naffeh had pissed at all, saying that he had vomited.

Harran slept that night with the feeling that a harsh black future awaited them.

That same day, Amna's fawn died, and the little girl was inconsolable, crying so much that her mother began to worry about her and slapped her to make her stop.

Khazna cried more than ever, and people heard her say that now she awaited the return of two men: Awad and Mufaddi. Within a few months she went completely blind, but a strong milk-white light had been kindled within her, so she said with no sign of regret, and she continued to run her house as she had done for twenty years.

Life went on for Ibn Naffeh, but he maintained a grave silence.

The people of Harran were to remember Mufaddi al-Jeddan, and this particular day, for many, many years to come.

74

MUFADDI DIED AT NOON ON THURSDAY AND was buried that afternoon. As darkness fell in Harran, a strong, overwhelming grief stormed the quiet houses, leaving no home or heart unpenetrated. It spread as the darkness spread, like no sorrow they had ever known, moving as quickly and disruptively as water rushing downhill. People suddenly realized that they were more grief stricken than they had imagined, and they enumerated the many, many reasons why. When they met in Ibn Naffeh's house and said their evening prayers together, then went to dinner, they found that they had no appetite for food or drink. Their hands moved slowly toward the food; they tasted tears with the rice and the water seemed bitter, and when they had finished eating they stayed in their places and said nothing. None of them noticed Khazna al-Hassan enter.

"Mufaddi's blood is on you—on every one of you," she said hoarsely.

They looked at her, then at the mounds of uneaten food. The men dared not look at each other or speak. At last Dabbasi spoke. "We will strive for our reward—rest in peace, Mufaddi."

The men stirred, and stood up in unison. The dishes were cleared, and as the coffee was passed around they immersed themselves in conversation, discussing, in groups of two or three, how Mufaddi had been killed, where he had been found and who the killer might be. Their words were brief, whispered and anxious, and although they did not name the killer, the specter of Johar filled the room; while he had not killed Mufaddi himself, he was the likeliest murderer. They remembered how Johar had been only two or three years ago, and how he had changed, and they remembered Mufaddi.

Later that night most of the men left, including those from the emirate and two from the Desert Army, leaving only Salman al-Zamel, Fawaz al-Hathal, Abdu Muhammad, Ibn Naffeh and two of his relatives. Abdu Muhammad sighed deeply. "If I don't avenge you, Mufaddi, my name isn't Abdu."

"There was more than one killer," said Salman slowly.

Ibn Naffeh was listening, his eyes half closed. He turned to look at Ibn Zamel questioningly.

"Yes, there are more than one. Mufaddi died twice."

Everyone twisted around to look at Salman.

"There was one killer," said Ibn Naffeh. "It's as plain as day, and everyone knows who it was."

"I don't care who he is, he won't escape from Abdu," said Abdu angrily.

Salman went on as if he had not heard a word Ibn Naffeh said. "The first time, Emir Golden Teeth's gang killed him, and then the Albanian killed him. Johar and his gang are soaked in his blood. They dragged him to the water tanks and thought that was that, and the Albanian finished the job, that bastard of an Albanian who has no business in Harran but stealing people's money and kissing the emir's ass. When the men went to see him he said, 'I'm busy, I'm in the middle of an operation,' as if Mufaddi weren't a human being, as if he were a dog.''

"That's true, by God," said one of Ibn Naffeh's relatives. "If the doctor had come to help him, he might be alive now."

"Don't talk nonsense," snapped Ibn Naffeh. "It was the Americans who killed Mufaddi—they're the whole reason, they're the root of the problem."

"By God, tht's the truth, uncle, Abu Othman," said Abdu Muhammad despairingly. He added sharply, between his teeth, "By God, if I were alone, with no one helping me, that son of a whore Johar wouldn't escape."

"From the first day they came and set their stinking feet in Harran, we've been no better than camel piss. Every day it's gotten worse," said Ibn Naffeh, pointing to the American compound. "I told you, I told every one of you, the Americans are the disease, they're the root of the problem, and what's happened now is nothing compared to what they have in store for us. Someday you'll say, 'God rest your soul, Abu Othman, everything you said was true.' "

This same conversation, or different versions of it, took place throughout the workers' camp and in every house that night. While the men raised their voices and swore, the women listened silently and wept. The young men, afraid at first, forgot their fear and talked a great deal about Mufaddi, how he used to run races with the gazelles and beat them, how he remained in the desert for days without food, afraid of nothing and no one; how, when he rolled up his sleeves to treat a patient with his irons, he could hold down the biggest and strongest men by himself; how he had restored life to many patients who had died, only moments before they were nearly buried. They said that he himself might return; no one could kill him. They recalled the many mysterious occurrences in the coffeehouse and the quarry at twelve noon exactly, the instant of Mufaddi's death, and told of how at the same moment the children on the beach had seen a gazelle leap into the sea. Children returning from school to the western hill had seen men running toward Ibn Naffeh's house, and when they stopped to watch, they heard a piercing scream followed by flocks of white birds flying out of the windows and door. They were the largest birds they had ever seen. The birds sitting on the wall of the courtyard all fell off at the same moment and were eaten by the circling dogs, who had been barking eerily.

Everyone in Harran had something to say about Mufaddi that night; even Dr. Subhi, who heard of the death, gave Muhammad Eid a story, since he was planning to go on a trip the next day.

"Say, 'The doctor was in the operating room; it was a major operation, but even so he told the men to bring Mufaddi immediately. He would have gone with them, but the operation . . . the poor man on the table was dying. In the afternoon, when the operation was finished, he changed his clothes and got his bag ready to leave, but . . .' "

Muhammad Eid smirked. "We have to decide who the poor patient was, Doctor."

"Anybody." The doctor laughed. "Who's going to check? Forget it, and forget that dog. He isn't worth telling lies for."

Harran's sleep that night was intermittent and fraught with nightmares. Mothers were surprised that their children woke constantly, while adults felt thirsty and asked for water, though on other occasions they usually fetched it themselves. Babies cried all night, as though afraid or in pain.

The next day, Friday, Abdu Muhammad baked more bread than he ever had and distributed it all free, always refusing the money offered him with the same short words: "Today's bread is for the memory of the deceased."

He could not bring himself to mention Mufaddi's name, and no one needed to ask him. They all understood, and this secret understanding was a way of expressing their feelings.

Abu As'ad al-Helwani did the same as Abdu Muhammad, though neither man knew what the other was doing.

Men who were not used to going to the coffeehouse found time hanging heavy on their hands, with long hours remaining until prayers, so they went, and some of them went back in the afternoon, so the coffeehouse was full all day. When noon prayers were called, however, they all got up and left. That had never happened before, but their feet and actions were guided by mysterious feelings and desires they themselves did not understand. Some of them, who usually hid or slipped away when it was prayer time, were among the first to head for the mosque, and some of them were zealous enough to ask the others whether it was preferable to go immediately or wait a little, although they were generally annoyed by the call to Friday prayers.

Although it had never been a habit in Harran to visit cemeteries, Khazna did so involuntarily. She found the burial site without having to ask, perhaps from the freshness of the soil or some other indication, and when she sat there she saw two other women, Naama Dakhlallah and Sabha, Umm Othman, Ibn Naffeh's wife. They did not ask her why she had come, and she did not ask them; there was no need for words. Khazna began to recite in her own special way, saying things that could not possibly have been from the Koran, though the other women were not certain of that. When Sabha told her husband that night that Khazna had been reciting the Koran over Mufaddi's grave, she paused and then asked him if there were any verses in the Koran that cursed kings and princes, saying that they brought only corruption. Abu Othman told her that there were indeed such verses in the holy scripture, but Sabha was not convinced. Surely the Koran could not contain curses such as those Khazna had

pronounced, which Sabha could scarcely bear to remember. Abu
Othman was surprised that his wife would visit a graveyard,
but he did not get angry, though he was often angered by much
more trivial things.

Although the townspeople had all sat up late the night before,
tonight found them less able and less willing to stay up, so most
of them went to bed shortly after evening prayers. While some
of them found rest in their beds, however, most of them re-
gretted the long night's sleep, which brought nightmares that
weighed on their chests like boulders and lasted until morning.
Some men left their beds while the night was still black and
went to the mosque, but they found it still and silent. They sat
there to wait for the sheikh to wake up and call them to prayer,
but that would not happen for many hours. Abdu Muhammad
was surprised by the numbers of Harranis who came to him
before dawn, and much the same thing happened to Abu As'ad
al-Helwani.

Saturday was a strange day. At noon, or shortly before, the
emirate issued a statement: "In the investigation conducted by
the emirate with regard to the murder of the bedouin Mufaddi
al-Jeddan, profession retailer, it has come to light that the above
mentioned had several enemies outside Harran. The investigation has not proven the charge against any person or persons,
and His Highness the Emir has therefore ordered the case closed
and the killer deemed unknown."

That same Saturday, the company informed twenty-three
workers that they were no longer needed and requested them
to report to the personnel office to collect their severance pay.
The announcement, which was posted in several locations, said
that in the event of vacancies occurring in the future, those
currently leaving employment would be given hiring priority.

Ibn Hathal read the notice aloud at the request of the workers.
He read it twice, in two different places. Before he had finished

reading it a third time, one of the workers stepped forward and tore it up. Some of the workers whose names were listed did not believe it. They followed Ibn Hathal from one place to another and insisted that he check again, and some of them were not even satisfied with that, asking him to point out each name with his finger, and to read more clearly. This was in the late morning, contrary to usual practice, whereby notices were always posted in the early morning; some were even posted before the morning shift came on. This time they were posted late in the first break period, and even though the ten-thirty whistle blew, marking the end of the break, not all the men reported back to their jobs. Some officials from the personnel office intervened to pressure and threaten the workers, saying that those who did not report back to work immediately would suffer the same fate as those who had been laid off, but no one paid them any attention. Shortly thereafter five of the emir's men stepped in and shouted at all of the workers indiscriminately, using any means possible to convince them to return to work.

When word reached Johar, he was busy dictating a memorandum to one of his assistants, one that made it compulsory for all those seeking work in the company to report first to the Command Center for clearance. He was planning to post the announcement in the mosque, the Desert Travel garage and Abu As'ad al-Helwani's coffeehouse. When he heard the news he was frightened, or rather shocked, but he did not let his emotions show. He smiled broadly at his assistant.

"If you laugh with a bedouin, if you tell him 'Welcome,' he thinks you're afraid of him. Those bedouin sons of bitches are like children; you just have to break their heads."

He immediately orderd that an armored vehicle be brought, with seven men to accompany him, and turned to his assistant. "It looks like our friends either don't know Johar or never saw him in action." He adjusted his uniform and struck the windowsill with his baton. "We'll see if they have any real men among them."

He peevishly asked if his troops were ready, though they already stood waiting in front of the armored vehicle. He strode past them and looked at them with a quick and appraising, almost hostile glance, and when he was satisfied he spoke sharply. "I want you to teach them what red death is. Break their bones. Curse their grandfathers and have no mercy."

His words were arousing but mysterious to the men. They did not know what their commander was talking about, but they sensed that their mission was important and even momentous, that he was depending on them and had placed all his trust in them, so when they jumped into the two cars—six of them in the armored car and Johar and his assistant in the other, though he presently asked a third soldier, who was immensely tall and black, to join him—they were like hungry wolves. They were filled with hatred and the desire to fight and destroy. When the vehicles began to move, the soldiers looked at those left behind and shook their fists to show that they had already begun to follow Johar's orders.

Johar gave his mission an innocent pretext: a routine inspection tour. First, they headed for the market, driving up Harithy Street to the Rashediya district and the workers' camp. They did not stop there, but Johar ordered his driver to drive as slowly as possible, and when he saw three groups of workers on their way back from the American compound, he stared at them with a mixture of scorn and hatred; he said nothing, though, and did not stop them. When he reached the American compound he saw a small crowd at the workers' entrance, and though the vehicle passed near them, it did not stop there either. He headed for the main gate of the compound and drove in. He had not yet decided what to do. He wanted to choose the right moment, and identify their weak point. He was not in a hurry or under compulsion to act. He was sure that he would crush the heads of those who were intent on making trouble in the compound, and sure of his power. He knew the bedouin, he knew how to come at them and from which direction. He said to himself, "A loud voice is not always a sign of power, and the man leading them is not always the strongest or bravest of them. The bedouin, sons of bitches, are impossible to understand. One of them might be an inch tall, but if he's wronged, or thinks he is, he turns into a snake, into the worst devil. The thing is to know when to strike and who to strike!" This is what he was saying to himself as he entered the main gate of the compound after surveying the crowd of workers at the other gate.

"What do you say the men get off here and give them a hand, Abu Sultan?" his assistant asked.

"Don't worry," said Johar. He turned his profile and smiled. "They'll get what's coming to them and more. They'll bleed." He paused. "I'll find the snake among them. When I strike a blow, even Antar bin Shaddad rubs his head and says, 'Intercede, O Prophet, O messenger of God!' "

The Americans told them that the dismissal of the workers was a strictly "routine" measure, and that they had often taken such steps in the past—there was no special significance to it. The workers' failure to report back to work was a result of their inability to read or write—they did not understand who had been laid off and who was still employed. The Americans said that to avoid this problem in the future, such notices would be posted earlier and read aloud before they were put on the bulletin boards. The workers who had been laid off were to report to the personnel office to settle their accounts and take what was due them.

Johar was perplexed as he made his way out. Should he go back to the Command Center without doing anything? Should he tell the emir that he could not describe the Americans' decision to lay off the workers, that it was like other decisions they had made, and that the bedouin, who had previously not owned so much as a crust of bread, and did not even know where they came from, had become so used to playing with money after working in the company that they would start trouble if they were put at liberty again?

He passed near the workers' gate. The workers were still there. He stopped the car a short distance away and motioned for the workers to come to him. It was an easily understood gesture, but the workers hesitated.

"Come here, boy!" shouted Johar roughly. "And you, and you!"

The workers looked around and then at each other, wondering which of them he was addressing.

"You, come here—you, boy."

Salman al-Zamel and two others approached. Two soldiers of the emirate approached from the guard's post.

"Hah! Don't you have work to do?" asked Johar angrily. "Why are you standing here?"

At this point a large group of workers drifted over and surrounded the vehicle, and the soldiers jumped out and pushed them away. Johar looked closely at their faces and saw a menacing anger. He changed his tone to sarcasm. "Don't be afraid, my boy, speak. Say something."

"They threw out the workers."

"They threw out the workers?"

"They told them, you have no work here, go find work somewhere else."

"You—they threw you out?"

"No, they didn't throw me out, but they threw my brothers out."

"So what's your problem?"

"My brothers, sir."

"You just look after yourself and don't bother with others."

"God is great! I shouldn't bother with my brothers?"

There was a babble of voices, and the soldiers pushed away the workers who had gathered and surrounded the riders. Johar laughed. "My friends, be reasonable, and stay out of affairs that can mean only trouble for you." He paused and then added, in a fatherly tone, "Come on now. Back to work, all of you."

There was a shout from one of the workers in the rear of the crowd, invisible to Johar. "What about the ones thrown out of work? The ones who don't have work?"

"There is no lack of work here."

"They just threw us out without giving a reason, as if we had no rights."

"Don't raise your voice, you bedouin! Thank God that you have enough to eat." Johar had begun to tremble. He changed his tone. "We told you to be reasonable, and we've heard enough of this stupid talk. If you don't understand me, there are other ways of making you understand."

He paused again and sighed as he looked at the men encircling the vehicle.

"From now until the afternoon, we have no quarrel with any of you who understand, but those who want to oppose us or be stubborn, God help them!"

Even before Johar's car and the armored vehicle were out of sight the workers smashed the gate, tore up the notices and destroyed the bulletin board. They brought some empty barrels and blocked the main gate and the other gate, then filled the barrels with sand. Juma tried to escape from them. He protested and shouted and tried to use his whip, but they tied him to the cement gatepost and left him there after taking away the whip. The other guards had already begun to move away when Johar's car drove off, but when the workers smashed the gate they withdrew hurriedly and ran away, though no one noticed.

At noon the workers headed from the compound to Harran. No one knew who had proposed that course of action or why they followed it. As they neared Harran they were joined by others, all of those who had been living in the tents near the beach, who had come long weeks and months ago, and many more recent arrivals. A large number of the townspeople of Harran joined them as well. Small delighted boys ran in all directions, and some of them ran as far as Arab Harran, on the western hills, to spread the news that all of the workers had come to Harran. Soon all the townspeople and everyone who had been in the markets came out. The coffeehouse emptied when the marchers came by, and the air rang with the cheers and applause of all of those who stood up and joined them. Within minutes they were all inside the mosque.

Naim Sh'eira, Nusayis, who was translating for Hamilton, trembled slightly as he told the emir, "The important thing now is that the strikers keep away from the oil installations."

The emir nodded to show that he understood, and Naim went on in a different tone. "We've instructed our people to try to convince the workers to head to Harran instead of going back to their camp and attacking installations or starting fires."

Hamilton paused a moment, looking worried, then went on. "We're convinced that the matter goes beyond the firing of the twenty-three workers. The company has laid off workers in the past and there was no reaction at all. Not only that, the company subsequently rehired them, or some of them. But this time our preliminary assessments indicate the existence of other reasons, of acts of incitement that did not obtain in previous instances. We believe that these causes, these acts have nothing to do with the company."

The emir listened silently and nodded but had no clear understanding of what Hamilton was saying. True, the translator was speaking to him in Arabic, and had interpreted for the men many times in the past, and his words had been intelligible then, but now the meaning was unclear. There was a pause.

"You say you told them to go to Harran?" asked the emir.

"When the commotion got out of control, and they smashed the gates and windows, some of them wanted to get to the company installations and start fires, so our men began to implement a contingency plan, a plan formulated some time ago in the event of any disturbances facing the company. Our men suggested that the workers head for Harran rather than the camp."

Echoing shouts could be heard from the direction of Harran as they spoke. The emir picked up his telescope and saw an astonishing sight: the workers were in a state of total anarchy. Sweat poured from their faces and their fists were high in the air. Some workers rode on the shoulders of others, but they were all waving their arms and shouting or perhaps cursing, he guessed, but he could not be sure.

The emir would have watched the demonstration for a long time had Hamilton's voice not intruded. "What is your opinion, Your Highness? Do you think there could be reasons unknown to the company?"

"Reasons? What reasons?"

"The company wants to know: does the palace of the emirate have any idea, any assessment of what might be causing the disturbances? Do you think the strike came as the result of the layoffs, or that there might perhaps be other reasons?"

The emir was confused, not knowing how to answer such a complicated question. He shrugged to show that he did not know and said, staring at a point in space behind the two men, "Who knows? God knows."

Hamilton looked straight into the emir's eyes. "Do you think Miteb al-Hathal has had anything to do with the disturbances?

Do you think there's any connection between these incidents and last year's troubles?"

"Miteb al-Hathal? My friends, Miteb no longer exists."

"The man who was killed two days ago, do you think there is any connection between him and these disturbances?"

"What has the company got to do with Mufaddi al-Jeddan?"

"The company has nothing whatever to do with the man, as he had never been employed by us."

"That bedouin was just a complainer. Every day he had a new problem. No one knows who killed him!"

"Might his killer have anything to do with the workers?"

"With the workers?"

"The company means, did his killer influence the workers or incite them?"

"Nobody knows!"

They moved on to other matters. Hamilton asked the emir to provide guard units for the installations, at least twenty men, adding that the company would give them food and living quarters. Their mission would be to protect the installations and bar all approaches to them, in coordination with the American emergency forces in the compound. Hamilton also asked the emir not to resort to force to settle the strike. He emphasized that if that day passed without clashes, things would gradually cool off, and everything would return to normal. Lastly, Hamilton proposed that an operations group be set up to monitor the crisis, a group made up of five people: two Americans, two of the emir's men and a representative of the merchants of Harran. They would meet twice daily, and would if necessary remain in constant open session, especially in the early stages of the crisis.

"Our men are at full readiness at all times, Your Highness," said Hamilton as he rose to leave. "Naim will visit you two hours from now to receive your instructions with regard to when the operations group will meet, and any other matters."

The emir liked the idea; in fact he took to it immediately and told himself that the Americans thought of everything, that they were ready for anything.

"I believe we have reached agreement on all points, Your Highness, am I right?" asked Hamilton, who was now standing.

The emir's thoughts were unsettled and confused. "Trust in God," he said. "God willing, everything will turn out fine."

The emir asked for Johar, but he could not be found, He was told that the officer had gone down to the market with three of his men before the workers had arrived at the mosque, and that he was expected back at any moment. After conferring with his deputy, the emir decided to postpone all decisions until Johar returned, and he occupied himself with surveying the market and the crowds of people, not forgetting to inspect the sea and the Americans' compound.

Johar had gone down to the market early, but after hearing that the strikers had set out for Harran, he felt uneasy about confronting them there, so he went instead to Hassan Rezaie's offices.

At first he was sure of himself and clearly angry, cursing and complaining. He promised that the disturbances would not go unpunished—there would be severe retaliation.

"When I find out who's behind all this, I'll leave his bones spread over every hill in Harran," he told Hassan. "And God help him who gives me the bad news of who it is."

Hassan tried to soothe Johar's anger by telling him that the incident was only a freak occurrence, and that it would die down as quickly as it had started, but his efforts did no good. Johar's anger turned to fear when the crowds came nearer. Their voices were becoming louder and clearer, and it occurred to Johar that the mob might discover where he was, and might attack and kill him. He turned nervously and angrily to his men and asked them repeatedly where his car was parked, and if anyone had seen them park and go up to Rezaie's office. He looked down from the window and saw the car parked directly in front of the office. He would surely be discovered.

"Where should we put the car, men, so that those madmen don't burn it?" he asked sarcastically.

One of Rezaie's men hurried out to move one of the company cars out of the garage and put Johar's inside. Suddenly this seemed to Johar to be a serious mistake. The approaching mob had surely noticed this reckless movement and might misunderstand it.

"Did anyone see you put the car in?" he asked the driver when he reentered.

The driver said nothing.

"Well, did you see anyone?"

"No . . . sir."

Although Johar had watched everything closely, he was still not reassured. He felt more frightened with every step the mob took toward him. Hassan Rezaie was deeply afraid, and paced the room like a caged beast.

"I think, Abu Sultan, we should go into the other room," said Hassan in a moment of weakness.

Without waiting for any discussion or comment from Johar—who had already stood up to follow him—he went into the small room.

It was a storeroom, full of crates and metal filing cabinets. With its steel door and strong walls, and despite its small size, this room filled Hassan Rezaie with relief.

The two men entered the room and locked the door from the inside, but from the tall narrow window, scarcely wider than a fissure in the wall, and from behind the crude drapery, they could hear the shouts, at first, and then the arrival of the first strikers. Their fear mounted with every step, and Johar, who was doing his best to appear strong and firm, could hear his heart pound. His breath was short.

"We should have locked the downstairs door," he said restlessly.

"All the doors are locked, Abu Sultan," said Hassan Rezaie with a tentative smile.

When the crowd of workers passed under the window, all their faces seemed identical to Johar, like one face marching past hundreds of times over, and the tramping of their feet was like the regular blows of skilled hands on soft dough. Their chanting, led by Salman al-Zamel, was loud and rhythmical:

> "Johar, tell your rulers
> The pipeline was built by beasts of prey.
> We will safeguard our rights.
> The Americans do not own it.
> This land is our land."

"They're crazy, Abu Misfer," said Johar uneasily to the emir after sundown. "Any one of them would kill his own father. They're out of their minds, running around like dogs. What do they want? If God hadn't saved us, they'd have killed us."

The emir laughed and turned to Hassan Rezaie, who had driven Johar to the emirate in his own car.

"Bedouin have volatile moods, like a downpour that stops and moves on. If you left them to themselves, they'd start killing each other."

"If we leave them to themselves, Your Excellency, they'll kill everyone and everything," said Johar, still afraid.

"You know the bedouin, Johar."

"I know them, the sons of bitches, Your Excellency. Unless you break their noses they'll run mad."

"The Americans say to leave them alone."

"And what do the Americans know?" Johar shook his head sadly and said bitterly, "We know our people better than they do, Abu Misfer."

"What do you say, Abu Sadeq?" the emir asked Hassan Rezaie.

"They were like animals, down in the market," said Hassan worriedly. "They wanted to burn down Harran, to destroy everything. If they hadn't been prevented, God only knows what would have happened."

"Trust in God, my friends." The emir laughed. "We know the bedouin well enough. Let a day or two pass, and it will all be over, as if nothing ever happened."

"Abu Misfer, Your Excellency, they're not only bedouin— they are bedouin and townspeople together. All of Harran is with them, and our informers among them tell us that Miteb al-Hathal is closely involved. If we leave them alone, this is not going to come to a good end," said Johar.

When the deputy emir suggested that they leave the matter until the next day, to see whether things stayed at the same pitch or ended as they had begun, everyone agreed with him. When Naim Sh'eira showed up for the third time that evening, he was told that "the emir is meeting in constant session with officials." Hassan Rezaie had proposed that this message be passed on to the Americans, with the recommendation that Naim come again the next morning at eleven o'clock to be informed of whatever measures were deemed necessary and proper.

Harran fell silent shortly after sundown, pausing to unbend and then, by degrees, to relax. The crowds that had filled the streets had disappeared like salt in water: every house, in the market quarter and on the western hills, opened its doors to the workers. Every citizen of Harran went home that evening with two or three "guests of God," as the workers were known that day. Food and water were brought to those who insisted on spending the night in the mosque or the coffeehouse. Water was plentiful in Harran, and there was no need to fetch it from Arab Harran or anywhere else, but some of the poor insisted on fetching it, without being asked to, "for the soul of Mufaddi, who gave all Harran to drink."

The night was as long as the one in which Mufaddi had been mourned. The people were overwhelmed with pity and fear; these were obscure but powerful emotions. Perhaps they reflected upon the fact that if Mufaddi had died now, as he had, any one of them might die in the same way, for no reason, by an unknown hand; and like the workers expelled today, who now had nothing to do and nowhere to turn, any one of the workers might suffer the same fate at any time. Johar had told them to be thankful to God that they were alive and had food to eat, but no one knew for how much longer they would be alive or able to eat. True, the company was paying them now, but the next day workers paid out again what they had received. Prices went up every day, and their savings declined. The promises Ibn Rashed had made years before, as he herded them in from Ujra and elsewhere, about the houses they would find in Harran and the life they would enjoy, had predeceased even Ibn Rashed. The personnel office had promised that the company would build houses for the workers so that each man might bring his family and return from work every night to his own house and children—that had been years ago, and the promise had been repeated for years on end, but not a single house was built, and the workers remained huddled and cramped in the accursed barracks, which grew hotter and filthier with every passing day.

When the workers remembered this, and remembered their families, they felt a crushing depression. The people of Harran looked at their faces and then at each other, thinking how unhappy and oppressed they were, and grew sad when they reflected that there must be terrible reasons for the depression.

They felt afraid, but still dared to say things they would never have said had they not been so consumed with sorrow and anger. Why did they have to live like this, while the Americans lived so differently? Why were they barred from going near an American house, even from looking at the swimming pool or standing for a moment in the shade of one of their trees? Why did the Americans shout at them, telling them to move, to leave the place immediately, expelling them like dogs? Juma never hesitated to lash out with his whip when he found the workers in "restricted areas." The Americans had erected signposts warning them against loitering or going near most of the places, and they had even put barbed wire in the sea to keep them at a distance.

Why did the Americans make them perform tasks that they themselves would never dream of doing? Although the workers held their peace and showed nothing but contentment, the Americans were never satisfied by anything but constant work.

And the emir, was he their emir, there to defend and protect them, or was he the Americans' emir? He had been a different man when he first came to Harran. He used to stroll through the market and invite townsfolk to his house to drink coffee, but he changed abruptly when Hassan Rezaie and others started bringing him gifts—he was enthralled by those gadgets and left all of his responsibilities to Johar. And who was Johar? With the Americans he was a lamb: he kept silent and listened politely, nodding at every word they said to him. With Naim Sh'eira, Nusayis, he talked and laughed as if they were brothers or best friends. But if he turned around and saw Arabs, he loved to curse them, especially in front of the Americans; sometimes he even struck at them with his baton for no reason. And they remembered even stranger things: once, when he was making his rounds, Johar stopped to talk with a number of workers. This was a few months after he had begun wearing his military uniform, but he was very friendly. He asked them their names, where they came from and how long they had been with the company. The workers had gathered around him and were chatting eagerly when one of the Americans passed by; perhaps he wanted something from Johar, or perhaps he was only curious, but as soon as he came near and Johar saw him, he began cursing the workers and hitting them with his baton, telling them to get back to work before he threw them all into prison!

The workers were astonished, and could think of no excuse or explanation for his behavior. Another time, he asked a group of workers to come to the emirate on their day off to help him build a wall. He was genial and pleasant as they talked, and told them that the job would only take half a day. The workers agreed to come and help, but as soon as Naim joined them Johar underwent a complete change. He began to shout at them, and told the soldiers with him to arrest three of the workers and to take them directly to prison. They spent a week in the prison, and were released only when Naim intervened in their behalf!

There was no end to the stories about Johar, and every week brought still more. The people were inclined to forgive and forget, but they could not do so forever. When the news of Mufaddi's murder spread, their resentment rose to the surface; they felt unnecessarily, intolerably oppressed. They applauded when Salman al-Zamel stood on the wall of the mosque and said that the workers and citizens of Harran were against no one and had only two demands: the reinstatement of the workers who'd been fired and an inquiry to find Mufaddi's murderer. They shouted, *"Allahu akbar! Allahu akbar!"* The chants they instantly devised centered on these two demands:

> "Your blood, O Mufaddi, is not forgotten.
> All Harran is with you.
> Ruler of the northern hill,

Listen and give us an answer.
Your blood, O Mufaddi, is not forgotten!"

And

"Stone by stone, we constructed,
Inch by inch, we built the pipe.
Now that we have built and raised,
What do you say, O company, O God!
God is our witness, you have no rights.
Our rights are everlasting, they are ours.
With our blood and sweat we will achieve them!"

Just as Johar had been unable to distinguish one face from another from the window in the small room, their chants were confused and intermingled in his ears, like rolling thunder. He could not understand them. When some of his men came to him late that night to say that the whole population of Harran had joined in the demonstration, and that they had demanded vengeance for Mufaddi's death and the reinstatement of the workers, Johar got so angry that he cursed them for bringing bad news, called them cowards and said that he would make them pay.

The emir, who deemed postponing any decision the wisest course, was delighted when Hassan Rezaie visited him that night. This man filled him with a world of repose, for in addition to the wonderful inventions he brought, he had an inexhaustible fund of stories about his travels and experiences. The emir took his telescope and gazed unhurriedly at Harran after sundown, found it calm and quiet, then turned on the radio to listen to the BBC. After he, Hassan Rezaie and his deputy had listened to the news, he felt newly confident, even exhilarated, since he had a whole evening to spend with Hassan.

The conversation turned to the day's events. The emir said

with absolute certainty that the Americans thought of everything, and that they had told him of their conviction that the troubles would pass as suddenly as they had come; he was in complete agreement with them.

He smiled broadly and confidently, then asked Hassan to come near so that he could tell him a secret that no one knew. Hassan came over, and he beckoned to his deputy to approach too, and when all their heads were together he whispered, "In a few days we're going to get a marvelous thing. It will solve all our problems!"

Hassan Rezaie seemed surprised and a little puzzled; he did not entirely understand the emir, but he did not want to look as if he did not understand. When the emir nodded his head encouragingly, since it seemed to him that the new invention the Americans had shown him a few days before was too great and significant for Hassan Rezaie to grasp easily, he was delighted that he knew more about something than Hassan did. He rose quickly and from underneath a pile of cushions drew the marvelous thing. He carried it as a father would his infant son and placed it gently in Hassan's hands.

"Oh, yes, yes." Hassan laughed. "A telephone."

Surprised, the emir asked Hassan if he had ever seen such a device before, and if so where. He was even more suprised to hear that Hassan had seen it in many different places, and he asked him to tell him about it. How did it work? Did it work at night as well as during the day? Did it get tired and need to rest? Was it possible to use it to contact all manner of absent people—even the dead?

Hassan tried to explain, and said many incomprehensible things, but the emir understood the value of the device, how it could shorten distances and be helpful to men, so he had to reveal his secret.

"The American boss, the chief of their camp, told me that in

two weeks or a month at most, there will be permanent contact
between the emirate building and their compound, and that we
can talk day and night on this instrument."

The emir tried the device. "Hello. Hello, trunk. Hello, switch."
He used all the expressions he had heard on his visit to the
American compound a week before. When Hamilton told him
that steps had been taken to install a line between the compound
and the emirate he became excited and rapturously happy. He
dreamed of waking some night to the sound of the telephone's
bell. The bell was no less important or mysterious to him than
the instrument itself, even though there was something Christian
about it, he noted a little regretfully, but it impressed him, the
way it rang by itself. Could Muslims adjust it to say *"Allahu
akbar"* instead of making that sound?

The emir talked about the wonderful device all evening and
speculated on the numberless things that the great invention
could accomplish. He told his deputy that the line to Harran
could render undreamed-of services, even more than the telescope.

"The voice—yes, the voice, Abu Rashwan, is the most important thing. It's what people say, what they're thinking, not
how they look, that's important."

The emir began to relax, saying that he had fallen in love with
several women on the radio. Stretching out to recline peacefully
on the cushions, he told them, "Sometimes the ears fall in love
before the eyes!"

While the emir grew more excited about the telephone, Johar's
agitation mounted over other matters: How could he crush the
strike? How could he arrest those who had started the trouble?
He had been told that Salman al-Zamel was the one who had
stood on the mosque's courtyard wall and shouted those slogans,
and he tried as hard as he could to remember what the man
looked like. He remembered him, he certainly remembered him,

but the face blended in with the faces of the others and dwindled away to nothing. He called out to the men he had summoned. "So! Are we supposed to wait until the bastards start something? We'll start something, and curse their grandparents! Better that than they should take us by surprise. We'll move in on them and grab them. Don't kill that Ibn Zamel. Tell him, 'Come with us and everything will be fine.' And when I get my hands on him, he's a dead man."

The men listened but did not know what to do or what was expected of them. They looked at Johar's face and threw questioning glances at one another.

"At noon you'll be at the mosque, before the call to prayer. Before anyone speaks, before anyone says a word, say, 'They burned the company and cursed them who built it, that's the reason.' And don't worry about a thing."

Johar repeated his instructions several times, and when the men understood he said firmly, "No sleep tonight. Stay up and don't worry."

He went to instruct the units that would take up positions at the fence by the main gate and the workers' gate. For those assignments he would use all of the Desert Army except for the emir's guards.

No one slept that night, and Johar, who had asked his black assistant to wake him before dawn, could hardly close his eyes. He tossed in his bed, imagining the workers and people of Harran marching toward the compound. He saw the men he'd sent at night, clashing with the demonstrators, their blood flowing, and he imagined the Americans, the emir and all the people of Harran begging, pleading with him to put a stop to the terrible events. He knew everything and enjoyed boundless self-confidence, and he longed to arrest a few of the people to make an example of them.

It was too great an opportunity to let slip. He had agreed to stay in this small room and listen to the curses and threats, and endure the sight of the men he had shouted at and beaten as they scattered, but he could stand it no longer. The Americans did not know the bedouin as he did, and the emir was immersed in affairs he did not understand, and did not know what he was talking about. He could not let this opportunity slip. He was the man responsible for security, and the only man capable of action. If he did not act, no one else would be able to. If he managed to arrest those who were behind this anarchy, everyone would thank him. Harran did not need men like those, and it could not be expected to tolerate them anymore. Had things gone so far that they demanded vengeance for Mufaddi? If they were not punished, then tomorrow or the next day they would demand everything. The bedouin were greedier than wolves. He would not let them get away; they were cowards; if one head got broken the rest of them would be quiet as lambs. None of them would dare speak or even open his mouth.

The workers and citizens of Harran slept soundly. Even those who loved to play tricks and practical jokes at the last moment hardly indulged their passions. The workers slept in homes and in the mosque, and the ones who preferred to go back to their camp did not insist, because it was far off, and now they were more cautious.

Salman al-Zamel, who was, with Ibn Hathal and two others, staying with Ibn Naffeh, appeared anxious and upset as they all drank their coffee after supper, in contrast to the feeling of self-confidence that had filled him all day as he chanted and shouted. When he had stood on the wall of the mosque, however, an uneasy doubt had displaced his confidence: Where was Johar? Why was he not confronting the demonstrators? Would the days to come be as easy as this one? Would the company respond to them and reinstate the workers, or remain deaf and distant behind the barbed wire?

He was beset by doubt, or rather by bewilderment. He needed the company of others, to listen to them and ask questions, in order to examine his own convictions before taking the next step. Ibn Naffeh read his mind and spoke to him. "Listen, my boy, listen and understand. If a camel goes astray or a bedouin stumbles, anywhere from al-Miyasem to Juweyreed, or from this sea to Egypt, those bastards will know about it."

Salman laughed, understanding that Ibn Naffeh meant the Americans.

"And Johar, Abu Othman?"

"That dog? He's worse than they are, a tramp, not worth a bean."

"And Mufaddi's killer?"

"God Almighty, are you asking me, nephew?"

"Didn't Johar kill him?"

"Yes, he did it, but what is Johar without them?"

"So where is our revenge, Abu Othman?"

"There are many to whom we owe revenge."

"What is your advice for tomorrow and the day after?"

"Just what you said in the mosque today: the reinstatement of the workers, and they have to say who killed Mufaddi."

"And if they don't listen?"

"They'll listen, my boy, yes, they'll listen. Even stones can be worn down, only unite—don't allow your ranks to be broken, and don't let them outsmart you, the bastards, because all the people are with you."

75

SUNDAY WAS A STRANGE DAY IN HARRAN. THE OLD men, who were used to solitude when they said their morning prayers, found themselves a minority among the crowd that filled the mosque at dawn; they found that a great number of the worshipers had preceded them here. The workers who stayed overnight in the mosque had slept only a few hours and spent the rest of the time telling stories and jokes, and some of them prayed. A number of them gave their places to the latecomers. Ibn Naffeh, who led the prayers because the imam was ill, or had stayed away on the pretense of illness, did not hesitate to speechify before and after the prayers. In the midst of the crowd that grew around him before prayers, he said that this was Harran's day, as the Arabs had had days both before and after the revelation of Islam. He said that if prayer was a Muslim duty, then resisting oppression was a duty as well; a Muslim's protection of his brother Muslims was a duty, as was the defense of truth and his land. He said that there was strength in unity, and that a loyal, fraternal group would never be defeated, whereas if they differed among themselves, if their aims and desires were in conflict, they were finished. Ibn Naffeh said all this and a great deal more besides. He chose his texts from the Koran carefully and recited them in clear and melodious tones so that they took root in the hearts of the congregation and affected them deeply. His listeners felt like a new breed of men, made of some new substance.

After the service, many of them said that they had sensed angels hovering over their heads. Others said that a powerful white light, brilliant as lightning, had filled the mosque when Ibn Naffeh concluded the prayers, saying, "The peace and blessings of God be upon you, the peace and blessings of God be upon you all." When the men poured out of the mosque, descending on the market to stroll around or rest a little in Abu As'ad al-Helwani's coffeehouse, they decided among themselves to meet again late in the morning, in the mosque.

With the exception of the bakeries and a few shops, all of Harran was silent and closed down. There was not a single rider for the Ujra bus, which departed daily at six in the morning; even the passengers who had bought their tickets days before, and made their plans with the intention of traveling this very day, did not show up. Some of the workers passed by in the late morning, on their way to the mosque, and asked the driver, who was busy repairing the bus, if it would leave for Ujra that day.

"The bus has broken down," he replied without raising his head. "It will take two or three days to fix."

Abu As'ad al-Helwani decided to join the strike and told the workers who filed in that he was happy to receive them but would not be serving anything today. Just as quickly, though, he changed his mind.

"I've spent five—no, six years serving the people of Harran," he said gaily. "Well, if you want to drink today, everything is here: tea, sugar, coffee—but roll up your sleeves, because today Abu As'ad is off duty. In plain Arabic, on strike."

The workers delightedly took Abu As'ad's place, but the numerous mistakes they made, and the anarchy that filled the coffeehouse, forced him to abandon his strike and go back to serving his customers.

All efforts to persuade or provoke the Harranis to violence and confrontation failed. Everything remained in the context of their demands that the fired workers be rehired and Mufaddi's murder be investigated. There was an attempt to burn one of Rezaie's cars, but they prevented it, saying, "One burned car will burn all of Harran. Johar is waiting for mischief so that he can start the big fire!" Some people proposed that they all go and attack the gates of the company and then smash everything they could lay their hands on, but Salman al-Zamel looked squarely into the eyes of the shouting bedouin who was trying to organize the march to the company, and answered him. "Listen. There's the gate to the company, go by yourself and tell them that the workers of Harran are waiting for them."

When the bedouin kept shouting, Fawaz al-Hathal seized him by the neck. "We told you," he said angrily. "This time we want the company to come to us, and it will have to come."

As had been the case the day before, nothing developed until the afternoon, when the crowds set off for the mosque. They marched through the town's three main streets and came back again, chanting the slogans they'd made up the day before, with some additions and revisions to make them clearer and stronger. Dabbasi, who was acting as a mediator between the people and the emirate of Harran, conveyed the emir's statement: the workers who had been laid off would surely be rehired sooner or later, so the workers should end their strike and go back to work; as to Mufaddi, he was dead and that was it—no one knew who had killed him.

Dabbasi reported what the emir had said or what he'd heard from others with some pain and a great deal of bitterness. It had become clear to him, after two visits to the emirate, one in the morning and one in the afternoon, that by the time he made a third attempt one of the two sides would surely become his enemy.

"My wife, the emir, and my son are all expecting the worst," he said almost to himself when he told the workers what the emir had said in their second meeting.

The workers looked at him. They had no idea what he was saying or getting at. He smiled. "The long and short of it is, it's all in your hands. You know the situation better than I do. I am, as you see, very much concerned but completely powerless."

He wanted to tell the workers to be steadfast, to persevere. His eyes shone with rage when one of the workers shouted, "And Mufaddi's blood, Abu Saleh?" but there was nothing he could say—anything he said would surely find its way to the emirate and he would be expelled from Harran. He could not trust the emir or confront him. He was confused and distracted; he prided himself on his ties with the north hill and his friendship with the emir, but he also felt that the murder of Mufaddi was inexcusable and must not go unpunished.

Silence fell. It was a heavy, rude silence, and Dabbasi had nothing else to say—he felt, furthermore, that words were useless now. It was clear even to the most optimistic and expectant citizens who had awaited Dabbasi's return from the emirate that the situation was too complicated to be resolved quickly, or to their satisfaction, and they could think of nothing to say to him. Dabbasi stood, leaning on his cane and eager to leave, but he asked Salman and Fawaz to come closer. As they approached and he stepped forward, he lost his balance and nearly fell down, but Salman caught him. Dabbasi supported himself against their bodies and whispered to them softly. "This is all I could do." He pointed his finger and added kindly, "If you need anything, come to me. Do you hear? Come to Abu Saleh before you go to anyone else. God willing, we may be able to do something." He looked at the ground. "God curse Satan and protect us from him."

Naim showed up at the emirate before eleven o'clock to inquire about Hamilton's proposal for setting up an operations group. When the emir was told, he grew a little uneasy, as if he had not been expecting Naim, and wished at that moment that the telephone, that marvelous invention, were working between himself and the compound. Had it been, he would have been able to solve everything; he could have had a long conversation with Hamilton or Hassan Rezaie or Johar or any number of others before responding to any question or request. He dwelled for a moment on this wish. His secretary was still there, looking at him and wondering what to tell Naim.

"Johar, where is Johar?" the emir said at last.

Johar was summoned, and the emir addressed him with a resoluteness he did not feel. "Go, you and the translator, and take Najm and Abu Sadeq. Go talk to the people and see what you can do."

Naim read out from a written text prepared by Philip, one of the company representatives in the operations group, translating as he went along. "The company will not comply with the workers' demands and will not reinstate under pressure or threats those who have been terminated. Such a precedent would only cost the company prestige and encourage the workers to make other demands, number one. Number two, the company does not wish to resort to force at the present time, because the current situation does not call for it. We are ready to promise to study the matter on condition the striking workers return to work immediately, and we reiterate that, in the event of new vacancies, the company will give hiring priority to previously terminated workers. Third and lastly, the management of the company emphasizes that the causes of the strike that began recently go far beyond the termination of a handful of workers. We wonder, but we cannot be certain."

Although Johar pretended to pay close attention, his mind kept wandering. He did not understand several of the phrases Naim used. All eyes drifted to Johar, as if beseeching him to speak, to say something. He felt besieged and uncomfortable, but he gripped his baton and gave the table a sudden loud whack.

"If we don't break their heads, if we don't smash their bones, they'll make fools of us."

Arnold laughed when Naim translated Johar's remark, though the translator had to ask Johar to explain his slang word for *smash*. Johar felt confident, inferring that the Americans were with him. He went on. "They're our people and we know them well. Slap their noses and they'll cry, but beat them, break their bones, and everything will return to normal."

"Is there any connection between the strike and the killing of that bedouin?" asked Philip.

Johar flinched when Philip's question was translated, and the color drained from his face, but when he spoke it was in a very sharp if somewhat unsteady voice. "That's one story and this is another."

This was translated, but the Americans did not understand. Their eyes did not leave his.

"My friends," he said, "Mufaddi was killed by his own complaints. He's dead and gone, and the bedouin who work in the company have nothing to do with it."

"Why have we never seen strikes like this before? Why didn't they strike two months ago, or after the pipeline was completed, when we laid off a lot more workers?"

" 'You clink one goblet on another, and a thousand dancers come running,' " suggested Johar. "They needed an excuse, and they found one!"

"The phenomenon facing us today must be examined and treated on two levels," said Philip, reading from a sheet of paper. "The first level is the immediate one—the strike. It must end without the company giving in, and without acts of violence. The second concerns the workers' conditions, which must be studied carefully to reveal their deep-seated causes: Are there political implications? Are there organizations or instigators at work? Are there factors outside the company and the workplace?"

"Yes, yes, it's all completely abnormal, that's for sure," said Hassan Rezaie. "Yes, something is wrong. We have to look at it closely and think of the future."

Johar had not been listening to them, but he was furious. "You don't know anything about the bedouin. You don't know how vile they are. They're worse than devils."

Hassan Rezaie nodded vigorously. "You are right, they're vile, yes, really wicked. They laugh at you and try to cheat you, and if they succeed they'll kill you without batting an eyelash."

Johar's eyes darted between Rezaie and the Americans. He did not want to miss a word Hassan said, or its effect on the Americans.

Philip returned to their discussion. "You know these people better than we do, but what concerns us now is ending the strike."

"Leave it to me," said Johar.

"That's fine with us, as long as it does not get violent, not yet at least."

The meeting ended with no final decisions being made. Rezaie asked that the situation be monitored all day and that they meet again in the evening or at a time to be determined later.

Johar was convinced that no one knew how to handle the situation as he did. The Americans talked about complicated notions that had nothing to do with what was happening. They said this was fine and that was not, but they did not know what they were talking about. They knew nothing about the bedouin; they supposed them to be simple, peaceable people. They knew nothing!

Johar decided to act quickly. It was clear to him that the units sent to the mosque that morning had accomplished nothing, and even clearer that the workers wanted to avoid clashing with him.

76

GUNSHOTS WERE HEARD BETWEEN MIDAFTER-
noon and sundown, as the men lay in the shade
of the mosque and the nearby shops. They
were napping after having marched twice through Harran as far
as Harithy Street, waiting for the intensity of the sun to abate
before starting the third and last phase of the day's action, waiting
for the end of their second long, strenuous day, and for the
return of the men who had gone back to the camp to fetch
supplies. The gunfire was distant and sporadic, from the direction of the camp.

"That bastard Johar, it's him," said Salman al-Zamel.

"God help us," said Ibn Naffeh, who was in the midst of a
discussion with a group of men.

Some of the men ran off to see what was happening, and a
tense silence settled. They saw a group of workers racing toward

Harran and heard another burst of gunfire. It was now clear that something terrible was happening.

The people of Harran, who until this time had been laughing and joking, and inclined to be indulgent, felt something changing inside them. They felt heartache; they felt that they could no longer bear to stay in this place. They no longer heard what Ibn Naffeh or anyone else was saying. Even the strength and discipline in the face of adversity that some of them possessed now failed. Within minutes three workers arrived, pale, wild-eyed and out of breath. From the few brief words they gasped the men understood that two workers had been wounded or killed and that others were trapped between the electric station and warehouses and needed help; left alone, they would be massacred by the soldiers.

These words sounded in their ears like drumbeats and roared like a tempest, driving the men to a mounting anger that made the blood pound and throb in their temples. They gazed at the panting men before them and at the electric station and warehouses where the men were besieged.

"Today is our day, men," said one of them, hefting an iron pipe.

He ran, and the rest ran behind him, grabbing whatever came to their hands: iron pipes, sticks, rocks and wooden poles. They ran like camels, and a song they knew from long ago sprang to their lips, from the need they felt to inflame their thoughts and emotions.

How had these human waves come together? Where had they come from? How did the people of Harran arrive so quickly— how did the women get there before the men?

Something like magic was at work in this hour. Ibn Zamel, who shouted to slow the people down, and cursed as he grabbed some of the men, realized that his voice was lost. The men he grabbed gave him a certain look; his hands fell and he stood, confused, not knowing what to do, then suddenly found himself running along with the rest of them, even pulling ahead of them. Ibn Naffeh, who grasped his staff and shook it in the air, found himself chanting along with the others. Although he did not move as the younger men did—he could not run, or even walk very fast—a sudden piercing strength surged through him, and he was amazed at how quickly he arrived at the compound. Khazna was on her way to Arab Harran with a loaf of bread under her arm after having spent the whole day by the mosque or strolling through the market, repeating one phrase over and over again every time she saw a group of people: "God give you strength; God give you victory." When she set foot on the slope of the hill, the water tank loomed over her like a boulder, and a black cloud seemed to envelop her as she heard the shooting. She turned for a brief moment, then began running back toward the mosque. Many said that she was singing and shouting, and that tears flowed from her eyes, whether from joy or fear they did not know, but everyone who saw her running toward the camp was struck by her peculiar exhilaration and vigor, and though she was one of the last to arrive, her chant was clear and loud, and deeply affecting.

The masses of people moved as one man, and their voices rose to reach the farthest places, even drowning out the sound of the gunshots and the screams that came from the other direction.

It had all started when Johar went to the American compound. Two of the soldiers at the gate told him that a group of workers had come to the compound, and they had been allowed to enter after being searched. When he heard this Johar began to howl like a wolf. "You let them in, you sons of bitches?"

The soldiers said nothing but hung their heads and looked at the ground.

Johar shouted more loudly than before. "You stupid bastards! I swear to God I'll break your heads before I break theirs!" He grabbed one of the soldiers nearest him and beat him with his baton.

"Where are they? Where did they go?"

When Johar reached the American compound, he gave orders to open fire, and to forestall any hesitancy or delay in doing so he drew his pistol and began firing himself. Within moments the air was filled with a hail of bullets. The three workers who crossed the barbed wire to reach the mosque were able to report only the first events. When the citizens of Harran arrived, escorted by crowds of workers, one cry filled the air: *Allahu akbar! Allahu akbar! Allahu akbar!*

Where was Johar? What was he planning? Where were the trapped workers?

In a moment of silence, Khaled al-Issa addressed the soldiers who stood behind the barrels, their rifles pointed at the gathering of people. "Leave the workers alone," he said. "You may shoot at us."

"One step closer and we'll open fire," said one of the soldiers uneasily.

"Gunpowder doesn't frighten us, my boy, gunpowder is a man's perfume. You had better leave them alone and shoot at us."

"One step . . . one step and we'll open fire."

"Listen, boy!" shouted Ibn Naffeh, coming forward. "Fear God, and leave the men you are holding. Shoot at us!"

The order came from afar, in a harsh but muffled voice, like a cry from a cave. "Fire!"

They said later that the sound of the shots intermingled with the shrill, drawn-out trilling of Khazna al-Hassan, as if she were at a wedding. They said that most of the men turned to Khazna instead of toward the sound of the shots, but when they saw Ibn Naffeh bow over his cane, then slip and fall to the ground, they were struck motionless for an instant. His cane rose into the air, as if he were playing with it. "He's killed me, the Americans' servant . . ."

He gasped and tried to smile. "But don't worry."

When they saw him and heard this they knew he had been hit. He made a heavy, difficult movement, and his face plainly showed the pain. When he rolled over, they saw the stream of blood beneath his back, and Khazna began to chant.

> "Death will die, but not you, Abu Othman!
> Pride of men, above us all, Abu Othman!
> Death will die, but not you, Abu Othman!"

What fury comes over men in a moment like this? What powers does it detonate?

As the wind sweeps through a tree, or as waves collide with rocks, gusts of anger flooded their faces and hearts, smashing the timorous prudence that had ruled them in the mosque and the marketplace. Within moments the people became like a flame, or a tempestuous wind. They feared nothing and cared for no consequences. Johar, who was still shouting "Fire . . . fire!" could not believe his eyes. The people were charging, a human flood, swarming forward like locusts; he could not believe that his armed soldiers were retreating and beginning to flee.

The concrete posts shook like empty branches and were uprooted like dead trees. In moments the barbed wire was buried under the sand, and the human waves plunged forth. The people later said that Fawaz al-Hathal and his brother Mugbel, who had arrived in Harran a few weeks before, were seen flying through the air like birds, crying, "We have come, here we are, Father!" and that Fawaz was the first to reach the side of the wounded. They said that they saw him carrying Ibrahim al-Dosari all by himself, even though Ibrahim was much heavier than he. He was the first, or one of the first two, to locate all the wounded, to find where the four workers were hidden, and to free them. Johar saw the crowd charging and attacking, and his men retreating, and he did not delay long in fleeing himself. He headed for the American compound, but before he reached the gate Fawaz al-Hathal noticed him and dove to grab his leg, and Johar fell. Had he not bared his teeth and bitten Fawaz's hand, so hard that the teeth marks did not disappear for weeks, he would not have escaped.

Those who arrived at the compound late said that they had seen from afar a man on a white camel pursuing the soldiers and firing at them and attacking the main gate of the compound, and many of them said that the man was Miteb al- Hathal. Still others swore with absolute certainty that they saw a phantom shaped like a man flying above their heads, and it looked exactly like Mufaddi al-Jeddan. They said that the soldiers who fired their rifles were frightened to the point of utter terror and that most of their bullets were fired at the phantom, at Mufaddi al-Jeddan. They reported that the man's clothing was full of holes made by the bullets.

After freeing the detained workers, the people would have pressed on with their attack had not Khaled al-Issa climbed to the top of the water tank and addressed them, panting and out of breath. "Enough, my friends, now we have to care for the wounded."

They hesitated, but not for long, then turned their attention to the wounded. Those among them who had seen Mufaddi al-Jeddan as they attacked the compound and Johar and his men fled, also saw him as they transported the wounded. They even felt his presence, for the wounded tried to break loose, and some of them flew from between their hands. They were as light as feathers or even lighter. Numberless unseen hands helped the men carry the wounded.

"The doctor is out of town," Muhammad Eid told a small

group of them when they came to fetch Dr. Subhi. "He'll be back in a week."

Dabbasi sent his son Saleh to the American compound to explore the possibility of getting treatment for the wounded there and received an unambiguous response: "The company may provide on-site first aid to the wounded, with the express approval of the Emir Khaled, and after that the wounded may be taken to Ujra or elsewhere."

Saleh al-Dabbasi told Naim and one of the Americans, whom he had never seen before, that two of the wounded were in serious condition and needed attention immediately, and he got a firm answer: "No action can be taken on this request until Mr. Hamilton and his deputy return. They have been out at sea since early morning and are not expected back before midnight."

The people were not awaiting word from Dr. Mahmilji or Muhammad Eid the Needle, because they had not even thought of approaching them. They deemed Saleh al-Dabbasi's initiative at the American compound an unforgivable affront.

Ibn Naffeh was treated in the mosque. Khazna helped two of the workers clean the bullet wound in his thigh, then they carried him to his house. Dabbasi visited him that evening and told him about his son's visits to the American compound and what he had been told there.

"I don't think you really want that for us, Abu Saleh," said Ibn Naffeh. "If God wills us to die, it is better to die in our own houses, among our own people than to die among them, like dogs."

The two men who had been wounded in the beginning of the battle had not received dangerous or fatal injuries, but they were weakened by loss of blood, so that Khazna dared not touch them. She bit her lower lip worriedly until it bled.

"Where are you now, father of orphans, brother of widows?" she asked.

"I'm taking them to Ujra," said Raji, who was tightly bandaging the shoulder of one of the men to stop the bleeding. "We'll get them to a doctor within an hour or two, and they'll be fine."

They dressed the second man's wound. When Salman al-Zamel went to Dabbasi to borrow his truck to transport the two men to Ujra, Dabbasi sighed. "God curse the day the first stones of Harran were built up, and the day I came here. Nothing has come of it but misery." He paused and added despairingly, "Even the money here is black and worthless."

The truck soon sped off on its way. It did not stop at Mile 110 or at Mile 75. Al-Ghanem stood by the side of the road and waved at the oncoming truck, and for a moment he thought that Raji was playing a trick on him when it rushed past—surely it would stop and back up—but it flew past the coffeehouse and vanished.

"Has he become a thief in his old age?" mused al-Ghanem aloud. He stopped to think for a moment and shook his head in surprise. "Absence and travel are both alibis."

In under two hours the truck rolled into Ujra, as the evening calls to prayer were sounded, and headed straight for the National Hospital.

"We died over and over again," the two men who accompanied Raji and the patients later said. "The truck was flying— floating through the air, but Abu Yaacoub rode it like a champion, and here we are."

Khazna finished dressing the wounds of the remaining three with the help of others, even little Amna, who moved around the mosque as if she had lived there all her life. She fetched Khazna whatever she needed: hot water, bandages and woolen blankets—no one knew where she found them.

When Khazna had finished bandaging the men, she smiled,

showing her teeth in delight. "Thanks to God, and to the man you all know, they have been given new life."

Everyone understood that she meant Mufaddi. That night, Mufaddi appeared to countless people. He went back and forth from Arab Harran to the mosque, and every one of them examined his bullet-riddled robe. Three of them, one worker and two Harranis, said that they had felt the robe and seen that the edges of the bullet holes were singed. When Mufaddi saw them palpating the robe in a shocked manner, he laughed and said that someone should buy him some new clothes.

Raji, who slept with the wounded workers in the ward of the hospital after a great deal of protestation and argument when his request was initially refused, said good night to the two men who had accompanied him to the prison, where they answered questions about how the men had been wounded and who was responsible. He said that he saw Mufaddi twice that night: the first time when he covered one of the wounded men with a blanket, and the second time when he came in shortly after dawn bringing water to a patient at the far end of the ward.

Everyone in Harran saw Mufaddi at least once late that night. At first he seemed tired, perhaps from the long day's events, but after drinking tea at Ibn Naffeh's, where Abu Othman was supine on the floor, he vigorously helped him to rise, undid his bandage and moved the light closer to inspect the wound, then tied the bandage up again and said that Khazna had done better than he could have done. Then he excused himself to go and visit some of the other wounded, who were spending the night in various houses in Harran. He asked about them, and when he was asked whether he would come back the next day, he nodded and laughed but said nothing . . . then vanished.

When Emir Khaled heard the gunshots in the late afternoon as he was experimenting with the telephone, something came over him. He assured himself that it was not fear by any means, because when he looked into the face of his deputy, who was playing with his black cat—which he regarded as a good omen— the sound of gunfire intermixed with the meowing of the cat, and the emir said that at that very moment, a flash of light like a ray of sunshine glittered from his eyes, followed by a puff of blue smoke. This is how he explained his condition to the Pakistani doctor who was summoned urgently between sundown and night to examine him.

Hassan Rezaie and Dabbasi heard of the emir's sudden illness and came to visit him.

"Abu Misfer hasn't looked well these past two days," the emir's deputy told them. He shook his head sadly as he remembered. "He was fine the day before yesterday. He was talking and laughing; you saw him. Yesterday, after Abu Sadeq left, he said, 'It hurts here and here,' and pointed to his neck and the base of his skull. I told him, 'It's only tiredness, Abu Misfer,' and he said, 'It isn't tiredness, something's writhing; it doesn't go up or down, it's like a fiery skewer.' I told him, 'Trust in God. You'll be fine if you get some rest. You must sleep.' He said, 'I won't live to see tomorrow.' 'Trust in God, man,' I said, and I stayed with him until he fell asleep.

"Today he looked terrible; Abu Saleh saw him. You saw him, Abu Saleh. He looks into the air like he's lost, and won't eat or drink anything.

"When the shooting started, he said, 'It's all over,' and started in with the telephone. 'Hello, hello, reply, switch.' He said, 'The Americans aren't safe, they have no friends.' He looked around at me. 'Smoke! There's smoke coming out of your eyes and nose, Abu Rashwan. Black smoke, blue smoke, smoke everywhere.' It was the fever. I said to myself, fever makes a man rave. So we sent for the Indian doctor, but he didn't tell him where the pain was, he just kept talking about the smoke. Smoke here, smoke there. The doctor wanted to examine him but he wouldn't let him. He wouldn't let him lay a hand on him. The Indian said, 'Give him this medicine. It will make him sleep, and he'll feel better.' But, God help him, he wouldn't touch it. He sent for the Syrian doctor's assistant, and told him to bring his stethoscope. So he came."

As the deputy made this explanation to the two men, confused sounds came from the neighboring room. They could make out the emir's voice, as he raved and gave orders: "Hello. Hello! Switch." Then: "No, higher . . . a little higher. No, lower. To the right. More to the right."

Hassan Rezaie asked Dabbasi, with his eyes, whether it would be decorous for them to go in and visit the emir while he was in this state, or whether it would be better to tell his deputy that they wished him a speedy recovery, then to leave. But the deputy needed them and wanted their help in this difficult situation. He wanted them to stay by his side, but he was afraid that the emir would react badly if he learned that they had come but did not go in to see him.

Dabbasi tapped his cane on the floor and spoke wearily. "There is no power and no strength save in God."

He paused a moment before going on. "When troubles come, they come in a deluge, like a flood, and leave nothing behind but ruin."

"If only we get through these few days and the emir gets better, everything will be fine," replied Hassan Rezaie.

Dabbasi spoke slowly, as if to himself. "I don't think so, Abu Sadeq."

Shouts again sounded from the next room, and with the shouts curses, and the deputy looked at the two men, bewildered and helpless.

The door opened suddenly, and the emir peeked out. His robe was open, exposing his bare chest, and the stethoscope was hung around his neck. His eyes were red, and there was froth at the corners of his mouth. When he saw the seated men, their heads close as if whispering together, he struggled toward them with slow, uncertain steps, a small, malicious smile on his lips.

"This is an unsafe world!" he said as he drew close to them.

The three looked up at him with fear and pity.

"Are you feeling better, Abu Misfer?" his deputy asked uneasily.

The emir kept talking, ignoring what his deputy had said. "The Americans sent the Indian over here and told him: Kill him. Don't let him live another day. So here all of you are, saying: If the Americans don't kill him, we will. Right?"

"Trust in God, Abu Misfer," said Dabbasi in genuine despair. "Our hearts are with you. We want you to be cured as soon as possible."

"Nothing's wrong with me. You can see that I'm stronger than a camel."

He stepped closer until he stood directly above his deputy's head. His deputy started and drew away in fright.

"You are ill, Abu Rashwan," said the emir. "Tell me, where does it hurt?" He leaned over him more steeply and grasped the stethoscope. "Hah. Where is the pain? Don't be afraid, tell me where. Don't worry. Leave it to me."

With difficulty the three men escorted the emir back to the room he had come out of. They found Muhammad Eid in one corner, pale with fright and trembling; in the other corner they saw two of the emir's men. When the four had entered the room, urging the emir to lie down and rest, to sleep, he threw a hateful glance at Muhammad Eid and spoke to him slowly. "Out of town, eh? And when might we expect him?"

Muhammad Eid began to mumble indistinctly in reply, but the emir laughed and cut him off. "That stupid son of a bitch thinks I'm crazy. Does he think I swallow the poisons he gives me? No, no, he's wrong. I buried them all in the sand and pissed on them!"

"Abu Misfer, if you rest for an hour or two—" said Hassan Rezaie.

The emir turned to one of his men. "Come here. You."

The man came forward, frightened. The emir pointed to Muhammad Eid. "This one is just like his master, his boss; he doesn't tell the truth. And he doesn't know anything. I want you to tell me what this says."

He removed the stethoscope from his neck and placed it in the ears of the terrified man, who looked beseechingly at the other bewildered men, then at the emir.

The emir stretched out on his bed and motioned for the man to come closer and put the stethoscope on his chest, near the neck. The man did not know what to do; he was in a lamentable state, and the other men were utterly at a loss.

After several efforts and a great deal of pleading, cajoling and even firmness, they finally made the emir agree to lie on his bed and rest after Muhammad Eid and the other men had left the room; he may have obeyed out of exhaustion.

The emir slipped into a deep sleep before midnight. His deputy and Hassan Rezaie were able to remove the stethoscope he always insisted on putting in his ears and on his chest, and they laid it at the side of his bed. Dabbasi had left early, and he went to visit Ibn Naffeh before going home.

77

THURSDAY. SHORTLY AFTER SUNRISE, WORSHIP-
ers leaving the mosque said that they saw six
of the emirate's automobiles, including the
emir's own, stop briefly in Rashedi Street, in front of Hassan
Rezaie's offices, and take off again in the direction of the Ujra
road. They said they saw the emir in one of the automobiles,
toying with the stethoscope around his neck and holding a piece
of black iron, whose nature and use they did not know. It looked
like a long pestle or a ladle. The emir put it to his mouth, shouting
and cursing, and Hassan Rezaie, who was sitting beside him,
kept trying to hold on to him and calm him down. Johar was
lying down in another automobile. He raised his head when they
passed the cemetery; they were sure of this, because his black
assistant was sitting to the right of the driver and turned around

every now and then to look in the backseat. The other automobiles were filled with bodyguards, emirate staff and some members of the emir's family.

Abdu Muhammad said that one of the emirate automobiles had come to his shop three hours earlier than usual, and the two soldiers sent to buy the bread had to wait quite awhile for their order to be filled. He understood from their conversation that a group from the emirate was preparing for a journey, but he could not discern exactly how many were leaving or who they were.

Travelers arriving from Ujra early that morning said that they saw the emirate's automobiles at Mile 110. The vehicles paused for a few moments near the coffeehouse, perhaps because the passengers wanted to take a rest, but at the last minute they turned away and resumed their journey. Most of the bus passengers saw the emir putting the stethoscope around his neck and waving back at them, and they all said that they saw Johar's black assistant alone in the second car.

Khazna, who had kept vigil by Mufaddi's grave since dawn, said on Thursday afternoon that she had had a dream during a short nap she took by the graveside. She saw Mufaddi or someone else—she could not make out his features clearly—who pushed her away and tried to run away from her. She was frightened and cried. In the afternoon, she interpreted the dream as signifying "the departure and flight of the bastards," as she called the emir, Johar and soldiers who had opened fire.

Thursday was a sad and unsettling day, unlike the preceding days, and full of rumors. In the late morning, a number of visitors to Ibn Naffeh told him what the worshipers and the bus passengers in Ujra had reported, but he answered without looking at them. "They may have left, but we don't know whether they'll be back." He changed his tone of voice and went on,

"We've seen so many come and go before them, but the ones who take their place aren't always better. We may yet ask for God's blessing on those who left today!"

"The important thing is that we're rid of them, Abu Othman," said Abu Assaf, not hiding his joy. "They made our lives miserable, and we were sure they would be the death of us before they died."

"You know quite well what the problem was that made us miserable."

"Johar and all the Johars were the problem, Abu Othman," said Abu Assaf. He laughed. "God! The Ujra road—how much it has given and taken away!"

"What about the sea road?" asked Salman al-Zamel.

Ibn Naffeh shifted around in his bed and cleared his throat.

"It isn't the Ujra road, or the sea road. The only road, my friends, is the one that all our people follow and never diverge from." When they said nothing, he went on. "I told you all before. The Americans are the source of the illness and the root of the problem."

At noon the emirate issued a short statement:

"His Highness Emir Khaled departed Harran this morning for medical treatment. Before leaving, His Highness ordered the reinstatement of all workers to the company, and the company has acceded to his wishes. His Highness also ordered the formation of a committee to study and identify the responsibility for the recent events.

"The emirate therefore appeals to one and all to cooperate and do their utmost to see that reason and wisdom may prevail for the good of the country and the service of all citizens. 'Say: work, for God and His Prophet and the faithful witness your deeds.' "

"You said, Abu Othman, that Mufaddi's blood would not be lost," Khazna told Ibn Naffeh as she rebandaged his wound.

"Khazna"—he laughed—"Mufaddi's blood is lost . . . lost."

"Lost!"

"Woman, you should ask whose blood is next."

"Ours is a long story, Abu Othman."

"Long. How much longer?"

"Trust in God, man. All is well with the world."

"God only knows." He laughed sadly. "Hope for the best. No one can read the future."